STONE *and* ANVIL

To the brave crew and passengers of the *Kobayshi Maru* . . . sucks to be you.

STAR TREK
NEW FRONTIER®

STONE *and* ANVIL

PETER DAVID

Based on STAR TREK: THE NEXT GENERATION®
created by Gene Roddenberry

POCKET BOOKS
New York   London   Toronto   Sydney   Singapore

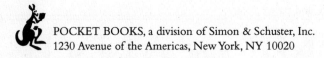

Chapter One

Now

On the *Trident,* Captain Elizabeth Shelby shook her head in disbelief as she and her husband, Captain Mackenzie Calhoun, walked down the corridor leading to the turbolift.

"So McHenry's gone?"

"That's right," said Calhoun.

"And Soleta's returned to the ship."

"Feeling very bewildered and, I think, rather embarrassed," Calhoun told her. "And the effects of the ambrosia are wearing off the rest of the Danteri as well. They've already been imploring Si Cwan to come back and take another stab at beginning a new Thallonian empire."

"Let me guess," said Shelby. "He doesn't want any part of it."

"No. The Danteri were no joy to work with even before the Beings got involved with them. Si Cwan is interested in keeping a safe distance from them. I think he's still enchanted with the idea of a new Thallonian empire, but he's convinced the Danteri aren't the way to go."

"Our remaining problem is the Tholians," said Shelby. "Fortunately enough, Ambassador Spock is with us. The Tholians are on their way, but we're thinking the ambassador will be able to forestall any problems. Especially when he explains that the downside of ambrosia is that it makes anyone who takes it extremely peaceful. I doubt that's going to be very attractive to the Tholians." She paused just before they got to the turbolift, turned, and said to Calhoun, "I'm very proud of the way you handled everything. I really am."

"Thank you. That means a lot, coming from you. And I love you."

She laughed softly. "You don't initiate that statement very often. And I love you, too."

"Tell me," he said, "do you think they'd miss me back on the *Excalibur* if I was gone for, oh . . . another half hour or so?"

"Even if they did, they'd probably figure out why and have the good taste not to comment on it."

"Your cabin?"

"By all means."

They walked forward into the turbolift, the door hissing open, and Shelby jumped back and barely stifled a shriek.

The ripped-up body of Lieutenant Commander Gleau tumbled out of the lift, staring with lifeless eyes up at them.

"This might take longer than a half hour," said Calhoun.

The offhand tone of Calhoun's comment didn't even register on Shelby. She was staring, goggle-eyed, at the corpse that had fallen out of the lift.

Gleau had always been one of the most strikingly handsome of the ship's crew. That had not simply been part of the Selelvian charm called "the Knack," which he wielded with such effortless—and occasionally divisive—results. By any Earthly standard of measurement, he was exceedingly good-looking. That was no longer the case. The front of his body had been completely torn up. Because of all the blood, it was hard to distinguish between uniform shreds and shreds of skin. The upper portion of his face was hanging half off the front of his skull.

It took herculean effort on Shelby's part to steady herself, and she started slightly when there was an unexpected pressure on her right shoulder. It was simply Calhoun's hand and he said from behind her, "Are you all right?"

Part of her mind could scarcely conceive it. He sounded so calm. Wasn't there *anything* that fazed the man?

But she didn't say that. She'd be damned if she'd let Calhoun see how affected she'd been by the abrupt discovery. If he could take unexpected corpses in stride, so could she. She managed a nod, then tapped her combadge and said, "Sickbay, this is the captain."

"Villers here, Captain," came the perpetually irritated, no-nonsense voice of the ship's CMO. She always seemed mildly perturbed to be distracted from whatever it was she was involved with at that moment.

Shelby didn't care. Without going into details, she said briskly, "Full medical team to deck seven, forward section nine, turbolift. Gleau is apparently dead."

Instantly Villers was all business. "On my way," she said.

"Hurry," said Shelby.

"All things considered, I don't think the doctor's attempts to 'hurry' are going to be a major factor," said Calhoun.

Shelby closed her eyes and counted to ten, as her mother had always suggested she do. "That's what I love about you, Mac," she sighed. "No matter the situation, you always know just what to say."

Then

M'k'n'zy of Calhoun had no idea what to say.

M'k'n'zy, a warlord of nineteen summers in age, had just witnessed a meeting with a representative of the Danteri that was likely going to result in the freedom of his people.

The young Xenexian had no idea what to think about that, no idea how to feel. For as long as he could remember—and sometimes, it seemed, past the point where he would have liked to forget—M'k'n'zy had been leading his people in a bloody and brutal civil war. Now it appeared as if it was coming to an end. Bragonier of the royal house of Danteri had just been summarily dismissed, sent back to the Danteri with his metaphorical tail between his legs. He'd be returning to them with a message they were not going to want to hear, but would be forced to accept: Xenex would tolerate no further attempts to be ruled by them. The Danteri domination of Xenex was in its death throes.

As was M'k'n'zy's importance.

He knew in his heart that he shouldn't be feeling that way. His own concerns, wants, and desires were secondary to the needs of his people. He had always known that and been eminently comfortable with it.

But if the Xenexians were not going to be at war . . .

. . . of what use was a warlord?

These notions had always floated around in the back of his head. He'd always been of a dual mind: fighting for a time of peace, and secretly dreading what would happen to him if that peace was achieved. The latter concern had never caused him to hesitate in his pursuit of the former. Now that it was confronting him, however, it dominated the entirety of his mind rather than allowing itself to be shoved to the deepest recesses.

Part of what had brought it to the forefront was the gentle, probing questions of the thinning-haired man who was standing before him. He had the odd, nearly unpronounceable name of "Jean-Luc Picard." M'k'n'zy couldn't begin to handle "Jean-Luc." The combination of vowels and consonants tripped up his tongue and teeth. The last name he said after a fashion: PEE-cahd. It was as close as his normal pattern of speech would allow.

This PEE-cahd was from something called "Starfleet," which was, as near as M'k'n'zy could determine, the military arm of something else called the "United Federation of Planets."

M'k'n'zy had heard tell of the Federation when he was younger. His late father had made it sound very important. Assorted planets, uniting for the common good, to seek out new life and new civilizations. As for M'k'n'zy, he'd never given much consideration to planets. They were far too esoteric a concern for someone whose worries were so completely bound to the reality of the ground beneath his feet. Still, he had to admit that the name of the organization sounded very powerful, very important. It was the kind of name that put opponents on notice that they were dealing with a force to be reckoned with.

PEE-cahd had shown up, purporting to be captain of a ship called the *Stargazer*. M'k'n'zy was unimpressed by the name. If the tales of the Federation were to be believed, these Federation star vessels packed considerable weaponry. The word "stargazer" was too soft for such a ship. It made it sound as if the ship just sat around staring at the stars all the time. *Killcruiser*. Now, *there* was a name for a ship. *Annihilator* was also acceptable.

Still, for the commander of such an ineptly named ship, PEE-cahd was bearing a potent message. He spoke to the Danteri representative of an "understanding." Of reaching "a compromise," so "the bloodshed will end."

M'k'n'zy would have none of it, however. He knew there would be no compromising with the Danteri. He could just see it: If the Danteri gave something back, the Xenexians would give something back. Strategic withdrawal, or overseeing the Xenexians in their assembling of their own government. Promises that could be bent or broken as time passed and PEE-cahd and his associates moved on to something else.

Only one option was available when dealing with the Danteri. They were to get off Xenex and never come back. Period, done, end of discussion. When Bragonier balked, M'k'n'zy was interested in hearing nothing more. When Bragonier declared that such as he could not be so easily dismissed, M'k'n'zy dismissed him. Telling M'k'n'zy that he could not do something was the equivalent of telling someone else that he could.

PEE-cahd had chided him, which M'k'n'zy had expected and ignored. The Federation man was an outsider. He had not witnessed *his* father being brutally beaten to death by oppressors. He had not had *his* entire youth swallowed up in pain, blood, and brutality. He had not hated for year upon year upon year. How could he? The Federation, after all, was entirely about cooperation and understanding, or at least so the stories went. How could someone who was a product of such an environment come close to comprehending M'k'n'zy?

He couldn't.

And yet . . . the things PEE-cahd said to him upon Bragonier's huffy exit made M'k'n'zy believe PEE-cahd was on his side. That he would force the arrogant Danteri to realize that their domination of Xenex was at an end. It gave M'k'n'zy the first flicker of hope he'd had in . . . well, ever, really. Simultaneously it fanned the flames of uncertainty as to his own future. Would there be a place for him in a Xenex that knew peace?

M'k'n'zy's confusion as to his status was brought home when, in a private moment, PEE-cahd point-blank asked him what would happen to him in the long term. "Perhaps I shall continue to lead my people here," M'k'n'zy had replied.

"Perhaps," the Federation man had said. He sounded agreeable enough about it, but there was a dash of uncertainty and even curiosity in the way he regarded the young Xenexian. "Will that satisfy you?"

That had been the question which had left M'k'n'zy in the rare position of not having the faintest idea of what to say. "I . . ." He hesitated. It seemed such a simple question. Why did the answer elude him so? "I . . . don't know," he admitted, sounding confused, hating himself for it.

"Well," said PEE-cahd, sounding reasonable enough, "at the point when you do know . . . let me know."

The response immediately caused M'k'n'zy's suspicions to flare. What was it that this man had in mind for him? He didn't strike M'k'n'zy as the type to make random comments for no reason. Furthermore, most people that M'k'n'zy encountered did nothing out of any sense of altruism, but rather were driven by self-interest. He couldn't begin to guess what manner of self-interest was motivating PEE-cahd. "Why are you so interested in me?" he demanded.

PEE-cahd shrugged. "A hunch," he said. "Nothing more than that. But captains learn to play their hunches. It's how they become captains."

"I see," M'k'n'zy mused. "So . . . if I had a hunch . . . that you were important to my future . . . that in itself might be indicative of something significant."

"Possibly," said PEE-cahd.

The captain could not possibly know what was going through M'k'n'zy's mind. Couldn't know that not long before, M'k'n'zy had been close to dying in the desert (not that M'k'n'zy was willing to admit to himself that wounds from Danteri slime would have been sufficient to kill him). And during that time, when he had drifted in and out of awareness, he had seen visions. Visions of this man shouting at him, telling him he was a "Starfleet officer," that he had a destiny, and that he couldn't let that destiny slip away by doing something as inconsiderate as dying.

And there had been someone else . . . a woman. A blond woman. A naked blond woman. Fair of skin, luminous of eyes, and the way she had looked at him had fairly burned into his soul.

It was said that in the desert strange things could and did happen. Men had often claimed that they'd seen echoes, shades of their past or their future, particularly when they themselves were in dire straits, with possible death drawing near. M'k'n'zy had never given much credence to such claims, but they were certainly sounding more convincing now.

He noticed abruptly that PEE-cahd was heading for the door of the small room. He realized that he'd just been standing there, lost in thought, and PEE-cahd had doubtless thought that the meeting was over. "PEE-cahd?" he ventured.

PEE-cahd turned and looked at him coolly. "Yes?"

"You, uhm," and M'k'n'zy cleared his throat. "You wouldn't happen to have brought a naked blond woman with you . . . ?"

Whatever PEE-cahd might have been expecting him to ask, that certainly wasn't it. "I beg your pardon?"

M'k'n'zy shrugged it off. It seemed pointless, even embarrassing to try and explain it. So instead he just said, "Never mind."

PEE-cahd didn't appear inclined to let it go immediately. "If you don't mind my saying so, that was a rather curious question."

"Yes, well . . ." M'k'n'zy, seeing a chance to give back a bit in the spirit of what PEE-cahd had said, replied, "Call it a hunch, for what it's worth."

The captain seemed to consider the comment with great deliberation. "Well," he said at last, "I didn't say all hunches were good ones. A captain has to pick and choose."

"I'll remember that," said M'k'n'zy.

PEE-cahd walked out, and M'k'n'zy suddenly had the feeling that he had just made a terrible mistake, letting the man depart. M'k'n'zy had never been one for deep consideration of topics at hand. He was a creature of instinct, operating almost entirely on a gut level. His decisions were not always right. But they were quick, they were decisive, and they were unwavering.

He knew what was running through his head was nothing less than a major life-changing concept. Any other person—certainly any sane person—would have looked the notion over from many varied directions. At the very least, they would never have been moved into immediate action.

But M'k'n'zy was unlike any of those others. It was very possible that he was unlike anyone else on Xenex. Because for M'k'n'zy, concept transformed into decision, and decision into action.

PEE-cahd was standing outside several feet away. Passing Xenexians cast furtive glances in his direction, clearly finding him a curious creature, but no one wanted to say anything to him. Perhaps they thought he carried dangerous diseases or some such. He had just tapped his chest and he was saying, "One to beam—" But he stopped when he saw M'k'n'zy, and the urgency in his face. "Belay that," he continued. "I'll be back with you."

M'k'n'zy didn't have a clue to whom PEE-cahd was speaking. Perhaps he was praying to whatever his deities were. It seemed an odd moment to pray, but M'k'n'zy was fairly generous-minded with such endeavors. He was far too pragmatic an individual to think that some mysterious beings were always listening in, but he was hardly going to tell others they were wasting their time.

PEE-cahd watched as M'k'n'zy slowly, cautiously approached him. M'k'n'zy was annoyed with himself. He was feeling tentative, uncertain, and that sensation repulsed him. If he'd experienced this sort of hesitation when planning strategies or leading troops into battle, Xenex would still be bending under the Danteri yoke instead of standing on the verge of shaking it off forever. Forcing himself to focus on the business at hand, he drew himself up straight and fixed a gaze upon the Federation man. "How would it be done?" he demanded.

"It?"

"Being a CAP-tane. How would I go about achieving it?"

PEE-cahd smiled slightly. "You mean a captain? Like me?"

"Like you?" M'k'n'zy looked at him askance. "Is lack of hair a requirement?"

The captain didn't quite seem to know whether to be annoyed or amused, and opted for a slight chuckle. "No. That's not a requirement. Although there will certainly be times along the road where you'll want to tear your hair out, metaphorically speaking." He paused and studied M'k'n'zy. "Are you sure about this, M'k'n'zy? You haven't had time to give it much thought . . ."

"That's not true," replied M'k'n'zy. "I've given a lot of thought to my place in the world once we're free. I just . . . haven't come up with anything I liked. Perhaps that's because my place is somewhere else. At the very least, it's something I'd like to try."

"All right," PEE-cahd said gamely. "It . . . wouldn't be something that could be arranged overnight."

"That doesn't concern me," replied M'k'n'zy. "I've spent my entire life looking toward gains years down the line rather than immediately. I can wait." He paused, then asked, "What . . . exactly . . . am I waiting for?"

"Well . . ." PEE-cahd scratched his chin thoughtfully. "As I'm sure you can guess, Starfleet doesn't simply tap you on the head and say you're a captain."

"Why not?" said M'k'n'zy. He was genuinely surprised. Although he hadn't given much consideration to precisely what was involved, it certainly seemed straightforward enough. He'd been a leader of men for most of his life. Being a captain, why . . . that simply involved leading other men while wearing some sort of uniform.

"To start out," said a clearly amused PEE-cahd, "you have to learn your way around a starship. That's a rather daunting undertaking."

"Daunting? Why? How long could it take? A day?"

"It's a *starship*, M'k'n'zy."

"So." M'k'n'zy shrugged. "How big could it be, PEE-cahd?"

PEE-cahd studied him for a moment, then tapped his chest again. "Picard to Crusher."

"Crusher here, Captain," came back the voice of the man who'd earlier been standing near PEE-cahd when he'd first arrived on Xenex. M'k'n'zy was taken aback. It seemed almost magical to him.

"Jack . . . send down the *Columbus* to these coordinates, would you? Unmanned. Autonav should suffice, I'd think."

"You're not simply beaming up to the ship, sir?"

"I'm taking the pretty route . . . or as you'd call it, the scenic route."

"Not much scenic about this route, sir, with all respect."

"Oh, you'd be surprised. Picard out." He smiled at M'k'n'zy and there was something challenging in his look. "Would you care to go for a ride? If you're reluctant to, I'd understan—"

M'k'n'zy looked at him defiantly. "What, PEE-cahd, you think I'm afraid? I'm not afraid. Of anything."

"Good. By the way, it's 'Picard.' Short 'i,' accent on the second syllable."

By the time the *Columbus* arrived, M'k'n'zy more or less had down the correct pronunciation of Picard's name. He heard the vessel arriving before he saw it, the engine's roar alerting him. He looked up and saw it descending from the sky. Other Xenexians had stopped to watch as well. They weren't entirely primitive as a people; they'd seen flying ships before. Still, it wasn't all that common a sight. And when they did see them, more often than not it was in the form of troop transports for Danteri soldiers. So there was understandable tension in the air as a crowd gathered, and M'k'n'zy noticed that more than a few were reaching for weapons. Immediately he calmed them, assuring them that there was no threat nor did Picard pose one.

The ship settled to the ground and a door opened in the side. Picard stepped in, turned, and gestured for M'k'n'zy to follow him. The

Xenexian did so cautiously and, once inside, glanced around the interior of the ship. Picard settled himself in at helm and glanced over at M'k'n'zy. "Take a seat," he said.

M'k'n'zy did so, and suddenly his stomach was jolted as the vessel eased into the air. Picard glanced back at him. "Ever been off the ground before?" M'k'n'zy shook his head, a bit more frantically than he would have liked. A thin smile crossed Picard's face. "It can be quite disorienting for the uninitiated."

"I'm fine," M'k'n'zy said immediately.

"I'll take it easy on you. I'll minimize the barrel rolls."

"Fly however you want. I can handle it."

"You know . . . I suspect you could."

The ship moved skyward. Surreptitiously, M'k'n'zy gripped the underside of the chair, digging his fingers into it. Grozit, *what the hell have you gotten yourself into?* M'k'n'zy demanded of himself silently. After a minute or two, however, his initial, albeit unspoken, fears eased up. He began to relax into it. He discovered that he liked the relative quiet, broken only by the gentle humming of the engines.

From his seat, he looked around the interior of the vessel. There were lights and panels and all manner of things that he couldn't comprehend. But he knew he was a fast learner. He was confident that he could pick it all up pretty quickly.

Then he looked out the front viewscreen. The stars were so much closer, and he gazed with wonderment and awe.

"Impressive, isn't it," said Picard as if he could read the boy's mind.

"They're not twinkling. Why aren't they twinkling?"

"Because you're seeing them without an atmosphere between you. There's no refraction of the light."

"Oh," said M'k'n'zy, acting as if he understood. He paused and then went on, "When I was a child, there were stories that the night sky was a solid object—a screen that stood between us and great and terrible gods. And that no one could venture near it lest they tear a hole in the sky and the great and terrible gods come pouring through it to wreak havoc upon us."

"You'll find no screens nor fearsome gods up here, M'k'n'zy. Although there is the odd hole or two, but you can learn about that later."

"Learn how? Where?"

"Well, there's an academy. A school, back on the planet where I was born. The best, the brightest, the most gifted of young people attend it to learn and grow and, ultimately, see if they have what it takes to be a Starfleet officer."

"Are you in charge of it?"

"No, no." Picard smiled. "I couldn't exactly see myself running a school for gifted youngsters. Not sure I'd have the patience. But there are excellent people in charge of it. It's called Starfleet Academy."

"How long would I attend it?"

"Four years."

"Four years?"

"If it's of any consolation, that's Earth years. I believe each one is a few days shorter than a Xenexian year. Oh, come now, M'k'n'zy. You said you always looked toward the long term."

"Yes, but . . ." He shook his head. "It just seems such a waste of time. Four years to learn about a ship like this? I mean, yes, we have nothing like this on Xenex, but—"

"A ship like *this?*" Picard laughed.

M'k'n'zy bristled at the response. "What's so funny?" he demanded.

"It's not your fault, M'k'n'zy. It's mine. Obviously, I didn't make it clear to you. This ship . . . it's called a shuttle. It takes us to the actual ship . . . which, as you can see on the screen, is just ahead, orbiting your world."

M'k'n'zy stared at the vessel they were approaching. "Well, that doesn't seem . . ."

They drew closer.

". . . so . . ." he finished, but he could barely form the words.

The closer they got, the more gargantuan it became. All the blood drained out of M'k'n'zy's face. *"Grozit,"* he said softly. "It's . . . it's huge! You . . . you gave me no idea . . . it's gargantuan!"

"Well, I don't like to brag," said Picard.

They drew to within one hundred kilometers of the vessel, and it took up the entire viewscreen. Slowly Picard piloted the shuttle around the *Stargazer,* pointing out various sections of the ship such as the engines, the bridge, and other highlights. M'k'n'zy only partly took it all in. He was busy trying to comprehend what he was seeing, and being only marginally successful. "Can I go inside?"

"No," Picard said firmly.

"Why not?"

"Because frankly," he said, "I'm not quite sure you're ready for it, M'k'n'zy. My concern is you might find it so overwhelming that it could prove a disincentive for you to pursue studies at the Academy. That would be unfortunate. I think you have vast potential."

"Potential? To rule one of those?"

"We prefer the term 'command,' although the monarchist in me finds your description entertaining," admitted Picard.

M'k'n'zy wanted to argue the point with him but decided against it. He was beginning to sense that this man, this Picard, had great wisdom to him. And if he said he felt it would be counterproductive to bring M'k'n'zy aboard now, then he would abide by that.

"Can we go around it again?" he asked.

"Why not?" said Picard, and continued the shuttle on its circular course.

"It's . . ." M'k'n'zy shook his head. "It must be the biggest spaceship in the galaxy."

Picard again chuckled. "Actually, it's not even the biggest ship in the fleet. There are others far larger, with crew complements of over a thousand. The *Stargazer* has just over six hundred people aboard."

M'k'n'zy stared at Picard, stared at the ship, stared back at Picard.

"I'm starting to think," said M'k'n'zy, "that four years of schooling may not be enough to learn everything."

"It's not," Picard assured him, as the stars shone temptingly in the sky. "The actual learning starts when you graduate."

Chapter Two

Now

In the Ten-Forward lounge of the *Trident,* M'Ress sat nursing a drink without having the slightest idea of how she was supposed to feel.

It was silent in the lounge, which was unusual considering the time of day. Usually at this point there was boisterousness and loud chatting, laughing and men and women cozying up to each other. There had been nothing like this lounge on the *Enterprise,* nearly a century gone, that M'Ress had served on. If one wanted to go and knock back drinks, one visited with Dr. McCoy or (M'Ress's preference) Montgomery Scott. Private parties would be staged and good times were had by all.

There were no good times being had this day.

Word was out all over the ship of the brutal, hideous murder of Lieutenant Commander Gleau. And because there were no secrets aboard a starship, the history between Gleau and M'Ress had become common knowledge.

She glanced around the Ten-Forward, holding her drink tightly as she did so. She realized that she was squeezing it to the point where, if she didn't ease up, she might shatter the glass. That wouldn't look particularly good, and would feel even worse. Then her hand began shaking violently, and she put the glass down lest she drop it.

She was certain that all eyes were upon her. Lieutenant Gold was at a table, and he was trying not to look at her, but kept doing so. And over there was Ensign Yarborough, and she was looking as well, and there was Ensign Janos, and he was staring at her openly, except thanks to the white-furred security man's superb intellect, he looked more as if he were studying a specimen under a microscope. And there were several crewmen whose names she didn't know, but they were looking at her, too.

She wanted to scream. She wanted to run, or howl, because she knew what they were all thinking: They thought she had done it. They thought she had just shredded Gleau with her claws, and the dually horrific aspect of it was that on the one hand she was appalled that they would think that of her, and on the other she couldn't blame them. If she were on the outside looking in, she'd have thought the same thing.

Even though she was seated in a secluded corner of the lounge, she nevertheless felt as if all eyes were boring into her. Finally, unable to take it anymore, she got to her feet with the intention of bolting. But she stopped cold when she realized there was someone directly in her path. It was a mark of just how distracted she was that she didn't detect the scent of the new arrival before actually seeing her.

Katerina Mueller, executive officer of the *Trident,* was standing there with her hands draped behind her back. "Going somewhere, Lieutenant?" she asked.

"I was thinking . . . back to my quarters, ma'am," said M'Ress.

"Ma'am?" Mueller looked at her skeptically.

"Sir?" M'Ress ventured.

"Generally 'XO' will do. Or 'Commander,' " said Mueller, and it was at that point that M'Ress noticed that Mueller was holding a bottle of clear liquid that didn't look at all like synthehol. Furthermore, the scent of alcohol was wafting off her breath. She hadn't consumed sufficient drink to be remotely inebriated, apparently, but she was certainly relaxed. "But in this case . . . call me Kat. Appropriate, don't you think, what with you and your feline . . . thing." She gestured vaguely. "Mind if I sit?" Not only did she not wait for M'Ress's invitation, but she was perched upon the chair opposite M'Ress before getting past the word "I." M'Ress, perplexed, slowly sat back down.

Swirling the glass's contents, Mueller said, "Would you like some?"

"No thank you."

"Good," said Mueller, and promptly refilled half of M'Ress's glass with the contents of the bottle.

M'Ress stared at it, and then looked up at Mueller. Mueller managed a ragged smile. Cautiously, M'Ress said, "XO," and quickly amended it when Mueller waggled a finger at her. "Kat . . . I . . . thought you didn't like me."

"I don't. I didn't," said Mueller, running a finger around the lip of the glass. "I felt that you were getting preferential treatment. 'Kid gloves,' as they used to say."

"I'm no child. No kid."

"Actually, it refers to very soft gloves, made from a 'kid' or calf. It means to be handled gently."

"Oh. I knew that," said M'Ress quickly.

Mueller ignored her. M'Ress wasn't even sure she'd heard her. "Anyway," continued Mueller, "because of that—because I felt that everyone was tiptoeing around hurting your feelings since you were the poor, time-displaced Starfleet officer who'd lost friends, family, everyone and everything to the passage of time—"

"You decided to go out of your way to make me feel unwelcome?" M'Ress wasn't thrilled about her choice of words, but she really couldn't think of any other way to put it.

"More or less," agreed Mueller with candor. "And now, because of that . . . I'm temporarily relieved of duty." As M'Ress's jaw dropped, she held up the bottle proudly. "What, you didn't think I'd be drinking *on* duty, did you?"

"Why?" asked an astounded M'Ress.

"It was a mutual decision," said Mueller. She was about to keep speaking, but she decided to fill up her glass again. She tilted the bottle but unfortunately missed the glass, sending liquid splattering on the tabletop. Heaving a sigh over the waste, she put the bottle to her lips and just drank it straight out. Then she lowered it and fixed her gaze on a point about six inches to the right of where M'Ress was actually sitting. "I went to the captain and explained to her that I would not be the best person to become involved in an investigation of Gleau's murder."

"They . . . definitely know it's murder," M'Ress asked, her voice wavering slightly as she asked it.

Mueller managed to figure out where M'Ress was sitting and locked her gaze on to the Caitian. "He was torn apart. Hardly sounds like suicide to me. If it is, then Gleau found the single most painful means of terminating one's own existence in history."

"Yes, I . . . I suppose," said M'Ress with a sigh. "It's just . . . wait," as Mueller's words suddenly got through to her. "What do you mean, you're not the best person?"

"Oh, he and I had a semipublic spat."

"A 'spat'?"

Mueller bobbed her head. "I slammed him around a little because I became convinced he was dropping into your dreams and threatening you."

M'Ress gasped. Her eyes wide, she said, "I . . . I don't know what to say. . . . I . . . I thought you—"

"You thought I believed you were crazy. Or looking for attention. Or out to make Gleau's life miserable because he had sex with you thanks to the Selelvian mind technique called the Knack. Those and other possibilities all occurred to me, and you didn't come out looking good in any of them." She pursed her lips and, without even being aware she was doing it, she traced the slim line of the Heidelberg fencing scar that adorned the left side of her face.

"But you came to believe me! Commander, I can't . . ." She realized her voice was getting louder, drawing unwanted notice from everyone. Everyone except Janos, who was simply staring in front of him, looking thoughtful. She lowered her tone to just above a whisper and said, "I can't tell you how much it means that you—"

"Save it," Mueller interrupted her curtly. "I allowed my personal perceptions of you to color how I handled the Gleau situation. If I'd believed you more quickly, if I'd done something else instead of just dismissing you out of hand . . ."

"You couldn't have known."

"I should have," she said brusquely. "But I didn't. And when my own investigations, coupled with the oddly incomplete psych profile on Gleau, led me to conclude something might well be wrong—I botched it. Handled it badly. I made matters worse. If I'd realized earlier on that Gleau posed a threat . . ."

"A threat?" M'Ress echoed the word. She felt as if her world were spiraling dizzyingly, threatening to throw her off. It had seemed forever that she'd been worrying, all on her own, about Gleau. Feeling isolated, bereft of any support. And now what Mueller was saying was tantamount to vindication. "A threat to someone other than me, you mean?"

"I don't know," said Mueller. She rapped her knuckles on the table in vague frustration. "When I confronted him, there was something in his eyes . . . I just knew. Knew there was more trouble there than I'd thought. But I had nothing really concrete. It was just—"

"Instinct?" M'Ress asked. "Believe me, Kat, I can completely understand that concept." Then her mind raced back along the conversation. "So . . . are you saying that you and the captain mutually relieved you of duty . . . because they suspect you might have had something to do with it?"

She nodded. "Anything is possible."

"But . . . the way it was done! How could they possibly think that you'd have just . . . just torn him up like that? That you *could?*"

"It doesn't seem reasonable, does it."

"No! Why, given opportunity and motive, it only makes sense that I would have—"

She stopped and stared at Mueller, and her eyes narrowed. Her nostrils began to twitch. "Ohhhh . . . I get it."

"Get it?" Mueller stared at her levelly. "M'Ress, you seem tense."

"How can you tell?"

"Your ears are down and your tail is straight back."

"Are they?" M'Ress's laugh was brittle. "Well, that's a surprise. Then again, none of it should be a surprise, should it. I should have realized you were no different than they are. *No different!*" Her voice carried, and now no one in the Ten-Forward was making the slightest pretense of looking the other way. "You weren't trying to be nice to me! You weren't taking my side! You were trying to trick me into confessing!"

"Do you have something to confess to?" Mueller asked. Any trace of inebriation was gone from her face, if there'd ever been any there at all.

"Oh, you'd like that, wouldn't you. It'd make your job so nice and simple. The outsider, the Starfleet officer from years ago, brought her hundred-year-old hands-on sense of justice to the modern era. Well, forget it, *Commander!*"

"Lieutenant, sit down," said Mueller, sounding a bit tired. "You're getting the wrong idea. . . ."

"No, I think I've got exactly the right idea! You're sniffing around, investigating . . ."

"Nothing has to be sniffed around," Mueller told her, and she got to her feet. "Doc Villers is doing a thorough forensics sweep of the turbo-lift and Gleau's body. It's taking a little while to sort out because the lift is so heavily trafficked an area. But once that's done, we'll know. And that will be that."

"And you were figuring . . . what?" she demanded with a slight toss of her mane. "That if the evidence proved conclusively it was me, you were going to try and make it easier on me? Perhaps get me to confess so it would look better in the final report? If I show some remorse, it might take a few years off my sentence?"

"Something like that," admitted Mueller.

"Well, forget it!" M'Ress started circling the Ten-Forward, moving like a great stalking feline, and she felt some inner degree of pleasure that the others were flinching back from her. All except Janos, whose infinitely sad gaze followed her around the room. "Because if any of you are expecting me to shed one tear over him, you can forget it! He made my life a living hell. And I couldn't be happier that he's dead! And I can see what's going through all your minds. You're thinking, 'How can she say that? Doesn't she know how guilty that makes her sound?' "

"I have to admit, it did occur to me," Janos spoke up.

"Oh? Then how about this: Only someone with a completely clear conscience would dare express happiness that someone who was a dan-ger to her isn't around to pose it anymore. And that's me! Clear con-science up and down the line." She turned back to face Mueller, pivoting noiselessly on her padded feet. "You want 'sorry,' Commander? Here's your 'sorry': I'm sorry I didn't put the bastard down myself. I'd never, ever have done it, because I'm a decent and ethical being. But in-side me, Commander," and she leaned forward, balancing on the edge of the table, "inside me there's a primal, feral part that would have de-lighted in feeling his blood pumping out of an artery severed by my own hand. Delighted in it. And if in this century, thinking about some-thing is the same as actually doing it, *then send in security to cart me away!*"

At that moment, the door to the Ten-Forward opened. M'Ress caught the familiar scent of Arex before he even came through the door. Three security guards were with him, and all of them had their phasers out. Clearly they were expecting some sort of struggle.

There were captains on either side of them: Shelby on the left, Cal-houn on the right. In both cases, their faces were grim. M'Ress suspected that Calhoun in particular was upset; the scar on his face was standing out bright crimson against his skin. They did not have weapons drawn. Obviously they were confident the security team was packing enough firepower.

Pushed to extremes and beyond, M'Ress didn't hesitate. With a snarl, she vaulted across the room, dropping right in front of the security squad. Arex looked slightly taken aback and stared at her questioningly.

"So how are we going to do this, Arex?" she demanded. "Going to drag me into a small room? Going to keep me from having food and water for hour after hour until I tell you what you want to hear, whether it's true or not?"

His eyes widened. "Shib, what the *hell* are you talking about?"

She was taken aback by his obvious confusion.

"Lieutenant," said Shelby, taking a step forward, a hardness in her eyes that would brook no further interference. "I know you've been under a strain lately, and that's being taken into account. But I'm giving you a direct order to stand aside immediately."

"Stand . . . aside?" She didn't comprehend, and yet automatically she moved to the side of the security squad. It was then she realized they were looking right past her.

"Ensign Janos, will you come with us, please?" said Shelby.

M'Ress felt a cold chill down her spine as she turned and saw Janos rise. The way in which he did it, the slow uncoiling, helped underscore just how fast and deadly he could be when he put his mind to it. But he did not seem troubled in his manner; just mildly perplexed. "Is there a problem?"

"Janos," said Calhoun, and there was tension in his voice. "Don't make this more difficult than it need be."

"I'm not quite sure what the required difficulty level might be, since the issue at hand has not been properly illuminated," Janos said. "Would someone be so kind as to enlighten me?"

"You want to be formal?" asked Shelby. "Very well: We can be formal. Ensign Janos, you are under arrest for the murder of Lieutenant Commander Gleau, and direct contravention of Regulation Thirty-eight, Sections One through Four."

There was dead silence in the Ten-Forward for a moment. M'Ress felt the hackles rising on the back of her neck. Janos, for his part, appeared unperturbed. "You know, if they felt the need to make a specific regulation against murdering officers, you'd think they'd have given it a bit more priority than placing it at number thirty-eight."

"Ensign, this is hardly a joking matter," said Calhoun.

"With all respect, sir, to me it is. It has to be a joke. I was not responsible for Gleau's death."

"The evidence indicates differently, Ensign. You are now being ordered to accompany us to the brig, pursuant to further investigation."

Another silence, this one even longer.

"Very well," said Janos quietly. He seemed more resentful than anything else. "Let us attend to this immediately so we can clear up this misunderstanding as briskly as possible. Gentlemen . . . ladies . . ." and he bowed deeply, like a magician about to disappear off the stage after having put on an incredibly good show. He turned back to the security team. "Would you care for me to walk around so that I'm in front of you? I mean, you could keep your weapons aimed at me and then walk backward the whole way. Or we can make this easy on you. Your discretion."

Calhoun gestured for Janos to precede them. "After you," he said.

"Thank you, Captain." With his head held high, Janos swayed slightly from side to side as he moved in his standard anthropoid gait.

"As you were," Shelby called out to the rest of Ten-Forward. "XO, if it wouldn't be too much of a problem . . ."

"On my way to take the conn, Captain," Mueller said immediately.

"Thank you, XO," said Shelby.

Mueller turned quickly to M'Ress and paused long enough to say, "We'll chat more later." Then she was out the door after Shelby.

The moment they were gone, hushed conversation filled the air of the Ten-Forward. They were all looking toward the door, as if expecting Janos to come back through there at any time. All interest in speculating about M'Ress, silently or otherwise, had abruptly ended.

She had never felt so relieved, and so simultaneously distraught, in her life.

Then

i.

Joshua Kemper was a tall, good-looking, square-jawed example of Starfleet, with broad shoulders and closely cropped black hair.

He stood leaning against the entrance to the main building of Starfleet Academy, shielding his eyes against the sun as he looked up and watched the shuttles arriving in a steady stream, each carrying with it a new crop of Starfleet recruits. The brisk salt air of San Francisco Bay wafted toward him on the stiff breeze. He inhaled deeply, finding the scent exhilarating.

"Bringing back memories?"

He glanced over to see his best friend, Ray Williams, approaching. Williams bore a resemblance to Kemper, but he was taller and his face was more open; he always looked on the brink of laughing at a joke. Kemper chuckled when he saw him and reached over, patting Williams on the stomach. "Let yourself go during the summer, Ray."

"Nonsense. My mother's cooking would do this to anyone," he replied, thumping his gut. "I'll have it worked off within two weeks, Kemp. Mark me." He saw where Kemper was looking and shook his head. "The new arrivals. How they looking?"

"More raw every year," said Kemper.

"Were we ever that young and stupid-looking?" Williams wondered.

Kemper firmly shook his head. "Never."

"Good, I thought as much."

As the students arrived, they would head one by one or in groups toward an orientation center, guided there by various senior students who had been given the specific duty or, in some cases, had even volunteered. To Kemper, volunteering for such a thing seemed a waste of material and possibilities.

More shuttles were arriving, and Kemper felt stirred to action. "Come on, Ray. Too gorgeous a day to let opportunities slip past us."

"Awww, Kemp," moaned Williams. "Why try to start up trouble, huh?"

"Because it lets the plebes know just exactly where they stand and where we stand." He clapped Williams on the back and spoke expansively, like a Roman senator putting forward declarations for an attentive senate, striding toward the arrival pads as he spoke. "It's not truly up to us, Ray. Our actions in this matter are dictated by time-honored tradition. We are not endeavoring to 'start up' anything. We are merely carrying on in the long—"

"If I come along, will you shut up?" said Williams.

"Of course!"

"Because God forbid you could just do this for your own amusement. You need an audience, and I'm elected."

"You could participate . . ."

"Ohhh, this is much more your thing than mine. But I'll cheer you on, because that's what friends are for."

"You are an officer and a gentleman," said Kemper approvingly.

A new shuttle, this one just arrived from the switching station on Titan, disgorged more passengers, just as Kemper and Williams drew close. The cadets were standing there, clutching their bags, looking variously excited, nervous, confident, scared. There were half a dozen of them . . .

No. Half a dozen plus one more.

Williams saw him at the same time. "Ohhh, he seems ripe."

"Your excellent eye for talent has not diminished," said Kemper approvingly.

The "one more" was standing several feet from the others, who were clustered together and talking excitedly among themselves. He was just standing there, staring at the buildings surrounding Academy Plaza as if he'd never seen anything like them. He very likely hadn't.

"Would you like to know his story?" Kemper asked.

"You know his story?"

"Of course," said Kemper, tapping the side of his head. "My practiced eye misses nothing. The likelihood is that he was raised on some small farming colony somewhere, possibly in one of the outer systems. He took the entrance exam, tested well—possibly he cheated or had an old family friend administering it who was willing to look the other way . . . you know the type . . . and then his parents pulled together the where-withal to send him here so he could aspire to some sort of better life than they have."

"You can tell all that," said Williams skeptically, "just by looking at him."

"Absolutely." He smiled in anticipation. "I'll bet you he's never even seen a Starfleet officer. Probably worships the mere notion of us, like gods."

"I see someone became full of himself during the summer."

"Better that than full of Mom's home cooking," Kemper chided him. "Come on. Let's do our duty."

Kemper and Williams picked up the pace and arrived at the group of cadets at exactly the same time as another upperclassman. She was hold-ing a padd and was clearly one of those guiding the plebes to where they were supposed to be. Her name was Theresa Detwiler, and Kemper had seen her socially for a while before the relationship self-destructed, as so many tended to do during the crucible of Academy life. Detwiler saw him coming, and she ran her fingers through her lengthy red hair in that way she did when she anticipated problems.

The cadets saw Kemper and Williams coming as well, and uncon-sciously—or perhaps deliberately, in some cases—they straightened up. Kemper could well understand why. He and Ray certainly cut impres-sive figures in their sharp fourth-year uniforms. *We are as gods,* he thought again, and took amused pleasure from that.

Only the bumpkin from the farming colony didn't snap to. He didn't even appear to notice the upperclassmen. He was still too busy staring at the buildings.

"Welcome, Cadets," Detwiler was saying, although Kemper could see that her peripheral vision was fixed on him. "I'm Theresa Detwiler, a third-year cadet, and I'm your orientation guide here at . . ."

"I'll take it from here, Terry," Kemper said confidently, striding forward, arms draped behind his back.

"I believe, Mr. Kemper, I have matters in hand," said Detwiler.

He smiled pleasantly. "I'm sure you do. But, fourth-year prerogative . . . I thought I'd see the kind of stuff that's being sent to the Academy these days. You!" he said abruptly, his entire tone changing. "With the scar. Eyes front."

Closer up, Kemper had a better chance to study the young man who had caught his attention. His clothes were extremely plain and seemed thrown together with little concept of fashion sense. His hair was trimmed but hung about his face carelessly, as if he'd had it cut and styled recently, but couldn't be bothered to worry about maintaining it. His eyes were . . .

Kemper froze.

It wasn't the color of the eyes that caused him to be taken aback. Purple was unusual, granted, but not so unusual that it would disturb a fourth-year cadet. No, it was the coldness that he saw in them. Eyes that were sizing him up, burning with chill fire, looking to see . . .

Looking to see the best way to kill him.

Yes. That was it. Pure, undiluted savagery that was assessing in a heartbeat whether this man was an enemy and, if so, what would be the most efficient way of dispatching him.

And then, just like that, the farmboy (for so Kemper had dubbed him) pulled a virtual veil across his eyes. Only for an instant had Kemper seen the undiluted ferocity of what was facing him, and then it was gone . . . so quickly, in fact, that Kemper barely had time to process what he'd seen. It didn't fully register on him. And because of that, Kemper was able to convince himself that whatever he'd thought he'd spotted in that deadly gaze was merely his imagination. He'd been away from the Academy for too long. The summer break had made him rusty, that's all there was to it. Rusty and second-guessing himself.

"What's your name, scar face?" demanded Kemper, squaring his shoulders to look even more impressive than he already was.

The boy stared impassively at him. Whatever emotions he felt over the comment on his scar were kept tightly wrapped. Kemper couldn't help but approve. A Starfleet officer needed self-control, and this young man obviously had it in spades. But this was hardly the time or situation to start bandying about compliments.

"Your name," he said again when the boy didn't answer.

When the boy finally replied, Kemper blinked. It didn't sound like a name. It sounded as if the boy were gargling. There was a "Mah" sound in there, followed by what seemed to be random consonants slapped together. "What the hell kind of name is that?" he demanded.

"Mr. Kemper," said Detwiler sharply, "I really must insist . . ."

"Xenexian," the boy said, speaking over Detwiler.

"Xenexian." He tried to recall what he knew about Xenexians. Not much. So the boy wasn't a farmer; instead he was from some backwater planet that was barely up to Federation standards. Perhaps he was someone's idea of a charity case. He certainly didn't seem particularly impressive or imposing. Slowly Kemper started to walk back and forth with a slight swagger. He cast a glance at Williams, mutely seeking approval, but Williams was just watching scar face as if he was concerned something was going to go horribly wrong. Well, that was typical Williams: always worrying about nothing. "I hear," continued Kemper, "that only two things ever come out of Xenex: fools and mules. You don't look like a mule, so you must be a fool. Is that right?"

"Josh, for crying out loud—!" said Detwiler.

He silenced her with a look. His seniority over her was marginal at best, but it was still there, and Detwiler understood and respected the chain of command as well as anyone. She smoldered but fell silent.

"Well? Which is it?" demanded Kemper.

Scar face said nothing. Just stared at him.

Kemper stepped in closer to him. "Are you giving me eye, boy? You don't give me eye! You respect your senior officers, one of whom happens to be me."

He was astounded when the boy replied, "Respect is earned, not given."

Kemper's mouth opened and closed without a word uttered. A moment later he had composed himself, and then he said, "Respect, boy, is what rank entitles one to. An officer in Starfleet is granted it automatically. He doesn't have to jump through hoops to earn your respect. You give it and you're glad to give it, do you understand?" When an answer wasn't instantly forthcoming, he repeated louder, "I said *do you understand?*"

"No," said the boy.

The other cadets were watching the proceedings with mute shock. The reactions were mixed: Clearly some admired the young man for his nerve, while others thought he was insane for giving a senior student this much grief. This angered Kemper. As far as he was concerned, reactions shouldn't be mixed. There should be one and only one: anger that someone who clearly had no concept of how Starfleet operated was being allowed anywhere near the Academy. Well, lessons were going to have to be taught immediately.

"Drop," he said, "and give me forty."

The boy whom he'd taken to calling "scar face" rather than "farmboy" simply stared blankly at him.

"I said drop and give me forty!"

"Drop what? Forty what?"

Looking somewhat embarrassed, Detwiler said, "He wants you to lower yourself to the ground and do forty pushups for him. You know: like this." She demonstrated with her arms pumping up and down.

The boy said nothing. Just stared at Detwiler, then at Kemper.

A slow smile spread across the boy's face.

"Do you think this is some sort of joke?" Kemper asked him. And when the smile widened, he said, "Perhaps I should call Xenex and tell your daddy his son has got no chance of ever being a Starfleet officer."

The smile faded instantly. Even more curiously, the scar on his face became slightly brighter against the skin. "You," he said, "do not speak of my father."

Kemper advanced on him, and as he drew closer, his voice got louder and his manner angrier. "I will speak of whomever I wish to speak whenever I wish to speak of him. You have no say in the matter, because you are a plebe, and you will do as you are ordered, when you are ordered, with no question, no thought, but simple obedience, and if you don't like it then you can climb right back on the shuttle and head back to Xenex, and tell your daddy that—"

It was the last thing he remembered before he woke up in the infirmary three hours later.

ii.

Commander Edward Jellico, dean of students, looked up from the report on his computer . . . the one that had been dutifully filed by Cadets Detwiler and Sullivan at the time of the incident. The descriptions of the event matched up so perfectly that Jellico was almost inclined to suspect collusion. It seemed preferable, because the truth of the matter was harder to absorb.

The young man known as M'k'n'zy of Calhoun sat on the other side of Jellico's desk, his hands folded on his lap. He wasn't moving at all. He might have been carved from a block of marble. Jellico had seen dead people who were livelier. He tried to imagine for a moment what it would be like entering a darkened room, knowing this M'k'n'zy was waiting for you, trying to locate him with your normal five senses and hoping that movement on his part might give his position away. He had to believe that anyone in that predicament wouldn't be getting out of it in one piece.

"You broke his jaw," said an incredulous Jellico.

M'k'n'zy said nothing.

"With one punch."

Still nothing.

"That he never saw coming." He looked at the screen again. "His friend, Cadet Williams, says he never even saw you throw it although he swears he was looking right at you. Cadet Detwiler says she spotted a 'slight movement' on your part, but didn't know it was a punch until Mr. Kemper collapsed. And Mr. Kemper, when it comes to the art of self-defense, is in the top one percent of his class." Jellico leaned back a moment, shutting off the computer screen and simply taking in the situation. "You've made quite a first impression, and I don't mean that in a positive sense."

M'k'n'zy continued to say nothing. He just sat there and stared. It was unnerving. Finally Jellico prompted, "Well? Do you have anything to say for yourself?"

"I warned him," said M'k'n'zy after a moment.

Jellico stood, walking forcefully around his desk. "You don't understand, Mach . . . Muckuh . . . Much . . ." He grimaced over his inability to say the name correctly and then tried to glide by. "It's not your place to warn a fellow cadet of anything. There is no excuse for such behavior, and whatever excuse you may offer is of no relevance."

"It is to me," M'k'n'zy told him.

"Don't you understand? This is not Xenex! You don't get to just smack people around if you don't like what they have to say. You're not a warlord here!"

"No. I am a warlord . . . here." And he tapped his chest, over his heart.

Jellico stared at him. "Just out of a sense of morbid curiosity," he said at last, "what *did* Kemper say?"

"He spoke disrespectfully of my father."

"I see," said Jellico. "And you hospitalized him for it. Doesn't that strike you as something of an overreaction? If I contacted your father, what do you think he would say?"

And M'k'n'zy looked up at him with just the slightest flash of pain in his eyes, which was quickly replaced with steel. "I think my father would approve. Then again . . . my father was beaten to death by our oppressors years ago. I saw it happen. I was helpless to stop him. So I'm just guessing."

Then M'k'n'zy looked away. Jellico felt a coldness in his chest, a sense of quiet frustration . . . and also chagrin.

"Shall I go home now?" asked M'k'n'zy after a long silence.

Jellico felt that, in some respects, that would probably be the best move. But he couldn't find it in himself to send the first Xenexian Starfleet candidate packing. He thought of his oath. *To seek out new life.* Well, new life had come knocking on the Academy door. Slamming it in the new life's face somehow seemed . . . lazy, if nothing else.

With a tone that was slightly softer, but still firm, he said, "You don't get off quite that easily, mister. Look . . . I don't think you're really understanding what I'm saying. You're here to learn rules. Our rules. Rules that have been developed over a period of many, many years. Rules without which Starfleet could not function. If you cannot learn them, cannot abide by them, then you have no place in Starfleet and no place here." He paused. M'k'n'zy said nothing. "Well? Do you have a response to that?"

"Was one required?"

Jellico sighed and sagged against his desk, rubbing the bridge of his nose tiredly. "Frankly, there're only two reasons I'm not packing you back off to Xenex right now. First, the strong opinion of Cadet Detwiler, a fine third-year student, who asserts that Cadet Kemper was endeavoring to provoke you into a display, and that Kemper got what he deserved. And the second is that Captain Jean-Luc Picard went to a great deal of time and effort to arrange for your enrollment here at the Academy. He wouldn't have done that if he didn't firmly believe you had tremendous potential. If he feels that strongly, then attention must be paid.

"Look . . . Cadet . . ." Jellico continued. "I know this is an adjustment for you to make. From what I understand, on Xenex you're something of a planetary hero. Legions of men fought and died on your behalf."

"They fought and died on behalf of independence," M'k'n'zy said. "I was an instrument of an ideal, not the ideal itself."

"Well, Starfleet is an ideal as well, Cadet," said Jellico. "An ideal of discovery, of exploration, and of mutual cooperation. That means we all work together. And that's not going to be possible if you knock out your co-workers. Whatever it is you've accomplished, whoever it is that you were, back on Xenex . . . here you're simply a first-year cadet, the lowest rung on the ladder. As such, you don't get to just go around breaking the jaws of upperclassmen. A superior officer must be obeyed."

"He's not superior to me."

"In rank, yes, he is. Is it possible that you're the better man? Perhaps. Perhaps not. But you don't get to prove it by dislocating his jaw. Otherwise the entire command structure of a starship would fall apart, if every order had to be backed up by a clenched fist and a willingness to use force to have an order carried out.

"You've had one cause for the entirety of your life. That has been achieved. Now you must find a new cause. And if you want this place to be your cause, then you must learn the best way to pursue it. Because unlike your previous situation, where the enemy was right in front of you and you could hack away at him . . . here, your greatest enemies come from within. Your own uncertainty, your own fear, may make you doubt yourself and even turn away from the fleet. You see, you . . ."

"All right," the young man said abruptly. "You've made yourself clear."

Jellico paused, and then said, "It will help you greatly in getting through the Academy, when addressing those who are your teachers, to add the word 'sir' at the end of declarative statements."

"Why?" asked M'k'n'zy.

Opting for the better part of valor, Jellico said, "It's a grammatical societal custom. Like 'please' and 'thank you.' "

"Oh." M'k'n'zy nodded thoughtfully, then said, "You've made yourself clear . . . sir."

"And your decision?" he said immediately.

"I need a new cause in my life, so . . . I will learn."

"I'm pleased to hear that. To be honest, considering the way you took Kemper down, I think you might best be suited to a career in Starfleet security. Or perhaps in one of our special armed services divisions. The ground pounders. You might be a formidable—"

"Command," said M'k'n'zy.

"I beg your par—?"

"I will lead," M'k'n'zy said with quiet conviction. "I will be a leader of men. That is what I must do. I . . . do not know how else to be . . . sir."

"The command track would be somewhat challenging for you."

"More challenging than liberating a world?"

"There are different kinds of challenges, Cadet. Furthermore, you have to understand: There cannot be a replay of what happened," he said, his face grim. "Despite the recommendations of both Detwiler and Picard, the bottom line is that—purely officially—you weren't yet in attendance at the Academy. You hadn't gone through orientation and indoctrination. So your assault on Cadet Kemper can technically be seen as something that occurred prior to your attending Starfleet Academy and, hence, outside of my jurisdiction. But now you're officially here, and that particular loophole has been closed up. You cannot beat up a fellow cadet again."

"Can I beat up a teacher?" asked M'k'n'zy.

Jellico blinked. "Are you trying to be funny?"

"No. Simply trying to understand limits."

"No. You can't beat up a teacher. You can't beat up anybody. If you're serious about following a command track, you're going to have to find ways to make people want to follow you that don't involve brute force or leadership through the example of slaughtering an enemy. Is that clear?"

"Yes." He paused. "Is this a grammatical 'sir' situation?"

"Never hurts to play it safe," said Jellico.

"Very well. Yes sir."

"Good."

Sensing that they were done, M'k'n'zy rose. So did Jellico, who then said, "By the way . . . just a suggestion. Your name is a bit of a mouthful. To accommodate non-Xenexian tongues, you might want to consider a variation of it."

"Such as?"

"Well . . ." He glanced back at M'k'n'zy's name as it appeared on his computer screen. "From the phonetic spelling of your name, I'd say something like 'Mackenzie' would be about right. And the name of both your home village and clan is 'Calhoun.' So 'Mackenzie Calhoun' might be easier for people to say."

"I'm not sure if *I* can say it." M'k'n'zy tried "Mackenzie" several times, allowing it to roll off his tongue. The fifth time he said it, Jellico nodded approvingly. The Xenexian shrugged. It meant little to him. "Mackenzie Calhoun."

"Excellent. Well, then . . ." and he clapped a hand on M'k'n'zy's shoulder. "You have a lot of work ahead of you, then."

"Yes sir."

"But I have confidence in you."

"Yes sir," he said again, as if confidence in him was the most expected thing in the world. "As do I."

"Good. You see, it's—"

"But if Kemper mentions my father again, next time I will break him."

Jellico sagged back into his chair.

"Sit down, Calhoun," he said.

Calhoun sat.

The meeting took a while longer than Jellico had previously estimated.

iii.

"So! You're One-Punch Calhoun."

The newly dubbed Mackenzie Calhoun stood in the doorway of the room he'd been assigned to. The bags containing his few possessions were already waiting for him. The room was simple, functional, stark. Calhoun had certainly had less posh accommodations in his life, so the room didn't seem so terrible to him.

He was slightly thrown off, however, by the presence of the other student. For one thing, he had the longest chin Calhoun had ever seen. His hair was brown and shaggy, and there was an air of mischief about him which Calhoun automatically found appealing. In the accent of his voice, he sounded a bit like Picard. Furthermore, Calhoun's innate knack for sensing danger told him that this fellow posed no threat to him. Nevertheless, being a territorial creature, Calhoun was not ecstatic over the fact that this man was standing here in what was supposed to be *his* room.

"Who are you?" Calhoun demanded.

The other young man put up his hands in mock defensive posture. "Hey, don't hit me, squire. I'm just unpacking my things." That was indeed what he appeared to be doing, putting his clothing away into a cabinet.

"I thought I was staying here."

"You are. I'm your roommate. Everyone doubles up at the Academy. You didn't know?" Calhoun shook his head. "Hope that doesn't pose a problem, squire."

"It may if you keep calling me 'squire.' "

"Fair enough," said the other cadet. He extended a hand, grinning. "Vincent Wexler's the name."

Calhoun stared at the outstretched hand a moment and then, sensing he was supposed to do something, put out his own right hand. "Mackenzie Calhoun," he said. They both stood there a moment, their respective hands facing each other. Finally Wexler reached over, took Calhoun's right hand with his own right, and then very slowly raised it up and down. Calhoun stared at him. "Another custom?" he said.

"One of many," affirmed Wexler. Then he turned back to unpacking the rest of his belongings into a cabinet. "I took this dresser if you don't mind. Somewhat random choice, really. So if you have a strong preference, I can unpack—"

"I don't care," said Calhoun.

"Fine then. So . . . is it true what they say?" He put away the last of his things, slid the drawer closed, then flopped down onto a bed and grinned at Calhoun. "Did you really take down a fourth-year cadet with one punch?"

"Yes."

"Supposedly he's over in the infirmary getting a broken jaw patched up. Even with the rebuilt bone, he'll still be talking out the side of his face for a week. Amazing. How did you do it?"

Calhoun shrugged. He couldn't quite understand the fascination everyone at the Academy seemed to have with his encounter with Kemper. He hadn't been able to express to Jellico what he was really feeling: that it was something between two men. One clearly goading the other, and the person who was being goaded retaliating. To Calhoun's mind, it was something that should be of little to no interest to anyone else. Disagreements happened on Xenex all the time. If Xenexians spent time prattling on and on about every fistfight or violent encounter, nothing would ever get done.

"I hit him," said Calhoun, unable to think of any other way to put it.

"Pardon my saying so," said Wexler, looking him up and down, "but you don't seem the muscular, burly type."

"Muscles are measured in quality, not quantity," Calhoun told him. "Strength isn't needed to break bones. Just speed and leverage."

"I'll definitely keep that in mind." His eyes glistened with curiosity. "So you were some sort of army captain back where you come from? Hard to believe. You seem so young."

"Xenex tends to age you."

"What did you do back there? I bet it was absolutely fascinating."

Calhoun didn't feel absolutely fascinating. He felt more and more uncomfortable. As if he was being subjected to intense scrutiny from everyone around him. How much of an outsider did he have to be, anyway?

"Nothing," Calhoun said abruptly. "Nothing that interesting. There's no point dwelling on the past."

Wexler seemed briefly surprised, but then he nodded approvingly. "Abso-bloody-lutely. That's why they call it the past, after all. Because it's past. Although," he added with a lopsided smile, "you will allow me my indulgences, I hope, if I embrace my own past."

"Meaning?"

"Meaning Wexlers have a long and proud history of service to

Starfleet," Wexler told him. "My parents, for example, are brilliant scientists, and have served Starfleet medical and biological research for many years. And I've been told I have this frankly annoying habit of bringing it up at every opportunity. So I apologize in advance if you find it annoying."

"Don't concern yourself. I'll simply ignore you," said Calhoun as he proceeded to unpack his belongings.

Wexler continued to chat politely and meaninglessly about this and that. It was when Calhoun pulled out a long object wrapped in cloth that Wexler fell suddenly silent. "Is that," he asked finally, "what I think it is?"

"I don't know," said Calhoun. "What do you think it is?"

"A sword of some kind?"

"Yes." Calhoun unwrapped it. The polished metal gleamed even in the muted lighting of the room.

"Where did you get it? Some sort of war souvenir?"

"Yes." He touched the side of his face, running his finger along the scar. "It gave me this."

"Really!" said Wexler, intrigued. "Presuming you don't mean that you cut yourself shaving . . . may I ask what happened to the sword's previous owner, your attacker."

Calhoun hesitated and then said, without looking up at Wexler, "I think you'd be more comfortable not knowing."

"Ah," Wexler said. "Very well. I . . . defer to your wisdom on the matter."

There was a sudden buzz, and instantly Calhoun brought the sword up and around, looking about suspiciously for danger.

Wexler saw and tried not to laugh. "You are a bit high-strung, aren't you. You've never heard a door chime?"

Calhoun looked bewildered. "Door chime?"

"You must tell me about your homeworld. I imagine it's very quiet."

"When people aren't screaming in death agonies, yes, it can be relaxing."

The bell chimed once more and Wexler called, "Come."

The door slid open and Calhoun turned and faced a vision.

"Hi, lover," said the blond woman at the door. She was wearing a cadet uniform, same as Wexler.

Calhoun felt as if his feet had become rooted to the spot. His mind couldn't process what his eyes were telling him. The woman looked at him askance for a moment, as if she was trying to place him. "Have we met?" she asked.

He didn't know quite how to respond. *Well, not met exactly, but when I thought I was dying, I had a vision of you lying there stark naked and smiling at me. You are my future, come to life. You are everything that I could ever have wanted or needed, and I loved you before I've ever set eyes on you. . . .*

"I very much doubt you have," Wexler said. He held wide his arms and she came to him. He wrapped his arms around her and kissed her, and at that moment Calhoun unreasonably wanted to send Wexler's head bouncing across the room. They came up for air and Wexler stepped back, but kept an arm draped around her shoulders. "This is Betty Shelby. My fiancée. Betty, this is my roommate, Mackenzie Calhoun."

"One-Punch Calhoun?" she said in surprise. She looked him up and down. "I thought you'd be taller."

"Has everyone heard about it?" asked Wexler.

"I'd say so. Your roommate is famous, Wex."

He nuzzled his face against hers. "Should I be jealous?" he said teasingly.

Calhoun was no longer considering knocking Wexler's head across the room. Now he was envisioning what it would be like to carve his entire body into small bits.

"Have you been . . . engaged for long?" he managed to ask, hoping that he was keeping his voice steady.

"We're not exactly 'engaged,' " said Shelby, casting a look of annoyance at Wexler. "Wex here likes to say I'm his 'fiancée.' Makes him sound more important."

"And here I thought it gave you more credibility," he gibed back. She elbowed him teasingly.

"So . . . you're not betrothed?"

"Our families have been friends for years," said Wexler. "Both old-time Starfleet families. My parents are scientists . . ."

"So you mentioned."

"Oh, yes, so I did. Well, Betty and I . . . we've had an 'understanding,' " he said, hooking his fingers into quotation marks. "When the time is right, we'll get married. Not that I'd hesitate to give her a ring if I thought for a moment she'd wear it."

"Let's not start that again," said Shelby with mock annoyance. "I'm not going to wear a band on my finger that declares to all the world I'm your personal property."

"Would that shame you?" asked Calhoun.

She looked at him oddly. "What a strange thing to ask."

"Yes. So . . . would it?"

Shelby stared at Calhoun a moment longer, looked as if she wanted to say something, and then changed her mind. "You know what? I hardly know you. So we're not having this discussion."

"We're not?" He felt bewildered. "Oh." He realized that even when he'd been staggering around in the desert after he'd been wounded—in pain, suffering from thirst, hunger, and blood loss—he hadn't felt quite as disoriented as he did right then.

"You'll have to excuse Calhoun, Betty," said Wexler, coming to his rescue. "He's . . . not from around here."

"I'm Xenexian."

"So I've heard. All right . . . I'll let you off easily this time. Don't give me any more trouble, okay?"

Their conversation was becoming no clearer to Calhoun, but he was so eager to be quit of it that he said hastily, "Okay," and considered himself lucky.

"And one other thing," she said with a warning tone. "I don't care what you hear this big lug saying," and she elbowed Wexler gently in the ribs. "He calls me 'Betty' because he knows me from the old days, and that's fine. You, however, get to call me 'Elizabeth.' Or 'Shelby.' Not 'Betty.' Understood?"

He nodded. He didn't want to speak anymore. Talking served as a distraction. All he really wanted to do was stare at her, drink in her presence like water quenching a days-long thirst.

"Good. Just remember that, and I'm sure we'll all get along all right."

"Oh, Calhoun here will be just loads of fun, I can tell," said Wexler confidently. "He'll be like the little brother I always wanted but Mom and Dad never saw fit to provide. Damned selfish of them, I always thought."

"Do you have to keep staring at me like that?" she asked Calhoun.

"There's another way to stare?"

"It's . . . just impolite."

"I stare at the stars," he replied. "At the moons, and planets. I stare at beauty in nature. Why not you? You're part of nature."

She tried to find something to say in response, and couldn't think of anything. She settled for laughing in genuine amusement. "You always know just what to say, don't you, Mackenzie Calhoun."

"Sometimes. Sometimes I always know just what to say." But his mind wasn't really there. It was instead light-years away, seeing a vision of her in all her glory and wondering whether it was a cruel hallucination.

No, he decided. No, that wasn't the case at all. She was his future. That was all there was to it. He had received a vision, and she was in it, and she was meant to be his. No ring was required to tell the world that. Calhoun didn't care if the world knew it. He knew it, and that was more than enough.

He wondered if he was going to have to kill Wexler so she could be his. He hoped not. If he'd gotten in so much trouble just for breaking someone's jaw, certainly killing a fellow student would be frowned upon even more profoundly.

Chapter Three

Now

i.

Calhoun wasn't entirely sure that Zak Kebron, head of security on the *Excalibur,* had heard what he'd said.

They were seated in Calhoun's ready room back on the *Excalibur,* and Calhoun had laid out for the massive Brikar just what the situation was on the *Trident.* Both ships were maintaining orbit around Danter until the last remains of the business with the Beings and the Tholians could be sorted out. Calhoun was grateful that Ambassador Spock was attending to that, because there was enough on Calhoun's plate as it was.

"Zak," said Calhoun slowly, "did you get all that?"

"He did not do it," replied Kebron.

"That's not the point."

"Then I think we should make it the point," Kebron said flatly. "The point is that Ensign Janos is in no way, shape, or form the murderer of this Lieutenant Commander Gleau."

Although it had been a while since Kebron's change of biology had unleashed a previously hidden verbosity in the Brikar, it still surprised Calhoun to hear Kebron speak in sentences of more than two or three words. "Kebron, the evidence would—"

"To hell with the evidence," said the Brikar. "I'm telling you what I know. He may have been temporarily assigned to the *Trident* while we were drydocked with repairs, but he was still under my command, and I know him better than anyone here. And I'm telling you there's no way he could have done this thing."

"I've known him longer than you, Zak, and I'm telling you it's not impossible."

Kebron was taken aback by that. "How much longer have you known him, sir?"

"Since my Academy days."

"He was a fellow student? No, but . . . that makes no sense, you couldn't have attended at the same time and he's an ensign while . . ."

"It's complicated and not terribly relevant, Lieutenant," said Calhoun.

"With all respect, sir, it may indeed be relevant if—"

"It's not," Calhoun told him in a tone that indicated no further discussion along those lines would be tolerated. "Look, Kebron . . . the truth is that no one really knows what anyone else is or is not capable of. You'll have to take my word for it that his nature doesn't rule it out, and even if I thought it did, the DNA evidence makes any discussion of his capabilities moot."

"DNA evidence?" he argued.

"Of course. Kebron, we're not embarking on a grand murder mystery here. We're not looking for fragments of clues—some telltale ashes, or a partial fingerprint that might lead us to our killer. Doc Villers's people went over the scene with forensic tricorders. They were exceedingly thorough, and there is simply no mistake. Janos's DNA tracks are all over Gleau's body and all over the site of the murder itself."

"They could have been planted somehow," said Kebron.

"Planted? Zak, DNA traces from Janos's claws were found in the chunks of Gleau's body that had been ripped apart. That sort of thing can't be planted artificially."

"Just because it hasn't been done before doesn't mean it can't be done. Just that it hasn't yet."

"Granted. But if you're thinking to use this as a test case to prove Janos's innocence, then you've picked a hell of a case to try and make forensics history on. Elizabeth's people inform me that their investigation is more or less airtight."

"Even airtight seals can develop leaks when they're not properly constructed. What's Janos had to say about it?"

"Nothing."

"Nothing?" Kebron was astounded.

"Not a thing."

"But this is absurd. Certainly a simple bioscan would prove beyond a doubt whether he's telling the truth or not. He must be willing to submit to that."

"He's not," said Calhoun.

Kebron wasn't entirely sure he'd heard him right. "He's not willing? But why?"

"I don't know. He wasn't exactly forthcoming about it."

"But a bioscan would vindicate him. Isn't he aware of that?"

"Perhaps, Mr. Kebron," Calhoun said, not unkindly, "perhaps his concern is that it won't vindicate him at all. That it will simply make his problems worse."

"He stands to be prosecuted for murder. How could they conceivably get worse?"

"I'd rather not think about that," said Calhoun dryly.

"And of course he cannot be forced to take a scan."

"Not for a criminal investigation, no. It would be an abrogation of his rights. If he volunteers, he can do it in a heartbeat. But regulations protect him against self-incrimination. If he doesn't want to have it done, we can't force him. His refusal, however, can be used as evidence in his court-martial."

Kebron paused a moment, then said, "I want to be assigned to the case."

"We have no standing in the matter. It happened on the *Trident.*"

"He's my officer!" said Kebron with urgency. "More than that, he's my friend. We can't just abandon him!"

"No one's abandoning anyone, Kebron. He's still protected by Starfleet, no matter what—"

"He's alone over there, Captain," Kebron said firmly. "No matter how you look at it, he's surrounded by people who are not his crewmates, and he's accused of murdering one of them. He's not going to get a fair shake."

"My wife isn't going to railroad him, Kebron."

"Sir . . . respectfully, you don't have the luxury of thinking of her as your wife. She's the captain of a vessel that's probably already made up its mind about Janos's guilt and, as such, presents a threat."

"That's a crock, Kebron," and Calhoun was starting to get angry. "Captain Shelby is just as interested in learning the truth as anyone."

"Then my endeavoring to seek it out shouldn't pose a problem." He sounded eminently reasonable about it.

Calhoun leaned back, shaking his head. "You're something else, Kebron, you know that?"

"Yes, sir. I do. Now please . . . get me aboard *Trident* to start investigating. It may well be Janos's only chance at vindication."

ii.

Calhoun couldn't have been more surprised when Shelby readily agreed to have Kebron come aboard and handle his own investigation. "It's an excellent idea, Mac," she said. "Frankly, I'm amazed you didn't suggest it immediately."

"You are?"

"Of course." She was on the viewscreen as the two captains communicated ship to ship, and she was nodding slowly over the apparent wisdom of his request. "Not only does it make sense that you're concerned, since Janos is your crewman, but this Gleau business is a delicate situation. Apparently Gleau put a number of noses out of joint, including my executive officer's and my chief of security's. And, frankly, he didn't make my life any easier. All the logical people to take charge of an investigation on this ship have been compromised. I want everything done by the numbers, and Kebron would be an outsider who also has some familiarity with the principles. It's certainly better than bringing in a Starfleet IAD to handle it. Which, of course, we'll probably have to do eventually, but the more groundwork we can cover on our own, the better. But then, I'm sure you already thought of that."

"Well, naturally," said Calhoun immediately.

"Tell Mr. Kebron that we will be happy to extend our fullest cooperation."

"I never doubted it for a moment," Calhoun assured her.

iii.

Shelby was waiting for him in the transporter room when Zak Kebron materialized aboard the *Trident*. "Oh" was the first thing she said. Then, obviously recalling more appropriate reactions to have under such circumstances, she added, "Welcome aboard, Mr. Kebron. I only wish the circumstances were better for a reunion."

Kebron couldn't understand her initial reaction, but then he realized. "Ah. Yes," he said. "This is the first time you've seen me since my recent change."

"Yes, Captain Calhoun mentioned something about that." She looked him up and down. "Your skin seems so much smoother . . . and a different shade of brownish gray. And you seem . . . what's the word . . ."

"Chattier?"

"That's not what I was thinking," she said, "but it'll do. Come. You'll want to be seeing Mr. Janos, I suspect."

"If that doesn't pose a problem."

"Not at all." They headed out into the corridor. Kebron noticed that crewmen were staring at him as he passed. He'd forgotten what that was like, since the crew of the *Excalibur* had grown accustomed to him. There were not that many Brikar in Starfleet, so the sight of one of his hugely proportioned race was a novelty for the *Trident* crew.

"So you . . . grew up? Is that it? All at once?" she asked.

"I had been the equivalent of what you would consider a teenager, yes," said Kebron.

"Well, that would certainly explain the surliness and reticence. And then you . . . grew out of it?"

"More or less. But certainly the details of Brikar biology are secondary to the issue at hand, don't you agree?"

She looked taken aback at the way he'd expressed it, but she recovered quickly. "Yes, I'd definitely agree. Here. You should have this." She handed him a blue isolinear chip. "This is a record of the entire investigation up to this point, so you can bring yourself up to speed. I'll set you up with a space you can work out of. You can learn as much about this as we've learned, and take it from there."

"I'll have free access to all suspects?"

"Suspects?" She stopped, turned, and looked up at Kebron. "Mr. Kebron, just so we understand each other . . . there's no plural of 'suspect' here. Ensign Janos did it. The DNA information doesn't lie."

"To say the case is open-and-shut based on DNA information alone is premature, Captain. Any number of further explanations present themselves."

"Such as?"

He ticked off possibilities on his fingers. "The DNA information could have been falsified through means we have not discovered. Ensign Janos could have been under some sort of mind control. Some sort of duplicate, ranging from a clone to an alternate version from some parallel universe, could be responsible. Someone with a long-standing grudge against both Janos and Gleau could have committed the murder and then planted the evidence."

"Those don't sound like very likely scenarios, Lieutenant."

"Well, Captain, Ensign Janos as a cold-blooded murderer doesn't sound like a very likely scenario to me. That's why I'm here. To see which unlikely scenario is the truth."

"Very well, Lieutenant. You can certainly count on our help in discovering it. All we care about is the truth."

"I never doubted that, Captain Shelby."

The "command center" that Shelby had arranged for Kebron was perfectly adequate for his needs, and he reviewed the case information on the chip. It was more or less as Shelby had described it. All the physical evidence pointed to Janos. What was missing was motive. What possible reason did Janos have to shred Gleau?

It wasn't that Kebron truly thought that Janos was incapable of killing Gleau if he needed to. If a circumstance arose where someone presented an immediate threat to life and limb, there was no doubt in Kebron's mind that Janos would not hesitate to lay into that threat and rip him, her, or it to small pieces. Kebron wasn't kidding himself. Janos was big, white-furred, anthropoidal, with the heart of a beast buried deep within his outer air of refinement. If he needed to toss aside that curtain of civility, Kebron knew he could do it quickly, efficiently, and fatally.

The question, though, was whether he was capable of doing so in cold-blooded, meticulous style. And, making matters worse, if he could then endeavor to cover it up, to deny responsibility even when all the physical evidence pointed to him.

These thoughts and more whirled through Kebron's mind as he went down to the brig to confront his erstwhile friend and coworker. He wasn't entirely sure what to expect upon encountering him, for Janos was always a pleasant and upbeat sort . . . except, of course, if he had to be woken up from a sound sleep. Then he was capable of literally taking your head off . . .

Kebron realized those were not the best thoughts to dwell upon during a murder investigation.

Fortunately for all concerned, Janos was not asleep. Indeed, he looked as if he hadn't slept for quite some time. He was in the brig, crouched on the bunk, his arms resting lightly on his thighs. As did Kebron, he presented a problem when it came to finding a uniform that fit him properly. He had dispensed with boots entirely, his furred toes wrapped around the edge of the bunk. His fur looked bedraggled, which was an indicator of just how dire his straits were, for Janos always prided himself on superb grooming.

A guard stood on either side of the door outside, as was the custom in such incarcerations. They looked up at Kebron, and he could see it in their eyes: They were nervous. It was second nature for anyone in the field of security to size up anyone new they were encountering, to determine just how much of a threat they might pose if a problem erupted. Clearly they didn't like what they were seeing when it came to assessing the risk Kebron presented.

Fortunately, he'd anticipated that and planned ahead.

"At ease, men," came a high-pitched voice from behind Kebron. "He's on our side."

Security Chief Arex Na Eth scuttled up with that sideways walk of his, and nodded greeting to Kebron. "Lieutenant, good to see you. A pity it's under—"

"—these circumstances, yes," Kebron readily agreed. "Thank you for coming down here to meet me."

"Since you intend to question the prisoner, it's certainly standard operating procedure for me to be here," said Arex. "I hope you have better luck with him than we have."

"If by lack of luck you mean he hasn't confessed to the crime, there's always the unpleasant possibility that he didn't do it. Then again, I'd hate to see you so dreadfully inconvenienced."

Arex regarded him for a long, quiet moment. "Lieutenant, let's get two things straight. First, I know he's your friend, and so I understand your personal stake in this matter. And second, I'm not shedding a single tear over Lieutenant Commander Gleau. I wouldn't have wanted to see him murdered, but the threat he represented to this ship and to friends of mine was a tangible one as far as I'm concerned. I'm not going to miss him."

"You realize you've just painted yourself as a suspect."

"Someone with a clear conscience can do that," said Arex.

"A clear conscience, and forensics that would seem to point conclusively to someone else."

"True."

"Just for my own edification," Janos called, "are the two of you going to continue to chat out there as if I'm incapable of hearing every word you say?" He tilted his head slightly. "Is that a new look for you, Kebron? You look like you had yourself cleaned and pressed."

"I had it done just for you. Do you like it?"

"And you seem less surly." Janos looked at him thoughtfully. "You know, I think I liked you better the other way."

"Things change."

"Yes, they do." Janos glanced ruefully at his surroundings. "And not always for the better."

"Care to let me in?" Kebron asked Arex.

Arex nodded to one of the guards, and the guard stepped over to the security station and deactivated the forcefield. Kebron stepped through and it snapped promptly back on behind him. "So. Tell me what happened."

"Haven't you heard?" said Janos. "I'm public enemy number one. Now that I've been rounded up, people can sleep soundly in their beds and nervous fathers can allow their virginal daughters to wander the streets in safety."

"This isn't a laughing matter, Janos."

"As indicated by the absence of laughing. I assume you studied some sort of file with the investigation details?"

"Yes."

"Then you know as much as I do."

"No, I don't. I don't know why you refuse to submit to a bioscan."

Janos shrugged. "I don't see the point."

"Don't see the *point?*" Kebron was having trouble believing what he was hearing. "How about your freedom, for one? Your vindication, for another?"

"Kebron, I've known you to be many things, but I never thought of you as naive," said Janos. His pinkish eyes looked sad as they stood out against his white fur. "Let's say I take the bioscan. Let's say I pass with flying colors. Do you seriously think they're going to let me go? Of course not," he continued, without waiting for Kebron to answer. "They've got DNA evidence linking me with the crime. For all they know, I might be some deep-seated pathological liar who's actually convinced he's innocent when he is, in fact, guilty as hell. They can't take the risk. Would you? Honestly?"

"No. I suppose not," Kebron admitted.

"So there's no upside to my letting myself be scanned. If they find out something that benefits me, it will make no difference to my current status. And if they find out something damaging, then I've just hurt myself."

"And what would they find out that's damaging?"

Janos almost smiled, even though his physiognomy wasn't exactly built for it. "Nothing, Zak. Nothing at all. They would find nothing, for my heart is pure. Haven't you heard? Prisons are filled with people who haven't done anything illegal. Just ask any of them. They'd be the first to tell you."

Kebron sighed heavily. This was going to be more difficult than he'd originally envisioned. "Janos . . . where were you when Gleau was murdered?"

"I was taking samba lessons."

"Your earlier statement was that you were asleep in your quarters."

"I know what I said. And you know what I said. So why are you asking me?"

"Janos, would you stop being so damned defensive?"

"That's what happens when you're under attack."

"Not from me," he said, thumping himself on the chest. "You're not under attack from me. I'm here to help you."

"No. You're here to do your job as head of security," replied Janos. "So allow me to do my job as prime suspect and say nothing else, all right?"

And with that, he crisscrossed his arms over his knees as he maintained his crouch, and lowered his head so he was no longer looking at Kebron.

Kebron growled deep within his nonexistent throat. *And Janos was supposed to be the easy one to talk to,* he thought.

Then

Elizabeth Shelby, aka Betty, had no idea at the beginning of the evening that the annual Starfleet mixer, or meet-and-greet, or mill-and-swill as it was sometimes called, was going to end in complete disaster. And yet, in retrospect, she realized that she should have seen it coming a mile off.

The cadets had had a week to settle in, to learn their way around the campus, to be issued their uniforms. Despite all the advance preparation work that was routinely done to accommodate new students, there were always things that were overlooked and had to be attended to. Introductory classes were held. The new students eyed the teachers warily, and vice versa. And walking confidently through all the tentativeness from the plebes were the upperclassmen, the degree of swagger directly proportional to what year they were in in the program. Shelby believed that it was the third-year students who swaggered the most. The fourth-years actually seemed more interested in getting down to the serious business of an impending Starfleet career (the attitude of one Joshua Kemper notwithstanding).

As she went through her classes, Shelby kept bumping into Mackenzie Calhoun. It might have been her imagination, but it seemed as if she encountered him about five times more often than she did any other student. It could have been simply because she'd already met him and so was more aware of him. But slowly she realized that she was running into him more often than she ran into Wexler, and she'd known him for years.

It wasn't as if Calhoun were being annoying or trying to chat her up. He'd nod, smile, acknowledge her presence in some way, and then move on. That was it. And whenever she came by the quarters he shared with Wexler, Calhoun was always bent over a computer screen, reading.

He read the way he did everything else: with great intensity. In fact, when he was reading, he was completely oblivious of the fact that she was in the room. She had told Wexler she suspected that they could throw their clothes off and rut like rabbits, and Calhoun wouldn't notice them as long as he had text in front of him. Naturally, Wexler was more than happy to take her up on it. Equally naturally, she passed on the opportunity.

At the end of the week, the meet-and-greet was held in the main banquet hall, the area that was used for formal functions, presentations, awards ceremonies, and the like. Shelby arrived stylishly late, and had promised herself that upon arrival she would not let herself become caught up in the stunning tradition of it all. After all, her family was rich with Starfleet tradition of its own. Certainly this would just be a continuation of that to which she was already accustomed.

She thought that right up until she entered the main hall, and then she felt her breath being taken away.

Paintings—grand, old-style paintings rather than modern holos— lined the walls, each bearing distinguished miens that she had come to know as well as her own. Admirals, fleet captains from times past. The greatest heroes of the last few centuries. Men and women and beings who had spent their lives—and in some instances, given their lives—not only exploring the galaxy, but trying to make it safer. She knew it was overly sentimental to think of them in those terms, but it was true.

The hall was filling up with teachers and students. She recognized a number of the students as nervous, edgy new arrivals who had been with her on the shuttle. Now here they were, and without having learned much of anything yet, they were standing about with newfound confidence. Obviously it was the Academy uniforms they were sporting that were doing the job. She was reminded of the words of humorist Mark Twain: "Clothes make the man. Naked people have little or no influence on society." She smiled at that.

Her hands draped behind her back, Shelby moved through the great hall, deftly navigating the crowds while never taking her eyes from the paintings. Although she was not in a morbid frame of mind, she nevertheless felt as if she were rubbing elbows with the ghosts of the people enshrined upon the walls. Coming from a family with a history to it was one thing. But now she was walking floors that had been trod by the true greats. She might be standing, right now, where James Kirk had been standing. Over there was a bench where Hikaru Sulu might have sat. And over there in that corner, Garth of Izar might have leaned against that wall and developed new strategies.

Then again, considering what happened to Garth, perhaps she should stay out of that corner, just in case.

Ultimately, Shelby felt a sense of almost giddy exhilaration. People who had made history had been here. And it made her wonder: Thirty, forty, fifty years from now, would some new cadets be walking this same place, dwelling on the fact that at some point in their past, Elizabeth Paula Shelby had been here? Would she accomplish great things that would inspire those who came after her?

Or would she be forgotten?

Well . . . that was a silly thing to dwell on, wasn't it? She wasn't embarking on this life's work simply because she was seeking personal glory. It was about exploration and serving her fellow beings and . . .

But still . . .

Would she? Be remembered? Or forgotten? Or worse . . . never make any difference at all?

"My, my. You seem lost in thought."

Wexler was almost at her elbow when he spoke, and she started slightly before forcing a smile. He kissed her lightly on the lips; anything more demonstrative would have been woefully out of place. His uniform looked as sharp as anyone else's there, and he was holding a drink in one hand and a small cheese-puff hors d'oeuvre in the other. "So what topic has you in such a deep reverie?" he asked, popping the cheese puff in his mouth.

"Immortality," she replied.

"Really." He seemed impressed by that. "Here I thought you were simply interested in getting good grades. But obviously you have aspirations beyond anything I might have considered. So how precisely do you intend to become immortal?"

"I'm serious, Wex," she said. "And where did you get that drink?"

He led her over to the bar, where a smiling bartender served up one of the better martinis that Shelby had ever had. "Don't get too used to it, pet," said Wexler. "Once we're shipboard, it's synthehol from there on in. They say you can shake off any effects of inebriation in about two seconds."

"Horrors. Perhaps I'm not cut out for Starfleet after all," she said as she sipped her drink.

"So tell me, love, in all seriousness. What's this about immortality?"

"It's nothing," she said dismissively. Eager to change the subject, she continued, "And why are you bothering to talk to me? Shouldn't you be doing everything you can to make connections? Shake all the right hands, say all the right things? This is an excellent opportunity for you to make the rounds."

"True, very true," he said amiably. "Then again, the evening is young. Oh, look! There's One-Punch!"

"Wex, come on, enough with that," she said. "Just call him Mackenzie. Or Calhoun. Or . . ."

"Mac?"

"Sure, why not?" She shrugged.

At the far end of the room, Mackenzie Calhoun was simply standing there. He was pulling slightly at the collar of his uniform, looking vaguely uncomfortable in it. No one was coming up to him and talking to him, and he didn't seem inclined to walk up to anyone and strike up a conversation. He stood there for long moments more, and then headed out a door that stood open to the outside.

"Oh, look at him," Shelby said, tugging on Wexler's sleeve. "He's not even talking to anyone."

"Certainly, Betty, that's his decision and his own concern. It needn't impact us one little— Where are you going?"

"To talk to your friend," she retorted, heading toward the door through which Calhoun had exited.

"He's not my friend! He's my roommate!" called an exasperated Wexler, who nevertheless followed Shelby as she eased through the crowd and out after Calhoun.

She found him outside in the surprisingly chill night air, seated on a bench in the garden. It was a vast expanse of meticulously maintained greenery. According to one of her uncles, a fellow named Boothby oversaw it. Academy legend had it that Boothby and the garden had already been there before the complex was built, and they had simply built around them both rather than try and figure out how to get Boothby to leave.

There was no sign of Boothby now, however. Just Calhoun, seated on the bench, staring out at the greenery. As Wexler and Shelby approached, he called softly, "Hello, Shelby. Wexler."

"You didn't even look our way. How could you know it was us?" demanded Shelby.

"How could I not?" replied Calhoun.

It was hardly an answer that she considered satisfying, but she suspected—correctly—that it was all she was going to get out of him. "We were just concerned you were going to be lonely out here."

"You were both concerned?" he asked.

"Oh, yes," Wexler quickly stepped in. "Me, I was worried sick about it."

Shelby ignored what Wexler obviously fancied passed for desperately amusing repartee. She sat on the edge of the bench, a comfortable distance from Calhoun. "You know, there's a whole party in there you could be attending."

"I don't do well with parties."

"Why not?"

"Because," said Calhoun, "I dwell on all those who died and so could not attend."

She stared at him for a moment and then shook her head. "You're really the classic 'glass is half empty' kind of guy, aren't you."

"I think I know what you're saying," he said, "but it's not the case. It's more that . . . others look upon accomplishments and derive pleasure from what's been done. I look upon them and think about what is to be done next."

"That's not such a terrible attitude to have, Mackenzie . . . Mac. Can I call you Mac?"

He shrugged. "If you wish."

"Okay. Mac . . . always looking to the next thing to be done . . . that's a pretty positive way to think. There's nothing wrong in setting new goals constantly. But it's tragic if you can't appreciate that which you've already accomplished. Otherwise what's the point of accomplishing anything?"

"What indeed?" asked Calhoun.

Shelby was taken aback by this response, but Calhoun gave her no time to dwell on it. "I do not understand the purpose of this," he said suddenly.

"The purpose of this?" Wexler said. "The purpose is, it's a bench. You sit on it, as you are doing."

"No," said Calhoun, with the closest thing to a chuckle they'd heard from him. "I mean the purpose of this greenery. Its form serves no genuine function. This garden has nothing to do with anything in terms of learning or gaining experience. It is simply . . . here."

"That's right," Shelby told him. "That's the point of it: that there is no point to it. When life seems completely pointless, it's nice to have a place to go that serves no other purpose than to look nice and be green. It's a calming, steadying influence."

"I find little about it calming," said Calhoun.

"You'll get used to it," assured Shelby.

He shrugged. "If you say so."

"You know, Calhoun, I'm surprised to see you here," said Wexler, coming around the other side of the bench. "You've had your nose buried in text for most of the week. I'm surprised you came up for air."

"I'm practicing," said Calhoun.

Shelby and Wexler exchanged looks. "Practicing?" said Shelby. "Practicing what?"

"Reading."

"Reading?" Again they looked at each other, this time with utter perplexity. "What do you mean you're practicing reading?"

"Universal Translators are all well and good for speaking," said Calhoun, "but reading remains a learned skill."

"You mean you're illiterate?"

"I read Xenexian," Calhoun said, sounding a bit defensive. "But it's very . . . what's the word? Simplistic. A very simplistic language in comparison. Mostly symbols."

"You have an entire civilization built upon a language of symbols?" said an astonished Wexler. "Calhoun, no offense, mate . . . but what sort of society can accomplish anything of substance or lasting importance without any—" and then with no pause he continued, as Shelby glared at him, "—and I'm totally forgetting the Egyptians, who were a remarkably progressive society and left works of architectural magnificence which last to this day, and I feel it would be wisest if I shut up about now."

"Go with the feeling," Shelby told him.

Calhoun glanced suspiciously from one to the other, and then continued, "A . . . friend of mine arranged for me to go to a facility before I arrived here. I was there for several months, and during that time, accelerated learning techniques were used to teach me to read. But it's still a lot to absorb."

"I'd think so," said Shelby in wonderment. "I'm . . . that's . . . it's very impressive, Mackenzie. What you're doing."

And then a voice came from behind them. "Oh, absolutely. Very impressive."

Shelby turned and saw about half a dozen senior cadets approaching them. They were grinning, but there was no air of pleasantry in the grin. She didn't know any of them offhand, but that wasn't surprising. She'd hardly had the chance to meet anyone so far.

"So you just learned to read," said the one in the forefront, and there was cold anger in his expression, and a bruise on his cheek, and Shelby instantly put two and two together and realized this had to be Joshua Kemper. And he had friends. A lot of friends. "As the young lady said, Calhoun: impressive. Any other recently acquired skills we should know about? Cutting your own food, perhaps? And . . . you are housebroken, I hope. Wouldn't want any unfortunate accidents."

"No. We wouldn't," said Calhoun. And Shelby saw Calhoun get up from the bench. Something changed in his deep purple eyes then. A coldness emanated from them, as if he was taking something out of himself and locking it away so it wouldn't get in his way.

And what was that "something"? Hesitation. Uncertainty. The air of civilization. Or perhaps something as simple as mercy or pity.

Kemper and his friends had stopped several feet away, and then Wexler interposed himself. He stuck out a hand and said, "Hello. Vincent Wexler's the name. Glad to be here and am very much looking forward to the—"

"Quiet, Cadet," said Kemper.

"Right, then," Wexler said instantly, and stepped back.

Kemper swiveled his gaze to Shelby. "And you are?"

"Elizabeth Paula Shelby," she said. Her gaze was steady, her shoulders square. She kept reminding herself that this was Starfleet Academy, not a school playground. Certainly there had to be a higher standard for behavior at the former than one would find in the latter. Then again, the hormonal drive of men—be they human or Xenexian—and the folly that drive led them to, was rapidly appearing to be a universal constant.

"Welcome to the Academy, Shelby . . . Wexler." He nodded to each of them, but he never took his eyes off the Xenexian. "And Calhoun . . . we've already had the pleasure."

Calhoun said nothing. Just watched him.

Kemper rubbed his jaw. "Good work, eh? You'll find the medical facilities at the Academy are top-notch. You'd never know it was broken."

This time Calhoun did speak. "I'd know. I broke it."

"Yes. Yes, you did. A lucky punch while I wasn't looking."

"Is *that* what you're telling people?" asked Calhoun.

"Cadet, I can't say I like your tone of voice. Perhaps it'd be best if you said nothing at all for the moment."

Shelby was certain that, at that point, Calhoun was going to launch himself at Kemper. She could almost see the muscles straining for the lunge. His fists were clenched and the knuckles worked against each other. But then slowly the fists unclenched, and Calhoun remained exactly where he was. It was an impressive display of self-control.

Kemper actually seemed a bit surprised that Calhoun had indeed reined himself in. "Well . . . that's wise, Cadet. Not quite so precipitous when you're outnumbered, are you."

If Calhoun's gaze had been capable of generating the actual cold that was coming from it, Kemper would have been an icicle. Shelby saw the direction the situation was heading. Sooner or later, Calhoun was going to be goaded into attacking Kemper, who had targeted the Xenexian for singular "attention." And when Calhoun did that, he would get the crap kicked out of him by the six-to-one odds. And then he'd be expelled. Whatever odds he'd managed to beat for striking Kemper once, he'd never be able to get away with it a second time.

She didn't want that to happen. It seemed too unfair. Too arbitrary. Someone who worked that hard learning to read—something that the rest of them took for granted—deserved his opportunity.

"This is supposed to be a relaxing party," Shelby spoke up, "and in this cadet's opinion, this isn't—"

"I didn't ask for your opinion, Cadet. Did I?"

"No, sir, but I—"

"At attention, Cadet."

Reflexively, Shelby snapped to attention. Arms at her side, looking straight ahead.

Kemper slowly circled her, studying her intently. "Very good. Someone who knows how to obey orders. I hope you're taking notes on her behavior, Calhoun. She's someone on whom you should model yourself. And she seems concerned about you. That's commendable as well. But you know what? Standing at attention for too long can make the muscles stiffen up. Doesn't seem fair. Cadet Shelby: jumping jacks, until I say otherwise. Commencing now."

Instantly Shelby started doing jumping jacks.

There's always going to be one. The words of her father came to her unbidden. *There's always going to be one upperclassman. Someone who takes it upon himself to show plebes exactly who's boss. He will throw arbitrary orders at you, lord it over you. And he will do so in the firm belief that he is doing you a favor. That he's indoctrinating you, teaching you strict adherence to the chain of command in a way that professors can't. Because that chain of command can and will save your life. You may want to ignore him, to disobey him, to fight him. Instead, tolerate him. Tolerate him and deal with him in a professional manner, since if you can't handle something as mundane as an officious superior, then you'll never be able to deal with something as challenging as the vacuum of space.*

Her face set, she continued the jumping jacks. They weren't especially difficult; she was in excellent shape. She felt slow, burning anger within her, but she pushed it aside, remembering what her father said.

She looked to Wexler to say something, do something. She didn't know what that might be, but he was clever. He could come up with something. Instead he just stood there, looking saddened, even pitying. He pitied her. That made her stomach tighten, and she wanted to shout at him even though it was unreasonable to do so. He hadn't gotten her into this fix; she had done it herself. All herself. *In this cadet's opinion.* What had she been thinking? Kemper had a bone to pick with Calhoun, she'd gotten in the way of that, and now she was paying the price. As her arms and legs scissored, she thought, *Let that be a lesson to you. Stay out of the line of fire when some idiot superior is on the warpath. . . .*

And suddenly rough-hewn hands were grabbing her, and she realized

Calhoun was facing her, gripping her shoulders firmly and forcing her to stand still. She was completely taken aback. He wasn't that much taller than she, didn't look especially bulky. Yet she was completely immobilized by him. Whatever muscle he had must have been like corded steel.

"What the hell are you doing, Cadet?" demanded Kemper. "Preventing another cadet from obeying orders—?"

Calhoun turned and spat out, "Coward."

"Calhoun," Shelby tried to warn him off, but he'd have none of it. She felt as if she were inside a shuttle spiraling downward in a death roll.

"Coward?" Kemper walked slowly toward him, and there was genuine delight in his face. "You call me coward?"

"Yes."

"I'm not afraid of you."

"You should be."

That threw Kemper off his step for a moment, but he recovered quickly. "Well, well. Aren't you full of yourself. You are aware that this time you don't have the element of surprise?"

There was not the slightest hesitation on Calhoun's part. He moved Shelby to one side and faced Kemper squarely.

"I don't need it," he said.

"Calhoun, that's enough," said Shelby, trying to pull him away. "Get into a fight, they'll kick you out." But he wasn't budging. She might as well have been trying to move one of the Easter Island statues.

Then he looked at her with a face as inscrutable as one of those statues. "Right and wrong doesn't make allowance for consequences."

"Cadet Calhoun," said Kemper, "I am dealing with Cadet Shelby. Are you going to cease and desist in this interference or not?"

"No." And then as an afterthought, he added, "Sir." Shelby had to admit she was surprised. She'd never have thought he'd give even that much of a nod to respect where Kemper was concerned.

"Gentlemen," said Kemper, nodding toward Calhoun, "escort Mr. Calhoun out of the way, please. He's interfering with the chain of command."

The upperclassmen came around from either side, reaching out with the clear intention of taking Calhoun by either arm. One of them gripped Calhoun firmly by the wrist.

That was a mistake.

Instantly Calhoun reached around with his free hand and locked it around the hand on his wrist. This confused the upperclassman for as long as it took Calhoun to twist his encumbered arm around and down, and suddenly the upperclassman let out a startled shriek, the weight of his own body applying extreme pressure to his arm. He bent in half and Calhoun drove a knee up into his face. There was a snap as the upperclassman's nose broke and Calhoun shoved him aside, sending him tumbling to the ground.

The entire move took just over a second.

The man who'd been coming in from the other side didn't have time to register what had just happened before Calhoun whirled and drove a foot into his stomach. He doubled over and Calhoun swung an uppercut, catching him square in the chin and knocking him backward.

"Get him!" shouted Kemper, and all the games were over as the remaining men rushed him. Calhoun turned to greet their rush, and Shelby didn't see fear or even anger in his face. Instead a grim smile was playing across his lips. He was happy for this. Thrilled for it. He was in his element.

He met the attack, one against four, and went straight for Kemper. The speed of his charge drove Kemper back, away from the others. To Kemper's credit, he blocked the first several of Calhoun's punches and even landed one himself. It glanced off Calhoun's face, just above the scar. Calhoun didn't even seem to feel it.

And then Calhoun picked him up.

Shelby couldn't believe it, had never seen anything like it. "Compact," "wiry"—these were the words she would have used to describe Mackenzie Calhoun. But that wouldn't have begun to cover what she witnessed now as Calhoun grabbed Kemper by the waist and by the back of the neck and lifted him clear off the ground, over his head. Kemper kicked frantically in midair, helpless as a child, and the only acknowledgment of the weight he was bearing was the slightest grunt from Calhoun.

At that instant there was no doubt in Shelby's mind that he would have thrown Kemper to the ground as hard as he could and conceivably shattered his spine, his skull—anything breakable in his body.

Then the other three upperclassmen slammed into Calhoun, bowling him over. Kemper fell out of his grasp and hit the ground. Calhoun rolled over onto his back, brought his legs up and under his chin, and thrust upward. One of the cadets fell back and Calhoun grabbed the two others by either side of their heads and cracked their skulls together.

But the battle had been enough to attract other upperclassmen as well, friends of Kemper's by the look of them. They poured out of the hall and Calhoun lunged to his feet to meet them. His uniform was a colorful mingling of grass stains and bloodstains, and his upper lip was drawn back into a disdainful snarl, but his eyes remained level and he didn't even seem to be breathing hard.

The upperclassmen converged from in front and behind, and Calhoun almost managed to dodge to one side to get out of their way. If he had done so, there was no telling how long he might have held them off. But luck went against him as his toe snagged the root of a tree, and Calhoun went down. Instantly the pile of senior students was upon him, pinning him down. Other first-year students were now visible at the outer edge of the gardens, but they simply stood there and watched.

He never cried out, never shouted for help. Not once. It was entirely possible that doing so never even occurred to him.

Help came anyway.

Shelby charged the pileup and grabbed the first person she could find from behind. She clamped her arm around his throat and pulled, and he came off with a strangled yelp as she tossed him aside and started hammering on the backs of the others. She caught a glimpse of Calhoun below her. He wasn't shielding his head as another might do, trying to withstand the storm of fists upon him. Instead he was swinging wildly, lashing out, not caring who struck him. As if he felt that they couldn't possibly do him any damage.

And suddenly other first-years were there, including Wexler. They came in, and what they lacked in knowledge of self-defense, they made up for in sheer enthusiasm. Within moments the entire area had been reduced to a melee, and even after the teachers and deans finally arrived to break the whole thing up, the general consensus by everyone who attended was that this was, quite simply, the best Starfleet Academy mill-and-swill they'd had in years.

Chapter Four

Now

Zak Kebron had never admitted it to anyone, but he had a morbid fascination with old Earth murder mysteries.

His interest had gone all the way back to the Academy, when his roommate Worf had been reading one and sniffed disdainfully when he finished with it. Kebron had glanced over questioningly as Worf had tossed the reading padd onto the table between their beds. "A singular waste of energy," Worf had said.

"What?"

"The man in that book murders someone who was endeavoring to steal his spouse from him, and then spends the rest of the tale trying to cover it up, only to be found out by a detective in the end through some foolish mistake he let slip."

Kebron stared at the padd. "So?"

"He killed an enemy," Worf said with greater insistence, as if Kebron hadn't heard him the first time. "Why would he try to hide such a thing? He should boast of his accomplishment and use it as a warning to any others who might attempt to abscond with the affections of his mate. And this detective was a shambling, confusing, and annoying little man who boasted repeatedly of his 'little gray cells.' Not at all a worthy opponent."

Kebron had taken that in for a moment, then picked up the padd and looked at Worf questioningly. "Be my guest," Worf had said.

Whereupon the Brikar read the novel and had a reaction that was

180 degrees from the Klingon's. He found it fascinating, engrossing. The step-by-step solving of the mystery intrigued him no end. He did, however, agree with Worf in one respect. The detective was annoying.

But then he had stumbled upon other books in this genre referred to as "mystery." And there was a subgenre that intrigued him all the more: "hard-boiled detectives." Writers and detectives such as Raymond Chandler's "Philip Marlowe," Dashiell Hammett's "Sam Spade," Max Allan Collins's "Nate Heller," Robert Crais's "Elvis Cole," and of course the greatest of them all, Tracy Tormé's "Dixon Hill."

They had appealed to Kebron because they threw themselves into their cases, they were hardheaded, no one could stop them, and they always got to the truth of the matter. Best of all, they did not hesitate to smack people around in the pursuit of a case's solution, a tactic that far more effete detectives in other, less worthy works would never even dream of utilizing.

In short, they used the direct approach. Kebron liked that. A lot.

It wasn't as if Kebron was happy that an officer had been murdered. Murders were anarchic deeds and were not at all in keeping with the safe, secure running of a starship. Still, the prospect of investigating one, particularly when the odds were so stacked against the suspected killer, greatly appealed to him. He'd read enough detective novels to know that the obvious suspect was never the one who had actually performed the fatal deed. That the first person accused was always a red herring to throw pursuers off the scent. Usually it was a trick concocted by the genuine perpetrator. Solving a murder involved determining not simply opportunity and motive for the killer himself, but also opportunity and motive for the person who was accused. Trying to determine who might have it in for Gleau was one thing. But figure out who both resented Gleau and would also want to see Janos framed for it, and that would invariably lead Kebron to the guilty party.

The questioning would be the most challenging part of it. Going to one suspect after another, grilling each one, trying to determine who was telling the truth and who was lying.

Unfortunately, it didn't work out exactly that way for Kebron.

As it turned out, the only individual he spoke to who refused to speak under the monitoring of a bioscan was the lead suspect. Everyone else was willing to submit themselves to computer monitoring of their vital signs. Monitoring that guaranteed to an absolute certainty that they were speaking the truth at all times.

Kebron was truly disappointed, because each and every person he spoke to had some sort of grudge or disagreement or frustration with Gleau. Every one of them would have been an ideal suspect. Motive was all over the place, even though he didn't have a reasonable means of explaining the nature of Gleau's death as being the responsibility of someone other than Janos, or explaining how Janos's DNA was all over the corpse.

From the top officers on down, everyone was cooperative. He didn't even have to go to them. One by one, at his request, they came down to his temporary headquarters and willingly spoke under bioscan. No one held anything back. Captain Shelby spoke of her going head-to-head with Gleau over his oath of celibacy. Commander Mueller was brutally honest over her concerns that Gleau posed a threat and her rather violent encounter with him. Arex had practically been ready to beat Gleau up over his alleged harassment of Lieutenant M'Ress. The more Kebron heard, the more he began to think that Gleau's murder wasn't the shocking development others believed it to be. Instead what was shocking was that he had managed to live as long as he had.

And when he'd asked each of the interviewees the most obvious question—"Did you have anything to do with the death of Lieutenant Commander Gleau?"—the response was immediate and unhesitating and in the negative. Each time, the bioscan did not hesitate to confirm that they were telling the truth.

Sam Spade would have been bored out of his mind.

He expected the conversation with M'Ress to be the most revealing, however. She, after all, had voiced the loudest complaints about him. She had accused him of taking advantage of her, of badgering her after she'd filed her initial complaints, of—and Kebron had to double-check his notes upon hearing this one—threatening her in her dreams. This despite the fact that Selelvians had no known history of that sort of psychic power. But according to Mueller, M'Ress had been so strident on the subject that she'd begun to wonder whether there wasn't something to the accusation.

M'Ress, however, was late for their appointment. She had promised she would be there at 1400 hours, but as time stretched, there was no sign of her. Kebron sat there, drumming his three thick fingers on the table, which shook under the tapping. When it reached 1430 hours, he informed Arex that M'Ress had missed her appointment.

"That's odd," Arex's voice came over the combadge. "She's usually quite punctual."

"That doesn't seem to be the case here," replied Kebron. "I'll look for her."

"That won't be necessary," Arex assured him. "I can—"

"No, it's all right," said Kebron, and when he spoke there was a gravely, noir-ish cadence to his voice. "I'll check out every back hallway, every hangout, every possible hidey-hole she could have stowed herself in. I'll turn this town upside down if I have to, and I guarantee that by the end of the—"

The door chimed and slid open. M'Ress walked in. "Sorry I'm late," she said.

"Never mind, Arex. Kebron out," said Kebron, feeling deflated. "I was wondering where you were."

"Just had business to attend to."

"Really. And here I thought you might just be reluctant to talk to me."

She tilted her head, her green eyes narrowing. "Why would that be the case?"

"Why don't you tell me?"

"You want me to explain to you the reasons for why you believe something?"

Kebron paused. That was actually more or less the case, but it sounded kind of stupid the way she put it. "No," he said.

She shrugged. "All right, then." She moved toward the chair in a sleek and graceful manner. Then she easily vaulted onto it, and crouched on it a moment as if trying to make herself comfortable, before easing down into it. "So. You wanted to see me."

"That's right. But did you want to see me?" he asked challengingly.

M'Ress tilted her head in the other direction. "Are you ill?"

"Pardon?"

"Are you suffering from some sort of—I don't know—mental deficiency? I mean, I thought this was to be an interrogation, but you're going about it in a very strange way."

"This is my investigation, Lieutenant, and I will conduct it as I see fit."

She blew air impatiently through her lips.

He waited for her to say something.

She idly picked some stray fur off her uniform.

"I have fish," he said abruptly.

M'Ress stared at him. "Pardon?"

"Fish. In a tank. Back on the *Excalibur.* I keep them as pets."

"All right." She clearly didn't know what to make of it, which was exactly what Kebron wanted: to keep her off balance.

"Does that interest you?" he asked.

"In what sense?"

"If you were confronted with them, would you feel a genetic imperative to eat them?"

She hopped off the chair. "This is asinine. I have no idea what you're going on about, but I'm not going to waste time with this idiocy . . ."

"Sit down, Lieutenant," he rumbled. She glared at him a moment, then sat once more. "What I'm trying to determine," he continued, "is how much of your actions is governed by conscious control . . . and how much by irresistible instinct."

"Considering that my instinct is to walk out the door whether you tell me to sit down or not, I'd say conscious control."

"Good," he said, sounding reasonable. "I'm about to activate the bioscan to measure veracity. Do you have a problem with that?"

She hesitated ever so slightly, and that pause spoke volumes to Kebron. "No," she said after a moment. "Not at all."

"Good. Computer."

"Working."

"Activate bioscan."

"Bioscan activated," the voice told him with its customary serenity.

"Would you care to sit?" he said expansively. "Can I get you something? Saucer of milk?"

"You must find yourself endlessly amusing," said M'Ress, shifting in the chair.

"Yes. So . . . did you kill Lieutenant Commander Gleau?"

"No," she said immediately.

The bioscan had an automatic default built into it. If the speaker spoke an untruth, the computer would react. Anything else and the computer remained silent.

"Did you want him dead?"

"No."

"Incorrect," the computer said immediately.

She bared her teeth and growled low in her throat. "The computer doesn't know what it's talking about."

"Incorrect," came the voice once more, perhaps even a hair faster.

"This is stupid and I don't want to be a part of this."

" 'This is stupid' is a subjective statement. Unable to evaluate," said the computer.

"Thank you, that was very helpful," Kebron assured the computer. "M'Ress, I think you'll find this takes a lot less time if you choose to cooperate."

"I am cooperating. I'm here. Isn't that enough?"

"You seem very testy."

"I'm not testy. I'm annoyed. And I resent your implication that I know who killed Gleau!"

He stared at her for a long time then, so long that he might have been a statue. "What is it?" M'Ress finally demanded impatiently.

"At no point," Kebron noted, "did I claim or imply that you know who killed him. But since you bring it up: Do you know who killed him?"

"I don't have the faintest idea."

"Incorrect," the computer said instantly.

She glowered, but there was less of the brittle edge to it than there was before. She seemed a bit nervous, which was exactly what Kebron was seeking.

"I . . . don't know for sure," M'Ress slowly admitted.

"But you have a good idea."

"Yes."

He rose from behind the desk, looming over her. No one loomed quite like Kebron, although Si Cwan, the Thallonian ambassador, came close. "You overspoke before," he said with faint reproof. "If you'd simply said 'I don't know' to the previous question, the bioscan would never have picked up on it. As it is, I'm now constrained to ask you just who, precisely, you think killed Lieutenant Commander Gleau."

She took in a deep breath and then let it out slowly. "Ensign Janos," she said.

His face twitched. "Well, that was certainly the obvious answer, wasn't it?"

"You asked me, I answered."

Well, she was certainly right about that, but Kebron wasn't about to just let it go that easily. "All right," he said. "So you think he might have done it."

"Yes."

"Why do you think that?"

"I just do."

"Why?"

"I already told you."

"No," said Kebron. "You simply reiterated what you think, not why you think it."

"We're going around in circles, Lieutenant," said M'Ress with obvious irritation.

"All right then. Let me draw you a straight line." Kebron's mind was racing. He was stitching together in his mind an assortment of scenarios that he'd read in various novels, and he didn't entirely know what he was going to say before it came spilling out of his mouth. He only wished he had a slouch hat and a trench coat . . . which admittedly would have looked odd, since such accoutrements were designed for inclement weather, which was a rarity on starships. But it would have fit the mood for what he was about to say. "You were terrified of Gleau. You hated him. You wanted him out of the way. But you didn't have the stomach for it yourself. You knew that suspicion would point at you, and that the inevitable DNA evidence would seal the deal. So you found a sap. Someone whom you could cozy up to. Janos. Furred, like you. His animal aspects on the outside, like you. You figured he'd be an easy mark. You played him, took him as a lover, and then you dropped the bomb on him. You told him you wanted him to kill Gleau for you. But he wouldn't do it. You misjudged him. But it didn't matter. You're a science officer. While you were busy 'entertaining' him, you had equipment up and running that was analyzing his DNA, replicating it so that when you murdered Gleau—shredded him with your very own claws—you would be able to use scientific techniques to cover your tracks with Janos's. He takes the fall and you walk away clean. *Isn't that right!*"

Her lower jaw had dropped to somewhere below her collarbone. It was with effort that she managed to close it. She looked completely shocked.

Kebron waited for a reply.

Then she looked down.

"How did you figure out we were lovers? What gave it away?"

Kebron was rocked back on his heels. He couldn't believe it. But he recovered quickly, not wanting to be too obvious about the fact that he was utterly stunned. "When you've been in this business as long as I have, you learn to figure things out," he said while still managing to sound nonchalant. "So it's true then. You admit it."

"We were lovers, yes . . . but . . . I wasn't using him!" she said desperately, her façade of annoyance evaporated. "We became involved, and one night I woke up trembling, and he asked why, and the whole thing just . . . just spilled out of me. And he got so angry, Kebron, so very angry. He wanted to confront Gleau, but I told him not to. I told him that I didn't think he could trust himself, he was so worked up about it. I made him promise he wouldn't. He swore he wouldn't. But now I don't know. I don't know what he might have done."

Kebron regarded her thoughtfully and then said, "Computer? Status of subject?"

"Subject shows no physiological changes."

Which was the computer's way of saying that she wasn't lying.

Kebron had been bluffing. It had been one colossal bluff, and yet he had inadvertently stumbled upon a huge chunk of the truth. Or at least *a* truth.

"How . . . why did you get involved with Janos, then? If it wasn't to set him up?"

Her green eyes narrowed. "Why do you think?"

"I don't—"

"He . . ." She frowned then, as if being asked to articulate things that she hadn't actually given any thought to. "There's . . . something about him. He's not my race. I don't know what he is, actually. Nevertheless, I was drawn to him, as if I recognized something of my own Caitian background in him. When I asked him what actual race he was, he said 'One of a kind.' " She looked up at Kebron. "Do you know?"

"Not really. His file is classified on the matter."

"Classified?" She was obviously surprised by that. "Why would it be classified?"

"I don't know."

"Well, perhaps you ought to find out."

"Why?"

"Because," said M'Ress, "you don't know. And anything having to do with Janos that you don't know in regard to this . . . this predicament . . . might be important."

She was right, of course. He was slightly annoyed with himself that she'd had to point it out to him. He nodded—which, as always, meant inclining his body at the waist—and said, "Yes. I believe I will be looking into that. Thank you, Lieutenant."

M'Ress was startled. "Thank you? You mean . . . I can go?"

"You can go."

She didn't need a second invitation to depart as quickly as she could, leaving Kebron alone and frustrated. "Computer, discontinue bioscan," he said.

"Discontinued."

And then Kebron was alone in the room, alone with his thoughts. Thoughts that were going in a singularly unpleasant direction.

Unless Lieutenant M'Ress was a pathological liar, then everything she'd said was the truth. Which meant that not only had Kebron come no closer to clearing Janos, but he'd actually gone in the other direction.

He'd provided Janos with what had been lacking before: motive.

He wondered if Philip Marlowe ever made things worse than they were when he started. He thought yes, sometimes that did happen, even to the most hard-boiled of detectives. But in such cases, they were merely setbacks. Creative obstacles along the way that only delayed the inevitable moment when the detective would come through for his client and the true guilty party would be revealed.

Kebron didn't like what was being revealed. Not only was Janos's situation becoming bleaker, but Kebron was now stuck with an image in his head of Janos and M'Ress copulating. No amount of detection would make that one go away anytime soon.

Then

i.

Calhoun was busy packing his bags. He didn't expect it to take long. He did expect that it would be necessary.

Wexler was watching him do so, and was having no luck in convincing him to cease his activities. "The investigation is still pending, Calhoun!" he said. "They haven't even spoken to you yet!"

"Then this will save them the bother," Calhoun replied, never ceasing or slowing his movements.

"You don't know how this will come out!"

"Yes. Yes, I do. It will come out the only way it could have come out."

"Oh, Calhoun, don't be a git."

Calhoun stopped what he was doing and stared at Wexler. "I assume that's some sort of insult."

"A mild one, yes."

"Wexler . . . I was never going to fit in here. I knew it from the beginning."

"Really," said Wexler. He was leaning against a chest of drawers, shaking his head. "And this doesn't strike you, then, as some sort of self-fulfilling prophecy?"

"It would have been fulfilled with or without myself."

"Well, I have to say, Calhoun, that for someone who was so convinced he wouldn't succeed, you did a hell of a lot of work to prepare for it. Not exactly typical for someone who's certain he'll fail."

"I was simply trying to prepare myself."

"For failure? It's rot, Calhoun. You weren't afraid of failure. You were afraid of success."

"Success?" snorted Calhoun. "And why would I be afraid of success?"

"Because," Wexler said, stabbing a finger at him, "Xenex was the entirety of your existence, and you're terrified of the thought of outgrowing it. If you go back, carrying tales of how you kicked the asses of Starfleet cadets and were exiled for it, then you get to be a hero all over again. And that's all you care about being, isn't it. Not a Starfleet officer. Not a man. Just a hero. Well, heroes end up dead, sooner or later, Calhoun, and if that's really where your priorities are, then it's bloody lucky that you're taking off now, before you take down a starship with you."

There was a chilled silence, and then Calhoun said quietly, "You don't know me. So don't pretend to."

"I don't have to pretend anything, mate, thanks. And what about Betty, eh?"

"What about her?"

"Well," Wexler pointed out, "did you give one moment of thought to the fact that she jumped in to try and save your ass? And because of that, she's at much at risk of discipline as you? And unlike you, she isn't willing to just cut and run when things are looking difficult. This place is her dream, her be-all and end-all. She was there for you. You're not going to be there for her?"

"She has you to be there for her, and besides, I didn't ask for her help. For anybody's help."

"Well, that's not the way the world works, Calhoun," Wexler snapped. "Sometimes you wind up getting help whether you asked for it or not. And then you're supposed to show gratitude in return. That's how things operate in worlds other than Xenexian ones."

"I don't need to be lectured by you, Wexler."

"Since you're not staying around for the lectures of the teachers, I thought I'd take the opportunity."

"*You* take an opportunity?" Calhoun dropped his bags to the floor and stepped toward Wexler, his purple eyes burning with cold fury. "I noticed that when others were jumping in to my aid, you were standing to the side. Watching. Doing nothing."

"That's right."

"And that inaction doesn't seem the least cowardly to you?"

Wexler laughed curtly. "There's just no pleasing you, is there, Calhoun. You complain when people come to your aid, and you complain when they don't. Which do you prefer?"

"It wasn't just me. Elizabeth was in the midst of the melee. You could have helped her."

"Because I'm her significant other?"

"I would have said 'lover,' but yes."

"Elizabeth is capable of handling herself. She wouldn't want me to come to her defense," he said airily. "She'd consider it insulting. An indication that I didn't think she could take care of her own business."

"Maybe," said Calhoun icily. "Or maybe you just didn't have the guts to get your hands dirty."

Wexler gave a thin smile. "It always comes down to matters of bravery for you, doesn't it, Calhoun. Fortunately some of us think with our heads instead of our hubris."

"And some of us think too much," said Calhoun. He picked up his bags.

At that moment, the door chime rang. "That will be Betty," said Wexler. "Come!"

The door slid open. Dean Jellico was standing in the doorway.

Calhoun turned to Wexler. "You just never get tired of being right, do you."

Jellico nodded in acknowledgment to both of them. "Cadet Wexler," he said, "my understanding is that you kept your nose clean during this entire ugly business."

"Yes, sir. Squeaky."

"Very wise. That shows great restraint."

"It wasn't easy, sir."

"I'm guessing it was," muttered Calhoun, just loud enough for Wexler, but not Jellico, to hear. Wexler kept a smile on his face but gestured toward Calhoun with his upraised forefinger and middle finger extended. Calhoun didn't know what that meant, but suspected it couldn't be good.

The dean of students then turned to Calhoun. His face darkened. "And as for you, Cadet . . ."

"As you see, I'm prepared to leave," said Calhoun. "If you can just indicate when the next shuttle will be departing . . ."

"Mr. Kemper."

"What about Mr. Kem—?"

The question died on Calhoun's lips as Kemper entered. He looked more the worse for wear than did Calhoun, which was surprising considering that Calhoun had been under a pile of upperclassmen who were endeavoring to pummel him. He was wearing a crisp, clean uniform, leading Calhoun to believe he'd gone to change it. But his short hair was in disarray, there were some bruises swelling up on either side of his face, and overall he looked like exactly what he was: someone who'd gotten into a fight and come up with the short end of the stick.

Calhoun said nothing. There seemed to be nothing to say. Perhaps Kemper was going to take a swing at him. Calhoun was almost hoping he would . . . although he wasn't sure if it was because he believed he deserved it on some level . . . or because he just wanted one more opportunity to take Kemper apart before he left.

"Mr. Kemper," Jellico said slowly, "takes full responsibility for the incident."

"Of course he does," Calhoun replied. "He started it."

Wexler was standing near Calhoun, and rested a hand lightly on his shoulder. Calhoun looked at it with annoyance, but Wexler paid him no mind. "You don't understand," Wexler said.

"Yes, I understand. He says he started it. He did. Now, when is the next shuttle—"

"Sir," Wexler turned to Jellico, "may I have a moment to confer with my client?"

Jellico stared at Wexler with raised eyebrow, and there may have been the slightest hint of a twitch on the edges of his mouth. Then he said formally, "As you wish, Cadet."

Wexler pulled Calhoun toward the far side of the room. Calhoun, curious, went willingly . . . which was fortunate for Wexler, since if Calhoun had been *un*willing, he wouldn't have gone anywhere. Speaking in a rush, Wexler told him, "When he says he's taking full responsibility, it means that you're being held completely blameless. No action taken against you."

"What?" Calhoun was having trouble understanding what Wexler was talking about. "How can I be held 'completely blameless'? It takes two to fight."

"That's not the point. We're not talking about interpersonal dynamics. We're talking about crime and punishment. Who instigated the crime and who is to be penalized for it. Usually in such instances, people finger each other and penalties are dealt all around. Kemper is saying that only he should be penalized. If the dean accepts that, they'd have no reason to kick you out. You were just defending yourself."

Calhoun's eyes narrowed and he regarded Kemper suspiciously. "Why? Why would you do that?"

Kemper looked to Jellico, who nodded. "Because it's the truth," said Kemper.

"And why should that compel you?"

"Because he's a Starfleet officer, Calhoun," Jellico said. "That's sufficient reason."

The upperclassman let out a heavy sigh. "Look . . . the simple fact is that I let my ego run away with me. I was so busy convincing myself that plebes have to be shown their place . . . that I forgot to consider that four-year cadets also sometimes need to be shown their place. It didn't help that you put me down with one punch."

"I thought it was a 'lucky punch,' " said Calhoun.

Kemper grimaced. "So did I. At least, that's what I kept telling myself. I take a lot of pride in my self-defense skills."

"Well . . . you should," Calhoun said diplomatically. "For a human who's probably never had to fight for his life, you handled it quite well."

Wexler laughed softly at that, then saw that neither Jellico nor Kemper was amused, and promptly quieted.

"The thing of it is," continued Kemper, "I realized I allowed my ego to blind me to just how easily you took me down. And word was all over the Academy. *All* over. One-Punch Calhoun, meet Glass-Jaw Kemper."

"You didn't have your friends with you in order to outnumber me," Calhoun realized. "You just wanted as many witnesses as possible."

"Yes. I thought I'd take you down easily the second time out, because I wouldn't underestimate you twice. It didn't exactly work out that way. And then things, well . . . they just spiraled out of control."

"I would certainly call a melee 'spiraling out of control,' " agreed Calhoun. "I'm curious: Would your friends have claimed, on your behalf, that I was the one responsible?"

"They would have told the truth," Jellico said firmly.

But Calhoun was looking at Kemper, and when the latter was certain that Jellico wasn't noticing, he gave the slightest hint of a nod. Which was exactly what Calhoun thought. "It really doesn't matter," Kemper then said. "I'd never have put them in that position."

Calhoun looked very thoughtful then, and Jellico asked, "Something you wish to say, Cadet?"

"I suppose," he admitted, "if I had simply done the pushups when Mr. Kemper asked me to, none of this would have happened."

"True enough," said Jellico. "As you go through life, Calhoun . . . not just your career, but life . . . you'll find there's any number of times when you have to weigh immediate inconvenience against long-term benefits. Only you can make those decisions. Sometimes they'll be difficult, other times . . . less so."

"What's going to happen to Mr. Kemper?" asked Calhoun.

"Appropriate measures will be taken," Jellico said, "the exact nature of which will remain none of your business, Mr. Calhoun." He glanced from one to the other. "This might be an appropriate moment, gentlemen, to shake hands."

Kemper stuck his hand out in that same odd manner that Wexler had first displayed. By this point, however, Calhoun knew what to do, and he took it and shook it firmly.

"I have to know, Calhoun: What would I have to do to learn how to fight the way you do?"

"Know that you'll win."

"No one can know that for sure," Kemper said. "There's always possibilities, unforeseen—"

"Know that you'll win."

Slowly Kemper nodded. "Know that I'll win. Got it." He pumped Calhoun's hand once more. "By the way, just so you know . . . I still don't like you very much."

"I can live with that," Calhoun assured him.

Kemper nodded, then took two steps back and snapped to attention. Jellico turned on his heel and headed for the door, followed by Kemper. At the door Jellico paused, turned, and said, "I feel safe in saying you've used up all your good luck, Calhoun. Another incident like this, I don't give a damn who started it. Not only will you have your bags packed, but I personally will escort you to the curb. Understood?"

"Yes, sir."

"Good."

The door slid shut behind them, and Wexler shook his head wonderingly. "You are the luckiest son of a bitch I've ever met."

"Lucky." Calhoun snorted. "People keep picking fights with me. I don't feel especially lucky."

"You're lucky that Kemper had enough class to take full responsibility for what happened. Any number of upperclassmen would have been concerned solely about covering their own asses. But Kemper, for all the grief he gave you, believes in the Code of Conduct. He handled himself honorably. You should keep that in mind for the future for yourself."

"What is that supposed to mean?" demanded Calhoun.

"Nothing. It means nothing." Wexler put up his hands defensively and cowered in exaggerated fashion. "Don't hit me."

Calhoun rolled his eyes.

ii.

As the sun set, Calhoun stood outside the Academy and watched the great glowing orb descend past the Golden Gate Bridge. There was a structure that had stood for hundreds of years. He thought about the remarkably primitive humans who must have constructed it, and marveled that they could have managed it at all.

"What are you doing out here?"

Shelby approached from behind him. He liked the way the sun shone off her blond curls. "Just thinking," he said.

"Thinking about how lucky you are to still be here?"

"I'm not entirely sure that's lucky." He pointed to some words that were engraved above the main entrance. "That's not your common language. I've been trying to understand that. What is it?"

She looked where he indicated and smiled as if what he was asking was charming or cute somehow. "It's Latin. It reads, *'Ex astris, scientia.'* It means 'From the stars, knowledge.' It's the motto of Starfleet Academy."

"What is 'Latin'?"

"It's a dead language. No one really speaks it conversationally any-more."

He made a dismissive sound. "If they're interested in disseminating knowledge, they should think about sticking to languages people use."

Shelby chuckled at that. "You're probably right." Then she drew nearer to him. His look, his body language, everything about him told her that something was off. "What's bothering you, Calhoun?"

"What makes you say something is bothering me?"

"The fact that something's bothering you is what makes me say it. I'm funny that way. I mean, come on!" and she slapped him on the back. "You should be celebrating! Wex told me you were packing up to leave, and all of a sudden, boom! You're staying!"

"Boom," he echoed tonelessly.

All attempts at joviality on her part evaporated. With real concern, she drew closer to him and rested a hand on his shoulder. "Macken-zie . . . seriously . . ."

"Seriously?" He shook his head. "All right. Seriously then. I was out-numbered."

"When?" Then she realized. "Oh. Then. Yes, you were."

"Fighting all those cadets."

"Yes."

"And all those other first-years were just standing there, watching. No one making a move to help me."

"You didn't call for help."

He shrugged. "It never occurred to me."

"I had a feeling."

"Or I should say," he continued, "it never occurred to me until you jumped in . . . and suddenly the other cadets couldn't pitch in fast enough."

"Calhoun, where are you going with this?"

"Isn't it obvious?" he said. "They followed you, but not me."

"And that bothers you."

"I didn't think it would." He paused. "But the more I dwell on it . . ."

"Then stop dwelling on it."

He turned to face her. "Is it because you're a woman?"

Shelby stepped back from him, making no effort to hide her annoyance with him. It was an attitude she would come to adopt very often in the future. "Oh, well, that makes perfect sense. I mean, it's the only reasonable explanation. That it's because I'm a woman. Our fellow cadets were suddenly seized with a massive flood of chivalry and had to leap to my rescue."

"All right. I can accept that."

"Calhoun!" she said in frustration, her hands flexing as if she wanted to throttle him. "I was being sarcastic!" Then she frowned. "Or ironic. I always get those two mixed up."

"Ironic," said Calhoun. "Spoken irony between two parties generally requires that one of the two parties doesn't realize the speaker isn't serious. Sarcasm is broader, more easily recognizable, and generally more insulting."

"Well, thanks ever so for the lesson, Professor I'm-So-Well-Read Calhoun."

"See, that was sarcasm."

"Shut up."

"And that was just rude."

"Not as rude as automatically assuming that because I'm a female, men had to leap to my aid."

"I didn't say they had to. I thought maybe they felt compelled to."

"Or maybe," countered Shelby, "they saw me as someone who was more like them. Someone who has a basic respect for the rules, and an appreciation for the history of Starfleet. Someone with whom they had common ground. And because of that, they came to my aid because they felt I was one of them. As opposed to someone who treasures his outsider status, acts in a sullen and belligerent manner when *anyone* tries to approach him, and clearly thinks that his upbringing of oppression and deprivation makes him eminently more worthy than anyone else here."

He considered that for a long moment, and then shook his head. "No. I think it's because you're a woman."

She groaned and sat down on the edge of a base of a large statue, her face in her hands. "You are the most frustrating man I've ever met."

"Me?"

"Yes."

"Then you should really meet more men."

"Calhoun . . ."

"Who's that?" He was looking up at the statue, his face full of curiosity. Shelby craned her neck around to look and see just whose feet she was seated at.

"Zefram Cochrane," she said. "There're probably more statues of him on Earth than any other person. He invented warp drive. If it weren't for him, interstellar travel wouldn't have been possible."

"That's not true."

"Calhoun," said Shelby, her eyes wide, "you don't even know who he was! How can you say that?"

"Because if he hadn't done it, someone else would have. The times arrive for things to happen, and people arise to accomplish those things."

"So you're saying accomplishments shouldn't be celebrated? Commemorated?"

"No," said Calhoun. "I'm just saying that people find ways. Always."

"Except when they're busy packing their bags and getting ready to give up."

He stared at her, then lowered his gaze to the ground. "Point taken," he said.

"Tell me, Calhoun: Did it ever occur to you that, just as you weren't looking for help when those men were pounding on you, I wasn't looking for help when Kemper was giving me grief? If you'd stayed out of it, the fight would never have broken out."

"He was giving you grief because of me. I couldn't allow that."

"Not everything is about you, Calhoun."

"Maybe it should be."

She was taken aback, and was about to tear off the sternest dressing-down she could muster when she saw a slight twinkle of amusement in his eye. She laughed before she even knew she was going to. "Okay, now you're just screwing with me."

"A little," he admitted. "But the truth is . . . I had to help you. I had no choice."

"Why? Because it threatened your sense of maleness?"

"Because I had to," he repeated, and she knew she wasn't going to get any more of an answer from him than that. It was good enough for Calhoun, and she was never going to manage to shake him from that.

"All right," she said softly. "I'll accept that. Provided you accept that maybe, just maybe, there's an outside chance that you don't know everything."

"The reading's certainly proving that well enough."

"What do you mean? I thought you were—"

"Comprehending?" He shook his head. "I . . . suppose I made it sound easier than it is. The truth is, I'm working so hard to catch up I feel as if my head's going to explode. There are some words I just stare at for what seems like hours and still can't comprehend. So then I ask the computer to tell me what it means, and the definition is even more confusing."

"I'll help you."

Calhoun was clearly surprised. "You will? That's . . . you don't have to."

"Oh! Typical," she said, needling him. "First you complain when no one helps you, and then you complain when someone volunteers to. Make up your mind. Do you want help or no?"

"Yes."

"Good. So . . . I'll help. On one condition."

"That being?"

"You stop saying that other people helped me because I'm a woman."

"All right."

"Good."

And he looked her full in the face and said, "They helped you because you are the most beautiful creature walking this planet."

Her mouth moved and no words emerged at first. Then finally she nodded and said, "I can accept that."

Chapter Five

Now

Janos couldn't even look Kebron in the eye. Kebron understood why.

He stood there in the brig, a foot away from the white-furred security officer, his massive arms folded. "You refused to submit to the bioscan because you didn't want me to find out about M'Ress. Correct?"

Slowly Janos nodded.

"You were concerned that if I knew about that connection, it would provide motive for you to have killed Gleau."

Janos looked up in surprise and blinked rapidly. "Oh. I . . . suppose it does."

"You 'suppose it does.' Are you telling me it didn't occur to you?" Kebron was getting a dizzying sinking feeling. That he had, as the old Earth saying went, backed the wrong horse.

And yet when Janos spoke, it was with such utter sincerity that Kebron found it difficult not to be swayed by him. "That's absolutely correct, Lieutenant. And I suppose the reason it didn't was because I know that I did not do this thing. Therefore dwelling upon considerations that might make me 'look' guilty or not guilty simply didn't factor into my thinking."

"Before we go any further," said Kebron, "would you object if—now that your involvement with M'Ress is public knowledge—I activated the bioscan?"

Janos shrugged. It looked odd, that human gesture on a being so utterly inhuman. "Not at all. Be my guest."

"Computer," Kebron said immediately. "Voice activate and identify, file Kebron nine zero six."

"Activating," the computer's voice replied. "Bioscan online."

He nodded and then said, "Janos . . . did you kill Gleau?"

"No."

"Did you arrange to have him killed?"

"No."

"Do you have any knowledge of his murder?"

"Yes."

Kebron was taken aback, and then braced himself. "What knowledge do you have of Lieutenant Commander Gleau's murder?"

"It resulted in his death."

"Besides that," said Kebron in annoyance.

"Besides that? No."

The computer did not offer any negative assessment.

"You're a riot, Janos," Kebron said sourly.

"You used to have a sense of humor, Kebron. A dour one, to be sure, but it was there nevertheless. Whatever happened to it?"

"I lost it right around the same time that one of my best men got himself accused of murder."

"Yes, I can see how that would be a mood killer."

Kebron let the remark pass. Instead he said, "So . . . all right. You didn't want to submit to the bioscan because of your involvement with M'Ress."

"Yes."

"But you gave no consideration to the concept of this information incriminating you."

"None at all."

Still there was no reaction from the computer. Getting suspicious, Kebron said, "Janos . . . lie to me."

"I love your new, chatty personality," said Janos.

Immediately the computer said, "Subject displaying physiological changes consistent with false statement."

Janos smiled wanly. Considering that his face was not built for smiling, that was no mean trick.

"And the hilarity that is Janos just keeps on coming," said Kebron. "All right. Very well. But what, then, was your reason for initially refusing a bioscan?"

"Why, Kebron, I'm surprised I have to spell it out for you: A gentleman never tells."

"What?" He couldn't quite believe he was hearing him properly.

And yet Janos seemed appalled by the entire notion. "M'Ress, believe it or not, is a private person. As am I. I had no desire to broadcast our relationship because I was concerned the fact of it would be enough to cause her some embarrassment. Plus, naturally, the endless array of jokes about 'the fur flying' and such. She did not need that and neither, I must admit, did I. So we resolved to take all effort to keep it between ourselves. Submitting to a bioscan is hardly 'all effort.' "

"But refusing to submit to it is hardly the best way to go about clearing yourself of murder."

"I should not have to clear myself of something that I did not do."

"You'd think that, wouldn't you," said a grim-faced Kebron. "All right . . . computer. For the moment, end bioscan."

"Bioscan terminated," the computer replied readily.

It was an odd situation for Kebron. He'd never realized that computers on all ships had a voice that was evocative of Morgan Lefler's. And considering that Morgan was now in the computer of the *Excalibur,* it had become that much more difficult to grow accustomed to the sensation. Fortunately enough, this was the *Trident,* not the *Excal.* At least he didn't have to worry that she was actually residing within the computer.

"So am I free to go?" asked Janos, his face a question mark.

"I wish it was that simple."

"You have my statement, verified by bioscan, that I didn't do it. Why precisely isn't it that simple?"

"Because," said Kebron in annoyance, "there's still the matter of your DNA all over Gleau's corpse. We're going to have to figure this out."

"And in the meantime . . . I remain incarcerated here. Made to feel like . . ." He looked from side to side mournfully. ". . . like a freak. A caged animal on display. For two credits people can stroll by and point and be terrified of the wild beast, caged up the way he should always have been. They could make a reasonably impressive petting-zoo specimen of me if they weren't concerned I'd rip people's arms off."

"Janos!" Kebron admonished. "I'd never have thought of you as someone who wallows in self-pity."

"My self-confidence and self-respect have been taken from me,"

Janos said quietly. "So kindly leave me one of the few self-reflective pleasures I have left, if it's all the same to you." Then he leaned forward on the small bench and hung his head between his legs.

Kebron tried to think of something else to say, but he couldn't. Janos was his friend, his coworker, and he was suffering in the depths of despair with no way out. At least, none that Kebron could readily provide.

With a sigh that sounded like a shift in tectonic plates, Kebron turned and said, "Lower the shield." The forcefield that barred the doorway to the brig went out and Kebron headed for it. As he did so, his mind was spinning with possibilities. He was now more convinced than ever of Janos's innocence. Certainly the facility with which he'd passed the bioscan had been sufficient to sway any reasonable person. But, as he'd just told Janos, the DNA remained a problem. His initial research into the matter indicated that it was simply impossible to cover up one's own DNA traces while substituting genetic evidence pointing to someone else. That meant very little, though. Centuries ago, any reasonable person would have told you that traveling faster than light was a scientific impossibility. The fact that Kebron had no idea how such a DNA switch could be made was of no relevance to him. What he needed to learn was just who *was* capable of making the switch.

There was one other thing of which he was certain. Something that all his reading of hard-boiled detective novels had convinced him. The person who was responsible for this murder was going to be the last person he suspected of committing it.

The moment Kebron stepped through the door of the brig, Janos let out an ear-rattling roar and leaped.

The roar accomplished exactly what it was supposed to do. It froze Kebron for a split instant right in the doorframe. While he was there, the field couldn't be reactivated.

Janos, claws bared, face twisted in animal fury, sailed through the air, propelled by incredibly strong legs, and landed on Zak Kebron's back. There were few people on the ship—indeed, few people in existence—who would have been capable of knocking the towering Brikar off his feet, but Janos was one of them. His arms pinwheeling, unable to maintain his balance, Kebron toppled forward like a great stone pillar. He was on his chest and Janos swept down with his claws. They skidded off Kebron's tough hide, inflicting damage upon nothing except Kebron's pride.

There were security guards on either side. They went for their phasers, but Janos was snake-fast. He was upon the guard to his right in a heart-beat, knocking the phaser from his hand before it could be brought to bear. The guard tried to back up and Janos grabbed him by the uniform front, hoisting him into the air and roaring into his face. His teeth bared, he looked prepared to bite the guard's face right off his head.

The other guard had his phaser out and was circling, trying to get a clear shot. "Just shoot him!" howled the guard who was having his life threatened.

The circling guard thumbed his phaser from the lethal "disruption" down to "stun," praying it would be enough, and he fired. At the instant that he did so, however, Janos swung around the guard he was holding so that the man's body served as a shield that intercepted the blast. He let out a truncated yelp and then slumped in Janos's grasp. Janos, with a triumphant howl, threw the guard like a shot put. He collided with the guard who was still standing and they both went down in a tangle of arms and legs.

It had all happened so quickly that Kebron still hadn't quite gotten back onto his feet. Kebron was built for many things, but bouncing quickly from prone to standing wasn't one of them. Nevertheless he did finally clamber to standing. By that point, however, Janos was gone. Immediately Kebron thundered after him, hitting his combadge as he did so. "Kebron to Arex!" he shouted, and without waiting for Arex to respond, continued, "Security breach! Janos is loose on deck five, corridor thirteen-A! Am in pursuit!"

"On our way!" came Arex's reedy voice.

Kebron charged down the corridor, the floor trembling beneath his feet. Following Janos's trail was no great challenge. He simply looked for the fallen crewmen along the way. Janos hadn't killed any of them, thank God, but they were scattered to one side or the other, having been unceremoniously shoved out of the way. He heard a distant roaring and picked up speed. He hoped no one got in his way, because he didn't think he'd be able to stop in time, and he hated the notion of winding up with *Trident* crewmen on his boots.

He rounded a bend in the corridor and almost collided with Arex and five security men heading in the opposite direction. They skidded to a halt, Arex with greater skill than any of them thanks to his tripod structure. "Where is he?" demanded Kebron.

"I thought you had him!"

"If I had him, you'd know by the fact that he'd be in my hands!" Kebron said angrily.

"Well, he didn't get past us!"

"Then where—"

Suddenly they heard a distant, triumphant howling. They turned and saw the Jefferies tube in the wall.

Kebron was there first, looking into the depths of the equipment-access tube. It angled upward, out of sight. Unlike some other such tubes that were short runs, this particular Jefferies tube accessed far deeper. An uncontrolled, totally berserk Janos was gallivanting around the inner depths of the *Trident*.

And it was at that moment Kebron realized that Ensign Janos was— despite the DNA evidence—the last person Kebron had suspected of being the murderer.

"Shit," muttered Kebron.

Then

"Should I be jealous of you two?"

In Shelby's quarters, Wexler was lying in her bed, naked under the cover, his head propped up with one hand. Shelby was busy getting dressed, and she glanced over at him in confusion. "Pardon?" she asked. "Me too?"

"You two. You and Calhoun."

She stared at him as if he'd grown a third eye as she adjusted her uniform top. "Me and Calhoun? What about me and Calhoun?"

"Well, you've been spending so much time together. I was beginning to wonder."

She could scarcely believe it. "Oh my God," she laughed. "I mean . . . oh my God. After this? After what we . . . God, Wex! Was I so lousy that this didn't even qualify as quality time?"

"It's not that at all. You were great."

"I know."

"It's just . . ." He flopped back onto the mattress. "Forget it. The more I think about it, the more petulant I feel and the more absurd it becomes."

"Well, good. So we won't discuss this any further?"

"Not a word," Wexler assured her.

"Excellent." Shelby pulled on one boot, reached for the other, then stopped and turned back to him. *"Me and Calhoun?"*

"So much for not discussing it further," he sighed.

"It's just . . . that's so ridiculous . . ." Then she shook her head briskly

and yanked on the other boot. She stood, limping slightly because she'd
pulled it on wrong and had to worm her foot down into it so it would
fit properly. As she did so by walking in a small circle, she muttered,
"Calhoun! And me! Just because I've been helping him . . . and you . . .
that is the most idiotic . . . small-minded . . ." She flexed her foot, satisfied,
then turned back to Wexler and said, "Forget this. It's just too stupid, and
besides, I'm going to be late for xenobio. So we'll discuss this later."

"Or . . . not at all," Wexler offered.

"Not at all. Yes. Good plan. You can let yourself out." She grabbed up
her padd and headed out the door, which shut behind her.

Wexler lay there, staring up at the ceiling, his arms splayed to either
side. "And three . . . two . . . one," he counted down softly.

Shelby barreled back into the room right on cue, still clutching her
padd and waving it around. "You're something else, you know that,
Wex?"

"That's coming to my attention, yes," he sighed. "You know, Betty,
right now there's not a more regretful person on this planet—possibly
this quadrant—than I. I'm sorry I brought it up."

"Well, you should be."

"So can we drop it?"

"No, because *you* brought it up!"

He moaned and pulled the pillow over his head with the vague hope
that he might be able to smother himself.

"Here I am," she continued, "trying to offer aid to a fellow Starfleet
cadet . . . trying to help him succeed against greater odds than you and I
and anyone else have had to face . . . and you start getting jealous just
because I'm tutoring him in reading comprehension."

"I'm not jealous."

"You just *said!*"

"I asked if I should *be* jealous. It's a totally different thing."

"Don't start getting semantical on me, Wex."

" 'Semantical'? Is that even a word?"

"You want a word? Here's three. Go fu—"

"All right, now, that's enough," said Wexler. He got out of the bed, the
sheet wrapped around himself, giving him a passing resemblance to a
Roman orator. "Here's a wild and wacky notion: Let's completely over-
react to a casual question."

"There was nothing casual about it," and she thumped a finger against his bare chest. "You don't trust me."

"It has nothing to do with that. It's just—"

"Just what?"

"Well," and he looked uncomfortable, but soldiered forward. "It's just, in my opinion, Calhoun was managing just fine before you started 'tutoring' him. And I think he agreed to it because he was anxious to spend as much time with you as possible."

"That's . . ." She shook her head skeptically. "That's ridiculous."

"Is it?"

"It is," she said firmly. "I've been helping him for weeks now, and he hasn't said or done the slightest thing to indicate that he thinks of me as anything but a friend."

"Well, he wouldn't. He'd wait for the right time. He wouldn't rush into it."

"And wouldn't that make him a master strategist."

"He *is* a master strategist, Betty! Haven't you been paying attention to his history? He's a bleeding warlord who masterminded his race's freedom before he was old enough to shave! He thinks long-term."

"At least he is thinking. I don't believe you're giving any thought at all to what you're saying. The words are just . . . just falling out of your mouth." She put up her hands. "This is ridiculous. I'm now officially late for class." With that, Shelby pivoted and went out the door.

He stared after her and then said very calmly, "Three . . . two . . . one."

The door remained closed.

"Three . . . two . . . one," Wex repeated.

Again, no sign of her.

"Hunh," he said. "Well . . . so much for th—"

Whereupon Shelby bounded back in, slamming down her padd.

"One of us is losing his or her touch," said Wexler.

Not appearing to have heard what he said, Shelby demanded, "You want to know what I think?"

"There are no words to encapsulate just how much I do not wish to—"

"I'll tell you what I think."

"Yes," sighed Wexler, "I rather thought you might." He sagged onto the bed, looking a bit forlorn.

"What I think is that you don't understand about helping people."

He stared at her with raised eyebrows. "Beg pardon?"

"Your entire approach to life, Wex, is 'What's in it for me?' That and keeping your nose clean so you won't do anything to jeopardize your Starfleet career."

"What a splendid opinion you have of me," he said dryly.

"Do you think it's wrong?"

"I think it's unduly harsh. Why do you think I have no concept of helping peo—" Then it dawned on him. "Because I didn't rush to help you when Kemper was forcing you to do calisthenics."

"I . . . wasn't thinking about that specifically," said Shelby in a guarded tone, "but now that you mention it . . ."

"Betty, for God's sake! What would you have had me do? Run to the rescue as if you were incapable of handling it yourself? Then you would have been insulted, just as you were when Calhoun stepped in."

"Maybe," she admitted. "Maybe I would have been insulted. A little."

"Then what's the problem?"

"The problem is . . ." She fumbled for words. "The problem is that . . . at least I would have known you cared enough to try."

"I didn't try anything because I *do* care. I care too much about you as a person to think of you as . . . as a damsel in distress. Someone whom I just whisk up in my arms at the first sign of trouble and announce, in my best manly basso profundo voice, that everything is going to be just tickety-boo. What sort of way is that to think? It seems to run in utter contradiction to everything I know about you!"

There was a long silence, and finally she said—her head cocked slightly—"Tickety-boo?"

"Yes. Tickety-boo," he said with a widening smile.

"Don't you ever say anything normal?"

"I try not to. Betty," and he stood and rested his hands on her shoulders, "I was just being foolish. I should have known better than to be jealous, especially when all you're trying to do is be a good friend and good cadet. Can we simply write this entire, ugly business off to the concept that I'm churlish, an utter cad, and move on from here?"

"Absolutely a tickety-boo idea," she replied, stood up on her toes, and kissed him. "I have to go!" Then she turned and ran out the door.

Wexler reached down, picked up the note padd, and extended it while saying nothing. Moments later the door hissed open and Shelby charged in. She had her mouth open, ready to speak, and then saw that he was just standing there holding the padd. She bobbed her head once in appreciation, grabbed it, and bounded out of the room.

He watched her go, reasonably sure that this time she wouldn't be coming back. Wexler was alone with his thoughts.

His thoughts . . . and the image of a young Xenexian cadet side by side with the woman he loved.

And he knew things were not remotely tickety-boo.

Chapter Six

Now

i.

Shelby rose from behind her desk in her ready room, hardly able to credit what Arex was telling her. Kebron was standing next to Arex. He didn't look any happier about it.

"Are you serious?" she asked when she regained her voice.

"Captain, I know at the moment it looks bad . . ."

"Looks bad?" She came around the desk and looked up at the Brikar. "It's nice to know, Mr. Kebron, that after all this time, your knack for understatement remains consistent." She turned to Arex. "He's loose? In the bowels of the ship?"

"I wouldn't say 'loose' and 'bowels' so closely together," suggested Kebron, "simply because it suggests another image entirely, and—"

"Shut up, Kebron."

"Shutting up, Captain," he said promptly.

"My security teams are fully mobilized," Arex assured her. "The problem is being attended to. But we wanted to inform you immediately."

"Thanks ever so." She hit her combadge. "Shelby to transporter room."

"Transporter room, Heisenberg here," came the voice of the transporter chief.

"Heisenberg, I've just been informed," she said with a menacing stare at the security heads, "that Mr. Janos is running amok somewhere within the ship. Lock on to his combadge, grab him, and then redirect him straight into brig five-A, would you please?"

There was a brief pause and then his voice came back, sounding regretful. "We've got a lock on his combadge, Captain, but that's all it is. It's not giving us any life readings. He's ditched his badge."

"Perfect. All right, then: Access ship's internal sensors and locate his biosigns. There's no one else on the *Trident* with readings like his. It shouldn't take you more than sixty seconds to locate him."

"I'm . . . not so certain about that," he replied.

"Heisenberg, I don't need uncertainty from you right now," Shelby said. "Can you do it or not, and just for your information, the 'or not' is not intended as an acceptable option."

"Under ordinary circumstances, Captain, yes. But here's the problem," said a frustrated Heisenberg. "We're experiencing a rash of power and systems outages. Totally random, as if . . ."

"As if someone is ripping at operating systems in the innards of the ship?" suggested Arex.

"Yes," Heisenberg said. "Exactly like that."

Kebron moaned and put a hand to the side of his smallish head.

"So you're saying you can't lock on to him?"

"No, Captain, you're saying that. However, I wouldn't rush to disagree."

"Wonderful," snarled Shelby. "Perfect. All right. The orders are standing. Try to lock him down, de-mat him, and then dump him in the brig. The moment the situation changes and you have a shot at dematerializing him, inform me at once. Shelby out."

She stepped back, leaning against the wall, and very softly thudded the back of her head against it several times.

"Shall I inform Captain Calhoun?" asked Kebron, looking a bit cautious. "I just figured he should know, but I don't want to chance getting you even angrier than you already are."

"Lieutenant," she said through lips pulled so tight they looked like a rubber band stretched to its limit, "I don't think it's possible for me to be even angrier than I already am."

At which point the lights suddenly went out. "I stand corrected," she said even as the light snapped back on almost immediately. "Janos?" she demanded.

"Very likely."

"Get him. Gas the crawlways and ducts if you have to drive him out, but do whatever it takes."

"And Captain Calhoun . . . ?" asked Kebron.

"Leave him out of it for now. He'll find out soon enough. I want to get this resolved before we have to drop all this negative news on him."

Arex looked slightly concerned over that. Kebron was, as usual, deadpan. Even with his new, more outgoing attitude, a vast range of facial expressions was not his strength. They both muttered "Aye" and headed out of the ready room. Almost as soon as they were gone, Kat Mueller walked in.

"How'd you know I was going to send for you?" said Shelby.

"My job to know, Captain."

"I see. All right," she said. She circled around back to her chair, sat down, and leaned back with her arms folded. "Janos has gone berserk. He's running around in the inner workings of the ship, and apparently he's doing enough damage—by accident or design—to prevent us from beaming him out of there and into a holding cell."

"All right," said Mueller.

"You knew all this already, didn't you?"

"Yes, Captain," she said. "It's my job—"

"—to know, yes, I understand that. Arex and Kebron have people working on this situation, but I want you monitoring it and giving me updates every ten minutes. Understood?"

"Yes, Captain."

But Mueller didn't move from her spot, and Shelby regarded her questioningly. "Something else?"

"Captain Calhoun. Will you be informing him?"

"Not at present," she said slowly.

"It's his officer."

"It's my ship."

"But Captain—"

Shelby put up a hand, instantly silencing Mueller. "Many has been the time, XO, where Captain Calhoun has kept his cards close to the vest."

"Making this . . . what? Payback?"

"Hardly. I would simply rather this situation be resolved before he is informed of it."

"Permission to speak freely, Captain?"

"I think wild horses sitting on your face couldn't stop you from speaking freely, XO."

"You don't wish to tell Captain Calhoun because you think it makes you appear as if you're not in control of your own vessel. That you are incapable of handling matters yourself."

"That's not the case," Shelby lied. Deciding to turn the topic quickly away from what made her uncomfortable, she said, "Give me an update, please, on Ambassador Spock, the Danteri, and the Tholians."

"The personalities of the parties are somewhat unpredictable."

"Meaning?"

"Meaning," said Mueller, "that either he's on the verge of settling the matter amicably, or the Danteri and the Tholians are on the brink of all-out war."

"I see." Shelby took that in. "Let me know how that works out, will you?"

"If shots are fired across our bow, Captain, I assure you you'll be the first to know."

The lights went out.

"I feel better already," said Shelby from the darkness.

ii.

In the dim lighting, M'Ress made her way with supple grace through the gantries and catwalks of the *Trident*. Her ears were fully extended, her tail was straight out, and she wasn't moving on two legs, but four.

It had been a long, long time since she had felt like this, moved like this. For ages now, it seemed, her world had consisted of oppression and frustration, of moral gray areas. She hadn't remembered until just now how much she despised such things. How much more she preferred pure, unencumbered instinct. But that wasn't who she was *(or pretended to be?)*. She had responsibilities, rank, an image that she had carefully crafted and clung to for all she was worth.

Rarely did she have the opportunity to dispense with all that. But this was one of those rare times, and she was thriving on it. More, she was loving it, so much so that it made her wonder why in the world she would ever want to go back to what she had been.

She was not wearing her uniform. She knew that the slightest encumbrance of civilization would impede her ability to do what she needed to do. So, once having entered the cross junction, out of sight of anyone's eyes, she had stripped down to her fur and started moving. With the loss of every article of clothing she felt more alive, more vital than she thought possible. The only link she maintained to the world she left behind was her combadge, which she had attached to the back of her hand to make it easier to find in the darkness. Not that the dark was a huge problem for her; her eyes were wide and luminous and saw almost everything.

She made as much noise as a shadow as she glided through the twists and turns of the utilities ducts, her senses extended to their capacity. Her nostrils flared, picking up his scent. She made her way quickly, down and through gantries, up through catwalks. All maintenance people doing routine work had been cleared out. Everything was too unpredictable.

Part of her wanted to laugh. One being, with nothing but the claws at the ends of his fingers and some sort of basic animalistic instinct, was causing power outages throughout the ship. For all their sophistication, all their technology, they didn't know how to handle him. And the other part of her reminded herself that it wasn't funny. That he might die because of this. That someone *had* died, and she bore some responsibility for that. This wasn't a game.

And yet it was.

Cat and mouse.

But despite her feline trappings, she wasn't entirely sure which role she was playing.

She tracked him through to another cross junction, buried deep in the heart of the backup systems, and suddenly she lost him. It wasn't that his scent had vanished. It was that his scent was everywhere. He had crisscrossed this particular area several times, leaving his spoor all over it. And she was having trouble determining which was the most recent. Worse, she couldn't tell whether he had done it by happenstance or whether it was pure animal cunning.

That was when she heard him.

Her heart began to pound and she forced herself to slow her breathing, even as she curled up into a tight, feral crouch. Her tail whipped back and forth as the low growl from her prey echoed around her. That was the big problem. She couldn't tell for certain what direction the noise was coming from. Between the confusing scent trails and the ricocheting of the sound, it wasn't possible for her to determine which way to expect an attack from.

Or would it be an attack? As unlikely as it seemed, she was hoping that would not be the case. That she would be able to reach him somehow, get through to him.

But her hackles told her otherwise. Furthermore, every nerve ending was quivering. She was possessed by the oldest survival instinct in the universe: fight or flight. She had no intention of fleeing, but she wasn't certain that, if it came to a fight, she'd have any chance of winning. Or even surviving.

She steadied herself, reaching out with her senses, trying to determine where he was. Another roar, more echoing . . .

. . . and then another sound. The sound of talons, clacking on metal conduits behind her.

She spun, ready to lunge. He was perched not five feet away from her, his mouth drawn back in a snarl. She'd turned to face him just as he'd been about to pounce, and the fact that she suddenly was looking right at him froze him. For a heartbeat they locked eyes. His pupils were dilated, his nostrils wide as they drank in her scent.

"Janos," she said, and her voice sounded strangled because her throat was tense. "Janos . . . it's me. Do you recognize me?"

A voice came over her combadge. "Do you have him?"

She didn't move a muscle. She felt as if to do so would cause him to charge. "I see him, yes."

"Where is he?"

"Much too close." Her pink tongue darted across her lips, which had gone very, very dry. "Janos . . . listen to me—"

His pink eyes seemed to retract into his head, and with a deafening roar, he charged.

She tumbled back, letting out an alarmed yelp, twisting away from the furious sweep of his claws. The space she was in was far too narrow. She barely had any room to maneuver.

There was a cross junction just behind her, but he seemed intent on not letting her get to it. She was on her back and he scrambled toward her, arms outstretched. M'Ress curled up her legs, braced herself, and thrust her legs out. One slammed flat into his chest, halting his forward motion, and the other—with claws extended—raked across his face, just missing gouging out his eyes. Janos roared and swung blindly at her with a sweep that, had it come into contact, would have ripped her open. But she was no longer there, having thrown herself down into the cross junction.

She tumbled away, knowing he would follow. But the access tube was narrow. She slithered through it quickly, feeling as if she were reliving her birth, and she heard his grunting behind her. He was too out of his mind with fury to try and find another route around in hope of cutting her off. Instead, despite his wider shoulders, he muscled his way along, ripping up relays, uncaring of damage he was doing as he pursued her.

She emerged from the access tube into a crawlway. The entire time she kept imagining she could feel his hot breath upon her, his claws sinking into her. He roared once more, and this time there were no echoes fooling her, no question as to where he was. He was right behind her, and if she slowed down in the slightest, he'd have her.

Practically doubled over, she sprinted down the crawlway, and then it opened up wider. She was somewhere in the utility corridors, a maze of catwalks (the irony was not lost on her) above and below.

The ramping beneath her feet shook from the impact as he came right behind her. She started to run, but here in the relative open he was simply too fast. The bouncing ramps nearly shook her off, and then he was upon her and she did the only thing she could. She threw herself off the catwalk, allowing herself to fall down, down through the depths.

The catwalks whizzed past her and then she snagged one with a desperate, outreaching arm. It almost yanked the arm right out of the socket, and then she hauled herself up. She looked up. Janos was coming right after her, bouncing from one ramp to the next like a great gorilla. M'Ress knew she was athletic, but she'd never seen a display of physical dexterity like this.

Even as she watched him, he drew closer and closer with dizzying speed, and then she spotted a Jefferies tube to her right. A quick mental calculation warned her that it was exactly where Janos was going to land. She looked to her left. There was a solid wall.

Desperate, she broke to the right as fast as her feet would carry her. She got to the Jefferies tube bare seconds before he did and threw herself into it. She tumbled end over end, and still he pursued her. He was almost upon her. He wasn't about to let her get away.

She tumbled out of the Jefferies tube into a brightly lit corridor, blinking furiously against the sudden change in illumination. M'Ress barely had time to orient herself before the thundering roar of Janos was upon her, and she backrolled out of the way just as he crashed out of the tube into the corridor.

"Take him!"

It was Arex, with Captain Shelby and Kebron standing on either side and a brace of security guards surrounding him. Arex and the security guards had their phasers leveled upon him.

"Stun only unless I give the word!" shouted Shelby, and then phasers fired.

M'Ress crouched in a corner, watching with eyes wide. She gave no thought to her nudity. It was of no relevance to her. All she cared about was the intensity of the blasts as they hammered at Janos, staggering him.

He threw his arms up, trying to ward them off, and howled and bellowed and then incredibly, impossibly, began to stagger forward, batting at the phaser blasts as if they were irritating insects. It seemed to M'Ress that the corridor was shaking between his infuriated roars and the shrieking of the phasers.

And he was drawing closer, and closer still.

The security team fell back, retreating a few steps and continuing the barrage. And still Janos kept on coming. It almost seemed as if the longer he held on against the assault, the more his rage grew and the more powerful he became.

Then suddenly he lost his grip on the floor and was lifted clean off his feet, hurled back against a bulkhead. M'Ress held her breath, waiting to see if he was unconscious.

"Cease fire!" shouted Shelby, and the phaser barrage halted.

And then Janos was on his feet, looking irritated.

"Damn," muttered Arex.

Very slowly, and with clearly a great deal of regret, Shelby said, "Set phasers for—"

"No," Kebron suddenly said. "He's my responsibility."

"Kebron, wait!" Shelby called out to him, but it was far too late. Kebron was charging forward with the speed and power of an ava-

lanche. Janos, now on his feet, let out a defiant roar and leaped toward him. He covered eight feet in one vault and slammed into Kebron. Kebron staggered but did not go down, and he grabbed huge fistsful of Janos's fur and would not let go.

It was like trying to keep a grip on a white cyclone as Janos howled, bellowed in protest, and clawed everywhere on Kebron that he could reach. Kebron said nothing, merely grunted repeatedly, as Janos's talons kept skidding off his hide. Within seconds his uniform shirt was reduced to tatters, and his pants legs were badly shredded as well.

"Janos!" he finally shouted. "Snap out of it!"

And then he began to shake him, as hard as he could.

Janos's head snapped back and forth, and the noises that came out of his mouth were like nothing that M'Ress had ever heard, noises of such pure animal fury that it was impossible to believe that she'd shared her bed with him, or spoken with him, or done anything aside from trying to stay the hell out of his way.

Then Janos's head speared forward and he tried to tear apart Kebron's face with his teeth.

Kebron let out a yelp of alarm, and then with a roar that nearly dwarfed Janos's own, he slammed the white-furred berserker up against the bulkhead. M'Ress could feel the impact from where she was sitting.

And then he hit Janos against the bulkhead again. And a third time, and then a fourth time, and then M'Ress lost count. She had never seen anyone or anything take such punishment, withstand such teeth-jarring, bone-rattling impact.

Kebron might not have been out of control, but he was close to it. He swung Janos to the left and the right and the left again, then down against the floor and then up against the ceiling. "Kebron, you'll kill him!" shouted M'Ress, and then realized that if Janos somehow managed to defeat Kebron, the security guards would kill Janos.

Then Janos managed to get his feet planted as Kebron swung him up once more toward the ceiling, and he thrust downward, knocking Kebron off balance. Kebron went down with Janos on top of him, and Janos clawed at Kebron with renewed vigor.

There was only so much Kebron's hide could withstand. Rips began to appear, thick black liquid oozing out like tar.

For an instant, Janos made a perfect target, and M'Ress saw the security guards aim their phasers to put an end to it. And then Kebron rallied, shoving Janos over, and the two of them rolled back and forth on the floor. A lethal phaser barrage at Janos might well mean Kebron's demise as well.

And then Kebron was in the superior position, one knee pressing down on Janos's chest, and he hammered him in the face, arms swinging like mighty pendulums. Janos's head snapped to one side and the other under it, and his roars grew louder and suddenly . . .

. . . they were words.

"What the bloody hell is going on here?!"

Everything came to a halt as Janos's eyes focused upon Kebron, but without the pure blinding animal fury that they'd possessed only seconds earlier. Instead there was only bewilderment mixed with confusion and outrage. And then, very slowly, it began to dawn on Janos that where he had been in his last recollection, and where he was now, weren't matching up.

He looked around and saw M'Ress slowly getting to her feet. "Lieutenant," he said softly, "you're out of uniform." Then he spotted the security force with their phasers leveled at him, looked at the wounds that Kebron had sustained, looked at his own talons with Kebron's thick blood upon them, and the immensity of what must have occurred dawned upon him.

"I'm in even more trouble than I was before, aren't I," he said.

"Yes," said Kebron, "and here I wouldn't have thought it possible."

Then

i.

Mackenzie Calhoun sat on the edge of the island, staring at the rolling green waters, and felt a chill down his spine.

Rather than his standard Starfleet uniform, he was wearing a one-piece jumpsuit that had various rations and survival necessities attached in pouches along the legs and arms, and a belt with devices such as a laser torch dangling from it.

He heard footsteps approaching, and recognized them without even needing to glance over his shoulder.

"What are you doing over here?" asked Shelby. Wexler, as was frequently the case recently, was next to her. They were both clad in outfits identical to Calhoun's.

"Surviving," replied Calhoun. "Isn't that what this foolish exercise is all about?"

Wexler chuckled at that. "That's what I love about you, Mackenzie. Here you are, nearing the end of your first year, and you're just as capable of expressing disdain for the Academy curriculum as you were the day you started."

"We all have our individual gifts, Wex," Calhoun said.

The island's name was Platonis. It was entirely man-made, fifty miles across, out in the middle of the Atlantic. Far from being any sort of tropical paradise, it was singularly inhospitable. Vegetation grew upon it, but it was not edible. One could drink from the streams that ran through it if one had a particular interest in enduring sustained intestinal cramps.

It was, in short, a failure as far as being able to support life went. Its creators, however, did consider it to be something of a success since it had been artificially created. It was named, Calhoun had learned, after a noted ancient philosopher named Plato, who had been among the first to preserve tales of a continent called Atlantis believed to have been swallowed up by the raging seas millennia ago. The creators of this particular island had a long-term goal: to create a small continent right in the middle of the Atlantic Ocean. Their work was called "the Atlantis Project."

This, Calhoun had learned, was significantly different from terraforming, which was well within the capabilities of modern technology. Terraforming simply required taking inhospitable terrain on another world and changing it over into somewhere that humans could live. Building a continent from scratch in the middle of the ocean, on the other hand, was far more complicated. Not only did they have to construct an ecosystem that was just the right delicate balance for life to be sustained, but they had to be careful of environmental factors. They had to take into account everything from the impact upon local sea life to the water displacement for which a new continent would be responsible. One could hardly construct a new, "risen" Atlantis at the cost of flooding and sinking already existing terrain.

Although Platonis was a practical failure insofar as creating a livable environment was concerned, scientists did learn from it. A new island, Poseidonis, was under construction many miles away and was said to be going rather well. That left Platonis high and dry, so to speak, and aside from the occasional curiosity seeker cruising past in a low-flying shuttle, no one came to Platonis, and had not for many years.

That was why it was an ideal site for the Starfleet survival drills that the Academy engaged in at the end of the first year.

Calhoun had little patience for it.

He, along with twenty other cadets, had been dropped off on Platonis two days ago (other cadets having been brought to locations equally unappealing). They were expected to survive there for a week. To pull together as fellow castaways. Calhoun had participated in the work involved, but he had done so in a distant and even vaguely contemptuous manner that a number of his associates found very annoying.

"What's your problem, Calhoun?" he'd been asked. Always he would simply shrug, mutter "No problem," and go on with whatever task he was undertaking at that moment.

Now he sat on the edge of the shore, staring out at the water. Wexler and Shelby, standing several feet away, had stripped down to under-garments with the clear intention of swimming. The undergarments were hardly the norm for such items. They were made from stretchable, waterproof material designed to withstand floods, pouring rain, and other such soggy challenges that nature might decide to throw their way. Which wasn't to say Calhoun didn't think Shelby to be quite fetching in the blue one-piece outfit she was sporting. Plus she had spectacular legs.

"Mac, really . . . what's bothering you?" said Wexler. His voice had that familiar ring of concern about it. Calhoun hated to admit it, but over the past year he'd actually grown to like Wexler. Certainly there were things about the man that were irritating, particularly his tendency to talk a far better game than he played, and to act as if the world was his by some sort of divine entitlement. But he was also a surprisingly good listener, had a sharp sense of humor, and didn't treat Calhoun in any sort of condescending manner. Of course, the major problem was that Cal-houn had to fight, on a daily basis, a deep, burning envy any time he saw Wexler with Shelby.

After all, Wexler could think about divine entitlement all he wanted. But hadn't it been Calhoun who'd "seen" Shelby in a vision? Wasn't she fated to be his? What sense would it have made for her to come to him while he was struggling to survive in the desert, only to be destined for another man? It didn't make any sense, and whenever he saw them to-gether, it came across as a mute commentary by the universe that noth-ing was fair and that anyone who had ever preached chaos theory knew precisely what they were talking about.

"What's bothering me?" Calhoun asked. Normally he would have shrugged it off, but finally he decided to say something. "Look at the two of you. This is supposed to be survival training, and you look like you're on vacation, enjoying a day at the beach."

"We've done a hell of a lot of work at the campsite, Mac," retorted Wexler. "As have you, I freely admit, before you get your knickers in a twist. Should we be held responsible if you choose to use your free time by being sullen while we grab some relaxation?"

"I'm not being sullen," Calhoun said sullenly. "It's just that this . . . that all this," and he tugged at his survival gear, "it's all nonsense."

"How is it nonsense?" asked Shelby. "This is survival training. That's survival gear. I'm not seeing the conflict."

"Because survival isn't about being dropped into hostile terrain equipped with everything you need to sustain yourself," Calhoun retorted. "It's about having nothing on hand except your wits and determination. It's about lasting day after day after day, and when you've reached the limits of your endurance, you keep on going, and not dying for no other reason than that you're just too stubborn to give the gods the satisfaction."

"And you've had to do that, I suppose," said Wexler.

"Yes," Calhoun replied without hesitation.

"Do you want to tell us about it?" Shelby asked. She seemed genuinely interested. Perhaps he could even impress her somewhat.

But he shrugged. "Not much to tell. Someone tried to kill me. He failed. He left me this," and he touched the scar on his face. "And I was dying in the desert . . ."

And saw you, and you were naked and smiling at me and you gave me something to live for, and why can't you see that, why can't you realize that we're supposed to be together . . .

". . . but I didn't. Die."

"And what did you have with you?"

"A sword. A laser welder, not too dissimilar from this one," and he touched the one on his tool belt. "That was more or less it."

Shelby knelt down a few feet away from him, her eyes wide. "A laser welder? How was that any good to you?"

"I took it off the body of the man who had cut my face open. It was bleeding fairly profusely. So I used the welder to seal the wound."

"Bollocks!" exclaimed Wexler, but even as he expressed disbelief, he was staring at the scar on Calhoun's face. Shelby was as well, and she reached toward it. Calhoun flinched back slightly. He didn't know why he didn't want her to touch it, but his response was instinctive and she immediately withdrew her hand. Wexler, amazed, came closer, his eyes like saucers. "You *welded* your *face?*"

Calhoun shrugged. He could still feel the heat, the searing pain. His hand trembled ever so slightly just thinking about it, but he wanted to sound nonchalant. "I couldn't afford the blood loss," he said. "I did what I had to do. You see," and the tone of his voice changed, *"that's* survival. Doing what you have to do. If they wanted to give us a true test of survival skills, they'd have dropped us naked on this island and said, 'Good luck.' "

"Well, *that* would have been interesting. People would have been fighting to go on survival training," said Wexler, grinning so widely that Calhoun couldn't help himself and laughed in response. It was almost a relief. All this talk about what he'd had to tolerate in the desert, and the way he'd acquired the scar, had started to depress the hell out of him. "Although," Wexler added, "what with this place being Platonis, we would all have been stuck with Platonic relationships."

Calhoun stared at him blankly. "What?"

"Never mind," Shelby put in, and she got to her feet, brushing dirt from her knees. "Look, Mac, no matter how little you may think of what passes for survival training in the first-year Starfleet curriculum, the bottom line is that we're here, we're doing what we're supposed to do, and there's no harm in having a little relaxation. Come swimming with us."

"No."

"Why not?"

"I grew up on a desert world. You figure it out."

She folded her arms, her mouth twitching in annoyance. "You can't tell me you don't know how to swim. I've seen you in the pool back at the Academy. You swim fine."

"I swim because I have to," he replied. "I had to learn. I practiced when no one was around so I wouldn't be flailing about like an idiot while everyone watched. But I don't like it, and if given preferences, I'd much prefer to have ground beneath my feet instead of water. Besides . . ."

He stopped.

"Besides . . . what?" asked Wexler.

"There's something . . . wrong in there," said Calhoun, pointing toward the water that was lapping at the shoreline.

They looked where he was pointing, both of them shielding their eyes from the bright afternoon sun. "Wrong?" echoed Wexler. "Wrong how?"

"I don't know. I'm just getting a 'danger' feeling about it."

"A 'danger' feeling?"

"You know," said Calhoun, sounding a bit put out, "you don't have to keep repeating the ends of my sentences."

"I think Wex is just trying to understand," said Shelby. "I know I am. What do you mean you . . ."

"I mean," said Calhoun, "that when there's danger present, I have this sort of . . . I don't know. A sixth sense. Just an inner warning. It's not one hundred percent reliable, and it's probably just my noticing something that I can't realize for what it is, but I know it's there just the same. . . . It may be nothing," he said when he saw their looks. "But it may be something."

"It may be," Wexler said patiently, "that it's stemming from your basic antipathy toward the ocean. Couldn't that be it?"

"Maybe," he admitted. "Still . . ."

"Mac, we'll be fine," Shelby assured him. With a toss of her short hair, she loped across the shore and splashed into the water. A moment later, Wexler joined her. They grinned and waved at Calhoun, and he nodded and waved back. But he didn't budge from his spot.

Outwardly he was the picture of calm. Inwardly he was scolding himself fiercely, even as Wexler and Shelby gallivanted in the surf. Here he was, talking so grandly about what it took to survive. And then, of course, there was his grand history as the warlord of Xenex. He had proven his bravery time and time again . . .

. . . and now, here he was, sitting on a beach, daunted by the ocean, while the woman he loved was playing in the surf with . . .

The woman he loved?

He ran the phrase back in his own mind. Was that really the case? Did he truly love her? Just from having a vision of her? Yes, he had spent much time with her, but in many ways he hardly knew her at all. How could he possibly believe that he was in love with her, especially when she had made it quite clear that her affections lay elsewhere?

It was foolish of him even to contemplate it. She probably even considered him to be beneath her. Yes, that was very likely it. Beneath her. Wexler, the far more polished cadet with the family history of service to the fleet, that was what she was interested in. She wanted someone with whom she had common ground, someone she could relate to. How could she possibly relate to an alien who, less than two years ago, had been so close to pure savagery (at least by Federation standards) that she likely wouldn't have even recognized him?

He realized it would probably be better if he just tossed aside his feelings right now. It would only lead to disaster otherwise, make his time at the Academy even more uncomfortable than it frequently already was. Yes, best for all concerned if he . . .

He stopped, his mind suddenly registering something.

The splashing about had stopped.

Slowly he got to his feet, his attention fixed on the water, the surface of which was now clear and unbroken. Gentle waves continued to roll in, but there was no sign of either of the cadets who had been bouncing around in it as carelessly as children on holiday.

"Shelby?" he called out cautiously. "Wexler?" And then louder and with greater urgency, *"Shelby! Wexler!"*

Still nothing, and Calhoun had started toward the water when Wexler suddenly burst from beneath the surface, mouth wide open, desperately gasping for air. Calhoun sprinted toward him. He reached out, grabbed his arm, and hauled him to the shore. For a moment Calhoun thought this might be some sort of prank on Wexler's part, but one look at the deathly pallor of Wexler's face disabused him of that notion. Wexler looked haunted, terrified.

Calhoun's head whipped around. There was no sign of Shelby.

"Where's Elizabeth?" shouted Calhoun, shaking Wexler by the shoulders, suddenly not caring what sort of near-death experience Wexler had just endured. *"Where's Elizabeth?"*

Wexler turned with wide-eyed horror toward the water, and that was all Calhoun needed. He kicked off his boots as he sprinted toward the water. "Get help!" he shouted, sensing that Wexler was so shaken he'd be of no use anyway. Without hesitation, he dove into the water.

Calhoun's fear of the water was not forgotten, even in the heat of his concern over Shelby. But he simply didn't have time to dwell on it. Besides, what he needed to do at that moment was submerge anyway. Swimming was the challenge for him; sinking he could do with no problem.

He went down like a missile, arms and legs moving in an inelegant but nevertheless effective fashion as he dove. He squinted through the murk, looking for the slightest sign of Shelby without really knowing what it was he was going to see.

Then he spotted her. She was below him, and thrashing in frantic desperation. Something appeared to have her leg. At first he thought it might be some sort of vegetation, or perhaps she'd caught her foot on an undersea rock formation. But then she was yanked down another six inches, and he knew that something was hauling at her, trying to pull her down into darkness and oblivion. Even from his distance, he could see that her eyes were wide with terror, her cheeks puffed out as whatever air she had in her lungs tried to force its way out.

With a desperate thrust of his legs, he propelled himself downward. She spotted his movements, realized who it was, and tried to wave him off. Here she was on the brink of death, and instead of reaching toward him as potential salvation, she was concerned about his welfare and was trying to warn him away.

She was one hell of a woman. Be nice if they survived so he could tell her so.

Her outstretched hand was only a couple of feet away, and then Calhoun was able to see a dark form below her. Worse, he saw there was a tentacle wrapped around her ankle, pulling on her.

His impulse was to utter a battle cry, but he instantly realized what an astoundingly bad idea that would be. Instead he kicked down further still, trying to ignore the steady pressure building in his chest. His hands sought out the laser welder and as he reached Shelby's ankle, the darkness of their surroundings flared to life upon the welder's activation. It sliced through the tentacle and something below writhed in agony as Shelby floated up and away.

But she made no effort to swim. She hung limply, and a frantic Calhoun tried to get to her when another tentacle lashed upward and snagged him around the waist. The sudden yanking caused the laser welder to be jerked from his fingers and spiral away.

Calhoun did not fight against the pull. He realized he'd be wasting precious seconds if he did, and it would likely be futile besides. Instead he thrust down into the murk, toward the creature that was obviously expecting him to resist.

In an instant he was face-to-face with it, and whatever he'd been expecting, it wasn't remotely in accordance with what he had found.

The creature was built more like a biped than anything that should be at home in the sea. It had, by Calhoun's admittedly hurried count, four tentacles, two on either side, issuing from the area of its shoulders. It had a triangular head, a mouth pulled back and filled with razor-sharp teeth, dark, pitiless eyes, and skin that looked like dusky leather.

Calhoun couldn't believe what he was seeing, and then the creature tried to snake another tentacle around Calhoun's shoulder. Another person might have been paralyzed by impending death, but impending death was when Mackenzie Calhoun did his best work. The fearsome burning in his lungs spurred him on, aided by exercises they'd done in the Academy that involved maneuvering in zero-gravity environments. Rather than surrendering to rising panic, Calhoun drove his fist forward squarely into the creature's face. He felt something give under the impact, and the creature's hold loosened on him but didn't come entirely free. It was all Calhoun needed. He grabbed on to one of the creature's flailing tentacles, digging in as hard as he could with an iron grip. Even under the water he was able to detect a pained yelp from the thing, and he hauled himself forward and around so that suddenly he was behind the thing. It flailed at him, trying to bring its tentacles to bear, but Calhoun would not be dislodged. Instead he wrapped his legs around the thing's waist, brought one hand to the side of its head and another underneath. Then, with a grunt (during which he accidentally took a small amount of water into his lungs) he twisted as hard as he could. The corded muscles in his arms tightened, and the creature's head was twisted three-quarters of the way around. There was a *snap* that seemed to come from very far away and then the creature sagged in his arms.

Calhoun wasted no time. He kicked upward, bouncing off the creature's body as he angled toward the surface. He saw Shelby's limp body floating there and snagged her with one arm as he desperately paddled for the surface. His lungs were now screaming for release, and he felt a pounding behind his ears that threatened to blow out the front of his face. The surface seemed impossibly far away. For one moment he even panicked and thought he was swimming in the wrong direction, heading not for salvation but instead sinking the both of them down into a watery grave.

The thundering within his head was everywhere. He couldn't think, he couldn't feel, he was moving through sheer determination, and then his lungs gave out just as his head started to emerge from below. His chest reflexively contracted and he took in water. He started to sink again, but he was paying no attention to himself. Instead he was frantically trying to shove Shelby above the water's surface. He was giving no thought to the fact that if he didn't survive, she wouldn't float on her own. All that was on his desperate mind was *Get her above! Get her above!*

And suddenly rough hands were on him and he thought *Oh* grozit, *no!* right before voices all around him were shouting, "Here! They're here!"

The world spun around him and the next thing he knew he was flat on his back on the shore. Somebody was pushing on his chest and he coughed violently, sending a geyser of murky water exploding outward. He blinked and looked up and saw a female cadet, Clarke, staring at him with her dark hair soaked and the water he'd just vomited up all over her face. "Thanks," she muttered, drawing an arm across her eyes.

He wasted no time in apologies. Instead he shoved her aside and staggered forward on his knees, seeing Shelby lying some feet away. Wexler was there, other cadets gathered around, and he was applying mouth-to-mouth resuscitation to her. She wasn't moving.

No . . . please no went through Calhoun's mind as he tried to get to her. But he couldn't seem to make his body function correctly, and instead he flopped forward on his belly like a beached whale.

And then there was someone older, some man whom Calhoun had not seen, and he was shoving a spray hypo into Shelby's arm. For a moment there seemed to be no reaction, and then suddenly her body seized up violently and shook, and if the water from Calhoun's mouth had been a geyser, then Shelby's was a volcano. It blasted out of her, her eyes wide and buglike, her arms flapping about, her legs seizing up. More water and then more. Calhoun had learned that ninety percent of the human body was fluid; it seemed as if Shelby's were ninety-nine percent, and all of it was exiting through her mouth.

She rolled over onto her side, more water pouring out, and then her body shuddered and Wexler was behind her, a hand on her shoulder. "It's okay, Betty," he murmured, and she let out a low cry and clutched his hand, still trembling.

The man with the hypo stood. Calhoun saw he was wearing a senior Starfleet uniform. He was some sort of medical technician. He should have known: Survival exercise or not, Starfleet was monitoring the proceedings. The moment something went seriously awry, they'd sent in a medical technician to help save the day.

Calhoun managed to get to his feet. Clarke, still wiping the regurgitated water from her face, nevertheless extended an arm to help him. "You okay?" she asked. "What the hell happened here?"

He didn't respond. His entire focus was on Shelby, who in turn was holding tightly on to Wexler. Her chest was heaving rapidly, but she was starting to calm. The med tech said, "You're going to be fine. Everything's going to be fine." Then he looked to Calhoun. "What was down there?"

Calhoun was watching Shelby and Wexler, who were facing each other but both sitting. She leaned forward and rested her head on his chest. "Thank you," she whispered to Wexler. "Thank you for saving me."

There was a dead silence then, and Wexler said softly, "It . . . wasn't me. It was Calhoun. He was the one."

Slowly full comprehension came to her. "My . . . God . . . yes. That was . . . I saw him . . . Mac . . ." She looked up at him. "Mac . . . I owe you my life . . ."

"Yes," he said.

Wexler chuckled slightly, even though the situation didn't seem to call for it. "You have to appreciate a man with no comprehension of modesty." Then, more seriously, he continued, "Yes . . . Calhoun, thank you. Forever . . . everything I have is yours."

I'll take her, thanks, and we'll call it even, thought Calhoun.

"I appreciate the sentiment," Calhoun told him.

"Cadet, you didn't answer," said the med tech. "What was down there?"

"I'm not sure," Calhoun said. *And even if I told you . . . I doubt you'd believe me.*

ii.

The cadets were unusually quiet grouped around the campfire that night. Calhoun was off to one side, as he usually was, when Wexler came over to him and crouched beside him. He didn't look at Calhoun. In-

stead he joined him in staring off into space as the cadets read or studied
or just looked at the stars they hoped to one day tread among. Every so
often, one or a couple of them would steal a glance in Calhoun's direction. He pretended not to notice.

"I really meant that, you know," Wexler told him softly. "About what
I have is yours. Almost losing Betty . . . makes me realize just how
meaningless possessions are."

"So you're generously offering me a share of that which you don't
care about?" asked Calhoun.

Wexler opened his mouth and then closed it again. "Well . . . yes. I
guess so. You know, somehow that sounded so much better in my head
than when I said it aloud."

Calhoun shrugged.

"I ran," Wexler said.

"You ran to get help."

"I ran."

"If you hadn't gone to get help," Calhoun told him, looking straight
at him, "I might well be dead. The people you brought helped rescue
us."

Wexler didn't return the gaze. "Y'know, you always have this sort of
mental image, imagining how you'll react, what you'll be like, when
faced with real danger. You never picture yourself scarpering. You're always the hero of the piece. You. Not some other bloke. But you, Calhoun . . . you always really are the hero of the bloody piece, aren't you."

"Think what you want," said Calhoun indifferently. "Me, I think
you're being too hard on yourself. Besides, you didn't hesitate to correct
Elizabeth when she thought you were the one who'd saved her."

"Ah, but see . . . that's the killer."

"What is?"

He laughed bitterly. "I wasn't honest because of great, high moral
standards. I was honest because everyone there knew damned well what
had happened. I couldn't get away with the lie. But if I could have gotten away with it, I would have. I would have sucked up all the credit, no
two ways."

"No. You wouldn't have," Calhoun said firmly.

"Calhoun . . ." Wexler hesitated and said, "You know how they always
say, 'Let the better man win'?"

"Yes."

"Well . . . you're the better man," Wexler said. "I know that. I admit it, to you and myself. But I still don't want you to win."

"We're not in competition for anything, Wex."

Shelby emerged from a tent, straightening her hair. She smiled at the two of them, her eyes glistening in the evening light.

"Yes," Wexler said to Calhoun out of the side of his mouth. "Yes, we are. And you know it, and I know it."

She started over toward them, and Calhoun held his breath. He wondered what she was going to say. He wondered how he was going to react.

Abruptly there was a crashing in the woods nearby, and Calhoun, Wexler, and the other cadets were immediately on their feet. "Who's there?" shouted Wexler.

"At ease," came Clarke's wry voice from the darkness. "Just wanted to show you what the tide dragged in."

Clarke, grunting, staggered into the light, and Calhoun gaped at what she was hauling with her. It was dried out, and decidedly dead, but it was definitely the creature that Calhoun had struggled to the death with below the water.

He stepped forward to help Clarke, and together they dragged it toward the center of the encampment. The other cadets gathered around as they dropped it near the fire and studied it. From tip to toe, it measured about eight feet in length.

"*This* is a sea creature?" said one of the cadets, a somewhat dyspeptic young man named Lawford. "It's got humanoid legs. What sort of sea creature walks on two legs?"

"And has tentacles?" observed Wexler. "It's damned peculiar. Like some sort of throwback."

Calhoun noticed that Shelby had instinctively drawn closer to Wexler. He put an arm around her shoulders as she stared down at the monster in horrified fascination.

"Thing is," said Clarke, "if it was a real 'throwback,' we'd at least have some familiarity with the species it's being thrown back to. I don't recognize this thing at all."

"I do," said Calhoun quietly. All eyes went to him as he continued. "The tentacles are not exactly standard equipment . . . but that's a bahoon."

"A *what?*" Wexler asked.

"A bahoon. I thought that's what I was up against, but everything happened so fast, and we were under water. . . . I just didn't want to say anything because I wasn't sure. Now I am."

"I'm thrilled you're sure," said Lawford. "Now would you mind telling the rest of us what a bahoon is?"

"It's a creature that roams in some of the more mountainous terrain on Xenex," he said. "Despite their size and ferocity, they're more scavengers than anything. Tend to keep to themselves. And they're bullies besides. If you run into one, a show of determination—or even just making fierce faces—will generally be enough to scare them off. Unless you get one who's simply gone mad. Then he's as likely to tear your head off as anything else. . . ."

"I'll remember this handy advice the next time I go mountain climbing in Xenex," said Lawford. "But that's hardly the point. The main question confronting us is, What the hell is a creature from Xenex doing in the Atlantic Ocean, and how did it acquire tentacles?"

He was looking so challengingly at Calhoun that it seemed he expected Calhoun might have the answer at his fingertips. Or maybe he was even responsible somehow.

Rather than rise to the bait, Calhoun simply shrugged. "I haven't the slightest clue how to answer either of those questions."

Lawford looked at him suspiciously, as if Calhoun were trying to trick him somehow. "How did this Xenexian creature wind up on Earth?" he said slowly.

"He walked. How the hell should I know?"

Growling in anger, Lawford stepped forward, stabbed a finger at Calhoun, and said, "You," he said warningly, "had better figure it out. You need to find a clue."

He pivoted on his foot and stormed off, leaving Calhoun to mutter to Wexler, "Would be nice if he took his own advice."

Chapter Seven

Now

Mackenzie Calhoun was in shock. Not that he was paralyzed in any way. Still, the news he was being given was almost too overwhelming for him to process.

He was in the conference lounge of the *Excalibur* with Zak Kebron, Elizabeth Shelby, and Arex. Slowly he was shaking his head as if sheer disbelief could somehow cause the entire horrific situation simply to go away.

"He went berserk, you say?" he said again. Shelby nodded. "And tore through your ship? Almost killed M'Ress . . . and Kebron . . . ?"

"He didn't almost kill me," Kebron politely corrected his captain. "I had a handle on the situation the entire time."

"A handle on it?" a skeptical Shelby replied. "Zak, he almost killed you."

"He 'almost' did no such thing. Lieutenant Arex was there; he will most certainly concur."

Arex shifted uncomfortably in his seat, although that might have simply been owing to its not exactly being built to accommodate Triexians. "Although Lieutenant Kebron appeared to have the situation in hand . . ."

"*Appeared to?*" snorted Kebron.

Not allowing himself to be thrown off track, Arex continued, ". . . Janos was like a wild thing. There was the distinct possibility that Kebron might not have been able to hold matters together if they had continued. We would have had to kill Janos. . . ."

"If it came to that . . . if he weren't stoppable while I was going three rounds with him," Kebron told her forcefully, "then I would have made certain personally he didn't survive to commit any other crimes."

"That's very comforting to hear, Mr. Kebron." Calhoun was trying to sound diplomatic. "Unfortunately, it doesn't do much to address the current situation. So you're telling me that Janos has no recollection of snapping?"

"None whatsoever," said Kebron. "The last thing he remembers is being in the brig. Then it's all one great big blur and suddenly he 'came to' in the corridor with all of us around him."

"And you think he's telling the truth? You believe him?"

"Yes, sir. I do. My opinion, however, would be purely subjective. Fortunately, a bioscan backs him up. We subjected him to intense questioning under computer analysis, and everything he says tracks. From a mental point of view, he blacked out. Technically, he can't be held criminally responsible because he had no intent. He wasn't in his right mind."

"A very elegant defense, Kebron. Two things, however. First, you're not his attorney, nor are you qualified to be. And second, criminal prosecution wasn't the first thing on my mind. I'd like to think it wasn't up there on Captain Shelby's list, either," and he looked questioningly to her.

She shook her head. "I'm just relieved no one was seriously injured during his rampage. We're not out for vengeance here. We're out to understand what the hell is going on."

"Which is a challenge considering the subject of the inquiry doesn't seem to have any more of a clue than we do." Calhoun leaned back in his chair and looked to Shelby. "We've got a situation on our hands, wouldn't you say, Captain?"

"That would be an understatement." She shook her head. "Quite a security staff you have on *your* hands, Captain. One of them undergoes a personality change when he sheds his skin; the other has blackout periods during which he goes berserk and becomes a murderer."

"It's still not definite," Kebron said defensively, "that he was responsible for the death of Lieutenant Commander Gleau."

"Mr. Kebron, with all respect to your position and your loyalty to your officer, I think it's becoming increasingly obvious that Janos did indeed do it," Arex pointed out. "You've got someone with his DNA all over the crime scene and a track record of going out of his mind into berserker rages."

"*A* berserker rage," Kebron said. "We don't know that it's happened before."

"I have the shredded body of one of my people," said Shelby, making a very visible effort to remain patient. "I'm thinking we do know it's happened at least once before."

Kebron looked ready to protest again, but Calhoun interrupted him. "Zak . . . I'm as dedicated to Janos as you. More so. But I think we have to start facing facts. We have to consider the situation not the way we wish it were, but instead the way it is. It's reaching the point where defending Janos comes across more like denial of reality than searching out some sort of truth. I don't want to believe it any more than you do, but let's face facts: Janos killed Gleau."

Kebron was on his feet, moving more swiftly than Calhoun would have thought possible. "So have you lost faith as well, Captain?"

"Sit down, Zak."

"No! It is intolerable that—"

"I said . . . sit down."

His voice was ice, his purple eyes flashing in anger, and this time Kebron sank back down into his seat.

Calhoun's fingers were interlaced, his hands resting upon his desk. He spoke with pronounced, forced calm. "Faith, Lieutenant, is the province of religion. Faith is what you cling to in the absence of fact. In this case, we have far too many facts in hand. To draw any other conclusion than that Janos is responsible for the murder of Gleau is to fly in the face of those facts. It's irrational. Faith is an admirable trait. It's good to have faith in another person. But when faith is used as a substitute for reality, then it becomes a crutch for refusing to deal with that reality. If this investigation involved someone that you didn't know and care about personally, on the basis of the evidence on hand, you wouldn't think twice about having him locked away for good. You can't apply a different standard of evidence simply because you have personal loyalty to the suspect.

"At this point, I think we have to abandon the position that Janos wasn't responsible, because frankly I'm not interested in burying my head in that much sand. Are you?"

Kebron considered it for a long, long time. Calhoun didn't rush him.

To his mind, it was important to have Kebron honestly on board. Having a head of security involved with an investigation when he had a mind-set that flew in the face of all reasonable conclusions was hardly conducive to accomplishing anything.

Any number of times, Calhoun had heard someone die. It was always the same, with that faint surprised final sigh of life escaping from between their lips. Kebron made a similar, albeit not identical, noise now as he murmured, "All right." Calhoun understood. Kebron was saying a final good-bye to something in which he had fervently believed, and staked much of himself upon. "All right," he said again. "Let's say that Janos was indeed responsible for the physical act of killing Gleau."

"Physical?" said a puzzled Shelby. "There's another aspect of it, aside from the physical?"

"It's still possible," Kebron pointed out, "that someone is controlling him. That someone has taken over his mind."

"And was responsible for setting him on Gleau?" Arex asked. "And was even responsible for sending him into some sort of . . . of fugue state that sent him into a bestial rage?"

"Yes. Exactly. I'm saying our search for the murderer shouldn't begin and end with Janos. We might be taking down the cat's-paw while the cat gets away."

"But how could this alleged 'cat' be doing it?" asked Shelby, looking from Kebron to Calhoun. "Is such a thing possible?"

"This is a wide galaxy filled with possibilities," said Calhoun. "I think it's difficult to rule out anything without thoroughly investigating it."

"Okay," Shelby said, stroking her chin thoughtfully. "Okay, I can see that. The first thing to do is have Doc Villers check him over from stem to stern. Look for some evidence of an outside influence. See if there's any trace of some sort of—I don't know—tampering. A chip in his skull broadcasting directives would certainly be a step in the right direction. Perhaps she can monitor his brain waves so that, if he goes insane on us again, it will leave a trace of a controlling source."

"That could work," said Calhoun.

"There's one thing we have to keep in mind, though," Shelby continued, her tone serious. "Any further investigation has to be from the point of view that we're trying to determine the truth, rather than simply doing whatever it takes to clear one of our own officers."

"He's my officer, Captain."

"It's Starfleet, Captain," she replied. "We're all part of the one group."

"Yes, I know that. It's—"

Calhoun's combadge suddenly beeped. He tapped it. "Calhoun here."

"Burgy here, Captain. You're getting an incoming hail from Admiral Jellico."

Calhoun let out a slow sigh that bore a striking resemblance to the sound Kebron had made moments ago. "Stall him, Burgy."

"He said it was urgent."

"Tell him I'm having sexual congress."

"With your wife?"

"No, with Si Cwan. Yes, with my wife."

"All right, Captain," Burgoyne said reasonably. "How long shall I tell him to hold on?"

"Three minutes," piped up Shelby. "If that."

Calhoun fixed a level gaze on her as he said, "Burgy . . . just tell him I'll be right with him."

"Aye, Captain."

"Gentlemen," and Calhoun indicated the door with a nod of his head. "If you wouldn't mind . . ."

"Have Doc Villers get started on what we discussed, Arex."

"Yes, Captain," Arex said to Shelby.

Kebron went out the door first, and Calhoun thought that his shoulders looked decidedly more slumped than they were before. He hated to see the massive Brikar that way, but really . . . there just came a point where sometimes the blinders had to be tossed aside. Moments later, the two captains were alone in the conference lounge.

"Perfect," Calhoun grumbled. "Just perfect. As if I didn't have enough to worry about, I've got Jellico looking over my shoulder. How much does he know?"

"This was a homicide, Mac," replied Shelby. "Starfleet regs leave no wiggle room. I had to inform them immediately. And I've kept them apprised every step of the way since."

"Thanks a lot, Eppy. You're really doing me tremendous favors here."

"I've said it often before, Calhoun, and maybe it hasn't sunk in. Not everything is about you. I have a dead science officer and a part-time berserker suspect on my hands. I don't need to be hauled in front of a board of inquiry and be grilled as to why I didn't conduct the investigation in accordance with regs so I can explain that, gee, gentlemen, I was worried it might offend my husband's delicate sensibilities. You're telling Kebron he has to deal with reality? Deal with it yourself while you're at it."

"Fine," he said.

"You always do that," Shelby said in irritation. "Agree with me just to shut me up."

"Typical female thinking," shot back Calhoun. "If I disagree it's because I'm not listening, and if I agree it's because I don't want to listen. Does that pretty much cover it?"

"Just take the damned communication from Jellico. He's a man. You'll like talking to him."

He tapped the combadge and nearly snarled, "Calhoun to Burgoyne. Pipe Jellico down here."

A moment later the scowling face of Admiral Jellico appeared on the screen. He looked as ill-humored as ever. Privately, Calhoun felt that someone should send an away team into Jellico's ass, in order to determine just what had crawled up there and died years ago.

"Captain Calhoun," said Jellico with forced politeness, and then his gaze flickered over to Shelby. "And Mrs. Captain Calhoun."

"With all respect, Admiral, I prefer 'Captain Shelby,' " she said, maintaining her reserve.

"Simply endeavoring to lighten a very difficult situation, Captain . . . Captains. Where do we stand on the Gleau murder? When are you bringing in the perpetrator, Janos?"

Shelby opened her mouth to answer, but Calhoun broke in before she could respond. "We don't know for certain he *is* the perpetrator, Admiral."

"My understanding is that the physical evidence is fairly clear-cut."

"That's true, sir," Shelby said quickly, not allowing Calhoun to speak. "But since this incident runs contrary to Janos's history, we believe there may be more to this than the surface would indicate. We need time to do a thorough investigation, to determine—"

But Jellico was putting up a hand, and she fell silent. "I'm afraid that time is a commodity you don't have in abundance."

"Meaning?" Calhoun asked.

"Meaning, Captains, that the Selelvians are outraged over the murder of one of their own."

"You told them?"

"Yes, Captain Shelby, we told them," said Jellico. "That is standard operating procedure. We have regulations and procedures that we have to obey, the same as anyone else . . . except, of course, for you, Captain Calhoun, who seem to feel that regulations are mere guidelines rather than rules, and exist to direct others while you follow your own impulses."

"I'm pleased we've finally come to an understanding, Admiral," Calhoun said, unperturbed.

"In any event," he continued, "the Selelvians have demanded that Ensign Janos be turned over to them immediately for trial and execution."

Shelby and Calhoun exchanged glances. "The Selelvians are aware, Admiral," said Calhoun, "that the trial is theoretically supposed to determine the necessity of the execution, are they not?"

"Frankly, no, I don't think they are," Jellico said dryly. He didn't seem to be any more pleased about it than they were, which gave them at least some faint stirring of hope.

"Have you told them we're conducting an investigation?"

"Yes, Captain Shelby, we have. They stated they didn't care. We told them we did, and if they didn't like it, they could complain to the Federation."

"Which . . . they did," Calhoun surmised.

Jellico nodded. "That's exactly right. The Selelvians are filing formal complaints with the Federation Council even as we speak. They've asked for an expedited hearing. If they're granted that hearing, and if they convince the UFP of their position, then we'll have no choice but to turn Ensign Janos over to them."

"That's insane."

"No, Calhoun, that's the political reality. Starfleet, in case you've forgotten, is the scientific, exploratory, and defensive agency of the United Federation of Planets. We answer to them. They tell us what to do, and we do it. They tell us 'Warp,' we ask them 'How fast?' That's how this works. Their authority supersedes ours . . . and even yours. And if the UFP, in its wisdom, decides that they want to handle the Gleau matter, then that's what happens."

"They can't just hand a Starfleet officer over to be executed. There's only one regulation still on the books that calls for a death penalty, and last I heard, Janos hadn't set foot on Talos IV."

"True, Captain," and Jellico actually sounded regretful. "For that matter, there's no death penalty extant for crimes against humans, either. If Janos had killed a human, this wouldn't be a problem. But he didn't. He had the poor judgment, so the evidence indicates, to have killed a member of a race that's a big believer in an eye for an eye. And if that race convinces the UFP, then we have no choice in the matter. Janos would have to be turned over to the Selelvians. That's all there is to it."

"It's barbaric," said Shelby, her hands almost trembling with suppressed anger.

"I agree," Jellico said, very quietly. "And not only have I told my superiors at Starfleet that, but I have every intention of addressing the Federation Council and telling them the exact same thing. I'm going to do everything I can to keep this internal. Because I trust you to handle this business in a professional, fair, and thorough manner."

Calhoun, in spite of himself, felt touched. "Thank you, Admiral."

Jellico glanced at him dismissively. "I was talking to Captain Shelby, Calhoun. Not you."

"Sorry. I don't know what I was thinking."

"You I wouldn't trust as far as I could throw."

"Yes, I get that, Admiral," said Calhoun.

Looking back to Shelby, Jellico said, "Understand, Captain: I believe I'm fighting a losing battle on this one. But I'll fight it anyway. Prepare yourself, though, for the very real likelihood that we're going to lose this one. Jellico out." And with that, his image blinked off the screen.

Calhoun sighed heavily and said, "We should have stuck with the idea of telling him we were having sex and couldn't be disturbed. Well, this is just insane," and he stood up and began to pace the room. "Look, if they say they want Janos, we just tell them no. That's all. We need more time . . ."

"Mac," Shelby reminded him, "you just got done telling Kebron how important it is to face the facts of any given situation. In this case the fact is that, as the admiral said, we're going to lose Janos to the Selelvians. There's always a possibility it won't play out that way . . . but we have to adjust to the notion that it is. And we won't be doing any of our people any good if we continue to deny it."

"Yes, you're right, of course," he said, but his mind was racing a million miles away. And Shelby knew it. And he knew she knew it.

He wondered if she knew the sort of desperation ploys he was running through his head. Chances were she did. He liked the notion that she knew what was going on in his brain. He also hated it.

Then

i.

Shelby circled the cabin for what seemed the hundredth time and yet, despite that, she still felt intoxicated by the fresh air and sense of primal newness in the forest around her.

Wexler and she had been up there any number of times, but usually in the company of their parents. The Wexlers, whose cabin it was, loved having weekend excursions so that friends could "oooh" and "aaah" and admire the back-to-nature setting. Shelby remembered being a mindless teenager and despising the purity of the woods around them, the towering redwood trees that threatened to brush against the clouds. Her attitude was that holosuites offered the exact same experience, except you could program them so as not to have irritating insects zipping around and getting in your face. Or you could adjust the temperature to be just so, or make sure the wind wasn't going to muss your hair. She remembered her parents' faces flushing in embarrassment, but the Wexlers just laughed and said their own son had had much the same comments, and youth should not be judged too harshly. That sounded pretty damned patronizing as far as Shelby was concerned, and she spent most of their first outing there closed in her room and watching vids.

Amazing how so few years had really passed during that time, and yet now she looked at the great outdoors as if seeing it for the first time. She was chagrined to imagine that whining, annoying voice coming out of her own mouth, and she had even apologized to her parents for her behavior of years earlier. Their response had been satisfied smirks.

"Betty!"

Wexler was standing in the door to the cabin, looking around. She came in from the opposite direction he was searching for her, stood there, and waited for him to look in her direction. He did so and started slightly, then grinned at having been so easily taken off guard. "Very amusing, dear," he said.

"Thank you," she replied, and kissed him on the cheek. Then she walked past him into the cabin.

Both of them were casually dressed in outdoor garb. It felt odd to Shelby, not wearing her Starfleet Academy uniform. She almost felt as if a teacher was going to burst in and give them demerits for being out of uniform. Shelby flopped onto a soft, comfortable couch. There was a large rug in the middle of the living room that looked like a gigantic bear skin. Upset by it as a teen, she'd been assured that it was purely a synthetic bear skin, no doubt removed from a synthetic bear. She still regarded the thing suspiciously, hoping that she hadn't been lied to so she wouldn't get upset. A fire was burning steadily in the fireplace, fueled by an unseen source, and the walls were decorated in rich shades of cedar.

She noticed Wexler just standing in the doorway, staring at her oddly.

"You're letting in the bugs. Close the door," she said. He stepped in and did as she said, but there was still something in his face that was bothering her. "What is it? What's wrong?"

"You kissed me on the cheek," he said.

She raised an eyebrow. "So?"

"So . . . I was puckering."

"You were puckering."

"Yes."

"Your mouth was doing this," and she smooshed her lips together.

"Not quite that grotesquely, but yes."

"So fine. Come here and I'll kiss you on the mouth. I'll kiss you anywhere you want if it'll make you happy."

"That's hardly the point."

"Then what is?" she said, impatience rising.

"The point is that kissing me 'anywhere' used to make you happy."

"Used to?" She sat up, shaking her head in bewilderment. "Wex, what the hell are you talking about? I mean, where are you going with this? What are you saying, that I haven't been affectionate enough lately?"

"No, I wasn't saying that . . ." Then he hesitated and said, "Although, now that you mention it . . ."

"Oh, for God's sake. Fine. You want affection? C'mere, big boy. Where do you want it? Right here, maybe?" and she thrust her hips toward the ceiling as if she'd been jolted with electricity. Then she turned on the couch and pointed at the rug. "Or maybe there. On top of that big old allegedly synthetic bear rug."

"You know what?" said Wexler. "We're not going to discuss this now, because you're being totally unreasonable about this."

"About what? I don't know what you're talking about."

"No, you don't, and that's the upsetting thing, Betty—"

"Stop it!"

He was taken aback by the vehemence in her tone. "Stop what?"

"Betty! I can't stand it anymore! Stop calling me Betty! I hate it when you call me Betty!"

"I . . ." Wexler looked as if he'd been slammed in the face with a hammer, standing there with a decidedly stupid expression. "I thought it was my special nickname for you that you liked."

"Well, you're right about the first half. But the liking it part? No."

"I'm sorry, Liz . . ."

"Elizabeth, okay? I like my name. I like all the syllables. Not Betty. Not Liz, not Lizzy, not Eliza or Liza or Betty or Betsy or Elly or anything else, just . . . Elizabeth. Okay? Or Shelby. When we start second year in school, Shelby's fine, too."

Slowly he nodded and, his voice very, very cool, he said, "All right, Elizabeth. Thank you for setting me straight."

"Ohhhh," she moaned, and sagged back down onto the couch, rubbing the sides of her forehead. "Now you're all mad at me."

"No. No, I'm not all mad at you. I'm just wondering about the timing of this outburst."

"The timing?" She stared up at him. "I'm not following."

"Ever since we finished our first year . . . actually, ever since survival training . . . you've been distant."

"I've spent just as much time with you as ever."

"I'm not talking about physical distance," he said. "I mean emotional. I feel like, even when you're with me . . . you're not."

"What's that supposed to mean?"

"I think you know what it means."

"No, Wex, I don't," she said impatiently. "You could tell I don't know what it means by the way I said, 'What's that supposed to mean?' Not a lot of gray area in the question. I don't know what you're referring to, but I do know it's beginning to bug the hell out of me."

"Calhoun," Wexler said.

"And there we go again!" Shelby practically shouted. On her feet, she paced back and forth, taking care to step over the bear rug. "You can't get your mind off him! You keep accusing me of having feelings for him! Feelings stronger than what I have for you! Yes, I'm grateful he saved my life, and no, I don't resent you for the fact that you ran to get help rather than just dive down after me! You keep describing it as cowardice, but I call it smart thinking! You slipped away by luck! If you'd gone back down on your own, that thing would probably have gotten both of us, and might then have preyed on others! Plus the others were there to haul Mac and me to safety, plus the med tech was on the scene, none of which would have happened if you hadn't shown some basic common sense! What Calhoun did was incredibly dangerous, and he risked his life, and he got away with it because he was lucky. Which isn't to say I'm not grateful, but my God, you've got to stop bringing up his name every time—"

"Calhoun," he said again.

The insistent tone of his voice brought her up short. In exasperation, she said, "Look, are you repeating it now just to irritate me? Because—"

"No, I'm repeating it because I'm seeing him outside the window."

"What?"

"He's. Outside. The window."

Shelby turned and stared where Wexler was looking. Sure enough, there was Calhoun, striding back and forth at the edge of the forest. He seemed to have no idea what to do with his hands. They kept twitching, moving spasmodically, and he was muttering to himself. He was dressed in what Shelby could only think were Xenexian garments. Loose-fitting, rough-hewn. She also noticed that, in the days since the first year of school had ended, he had stopped shaving. His beard was coming in

fast and thick, somewhat darker than the hair on his head. She wondered
if it made him feel more in touch somehow with his roots.

"What's he doing out there?" she asked.

"I've no clue. How did he even know where we were?"

"Well . . . I suppose I told him."

He turned to her. "You *told* him?"

"I'm sorry, I wasn't aware it was supposed to be a state secret," she said
testily. "Next time you might want to alert me to that."

"It wasn't a . . . never mind." He continued watching Calhoun. "This
is ridiculous. He's come all the way up here. Why doesn't he just come
and knock on the door?"

"Why don't you go and open it and invite him in?"

"All right."

He walked over to the door, nearly bumping his face on it before remembering that he actually had to open it with his hands. It was the
old-fashioned kind, in keeping with the entire retro look of the cabin.
He pulled open the door and stepped out, and Calhoun froze in place,
like a rummaging animal caught out searching through trash.

"This is a surprise," said Wexler, and then added, "Actually, on second
thought, it's somewhat not."

Calhoun took a deep breath, let it out, and then pointed at Wexler
and said, "By the laws and traditions of Xenex, I challenge you for the
woman."

Standing just inside the cabin, Shelby heard that and reacted in the
only way she could: with a loud guffaw. She stepped out where Calhoun
could see her and said, "I *beg* your pardon?"

"I have issued a challenge," Calhoun said stoically. It was astonishing.
He could not have been more serious. "A challenge in keeping with the
laws and—"

"Traditions of Xenex, yes, I understand that, mate," Wexler said. "I
hate to point it out to you, though, that this is not Xenex. Your laws and
traditions don't mean a great deal here."

"They do to me."

"But not to me," and he nodded toward Shelby, "and I daresay not to
Elizabeth as well. Isn't that right, Elizabeth?"

She wasn't saying anything. She was too busy grinning.

"Elizabeth?" He looked at her, appalled. "Oh, Elizabeth, *honestly* now."

"Oh, Wex, where's your sense of humor?" she said, punching him lightly on the arm. "I mean, it's almost fascinating. We're seeing here an actual instance of alien behavior steeped in ancient customs. The kind of thing we've only read about until now."

"Yes, but the nice thing about reading about it is that it doesn't try to attack you." He glanced back at Calhoun. "I am correct in that, am I not? That this entire 'challenge' would involve some measure of attacking?"

"Hand-to-hand combat is the traditional means, yes," said Calhoun. He didn't look any less resolute.

"Bugger that. Elizabeth, tell him you're not amused."

"Well, I am. A little. It's . . . kind of sweet."

"*Sweet?* He's come all the way here threatening to pummel me! I should call the . . ." He shouted to Calhoun, "I'll call the authorities! *That's* what I'll do! You've *lost* it, Calhoun! You've gone around the bleeding *bend!*"

"Oh, is that how you'd respond to a challenge for the woman you say you love?" demanded Calhoun. "By hiding behind others to defend you?"

"Too right! I'm on the command track, Calhoun! If some alien git tries to get physical with me, I beam down a security team and have them beat the snot out of him for me! That's how it's done!"

"That's not how I do it. That's not how a real man does it."

"And is that the measure of a real man, then?" demanded Wexler. "His willingness to subject himself to brutality?"

"No. It's the willingness to risk everything for someone he loves."

Shelby's breath caught in her throat. The words had been said, and Calhoun looked at her with defiance, as if daring her to laugh again. "Yes. Someone I love. I can't take it anymore, Elizabeth," and rather than being strident, his voice took on an almost plaintive tone. "You're all I think about. All I dream about. When I spend time with you, I never want it to end, and when you are gone, I can only think about the next time I'll see you again. I can't . . ." He paused, his voice catching slightly, and then he continued, "I can't promise what will happen next. Life is too unexpected, too filled with twists and turns we'd never anticipate. All I can tell you is that right here, right now, I need to make you mine or I'll . . ."

"Or you'll what?" said Wexler, making no effort to keep the sarcasm from his voice. "Or you'll die?"

"No. But living won't mean anything."

He had said it so softly that Shelby had almost missed it. Almost as if he were ashamed for having said it, Calhoun drew himself up straight, squared his shoulders, and fixed his attention upon Wexler once more. "I'm waiting for your answer."

"My answer? My answer is that you're a complete prat."

Calhoun looked uncertainly at Wexler. "Thank you," he said cautiously. "But I'm not interested in idle flattery."

"Oh, for God's . . ." He turned to Shelby and said, "Would you tell him, please? Tell him that you're not my property, to give over to him or be taken in some pathetic show of force?"

"He's right, Mac," she said slowly.

"Thank the Lord," sighed Wexler.

"But I get what you're trying to do."

"You do?" Wexler couldn't quite believe it. "Well, then explain it to me, if you'd be so kind."

"Well, it's pretty obvious." She walked slowly toward Calhoun. "Mac here is trying to define the world . . . control it . . . on his own terms. But it doesn't work quite that way, Mac. You have to meet the world on *its* own terms."

"The world's terms are too confusing," said Calhoun. He was watching her steadily, his gaze unwavering. It was as if he'd forgotten Wexler entirely. "I need to make the world understand . . . to make you understand . . . to make myself understand . . ."

"Elizabeth, get away from him! Right now!"

Shelby stopped where she was and regarded Wexler as if he had lost his mind. "You're telling me what to do? After you were just lecturing Calhoun on how I'm not someone's property? Where do you get off . . . ?"

"Oh, well that's marvelous, innit?" Wexler demanded. He was getting more and more worked up, looking as if he were about to explode. "Calhoun shows up uninvited, demands to have a throwdown so he can . . . I don't know, whack you on the head with his cave club and drag you away somewhere. And you find the whole thing utterly charming. I tell you to keep your distance from him because I think he's totally around the bleeding bend, and therefore dangerous, and you react as if I'm a thoughtless brute!"

"I'm just saying . . ."

"No," he said abruptly. "No, it's pretty bloody obvious what you're saying, except you're not saying it. So I'm going to say it for you."

Without a word he pivoted and stomped back into the cabin, leaving Shelby and Calhoun staring blankly at one another. Shelby shifted uncomfortably from one foot to the other. Calhoun, bereft of the person he was challenging, likewise looked a bit disconcerted.

"You had it all worked out in your head, didn't you?" she said finally. "You were sure that he was going to react a certain way, and you were going to do something, and I was going to do something else, and it all just came together perfectly in your mind's-eye scenario. Right?"

"Something like that," he admitted.

"And how did you and I wind up?"

"Together. Naked. Making love. Drinking in each other's soul."

"That . . ." She felt a slight stinging in her cheeks and smiled at her own embarrassment. Here she thought she was a modern woman, and yet with a few words he was able to make her completely flustered. "That's very sweet." Then she considered it further and amended, "Or actually somewhat evocative of a horror novel, depending how you choose to interpret it. Listen . . . Mac . . ."

"Do you believe in predestination, Elizabeth?" he asked abruptly, with an urgency that caught her off guard. "Do you believe in something being meant to be?"

She paused, and then said, "I think there are certain . . . tendencies . . . that bring mankind inevitably in particular directions. But—"

"That's not what I meant, and I think you know that. Elizabeth . . ." He took a deep breath as if about to fling himself off a cliff. "I've mentioned how I was out in the desert. About how I survived."

"Yes."

"What I've never mentioned is that one of the main reasons I survived was because of you."

Shelby shook her head, not quite comprehending. "What do you mean?"

"I mean I knew that you were going to be in my future. I didn't . . . I don't . . . know in what capacity. How long we'll be together, or anything like that. But I just . . . just knew."

"Mac," she said with an uneasy laugh, "that was before we met. How can you possibly . . ."

"I can't possibly. It's impossible." He reached out, took one of her hands in both of his, and pressed it tightly. She felt as if a small charge of electricity were flowing into her, and her breath caught, and her eyes widened. "And I want to explore those impossibilities with you."

"But . . . Wex . . ."

"You don't love him. You're comfortable with him," Calhoun said tightly. "Is that what you want from your life? Comfort? Is that the ultimate goal of a future Starfleet officer?"

"You're oversimplifying it."

"And you're overcomplicating it. It's . . ."

A throat cleared loudly behind them. They turned and saw Wexler standing some feet away, holding his bags. They'd been hurriedly packed. His face was inscrutable. "I'm leaving now," he said loudly.

"What?" Calhoun and Shelby chorused.

"I said I'm leaving," he repeated. He took a step toward them, and although his voice was steady, she could tell he was forcing it to remain that way. "Understand something, Calhoun. If I thought she was mine . . . if I thought she was going to be with me . . . I would fight you. And trust me, I've seen you fight. I know you'd probably be able to break me in half. But I will still go head-to-head with you, and they'd have to pry my teeth off your throat. That's . . . if I thought she was mine. But she's not. I've come to realize that . . . before, I think, even she has. I despise untidiness, though. I didn't know . . . where she was supposed to be. So I didn't want to walk away." He shrugged. "Now I can."

"Wex . . ." Shelby began.

But he shook his head. "No. Save it. We're . . ." He smiled, and it also was forced, but not as much. There was sadness in his eyes, but he seemed determined not to let it pull him down. "We're adults here. Adults and future officers of the fleet. We're going to be proud people. No harm in displaying some of that pride now. No harm in acting like officers . . . and gentlemen." He bowed slightly, said, "Spend the rest of the week here if you so desire. You have enough food . . . although I admit I've copped all my personal lager. Man has to draw the line somewhere, don't you think?"

"Yes. Yes, he does," said Calhoun, and Shelby looked into his eyes and saw that he was deeply shamed. He hung his head and said quietly, "Wex . . . I . . . look, I handled this badly."

"Too right you have. And you owe me, squire. And you, too," and he pointed at Shelby. "You both owe me huge. And don't think I won't hesitate to collect when the time is right." He took a deep breath, let it out, and said, "I'll send a lift round for you end of the week. That should give you more than enough time to . . . whatever. Right then. Off I go. You two . . . at ease. Smoke 'em if you've got 'em." With that final benediction, he turned and headed off into the woods and, within moments, was swallowed by the trees.

Calhoun said to Shelby, "Smoke what?"

"I'm not sure. It's some holdover from years ago. So . . ."

She suddenly felt uncomfortable in her clothes, in her own skin. She smoothed her shirt, her hands moving in vague circles, and then she said to Calhoun, "Sooo . . . what now? I mean, you're the one who had the grand scheme to come up here and . . ."

He leaned forward, took her face in his hands, and drew her lips to his. He kissed her ferociously, like a parched man hurling himself with abandon into an oasis. She was startled by it at first, and her instinct was to pull away, for she felt as if she were going to drown in him. But then she did one of the most difficult things she had ever done in her life: She surrendered to him. To it. To the passion that was sweeping over her. The world spun away and suddenly she was flying as she felt him lift her in his arms, carrying her toward the cabin.

"No club to the head?" she murmured. "I'm impressed."

ii.

They made love on the bear rug, with the fire crackling nearby and Calhoun displaying near inexhaustible enthusiasm. And as they lay next to each other, curled up within the fur (which Shelby was beginning to suspect wasn't synthetic at all) there was a part of Shelby that believed if she never did anything else again in her life, she would die happy. She knew it was an absurd sentiment to have. There was so much more she wanted to do, so many accomplishments that awaited her.

She thought of Wexler and had never been more grateful to him in her life.

"You know," Calhoun said in her ear, startling her since she didn't know he was awake, "according to ancient Xenexian custom, we're engaged now."

"Really," she said playfully. "Is that the same Xenexian custom that had you challenging Wex for me?"

"Yes."

"But we're not on Xenex."

"I know."

"Do you miss it?"

"Not at the moment," he said, wrapping a strand of her hair around his finger.

"And are we engaged?"

He lowered his hand and fixed his eyes upon her. "Do you want to be?" he asked gently.

She was surprised by how briefly she had to consider that answer. "No," she said. Then she added, "Do you?"

"No."

"Are you lying?" she asked suspiciously.

"No." Then he half-smiled. "Maybe. Tell you what. Let's discuss it in six months."

"It's a date," she said, and snuggled closer to him.

Chapter Eight

Now

"No."

Zak Kebron sat opposite Soleta in the *Trident's* Ten-Forward. Her face was a study in mute determination. Kebron had the sinking feeling that he was more or less beaten before he'd even gotten started, but he knew he had to press onward. "You're Janos's only hope," he insisted. "He's passed every bioscan that we can throw at him. Either he did not commit the crime, or it's buried so deep that nothing known to modern technology can get at it. If it's the former, then, despite his rampage, a grave injustice is going to be done. If it's the latter, then we have to—"

"No," she repeated. She had a glass of synthehol in front of her and she was staring at it resolutely.

"I'm asking you as a friend."

"No."

"As chief of security in the midst of a murder investiga—"

"No."

He paused, and then said firmly, "I could ask Captain Calhoun to order you to do it."

She looked up at him, her hard gaze piercing even his tough hide. "You're going to ask Captain Calhoun to *order* me to perform a mind-meld with Janos? You would do that to me? You'd dare? You'd have the nerve to sit there and call on friendship and, when that doesn't work, prove the depth of your friendship by threatening to have me forced to—"

"It wasn't a threat, Soleta."

"It damned well was a threat!" she practically exploded, slamming an open hand on the table, jostling the half-drained bottle of synthehol that sat between them. The outburst brought the attention of everyone in the place to them until Kebron's glare prompted them to become very involved once more in whatever they'd just been doing.

Kebron realized that whatever confidence he'd had that discussing the matter in a public venue would keep a lid on feelings was obviously misplaced. "It wasn't intended as a threat," he amended. "If it came across that way, I apologize."

"Oh, you apologize," she snorted.

"Yes. I do. I was just trying to show you how strongly I feel about this."

She gave a short, bitter laugh. She'd never sounded less Vulcan than she did at that moment. "You are some piece of work, Kebron. You really are. I come over here to the *Trident* for twenty-four hours' personal leave, and you follow me over. You invite me here to the lounge, tell me you want to buy me a drink. And then you dump this on me."

"Soleta, it's not as if you haven't used your mind-meld capabilities before. And great good has always come from it."

"God," she shook her head. "You are so clueless. You truly are. You have no idea, no . . ."

"Then explain it to me."

"You wouldn't understand . . ."

"Explain it anyway."

She started to get up from the table. His every instinct was to rise as well, to try and block her way, but he fought the impulse because he knew it was going to bring him into direct conflict with *her* instinct. And her instinct right now was to get away from him. If he endeavored to battle it, all it would do would be to harden her even more. So he stayed right where he was.

Soleta strode halfway to the door, then slowed, then stopped. Her shoulders sagged, and she turned around and returned to the table, flopping back into the seat opposite him. Inwardly he breathed a sigh of relief even as, on the exterior, he remained as inscrutable as ever.

"Every time," she said, "that I've melded with someone, it's sapped me. Left me feeling drained, exposed. Someone truly skilled in the mind–meld is able to block that. No matter how much they blend minds with another, they still preserve their core, their true sense of self and identity. They keep it . . . I don't know, hidden away where nothing can touch it. I don't have the training or sophistication for that. So I just throw myself into it. It's the only way I can accomplish it, to utterly commit myself."

"Such dedication is commendable."

"Such foolhardiness is idiotic," she corrected him tartly. "And now . . . now of all times . . ."

"What do you mean, 'of all times . . . ' " Then slow comprehension began to dawn. "Oh. You are . . . referring to the recent business with the Beings . . ."

"Yes. That," she said, her tone dour. "In case you didn't notice, that ambrosia of theirs robbed me of my personality. Made me into their willing worshiper, their . . ."

"Their what?"

Her mouth snapped closed and brought a veil of detachment across herself to shut down the pain briefly reflected in her eyes. "Kebron . . . picture my sense of self as . . . I don't know . . . a blanket. After what happened to me, after all I've been through, that blanket is now shredded and filled with holes. It will recover, I assure you of that. But it will take time. Time for the blanket to . . . to heal."

"Blankets don't actually heal, since they're not sentient or alive in any—"

"Quiet."

"Okay."

"To be mended, then," she continued. "And during that time, the blanket has to be protected. Folded up, tucked away in a drawer, and no one or nothing comes near it. And you're coming to me and saying, Soleta, I want you to take this blanket and throw it on top of someone else. Someone who is, by all evidence, capable of such berserker behavior that he could shred the remains of this blanket beyond any possible hope of retrieval. Do you understand what I'm saying now?"

"I think so," he said slowly. "You're saying that if you went into Janos's mind, you'd be putting your own mind at grave risk."

"Zak . . . if he turned on me mentally . . . if by delving into his conscious or subconscious, I unleashed a savage aspect of his mind and then came into conflict with it . . . with my lowered defenses, he could psychically tear me to bits. I'd just . . ." Her chin began to tremble. The prospect of seeing her cry was horrifying to Kebron. "I'd just . . . there'd be nothing left of me. I'd just be a vegetable, I'd . . ."

He reached across the table and put one massive hand atop both of hers. The contact seemed to steady her and she looked at him, her eyes limpid and no longer fierce. "Zak . . . please . . ." she whispered.

"I am a terrible friend," said Zak Kebron. "I should never have been so selfish as to ask you to do such a thing against your will. I'm truly sorry."

The edges of her mouth twitched upward. "No . . . you're a good friend. In this case, you were trying to be a friend to Janos. You were caught between loyalties."

"I'd never really have asked Captain Calhoun to order you."

"Yes, you would have."

"Perhaps," he admitted. "But he never would have done it."

"He might have. At which point I'd have resigned my commission, and he'd have had no authority over me, so that would have been that."

"I'm relieved it didn't come to that."

"I'm not sure I am."

"What does that mean?"

She waved it off as she shook her head. "Nothing. It's meaningless. Forget I said anything."

"All right." He felt it was the wisest course to do as she requested.

"And . . . I'm sorry, Zak. I really am. I feel like I'm letting you down."

"Don't concern yourself. It was a long shot anyway. I had to do something." He sighed heavily, which, once again, sounded frighteningly similar to an earthquake rumbling in the distance. "I was foolish to undertake this. I'm friends with the accused murderer. I haven't been able to approach this investigation in anything remotely resembling a neutral fashion."

"What's done is done," Soleta said, sounding much more like her normal self.

He pondered the situation. "I could go to Dr. Selar, ask her if she would be willing . . . but no." He cut off the notion before it went anywhere. "No, she's even more reserved and distant than you. I doubt she would perform a mind-meld with Janos . . ."

"I think you're correct," she agreed. "At the most, I could see Selar engaging in a meld if it were of medical necessity, and even then she would be reluctant. This is in the context of a murder investigation. I just don't see her . . ."

Kebron glanced over at her as her voice trailed off. "What?" When she didn't reply immediately, he repeated, *"What?"*

"You never asked the reason I came here. To the *Trident."*

"I simply assumed you were visiting friends or acquaintances here."

"Well . . . you were right about that. But I came to visit a specific friend-or-acquaintance for a specific reason."

"That being?"

"I more or less told you already," she said. "After the ambrosia and the business with the Beings, I was mentally off balance. I couldn't find any sort of peaceful, calm center. Such a mental state can be crippling. If allowed to continue, it would have wound up affecting my work, my off-duty time . . . my entire life, really. So I wanted to talk to someone who has a great deal of experience with everything from losing control of one's faculties to encounters with creatures such as the Beings. Fortunately enough, he was right here on the *Trident,* just finishing up some sort of talks with the Tholians. He took the time to meet with me, to speak with me at length. Gave me some simple exercises to perform, designed to help restore balance."

"Have they worked?"

"They are working . . . or they were until you came here and put my equanimity out of joint."

"There are only so many ways, Soleta, that I can apologize."

"Don't worry about it," she assured him. "That's not the reason I'm bringing this up. The thing is, if anyone is capable of probing the depths of Janos's mind, it'd be the person I came here to talk to."

"And he wouldn't be afraid to do it?"

With a lopsided smile that looked completely out of place on her, Soleta said, "Truthfully . . . I don't think he's afraid of anything."

Then

Calhoun couldn't believe how quickly the six months had flown past.

He lay next to Shelby in her quarters, and reflected on the fact that it had actually all worked out for the best. Shelby had a stunning roommate named Leanne Gold. They had found much to commiserate on, since both of them had younger siblings who were intent to get into Starfleet at the earliest opportunity, and were wildly annoying besides. (Hardly a day went by when Leanne didn't comment about the latest correspondence from her annoying kid brother, Mickey, who seemed to delight in pushing all the buttons that annoyed Leanne when they were both much younger.) Calhoun considered the whole thing rather juvenile, but the upside was that Leanne had had her eye on Wexler for quite some time. As soon as Shelby confirmed that she and Wex had gone bust, Leanne made a serious pass, which was promptly and gratefully completed. It had all been so damned civilized that they'd actually become a friendly foursome, forming a study group, socializing, and generally solidifying the relationship that might have deteriorated still further considering the circumstances.

Calhoun's breathing was returning slowly to normal, and Shelby was curled up next to him, one bare leg draped across his. The sex had been spectacular, as always. He was drifting back to sleep, bathed in warmth, and then she pushed gently on his chest. "Get up," she said.

There was something about the way she said it, something about her voice, that triggered a recollection. He knew the words she was going to utter before she did so.

"Get up, sleepyhead," she said, not noticing that he was mouthing the words along with her.

Get up, Mac, we have things to do. . . .

She nudged him once more, playfully. "Get up, Mac. We have things to do." Which was certainly true enough. They had the day off, and were planning upon a number of relaxing and fun diversions in San Francisco.

Except his mind was as far away from those things as could possibly be. Instead he was back in the desert of Xenex, and he was dying, and there she was, his vision. A vision that had been a guidepost to him. A touchstone for the journey that he had undertaken that had led him so far away from his native world.

He had reached that point. He had found her, had found this moment.

And . . .

. . . now what?

The question in his mind left a chill in him that he was most surprised to discover. What was that supposed to mean, now what? Now . . . there was her. There was Elizabeth Paula Shelby.

He had tried calling her "Betty," since that was the affectionate name that Wexler had used. But she had reacted rather violently to that, and he had quickly set it aside. So more often than not, he simply addressed her as "Elizabeth."

Except when he was either feeling affectionate or just wanted to throw her off her stride a bit. Then he would call her "Eppy," an abbreviated form of the initials forming "Elizabeth Paula." Depending upon her mood, she would smile at it or be annoyed by it. To Calhoun it didn't matter particularly how she felt. He called her what he felt like calling her.

That vision he'd had in the desert . . . it had given him hints of what was to come. Picard had been there, as had Shelby, and Picard had shown up twice. One vision, of Picard, had already come true; another was from a period later in his life. And Shelby . . .

He'd seen nothing further of her beyond this moment.

What if . . .

What if this was as good as it got? What if this was all they were destined to have?

Mackenzie Calhoun was unaccustomed to uncertainty. Throughout his life, he had always known exactly what he wanted, and gone about getting it in as direct and straightforward a manner as he could. And his view of his relationship with Shelby, and where they were going, had likewise seemed clear.

Now, though, he felt hesitation creeping into the hidden recesses of his mind. What if he had seen up to this moment and no further because they were not truly meant to be together? The truth was that he had indeed thought of her as his fiancée from the moment they'd first coupled. That was the Xenexian way. Part of him had bridled against the fact that Shelby didn't feel likewise, or at least said she didn't.

But he might be wrong. It had happened, once or twice before, that he'd been wrong. So it wasn't without precedent.

And because uncertainty was such a foreign aspect of life to Mackenzie Calhoun, he fought against it with all his might. He had to know precisely what he was doing, exactly what was going to happen, every step of the way. He wanted, needed to have control over that which was to come, as unreasonable a goal as that was.

He had been so positive that he and Shelby would be together forever. But through the crack of hesitation that had opened in the dam of his mind, second-guessing now came flooding through. It washed through him, poured through every aspect of him, and just like that— just like that—everything that he'd ever concluded with conviction about himself and Shelby was thrown into mental disarray.

None of this showed in his demeanor.

No one would have been able to tell just by looking at him that he was adrift in a sea of incertitude. To any observer, he was simply smiling fixedly at Shelby in precisely the same way he had been before.

But Shelby wasn't just any observer.

He could see in her eyes that she knew something was up. She focused on him intently.

"What are you thinking, Mac?" she asked.

He felt defensive, which was yet another unusual sensation for him. "How can you tell I'm 'thinking' anything?"

"Your eyes spin counterclockwise," she said with such gravity that for a moment he thought she meant it. Then she smiled and tapped the side of his head. "C'mon . . . what's going through that Xenexian brain of yours?"

He wanted to lie to her. But he had never done so . . . certainly not about anything of importance. And he didn't want to start now. Still, he himself wasn't entirely certain of what was going through his head, or what conclusions he was rushing toward. Proceeding delicately, he said, "I'm thinking about us. Wondering if we're going to make it as a couple."

"Really," she said lightly. She nestled up against him, resting a hand on his chest. Probably she thought it was some sort of game. She figured she knew the answer even as she asked, "And what's your conclusion?"

If she had asked him five minutes earlier, or five minutes later, the chances were that she would have received an entirely different response. But at the moment she inquired, Calhoun—his mind racked with uncertainty—said with heavy candor, "That we won't."

The truly amazing thing was that he didn't know how she was going to react to that. He realized even as her body stiffened against his that he'd been a complete idiot. How could he have not known that she would do what she then did: get out of bed with a small grunt of anger, her back to him, striding away from him with her naked backside twitching angrily. If her body had been capable of projecting quills when upset, he would have been pincushioned.

"Now you're mad," he sighed, stating the painfully obvious. "I was just trying to be honest."

She whirled to face him, belting a robe around herself. "To hell with your honesty and to hell with you." She was trembling and then she took a long breath in through her nose and let it out slowly between her lips, a long sustained hiss that made it sound as if she was deflating. Calming herself in this way, she finally was able to say, "Dammit, Mac, you can never leave well enough alone," in a level tone rather than some annoyingly overemotional manner. "Here we're having a nice, peaceful morning, for once, and you had to go say something to wreck it. You just *had* to."

"I didn't know you'd get so upset, Eppy," he protested.

She gave him an incredulous look he knew all too well. "How could you *not know?*" she demanded. "Didn't you think about the *consequences* of your actions? Do you *ever?*"

"Yes."

"When?"

He didn't have a truly reasonable response to that, and so said with a weak look that he hoped came across as ingratiating, but no doubt was a bit simpering, "When I *remember* to."

She turned away from him, arms folded. She had let her hair grow out longer because he liked it that way. It cascaded around her shoulders like a strawberry blond waterfall. He wanted to reach out to it, to run his fingers through it. But he knew if he touched her, doubtless she would flinch away from him. What surprised him, however, was that she didn't simply sound angry. Instead her tone was a combination of frustration, annoyance, and just plain sadness. "God, Mac . . . how am I supposed to build a future with you when you say things like that? When I'm with you, it feels so right . . . but then something makes it go wrong."

He felt terrible, as if the bottom of his stomach were lurching out of him. He didn't know what was worse: that he'd felt the way he had, or that he'd been honest about it. But . . . what was he supposed to do? He couldn't control the direction of his feelings. He wasn't an android, an automaton. He was a living, breathing creature who didn't always say the exact right thing at the exact right time. Did she realize that? Understand that? *Grozit,* he'd never claimed he was perfect.

She wanted to build a future with him?

His mind suddenly reeled back, trying to grasp fully what she had just said. Build a future? With him? But in the past six months, she had made it quite clear that she wasn't interested in him as a permanent mate. She had insisted it was nothing personal; she claimed she didn't want to think of any man in that way right now. Her breakup with Wexler truly did suit her long-term plans, although it wasn't as if she'd maliciously figured it all out. Shelby was many things, but coldbloodedly manipulative was not one of them. Indeed, it was her coolness to the concept of a long-term relationship that had caused some of Calhoun's own fire to diminish in that regard. Not that he wanted to say that. It would make it sound as if he were trying to blame her. . . .

Women were very complicated creatures. He suddenly realized he was running through his head a list of everything he considered preferable to women. It was a long and most impressive imaginary document.

Realizing that he had spoken precipitously, Calhoun immediately decided to try and institute some damage control. "Come back to bed, Eppy," he said.

"To hell with bed!" she snapped at him. At that point, Calhoun would have given anything to be able to roll back time and stop himself from opening his big mouth. "Didn't you *hear* me?" she continued angrily. "What about our *future?* About building tomorrow!"

Calhoun knew there was nothing he could say. He'd already said too much . . . and too little. He'd spoken too openly of foolish doubts and concerns, while simultaneously speaking too little of just how much she meant to him. He had no one to blame but himself for his current predicament and her rising ire.

He sat up in bed. Knowing it would be pointless to try and smooth over what he'd said, he simply decided to approach from a different angle entirely. "Funny thing, Eppy—houses, palaces, starships . . . they don't exist unless we build them. But tomorrow? It shows up whether we build it or not. All we can do is build the best today possible—and hope that tomorrow copies it, as it sees fit." He stretched out a hand to her. "Let's do what's right for today . . . and let the future sort itself out."

She stared at his hand, and then at him. Then she seemed to laugh softly to herself and sighed, "You are such an idiot. Do you know that?"

"Yes. I know. And if I didn't know, I suspect I'll always have you to remind me."

She sat on the edge of the bed, took his hand, and said, "Yes. Always. And I think I know what this is about."

"You do?" he said guardedly.

She nodded, then hesitated. "Are you sure you want me to . . . ?"

"To tell me what you think? Of course. I always want to know what you think."

"All right. I think it's because you've lived such a violent life. And you think, deep down, anyone or anything you love is going to be taken from you violently. So you figure the best thing to do is push it away before that happens."

"Oh." The response seemed small and pathetic, but it was all he could think of to say. "That . . . well . . . that . . . I don't think that's the . . . but . . . I guess it . . . makes sense, but . . ."

She drew him to her, held him close. He could feel the warmth of her body through the thin robe. "Don't automatically say you agree. Don't even force yourself to. Just . . . promise me you'll think about it.

Because the best way to get through life is not just to do things, but to understand why you do them. Okay?"

"Okay."

"And the coming-back-to-bed part?"

"Yes?"

She kissed him warmly even as she shrugged off the robe. "Not one of your worst ideas."

Chapter Nine

Now

i.

Captains Shelby and Calhoun stood outside the *Trident* brig, both of them with their arms folded in a stern manner. Dr. Villers was between them, watching the proceedings hawklike, her stare unwavering. Behind them were Soleta, Kebron, and Arex, and Arex looked none too happy, either.

Inside the brig, Janos could not have had more restraints on him. There physically was no room on his body. Huge electronic clamps ran the length of his arms, his legs. There was a muzzle on his mouth. Not only was the metal of the bonds beyond his capability to break, but if he gave the slightest sign of a struggle, they would automatically hit him with enough of a jolt to take down ten Janoses. At least, that was the theory. Shelby hoped they didn't have to test it.

Her greatest concern, however, was reserved for the individual within the brig with Janos. Ambassador Spock was studying Janos thoughtfully, walking back and forth, studying him from one side and then the other as if he were trying to line up a particularly tricky golf putt.

"Ambassador," Shelby said apprehensively, "are you certain about this?"

Spock halted in his preparations and looked at her with an arched eyebrow. "Certain? Within what context?"

"Are you certain this is a good idea?"

"All ideas, Captain, seem like good ones at the time they are being undertaken. It is only with the full clarity of hindsight that we determine whether our initial impulses were correct or not."

"Terrific," muttered Shelby. She turned to Calhoun and said, "If anything happens to him, it's your fault."

"*My* fault? How is it my fault?"

"Because Kebron, Soleta, and Janos are all your people, and they're responsible for talking the ambassador into taking this risk."

"The ambassador decided to take 'this risk' entirely on his own. Besides," and he directed the question to Soleta, "what's the worst that could happen?"

"If Janos's mind proves too strong, Ambassador Spock's consciousness could be permanently damaged, triggering the onset of assorted neurological diseases and eventual death," replied Soleta.

"Oh, that's just perfect," said Shelby.

Spock paused in his preparations to look at the officers standing beyond the boundary of the brig. "I *am* capable of hearing every word you say, you know. The decision to aid in this matter was mine and mine alone. None are responsible except me."

"Well, that's not precisely true, is it." It was Janos, speaking in a muffled voice through the restraints upon his mouth. "I'm the one who's responsible for this. For all of it. Captain Calhoun, perhaps it would best serve all concerned if I were simply turned over to the Selelvians now and be done with it."

"Who told you about that?" demanded Calhoun, his eyes narrowing.

"Keeping a secret on a starship is always an exercise in futility, Captain," said Janos. "It doesn't matter how I found out about it. The facts at this point seem incontrovertible. I killed one of their people. They demand justice . . . or vengeance . . . or both. It doesn't matter. They are entitled to it, and in my opinion, it should be given to them."

"Your opinion is noted and logged," said Calhoun.

"I believe I am prepared," Spock announced. He was standing to one side of the bound Janos. His eyes were the merest slits, his fingertips barely touching one another. To Shelby, who had taken extensive martial-arts training, he looked for all the world as if he were summoning his "chi," his inner life force. Perhaps that was exactly what he was doing, and Vulcans simply had another name for it.

Janos was not looking at him. Every so often, his small pink/red eyes would glance in Spock's direction before gazing fixedly forward once more. "Now . . . you've done this before, have you?"

"Yes," said Spock. He stretched the fingers of either hand and stood directly in front of Janos, hands hovering on either side of Janos's face.

"But have you engaged in this 'meld' business with a life-form substantially different from your own? Something as pronouncedly non-human as myself?"

"Are you familiar with the Horta?"

Janos now looked right into Spock's eyes. "You melded with one of those? One of those rocklike animals?"

"The Horta are rocklike animals in the same sense that human beings are meatlike animals," replied Spock.

"What was that like? Blending your mind with something that alien?"

"Merely an extension of my day-to-day existence," Spock informed him. "Now . . . if you would be so good as to clear your mind of any extraneous thoughts."

"I'll do what I can," replied Janos, faintly sarcastic.

"That will be satisfactory," Spock said, giving no acknowledgment of Janos's tone of voice. His fingers brushed against Janos's white fur, and his fingertips pressed more tightly against his head. Janos's eyes widened and his breathing became slower, shallower.

Although Shelby knew it was her imagination, she felt as if the temperature in the area had dropped by at least five degrees, and was continuing to sink. Spock's gaze had appeared to turn inward, and he was murmuring softly to himself. He seemed to be saying, "Our minds are merging," and Janos's mouth moved in synch with Spock's.

Long, seemingly endless seconds passed. The murmuring had continued for some time, but eventually had tapered off, and now both Spock and Janos were simply holding their positions, at slight angles to one another. Nothing was being said by either. Janos's normally narrow eyes were wide, while Spock's were slits with the barest hint of white within.

"Is this normal?" Shelby asked Soleta.

"There's no such thing as normal when it comes to the Vulcan mindmeld," Soleta told her. "One experience can be calm, serene . . . while the next one can be—"

Suddenly Janos let out a low, challenging growl. So did Spock.

"—less so," finished Soleta.

Spock and Janos continued to snarl in synch, their voices on the rise, building in bestial anger. Spock's tone was lower, more intense, while Janos sounded far angrier. Janos started to rock, jerking his arms, clearly trying to break free.

"Why isn't the charge from the bonds stopping him?" demanded Shelby.

"Ambassador Spock shut them off," Soleta said.

"What?" Shelby and Calhoun chorused.

Soleta nodded calmly. "The bonds remain secure. It's simply the jolt that has been removed from the—"

"That jolt helps prevent him from building up enough strength to break the cuffs!" said Shelby. "Why didn't you tell me?"

"I am telling you."

"I mean earlier?"

"You didn't ask earlier."

"Stop screwing around, Soleta," said an obviously irritated Calhoun. "You should have stopped him and you know it."

"If I had, then he might truly be risking death," Soleta retorted. "The key to a mind-meld is keeping the two minds stable, in synch. If Janos were to flinch or spasm or place any sort of stress upon the cuffs that could be read as an attempt to escape, the subsequent jolt could disrupt the merge and cause a psychic backlash. That could cripple both of them."

"If Janos gets loose, there'll be more crippled than someone's psyche," said Calhoun.

Shelby was about to turn to Arex to instruct him to go in and reactivate the cuffs manually, and suddenly Ambassador Spock, the pride of Vulcan, let out a howl that was as primal as a wolf baying at the moon. His lips pulled back into an animalistic snarl, his shoulders swung back and forth. He wasn't speaking words, but instead a series of grunts and snarls. Janos was doing much the same. It was as if Shelby was peering back to the dawn of time, watching primitive ancestors celebrating some frightening ritual around a campfire. Janos's hands, still bound by the thick cuffs, spasmed and tore at empty air, and his screeches were so perfectly in line with Spock's own that it was like listening to two identical voices at the same time.

And suddenly Spock yanked free from Janos's face. Janos slumped back, his eyes still open, the noises from his voice fading to a distant growling. Spock stumbled back ungracefully, banged into the far wall, and sank to the floor. Wide-eyed, he stared down at his own hands as if he expected to see something upon them.

Shelby had a fairly good idea what that "something" might be.

"Release . . . me," he managed to gasp out.

"Did you see anything?" Kebron asked urgently.

"Release me," Spock said again, his voice no louder than before, but definitely with far greater vehemence and conviction.

Shelby nodded to Arex, and within moments the Triexian had Spock free from within the brig. Janos made no attempt to break his restraints. Instead he remained where he was, chest heaving, although the gasping for air was slowing.

"Ambassador, are you all right?" said Shelby.

Spock managed a nod. "I am . . . in satisfactory health." His face looked considerably less green than usual. Shelby wished she knew if that was a good thing or not.

"We can take you down to sickbay . . ."

"That will not be necessary." Spock had straightened up and was smoothing down the front of his clothing. "I do not require . . . medical attention."

Calhoun turned his attention to the occupant of the cell. "Janos? How about you? Are you all right?"

Slowly Janos managed to shake his head. "No," he croaked. "I shall . . . never be all right . . . again."

Even before she asked, Shelby knew. She knew it from Janos's expression and even from the neutral look on Spock's face.

"Ensign Janos," Spock said softly, "now has a much clearer recollection of the events surrounding Lieutenant Commander Gleau's passing. Do you not, Ensign?"

"I killed him," Janos said.

And then he brought his hands up and, even though they were buried within the sleeves of the cuffs, he began to sob into the area where his palms would have been. He did not, however, have any tear ducts, so no moisture flowed from his eyes. None was needed. His misery and despair were obvious for all to see.

ii.

Calhoun and Shelby sat in Shelby's ready room. Neither of them sat behind the desk, although certainly Shelby would have been entitled to. Instead Shelby was seated facing the desk on the far side, while Calhoun stared out at the stars hanging so close that sometimes it seemed, in Shelby's imaginings, that she could reach out and scoop them up with her hand. She remembered a time when she was very little, and her father had explained to her that the sun was actually no larger than the palm of his hand. He had sought to confirm this by simply holding his hand up so that it blocked out the sun. Little Elizabeth had been very impressed by this, and had jumped up and down trying to touch the sun.

"When you're older you can touch it," her father had said in that type of mock-consoling voice he so excelled in.

It had been only a few minutes ago that they had been down in the conference lounge. Ambassador Spock had been there, calmly offering his assessment of the situation to the people who had witnessed his mental bonding with Janos. The one who had seemed the most stunned was Kebron, who looked like someone had kicked him in the face. Not that kicking him in the face would actually have hurt him, but he still bore the look of the walking wounded.

"The recollection was buried so far down," Spock told them, "that he was not even aware it was there. If it occurred to him at all, it was in the context of a fleeting dream."

"And you're certain it was genuine? Not a false memory," Shelby had asked.

"He's sure, Captain," Soleta said.

"I believe, Lieutenant, I was asking the ambassador." Shelby sounded none too pleased. "It's simply that there has been so much discussion and investigation into the incident, I thought perhaps that . . ."

"He had imagined it?" Spock inquired. He shook his head. "No. This was a genuine recollection."

"Is it possible that someone was controlling his mind?" asked Kebron. "That he recalls it because he knows he did it at some level, but that someone else was manipulating his actions?"

Shelby was most interested to hear Spock's reply to that. She knew the "controlling outside force" concept was a pet theory of Kebron's.

But Kebron seemed to sink visibly when Spock gave the slightest shake of his head. "Were the actions compelled upon him by another . . . were his mind not truly his own . . . I would have viewed the murder through a sort of . . . prism of the mind. The images would have seemed distant, even refracted. That was not the case here."

"You actually witnessed the crime?" asked Arex.

There was silence then in the room as Spock nodded. His voice was low and gravelly as he said, "He struck with the remorseless ferocity of a hunting beast. There was no mercy in him . . . and not the slightest spark of human intelligence."

"My God," Shelby said softly.

"However, from a legal perspective," the Vulcan continued, "the situation would be . . . problematic."

"Meaning?"

"Meaning, Mr. Kebron," said Calhoun, "intent is an issue."

"Correct," Spock said. "First and foremost for consideration of a criminal action is *mens rea*. The state of mind of the accused, indicating culpability. If Ensign Janos were not in his right mind . . ."

"Then he's not guilty of anything," Kebron said quickly. He almost dared to look relieved. "If he didn't know right from wrong, he was temporarily insane. Which means . . ."

"I am afraid," Spock said, "that as far as the Selelvians are concerned, it will mean very, very little. I have had a few dealings with them in my time. They can be a most unreasonable race when they are so inclined. And from my understanding, they will not accept a simple notion that Ensign Janos did not know what he was doing and, therefore, should be held blameless."

"But . . . it's not fair," Kebron had said.

And Spock had nodded. "No. It is not. Unfortunately, Lieutenant, it appears I must belatedly inform you . . . that the universe is not a very fair place."

Shelby had adjourned the meeting then, even though Kebron had wanted to keep it going. He wanted answers. He wanted to comprehend how this could have happened. What sort of madness had seized hold of Janos? How could it be that he didn't remember what he was doing?

Why did he do it in the first place? None of it made any sense, no sense at all.

He had turned to Shelby and Calhoun as if wanting answers.

They provided him none.

Instead they headed up to the ready room where they now remained in silence. A silence finally broken by Shelby.

"Does he know?" she asked.

"Which 'he' are you referring to?" Calhoun replied.

"Kebron. Although either applies, I guess. But Kebron is who I meant."

"Kebron knows the official Starfleet line on Janos. He knows the information in Janos's file that's available to all. But he doesn't know the deep background. It stemmed from a top-secret mission and there was no way to make it part of Janos's file without violating that confidentiality. So unless Janos told him—and I suspect he didn't, because Janos isn't exactly proud of it—then no, he doesn't know."

"But Janos himself knows. You're sure?"

"Yes, of course." Calhoun hesitated. "I think he does. I suppose it's always possible that he's blanked out that which he doesn't wish to recall. The mind is a funny thing, after all."

"Oh, yeah. Funny. You can barely contain the hilarity here," said Shelby. She moaned softly, covering her face with her hands. "Mac, what the hell are we going to do?"

"I'll tell you what we're going to do," Calhoun replied. "We're going to stop pretending, that's what."

"I wasn't pretending, Mac, and neither were you," she said sharply. "Neither of us knew for sure."

"Yes, we did." His voice wasn't loud, but it was harsh. "We damn well did, you and I, the moment we knew that Janos's DNA was all over Gleau's corpse. But in our own way, we were just as much in denial of it as Kebron was. And we had even less excuse, because we knew better. We kept hoping an explanation we preferred would turn up. Well, it hasn't, Eppy. It's playing out exactly the way we knew deep down it was going to play out, and now we have to do something."

The challenge hung there in the air, and then Shelby said quietly, "And what would you suggest, Mac?"

"We go to Dr. Bethom."

"That's impossible."

"It's not impossible, Eppy," Calhoun said with growing urgency. "If Janos's mental acceleration is beginning to break down after all this time, then one of two things is happening. Either Bethom's process was flawed in some way to start out, or . . ."

"Or . . . Bethom's causing it somehow."

Slowly Calhoun nodded. "Causing it . . . perhaps to get back at us."

"God almighty."

"We have to find him," Calhoun said again, "before it's too late. Before there's nothing left of Janos's mind to scrape back together."

"And the Selelvians?" said Shelby.

"Let them come," said Calhoun. "Just let them come. And I'll convince them of the folly of their actions."

"What are you saying, Captain?"

He looked at her, and suddenly she felt as if he were staring at her from across a gulf of years and light-years.

"Perhaps more than I should be . . . *Captain,*" he replied. Then he tapped his combadge, said, "Calhoun to *Excalibur.* One to beam over," and just stood there, arms folded, as he dematerialized. To Shelby, the air seemed to hold his shape long after he was gone.

Then

As Calhoun approached the office of Dean Jellico, he heard raised voices coming from the other side of the closed door. One he recognized immediately, of course, as Jellico's. He couldn't understand what it was that could be getting Jellico so worked up. What did he have to worry about, after all? Everyone at the Academy had heard about Jellico's promotion to captain. Word was that as soon as the semester ended, Jellico was going to be given command of a starship—the *Cairo*, most likely—and he was going to be out of here. Given that situation, Jellico should be in a remarkably good mood, since whatever was happening around the Academy was certainly going to be of only passing importance to him.

The desk in the reception area outside Jellico's office was empty, and Calhoun paused outside the door, listening. He heard a female voice, and words being bandied about such as "third year" and "risky" and . . .

"Xenex."

Upon hearing the name of his home planet mentioned, Calhoun felt the world reeling around him.

It was obvious what was about to happen.

He was going to be kicked out of the Academy.

The second year had gone remarkably smoothly, all things considered. But the third year had been rougher. Elizabeth and he had officially become full-time roommates . . . officially in an unofficial capacity, since Starfleet Academy was still remarkably parochial when it came to such arrangements. The official policy stemmed from the notion that studies and relationships were an uneasy mix, and therefore "couples" were not permitted to room together.

The rule had been on the books for over a hundred years, and no one had bothered to change it. That was because, by this point in time, no one was bothering to enforce it, either. Academy faculty had more important things to do with their time than police the living arrangements of the students. Furthermore, since the simplistic notion of male/female cohabitation being forbidden totally overlooked same-sex couplings, of which there were a number, the faculty had adopted an ages-old policy loosely referred to as "Don't ask, don't tell." The fact that one's official residence might not be where one left his or her boots every night was of no consequence to any faculty unless, and until, it became of consequence. So the cadets knew enough to keep their private lives to themselves, and everyone peacefully coexisted for the most part.

With that in mind, Wexler had bid farewell to his roommate Mackenzie Calhoun and a cheerful hello to Elizabeth Shelby's former roommate, whose personal effects magically migrated into Wexler's room. Meanwhile Calhoun moved in with Shelby.

It seemed the ideal arrangement.

Calhoun had made his permanent home on Earth. The Academy had a special living facility arranged for offworld students who wanted to do precisely what Calhoun was doing: remain on Earth between semesters. That was where Calhoun had stayed during each summer, occasionally visiting Shelby at her parents' home in Silver Spring, Maryland. Shelby's parents hadn't known what to make of Calhoun, but had been polite enough overall, although Shelby's mother made little secret of the fact that she missed Wexler.

In all that time, he had not thought about going home to Xenex. Even though it had been just a few years, his existence on that world seemed a lifetime ago. A lifetime belonging to someone else entirely.

But he had gotten off to a poor start in his third year, overwhelmed by a sudden upsurge in coursework. He had always leaned heavily on Shelby to help him out, but she was likewise burdened, and was having a tough enough time keeping up herself. "This is your third year, Mac," she'd told him one night with blistering impatience. "Time to stand on your own damned two feet."

After that he had not asked her even once for help. This had made for some uneasy evenings of studying, to the point where the silence became so heavy that one or the other of them had gone out and studied elsewhere.

It had been a mighty struggle for him, and his grades had slipped. It wasn't for lack of trying, but his professors had been coming down hard on him. Calhoun had felt as if he was having to deal with too much from all sides. On some level, it seemed ridiculous. How could someone who had spent his teen years organizing an eventually successful revolt of independence feel overwhelmed by something as pedestrian as homework?

But he had been, and now he was in deep, deep trouble because of it. He leaned toward the door, trying to pick up entire sentences while not getting too close lest he cause it to open automatically.

"He's simply not ready," he heard Jellico say.

"Not ready to be sent back to his homeworld? I disagree," came the unfamiliar female voice.

He was right. His grades, his performance had been so subpar that he had been summoned to Jellico's office to be informed that he was being shipped home.

"Disgrace." The word echoed in his head. He had left Xenex with such high hopes, and now he would be returning in disgrace. The great liberator, the great savior of Xenex, had flunked out in the third year of Starfleet Academy. It was unthinkable. Despite his accomplishments, he would be considered some sort of failure. A fool.

Well, he wouldn't stand for it. Let them try to send him back. He wouldn't go. He'd find a way to stay on Earth, or even go somewhere else if that was what it took. But he would not return home a failure. That simply was not an op—

He whirled suddenly, sensing someone coming in behind him. His fist was cocked even as he looked into the shocked face of Ensign Bialer, Jellico's aide de camp, who had just returned to his desk. Bialer flinched, obviously convinced that One-Punch Calhoun was about to cave in his face.

Slowly Calhoun lowered his fist. "Sorry," he said sheepishly.

"It's all right," said Bialer, leaning against his desk and catching his breath. "I was wondering what I was going to do to get my heart rate sped up today. Now I know." He gestured toward the door. "They're waiting for you. Go on in."

"Fine. But I'll tell you this," Calhoun said, raising his voice so that he was reasonably sure those inside would hear him, "I'm not going to go quietly!"

"I believe you," said Bialer, who looked as if he was still nervous that Calhoun was going to strike him.

Calhoun strode into Jellico's office to see that Jellico was staring at him, looking utterly bewildered. There was a woman seated in a chair a few feet to Jellico's right. She had a weather-beaten look about her, but her eyes snapped with firm intelligence. Her uniform and pips indicated that she held the rank of captain. For no reason that he could articulate, Calhoun liked her instantly. Before Calhoun could say a word, Jellico demanded, "What the *hell* is your problem, Cadet?"

"Isn't that what you're here to tell me?" replied Calhoun. If they were going to treat him in such a cavalier manner, he saw no reason that he had to be polite in return.

"I don't know what you're talking about, Calhoun," said Jellico. "Then again, if you ask me, the whole world's going crazy. Calhoun, meet Captain Alynna Nechayev. Captain, Mackenzie Calhoun, cadet, third year."

"A pleasure, Cadet," said Nechayev. "I've heard a great deal about you." She looked him up and down, openly assessing him. "I thought you'd be taller," she decided.

"So did I," replied Calhoun.

"Captain Nechayev is attached to the Starfleet Internal Affairs office," Jellico said. "She handles matters of an unusual or delicate nature."

"Ah," said Calhoun, nodding in grim understanding. "She's the one you bring in when you have to do something like this, then."

Jellico looked at him blankly. "Like what?"

"Like this. I have to say, Dean Jellico, with all respect . . . I thought you man enough that you'd want to handle something like this yourself."

"Something like this?" Jellico's faced reddened. "Calhoun, have you completely lost your mind? I have no idea what you're . . . Nechayev, do you know what he's talking about?"

Nechayev, to Calhoun's surprise, laughed softly. "Unless I am very much mistaken," she almost purred, "the cadet is under the impression that he's in some sort of trouble. Correct, Cadet?"

"You ..." He hesitated, suddenly uncertain. "You ... mean I'm not?"

"You may be. But not the type you think. Tell me, Calhoun," and she rose to her feet, "have you heard of a Dr. Marius Bethom?"

Calhoun shook his head. "Should I have?"

"A former teacher of xenobiology here at the Academy, with a particular specialty in the area of xenomorphics."

"Oh. Well, my . . . friend Cadet Shelby probably has. She's taken a great interest in xenomorphics. The entire study of aliens that are able to change their shape or expedite their own evolution ... she finds it fascinating. I'm ... not sure why," he admitted, and then added in confusion, "and why are we discussing this?"

"What would you rather be discussing?" demanded Jellico. "Your grades?"

"No," Calhoun said quickly. "No, that won't be necessary. You were saying ... ?" and he shifted his attention back to Nechayev.

Nechayev made a slow circle of the office as she spoke. "Dr. Bethom's interests in xenomorphing were all well and good, as long as he stuck with teaching about those things that occurred in nature. But his dismissal from the Academy came as a result of his preaching the positive virtues of practices outlawed by the UFP. Practices such as gene manipulation ... cloning ... the creation of artificial life-forms."

"These are outlawed?" asked Calhoun.

"And with good reason," Jellico told him. "Going all the way back to the Eugenics Wars, attempts to set ourselves up as gods and muck with nature have always ended in disaster. We learn from our mistakes, and the ban on such activities as Bethom was advocating is a sound one."

"Bethom was released from his position five years ago," Nechayev said. "No action was taken beyond that, however. After all, he was simply advocating an outlawed practice, but it wasn't as if he were undertaking it himself. However, since then ..."

"He started putting his theories to practical applications?"

Nechayev nodded approvingly. "Correct, Calhoun. Tell me ... does this look at all familiar to you?"

She swiveled around the computer screen on Jellico's desk so Calhoun could see the image that appeared on it.

"Of course it does," he said immediately. "That's the creature that nearly killed Shelby and me during our survival training two years ago. The one that looked like a bahoon."

"The reason it looked like one," said Nechayev, "is because it *was* one."

"Bahoons don't have tentacles."

"This one did," said Jellico. "Courtesy of Dr. Bethom."

Calhoun stared at it once more and shuddered inwardly. "You're saying that this Bethom . . . he had some sort of facility set up around Platonis?"

"Nearby, yes. We believe he had a large submersible vessel in the vicinity. By moving around, he made himself that much less conspicuous. This creature was either something that escaped, or else he simply released it into the watery environment to see how it would survive. Judging by the way it nearly killed the two of you, I'd have to say it survived quite well."

"Have you found him? Arrested him?"

"No," said Nechayev, "and that's where you come in."

"I'm coming in?"

"Yes. You see, Calhoun, we believe that Bethom is no longer on Earth, and has not been for some time. Our intelligence reports place him on Xenex."

"Xenex?"

"Your old homeworld," she nodded. "We believe he has a hidden base there. We're going to be sending in a strike team to root him out. I want to know if you're interested in being a part of it."

Calhoun could scarcely believe it. Here he'd thought he was being summoned for dismissal, and instead he was being given an opportunity to embark on some sort of incredible covert mission. "Me?" he said.

"You," Jellico told him, sounding none too thrilled about it. "Frankly, Calhoun, I don't approve. I'm not a fan of sending third-year students out on hazardous assignments, although it's not unprecedented."

"In your case, Calhoun, special circumstances apply," Nechayev told him. "First, Xenex is your homeworld, and we could use a native. And second, you come highly recommended by the head of the strike team."

"The head of the strike team?"

The door hissed open behind them and a startlingly familiar voice said, "My apologies, Captain Nechayev, for running late. Dean Jellico, good to see you, sir. Congratulations on your promotion."

Calhoun turned, knowing who he was going to see and not quite believing it. Standing in the doorway in a clean, pressed Starfleet uniform was Joshua Kemper.

"Hello, One-Punch," he grinned. "Welcome to the big leagues."

Chapter Ten

Now

Robin Lefler stared at the holographic image of her mother that sat efficiently in the seat at the conn post next to her on the *Excalibur* bridge. They were still in orbit around Danter and she was beginning to think they'd never leave the damned planet. But that annoyance paled beside the uncanny sensation of having her dead mother as her coworker.

It wasn't as if the computer-bound Morgan actually required a body in order to function. She could reproduce her face on the front viewscreen whenever she wished, and she could operate the conn station from inside the ship's circuitry with perfect ease. However, both Calhoun and Burgoyne felt that issuing commands to an empty chair was a bit much. So the engineering chief, Craig Mitchell, had spent half a day rigging up the chair at conn with the proper circuitry, and now Morgan was seated happily at the station in a holographic incarnation.

Morgan noticed that Robin was staring at her, which wasn't difficult considering Robin was making no attempt to hide it. "Problem, dear?" she inquired.

"This is just weird, that's all," said Robin. "I mean . . . I look at you and I keep thinking you're my mother . . ."

"I am your mother, dear."

"No. You're not. My mother was flesh and blood. You're a hologram, for God's sake. It's . . . I don't know . . . confusing."

"Would it be easier for you, dear, if I wore a large letter 'H' for 'hologram' on my forehead?" asked Morgan solicitously.

"No. It wouldn't." She shook her head. "I don't want to get into a fight with you, Mother. It's silly. I just . . . I . . ."

"What, Robin?" Morgan swiveled in her chair to face Robin. She did not, however, try to get up. To do so would have caused her to vanish.

Robin glanced around the bridge to see if anyone was listening. Everyone appeared busy at their stations. That, of course, meant they were hanging on Robin's every word. Well, to hell with it. She leaned toward the image of her mother and asked, "What's it like?"

"Having a holographic body, you mean?" Robin nodded. Morgan pondered it a moment. "It's very quiet."

"Quiet?"

"You don't realize how noisy a body is until you don't have one anymore. The little creaks of joints, the smacking of your tongue on your lips. Sneezing or hiccuping. Breathing. Sighing. Your heart beating . . ."

"You can't hear your heart beat."

"Actually, yes. You can and you do. You hear it all the time. You just don't realize you're hearing it until you don't hear it anymore. I know it sounds a little strange, but it's true. Oh."

"Oh what?"

"Captain's coming," said Morgan. "He just got onto the turbolift and ordered the bridge as his destination."

"God, Mother, can you hear *everything* that goes on on this ship?"

"No. Just anything that's directly addressed to me. When he gave his voice command of his destination, that went straight to me. Arrival in three, two, one . . ."

Burgoyne, who had been seated in the command chair, was rising smoothly from it as Calhoun stepped out onto the bridge. Calhoun saw Burgoyne moving before s/he could possibly have seen that the captain had returned, and he glanced over at Morgan. "You knew I was coming?"

"Yes," said Morgan. "And yet I didn't bake a cake."

"What?"

"Never mind," she sighed. "Before your time."

"Burgy," Calhoun said briskly, "I need you to watch the store five more minutes. Morgan, a moment of your time." Without another word he headed into the ready room.

Naturally Morgan was there before he arrived. To be precise, her face was staring out at him from the desk monitor. "Captain?" she said politely.

"I need you to access something for me, Morgan." He leaned forward on his knuckles. "And I further need you to understand that whatever services I ask of you are to remain strictly between us."

She looked at him askance. "Are we discussing sexual services, Captain?"

"Wha—? No! *Grozit!* What gave you *that* idea?"

"No reason at all."

"I meant," he said very deliberately, "that anything we discuss stays within these walls."

"And ceiling," she reminded him.

"Yes, and ceiling."

"And floor."

The exchange was rapidly losing its charm. "I get it, Morgan. All right?"

"Good. How can I help you, sir?"

"I need you to check all records for the whereabouts of a Dr. Marius Bethom."

"Working." She looked thoughtful for a moment. "Marius Bothem. Doctor of Xenobiology. Born, Denver, Colorado, on July 11—"

"I don't need his full biography, Morgan. I just need to know where he is."

"Right now?"

"At this moment in time, yes, what's his location?"

"I'm sorry, Captain," said Morgan, "but I'm afraid I don't have that information."

"You should. He should be listed as being in Federation custody."

"That is correct, yes."

"Well, then—?"

"But you asked where he was. Knowing that he is in custody is not the same as knowing where in custody he is. The Federation has thirty-seven different custodial facilities where prisoners or enemies of the Federation can be incarcerated."

"Fine. Check the records of those facilities."

"I don't have that information."

"How can you not have it?" he demanded.

"Captain, there's no need to sound so angry," Morgan told him sharply. "I'm not omniscient. I'm simply a damned computer, and the information listings of who is where in the Federation justice system is confidential material to which I do not have access. That information is held privately in separate Federation data banks."

"Can you interface with those data banks?"

She blinked, and he realized that most of the time she did not blink, which was why it looked so odd when she did. "I suppose I can."

"Would you please?"

"All right." She blinked again. "Go to hell."

"What?"

"Not you, Captain," she assured him. "I just tried doing what you suggested, and that's what those data banks told me."

"They told you to go to hell," he said skeptically.

"That's the loosely translated version. What they actually said involved a lot more zeros and ones, and words like 'systems error' and such, but that was the long and short of it, yes."

"Terrific. The one man in the galaxy who may be able to help me, and the Federation central computer system decides to be territorial."

"It's always something, isn't it?" said Morgan, all sympathy. "Is there anything else I can help you with, Captain? You know, there are official channels you can go through to try and obtain this information."

Calhoun slowly drummed his fingers on the table. "Official channels ask a lot of official questions, none of which I'm sure I want to answer. But you may be on to something there. I want you to raise someone for me."

"Who?"

"Vice-Admiral Nechayev. Her whereabouts, at least, you should be able to track down. Find her and send her a message that I need to speak with her on a matter of some urgency."

"If I may, Captain," said Morgan, "Vice-Admiral Nechayev might ask some of those same official questions you have no interest in answering."

"I'm thinking actually she won't," replied Calhoun. "Because most of them she'd probably already know the answer to, and besides . . . I've done her some serious favors in the past. She owes me. And I think she'll be willing to repay her debts. At least, I hope so."

"Very well, Captain. I'll find her for you. And Captain . . . ?"

"Yes, Morgan?"

She smiled broadly. "Isn't it more fun talking to me than just an ordinary computer voice?"

In spite of the situation, he returned the smile. "Yes. Much more fun, Morgan. Tons more fun."

Then

He had forgotten what the Xenexian sun was like. It pounded down upon him, oppressive, almost impossible to take. And yet, it was like having an old friend greeting him once more.

An old friend he really, really hated.

The entire situation struck Calhoun as patently absurd. If there was one man he'd ever encountered whom he was quite certain he despised and would forever despise, it was the bully known as Joshua Kemper. Kemper, after all, had been largely responsible for much of what had gone wrong during his first year at the Academy. As a result, Kemper was unquestionably the last person he would ever trust in any sort of situation, from politely social to life-threatening.

Yet here he now was, making his way through a narrow mountain pass with Kemper directly behind him.

Calhoun knew these mountains all too well. The Ridge Mountains. There had been any number of occasions when he and his followers had eluded Danteri troops here. The Xenexians had stumbled over an unusual feature of the Ridge Mountains through sheerest chance: The mountains contained some sort of natural ore that scrambled most sensor devices. It was impossible for anyone using most scanner technology available to accurately detect life forms hiding within the Ridge. Instead the most they would get was bounce-backs, echoes . . . ghosts of whomever it was they were searching out. It had driven the Danteri mad with frustration. Just one of the many tricks that the rebels had learned as they used the properties of their world to thwart and frustrate the more technologically advanced Danteri, forcing them to fight the Xenexian sort of battle. A battle that, in the long term, the Danteri could not hope to win.

It was because of the Ridge's nature that Calhoun had been convinced it was the area where their target, Dr. Bethom, would be hiding. He would be concerned about Federation pursuit, and want to make his headquarters in an area that provided both natural cover and some means of thwarting standard sensor scans. The only way sensors would be able to garner any trace readings would be if they were practically on top of him. The Danteri had discovered that years before, much to their chagrin, as their efforts to detect the hiding Xenexians had only been successful mere moments before death by ambush would come raining down upon them.

Fortunately, there was a particular mountain tribe whom Calhoun had encountered during his forays into the Ridge, a tribe that had come to respect and revere the great M'k'n'zy of Calhoun. They were by nature a very peaceful people, and they had refused to lend a sword in the battle to liberate Xenex. This had angered the young warlord at first, but the tribe had also been willing to provide aid and succor. This naturally put them at great risk of reprisal should the Danteri find out. Not only had they earned M'k'n'zy's respect, but the warlord had come to realize that there were many aspects to any war, and all should be appreciated for whatever contributions they could make.

It was upon that tribe that Calhoun, in the company of the Starfleet strike team, had called. The elder tribesmen did not recognize Calhoun at first. It was fortunate that he had continued to sport his neatly trimmed beard or they might never have done so. Once they did, though, Calhoun explained his situation and who they were looking for.

The elder tribesmen had nodded, looking grim. "We know exactly of whom you speak, Great M'k'n'zy," they had said to him. "Occasionally he has turned loose one of his beasts upon us."

"Have they killed any of you?" Calhoun had asked with some urgency.

"No," he was told. "No, we have managed to destroy them each time."

Kemper had looked grim as he said, "Why would he be doing that? Setting his creatures on these people?"

"He's testing them," Calhoun had replied. "Testing his beasts in the most practical way available to him: combat conditions. Then he determines what his creatures' weaknesses are and fixes them on the next go-around."

"Hideous," Shelby had said. "My God, I read his texts . . . the man is brilliant. I had no idea of the circumstances surrounding his departure from the Academy. What a waste. What a damned waste."

Not for the first time, Calhoun had wondered about the wisdom of bringing Shelby. But he had no one else to blame, for it had been he who had insisted that she be added to the team. There was, first and foremost, her knowledge of the writings of Bethom and of the sort of technology that could lead to the creatures Bethom was creating. And second, she had almost died at the hands (well, tentacles) of one of Bethom's pets. Certainly from a closure point of view, she deserved the opportunity to join in the mission to put an end to his activities. Besides, he had figured (correctly, as it turned out) that she would absolutely insist on going. This naturally was enough to put Jellico practically into cardiac arrest, but Nechayev had gotten the necessary permissions and Shelby had been added to the team.

There were three other men along. None of them seemed to be typical Starfleet. They came across more like extremely experienced foot soldiers, and apparently this was not the first job they had done for Nechayev. Their names were Langdon, Fitzhugh, and Travers. Langdon, the senior of the three, was clearly the most experienced, a burly veteran of such escapades. Fitzhugh, slimmer and waspish, said barely more than one sentence at a time, but he had the cold indifference of a man who was used to killing. Calhoun wondered if, in another life, Fitzhugh was an assassin. Or maybe in this life. Travers was the youngest of the three, with a broad, open face that, according to Shelby, screamed Midwest. He had a ready grin and seemed almost oafish. He moved, however, with the speed and strength of a panther. Calhoun, as always a good judge of a man's capabilities, reckoned him to be a formidable fighter.

For their part, they regarded the two third-year cadets with some suspicion, seeming as enthused as Jellico had been about their participation in the mission. As for Calhoun, he still hadn't quite gotten over Kemper's suggesting him. Part of him was suspicious enough to wonder whether this wasn't actually part of some revenge scheme that Kemper had cooked up. But Kemper had been completely candid with him back in Jellico's office.

"Look, Calhoun," Kemper had said to him. "Believe it or not, two years ago when all that happened might as well have been a lifetime ago as far as I'm concerned. The bottom line is this: Someone who's so skilled that he's capable of kicking my ass is the kind of man I want covering my ass. Understood?" Calhoun said that he did, and hoped that wasn't an exaggeration.

All of that had brought him to this moment in time, this place in the Ridge Mountains. He was on point, leading the way through a narrow pass, all too aware that this was a perfect place for some sort of ambush. Kemper was directly behind him, Shelby behind Kemper, and Langdon, Fitzhugh, and Travers bringing up the rear. Shelby had a tricorder out, and she was carefully surveying the surrounding area.

"Getting anything?" asked Kemper.

She shook her head. "More of the bounce-back. Still having trouble locking on to any sort of emanations. But if he has a facility around here, there should be some sort of energy readings I can pick up. Wait!"

They all froze.

"What is it?" whispered Calhoun, every muscle in his body tense.

"Getting life readings," she said. "Five. Maybe six."

"Weapons out," snapped Kemper, and the others immediately unholstered their phasers. "Shelby, keep talking. Tell me what you've got. Are they moving?"

"Position's fixed. I think maybe they know we're here. Wait . . . I'm getting more precise bioreadings. It's . . . That's odd."

"What?"

"It's mostly humans. Five humans and . . . one . . ."

Her voice trailed off.

"And one Xenexian, you were going to say?" asked Calhoun, trying not to grin.

Shelby muttered, "Sorry."

"Shiiiit," groaned Langdon, holstering his phaser.

"What happened? Are we still being tracked?" Travers seemed confused.

Langdon turned and cuffed Travers on the side of the head. "It was us, you idiot. She was picking up our life readings."

"I said I'm sorry," Shelby told him, getting a bit defensive. "The echo these walls are creating is just murderous."

Fitzhugh simply grunted, not looking particularly sympathetic.

" 'S okay, Shelby," said Kemper. "Could happen to anyone."

"Yeah, well, I wish it would have happened to someone other than me," Shelby grumbled as she fine-tuned some of the tricorder controls. "That way I wouldn't have to— Wait."

"Now what?" Langdon asked. He didn't sound enthused.

"Now I'm getting energy readings."

"It's probably from our phasers."

"It's not."

"It could be," Kemper agreed.

Shelby fired them a furious glare. "It's not the damned phasers, okay? It's something else. Some sort of energy signature, probably from the devices Bethom is using in his experiments."

"If the tribe's accounts are correct, and it's this area from which his animals are originating, then we should practically be on top of them," said Calhoun.

"Shelby, you're going to have to lock it down," Kemper told her.

"You think you can do better?" Shelby demanded. She shoved the tricorder at him. "Fine. I have an idea. You lock it down." She moved toward one of the rock walls of the canyon and said, "I'll just stand over here and tell you about everything you're doing wro—"

She vanished, letting out a sharp cry as she did so.

"What the hell . . . ?" Travers cried out.

"I think she found him," said Kemper dryly. "Holowall. Nice." He reached forward into the area through which Shelby had disappeared. Calhoun tried to get to her, but Kemper put up a hand. "Keep back," he said, feeling around, his arm having disappeared up to the shoulder into the illusion of a wall. Then he grunted, pulled, and Shelby stumbled back into the bright Xenexian daylight. "Good work, Shelby," Kemper said.

"He must have found some sort of cave entrance and then created this to cover it," said Travers. He ran his fingers through it. "Clever bastard."

"What's on the other side, Shelby?" asked Kemper. "Give us a preview." But she shook her head. "Too dark to tell. I could have been surrounded by God knows what in there, five inches from my face, and I wouldn't have seen it. Hold on." She brought her tricorder right up to the phantom wall and took readings through it.

"You sure you can trust what you're getting off there?" asked Langdon.

She nodded with conviction. "Definitely. There's nothing actually here to deflect the readings. Tricorder's getting no life readings from the other side."

"All right. Goggles, everyone."

Within moments they had all pulled day/night goggles from their packs and adjusted them over their eyes. "On line," said Kemper, as the goggle-phaser interface came on, providing them with targeting arrays over their eyes to facilitate phaser fire.

In two-by-two formation they moved through the wall, emerging into a darkened area on the other side. Calhoun and Kemper were the first two through, back to back, aiming their phasers all around to make certain that the corners of the room were vacant. Then came Shelby and Langdon, followed by Fitzhugh and Travers. Each of them made damned sure that there was no imminent threat. There was, in fact, not much of anything. Just a large, empty room.

"He carved this out of solid rock," murmured Calhoun. "Very impressive."

"I want to see less impressive stuff and more targets," replied Kemper.

Carefully they made their way across the room, encountering no obstacles. They got to a door at the far wall, which was locked. Calhoun aimed his phaser and fired off a shot. It cut through the lock easily and he pulled the door open.

Something huge and black-furred and extremely crazed-looking screeched directly into his face.

Calhoun slammed the door and said, "We may have a problem."

And then from the shadows overhead, dark beyond even the ability of their goggles to penetrate, creatures started dropping down. Creatures of all shapes, all sizes. They hadn't been there moments before, but Calhoun spotted trapdoors and hidden entrances snapping open, pouring out more of the nightmarish, malformed monstrosities that were charging them with the clear intent of ripping them to pieces.

"We may have a big problem," amended Calhoun.

ii.

Dr. Marius Bethom could not have been happier.

He sat in the innermost chamber of his lab and smiled at the spectacle that was occurring on the viewscreen. In his lap was a very small animal that looked like a cross between a gerbil and a tribble, round and furry but with a small head and little legs. He called it "Gribble," which was intended to be amusing. He idly stroked Gribble as he watched the proceedings.

Another creature was also watching, barely a foot away from it. It was much larger than Gribble. It was almost as large as Bethom himself. Its gaze was as fixed on the viewscreen as Bethom's was.

Five or six Starfleet personnel had opted to intrude into his place of residence. Without so much as an invitation! The idea! It was . . . it was monstrous, was what it was. Bethom's sensibilities were sorely offended at the trespass.

Fortunately he had a remedy for such an offense, a remedy that he had just unleashed.

For some reason his mind spiraled back to his childhood, when his mother would read to him from a centuries-old writer named A. A. Milne, who liked to write about curiously mutated stuffed toys. Indeed, it had been those early readings that had first piqued Bethom's interest in such things as animals that were in some way beyond what nature had intended. And in those books, the mutated pig toy was convinced that he had an uncle named "Trespassers Will," which was undoubtedly short for "Trespassers William," all because of a sign erected nearby his domicile that bore that inscription. The humor of the moment was aimed purely at adults, of course, for children would not comprehend that the sign had obviously once said "Trespassers will be prosecuted" or perhaps simply "shot," but with part of the sign having fallen away in disrepair, the brainless toy had drawn a false conclusion.

Bethom decided that, once the Federation intruders had been disposed of, he would put up a sign that read "Trespassers Will" in the main entrance. It would amuse him, and perhaps even cause a mild chuckle for further intruders before they, likewise, were annihilated.

The good doctor was tall and thin, with black hair smoothed back into a widow's peak. His skin was sallow, which was not all that surprising considering that he'd spent much of the past several years remaining inside whenever possible. His eyes were set wide apart, his nose was large but not hideously so. When he was nervous, his hands tended to move in a fluttery manner. He was not nervous now, however. One of his hands was calmly petting Gribble, and with the other he reached out and ruffled the fur of the rather large creature nearby. It was one of which he had become particularly fond, and it appeared to show great potential for future endeavors. He ran his fingers affectionately through the beast's fur as he whispered, "Now watch. Watch your brothers and sisters have fun."

He watched the flashes of phaser fire, which he had known would come. He saw the ricochets off the sleek metal walls, heard the howls of pain. It had been so predictable. He knew perfectly well that if Starfleet sent in someone, they'd be armed with their precious directed-energy weapons. Not a problem to thwart at all, if one simply put a little brainpower to it. His animals had been specially bred to be highly resistant to any setting short of full demolecularization. The Starfleeters would naturally begin with something a little less lethal, not realizing just how dire their straits were. They would quickly discover that their assailants wouldn't be stopped by anything as routine as a stun setting. But any stray shots would bounce off the specially treated wall. Which meant that if the Starfleeters kicked the setting up to a lethal level but missed their targets—which, in this darkened space, would certainly be a likelihood—then they'd be dodging their own phaser shots. Chances were they wouldn't be able to dodge them for long. Yes, some of the animals would likely be killed, but Bethom could always make more animals.

Oh, but certainly their clever Starfleet devices had built-in targeting systems. He smiled thinly as he looked at the blinking lights on his console. The lights that informed him that the scrambling system was nicely on line, thoroughly frustrating any devices they might have with them that facilitated targeting.

He heard the shouts and cries, and laughed. A voice was shouting "Cease fire! We're hitting ourselves!" and another cried out, "They're everywhere!" and yet another called, "Like hell I'll cease fire!" More phaser blasts then, more shouts, more cries. Bethom laughed louder. The creature next to him looked at him in curiosity. "Don't mind me, my friend," Bethom told him. "I'm simply having a very, very good day."

There was always the chance they might send more. Certainly when these didn't report back, there would be that inclination. But more teams would meet the same fate. And for that matter, Bethom had back-ups, other places he could hide out. They would never catch him, and he would be able to continue his work unharassed.

Then Bethom heard a shriek. A shriek of pain, of fear, of pure terror, and a sudden death rattle. It was not, however, from a human throat. It was from one of his animals.

This piqued Bethom's curiosity. Was it possible that one of the Starfleeters had gotten lucky? Managed to pick off one of his animals?

But that was when Bethom realized the weapons fire had stopped. The animal screaming, however, was continuing. High-pitched, angry, wounded, frightened. And there was another death rattle, and some sort of thick "splutch" sounds, as if someone was halving watermelons, and then another sound, a snarl. But it wasn't one of the animals. Bethom was sure of that. It was a snarl from a human throat, except it sounded even more animalistic than some of the animals.

"What the hell is going on down there?" he wondered, even as the sounds of combat continued.

And then they stopped. Just like that, there was nothing.

Obviously the fighting was over. Yet Bethom would have thought that, once the initial battle was completed, he would hear more sounds. The sounds of flesh being rent, of bones being snapped up. Of tearing and chewing and slurping as the creatures dined upon the carcasses of their prey. Obviously it had to go in that direction. These were animals, after all. There were just some things that happened naturally.

Yet there was no noise at all. Just a deadly silence.

He reached forward to his control panel and brought up the lights. He had to see what was transpiring down in a room that should have been running red with human blood.

There was plenty of blood, all right. But for the most part, it wasn't human.

Most of the humans were either unconscious or barely conscious. But they were most definitely alive, because even from this distance Bethom could see that there were no mortal wounds on any of them. Some had been struck by stray phaser blasts, others had been physically roughed up by the animals. None of them were dead, though.

And there was one who was very, very active.

He was crouched over the fallen form of one of the Starfleeters, who appeared to be a female. She was waving him off, clearly trying to convey that she was all right. Slowly he stood then, flexing his arms. His clothes were torn and he was covered with blood, but Bethom had the sick feeling that almost none of it was his own.

He was clutching something in his right hand. It was a sword, the blade slick with blood.

And his creatures . . . his beautiful creations . . . they were everywhere, and none of them in one piece. Arms, legs, torsos, cut apart, brutalized.

The man was standing in profile, but Bethom could still make out that his mouth was curled back in a snarl. His hair was hanging all about his face, and it likewise was thick with blood. He had a beard, and there seemed to be some sort of throbbing red line down the side of his face that was pulsing steadily. He looked even less human than a number of the animals that lay scattered about the room.

He'd slaughtered them. Slaughtered them all. He had hauled out a sword (and what the hell was he doing carrying a sword) and had simply waded into the midst of the attack wave and he'd just . . . just cut them all to pieces.

Didn't the fool have any comprehension of what he'd done? He was the one who was in the wrong here. He was the villain of the piece, and yet he probably considered himself some sort of brave hero, fighting the forces of darkness and chopping them to bits all in the name of the glorious Federation.

"Butcher," he breathed, and then he shouted, *"Butcher!"*

Incredibly, the man on the screen suddenly turned and stared straight out of the monitor, as if he'd heard the doctor's defiant howl. *"Bethom!"* he snarled. "I know you're watching! I'm coming for you, you bastard!"

One of the men in the room shouted after him, saying something that sounded like "Calhoun." But this "Calhoun" ignored it. Instead he headed out the nearest door, swinging his sword in anticipation like the reaper with his scythe.

Bethom wasn't concerned at first. The place was like a labyrinth. Calhoun would be searching forever and still would never find the proper route to Bethom's location.

Except as he switched to views from other cameras, he was horrified to see that Calhoun was moving with swiftness and certainty. Any time he came to a junction which could potentially have sent him off in another direction, he paused a moment and then actually seemed to be sniffing the air. Then he would keep on going, heading invariably and inevitably in Bethom's direction.

"Are you afraid, Bethom?" Calhoun bellowed as he made his way through the corridors. "Afraid to fight me man-to-man? Afraid to face me without hiding behind these things you've created? At least they took me on! At least they attacked! You sent them to their deaths and didn't give a damn about it."

"They weren't supposed to die," snarled Bethom. "You were. And you will."

Calhoun couldn't hear him, or at least Bethom didn't *think* he could hear him. Then again, it seemed with this madman that anything was possible. He kept on coming, right turn, then another right, then left, and actually seemed to pick up speed.

Bethom stood quickly, sliding Gribble in his pocket to keep him safe, and collided squarely with the creature who was next to him, watching the monitor raptly. He looked down at the creature and said, "This is it. This is your moment of glory. He's heading here, but I'm going to be gone by the time he arrives. Instead he's going to find you waiting for him. Kill him. Or, failing that, buy me enough time to get away."

The creature, crouching low to the floor, stared up at Bethom. There was clear skepticism in his eyes. He looked back to the monitor, back to Bethom, and then determinedly shook his head.

"No?" Bethom could scarcely breathe. "You're telling *me* no? *Me?* How dare you!"

He kicked out at the creature, the blow taking the creature solidly in the shoulder and knocking him over. He wasn't at all concerned that the monster might turn on him. He had enough safeguards built into the creature's psyche to insure that such a happenstance could never occur. "You will do as I say!" he shouted, and kicked the creature once more while it was down. Then he drew in a few deep breaths to calm himself, and snapped, "Get up!" He pointed at the far door. "He'll come in through there! Get ready! Keep him busy so that I'll have enough time to slip out through there."

The creature lumbered toward the door. Bethom was certain it had a far better shot against this Calhoun than any of his other creations. For starters, it was more massive. And second, his experiments with the thing's intellect had succeeded beyond what he could have hoped for. It wasn't remotely as smart as a human yet, but it would be able to match Calhoun barbarian tactic for barbarian tactic.

The creature was standing directly in front of the door that Calhoun would inevitably have to enter, since it was the only way in or out. Bethom angrily chided himself for the oversight, but really, how could he possibly have foreseen this?

Bethom readied himself at the far end of the room. He risked a glance over at the monitor, saw that Calhoun was almost there. This would work. He was certain it would work. It had to work.

The door slid open and there was Calhoun, sword in hand, looking even more fearsome in person than he had on the screen.

The great furred creature was waiting for him.

Calhoun swung his sword down in a stroke that would have cleft the beast from sternum to crotch had it landed. But the creature was as agile as Bethom could have hoped for. He lunged to one side, avoiding the sweep of the sword, and grabbed Calhoun roughly with one hand from behind and another hand on Calhoun's sword arm. Calhoun twisted around, trying to get at him with his free hand, but the creature was too strong and it had happened too quickly.

I'm not going to have to escape after all! He's going to kill him! Bethom thought with joy.

And then Bethom saw a glint of grim satisfaction in the creature's eye, right before it heaved Calhoun straight at Bethom himself.

Bethom gave an alarmed yelp and tried to get out of the way, but it did no good. Calhoun crashed into him and they both tumbled to the floor in a tangle of arms and legs. Bethom tried to extricate himself, to go for the sword that Calhoun had in his hand. No chance. In an instant Calhoun was atop Bethom, and he had the sword whipped around and pointed right at Bethom's throat.

"Dr. Bethom, I presume," he grated.

"Get him!" Bethom shouted to the crouching creature nearby. *"Kill him,* you great furry oaf!"

But the animal to whom he was shouting was busy picking small bugs out of his fur. He paused in his idle pursuit to exchange looks with Calhoun.

"Nice watchdog you got there," Calhoun said to the cowering Bethom, who now had his hands up in the universal sign of surrender.

And then very slowly . . . very deliberately . . . the "watchdog" said, "Thank . . . you . . ."

Both men froze and stared at him. He tilted his head and although he didn't—couldn't—smile, there was still a faint merriment in his eyes.

"It talks." Calhoun looked at Bethom. "It talks?"

"I . . . I was working toward it . . . but I . . . I didn't think . . . the chemical balances, I didn't think I'd gotten them right, I . . ."

"You . . . did . . ." said the furry creature, again taking excessive time between each word, as if it took every bit of focus and concentration he had to produce the sounds.

"But . . . but why haven't you said anything until now?"

"Be . . . cause . . . I . . . don't . . . like . . . you . . ."

"Just what I've always wanted to meet," said Calhoun, as he hauled the stunned Bethom to his feet. "A genetic monstrosity with good taste."

In one of the most bizarrely self-contradictory things that either man had ever seen, the creature bowed slightly and said, "Now . . . you . . . have."

Bethom watched his creation and, even though the thing had betrayed him to his enemies, he nevertheless felt a brief swell of pride.

"Damn, I'm good," he said.

Chapter Eleven

Now

"You might as well stand in front of me. I can smell you from here."

M'Ress had been holding back, reluctant to approach the brig. The security guards standing on either side gave no indication to Janos that she was anywhere nearby, but his pronouncement reminded her that his senses were easily just as sharp as hers, if not more so.

But Janos's wryly sarcastic voice floated to her and she knew there was no point in being paralyzed by indecision. "Am I that pungent?" she asked.

"I think I might have preferred the term 'piquant,' but yes, I suppose you are. But that's not necessarily a bad thing. You can come here. It's okay. I won't bite."

She came around the corner and stood in front of the brig. She gasped when she saw him there, shackled and with the muzzle on him.

"Quite an ensemble, isn't it," said Janos. "I hate it. It clashes with absolutely everything I own."

"Oh, Janos," she moaned. "Oh, look what they've done to you. I'm . . . I'm going to go talk to somebody, I . . ."

"No, M'Ress . . . it's all right," he assured her, and she thought he was forcing himself to keep his voice steady. "No, I'd . . . rather they did this. After what happened earlier, they can't take any chances. I wouldn't want them to. I . . . well, it seems I don't know my own strength. And by the way, it was extremely brave of you to search me out the way you did. You risked a great deal. I could have . . ." He hesitated, then shook his head. "I don't like to think about it. The possibilities, the . . ."

"You aren't yourself, Janos."

"Well, that's what it comes down to now, doesn't it," he said bitterly. "I'm not exactly sure who or what I am anymore. 'Greetings, everyone, this is Ensign Janos. Tonight he'll be a dashing, erudite man-about-town . . . unless, of course, a bizarre berserker rage seizes him and he rampages around the ship. You just never know *what* that wacky Janos is going to do next.' "

"This is all my fault," she said. "All my fault."

The two security guards glanced at each other, looking increasingly uncomfortable. In annoyance, M'Ress said, "If you don't like what you're hearing, feel free to leave."

"We can't exactly desert our posts, Lieutenant."

"It won't be deserting. Just . . . go a little ways down the hall or something. I mean, come on. You know I'm not going to let him out. He tried to kill me last time. Anyway, I don't know the security codes that have the cuffs in place."

The guards exchanged another look, then one of them said grimly, "We'll be right around the corner. He escapes, Lieutenant, and it'll be your ass in a sling."

"He escapes, and there won't be enough *left* of my ass to put in a sling," she retorted.

They moved off and M'Ress approached the barrier, but didn't get too near. Janos noticed it. "You're keeping your distance," he said. "That's probably wise."

"Oh, Janos . . . this is all—"

"Your fault, yes, so you said. The thing is, M'Ress, it doesn't matter how many times you say it. That doesn't make it true."

"It doesn't have to make it true. It *is* true. Everything that happened, happened because of me. The whole business with Gleau . . . I had so many opportunities to just . . . just let it go. Not make an issue of it. If I'd taken any of them, it wouldn't have spiraled out of control and you wouldn't be here. You went after Gleau because of me, Janos, and there's really no denying that, is there?"

"No," he sighed. "No, there's not. But here's the thing, M'Ress. Sooner or later, I would have gone after somebody. If not Gleau, then someone else."

Clearly she didn't comprehend. "Wh . . . what are you talking about? What do you mean?"

"I mean, my dear . . . that no one is ever what they seem . . . sometimes not even to themselves."

"I still don't understand."

"That is because I haven't explained it to you."

"Are you going to?"

Sadly he shook his head. "I'm afraid not. It's a long and tortured story and rather personal."

"Personal? Janos, we were lovers. It doesn't *get* more personal than that."

"Of course it does," he replied. "Lovers betray each other all the time. It's quite common. But I betrayed myself. That's far more rare. . . ."

"Janos . . ."

And his voice was suddenly hard-edged, laced with impatience. "M'Ress . . . what did you come here for? Absolution? Forgiveness? You want me to find the right words to make you feel all better? I'm sorry, I don't have them. Only you can make you feel better about yourself, about Gleau, about all of it. I can't do it, and I think it would probably be better if you didn't come by to see me again. I'd just as soon you not watch me trussed up like a prize steer in any event. It's humiliating, and I've tried to keep a stiff upper lip about it, but there's only so much even I can withstand. So please run along now."

"But I don't . . ."

"Leave!" The word erupted from his throat, and his eyes burned with self-loathing and anger.

And M'Ress turned quickly and sprinted down the hallway, not looking back.

Then

Shelby had never felt as lucky to be alive as she did at that moment, heading out of Bethom's hidden lair with the entire party intact and only mild bumps and bruises to show for it.

She was still unclear as to exactly what had happened. Her reasoning mind told her it was impossible that Calhoun had yanked out his sword from the sheath he'd been carrying it in and carved up everything that was attacking them. It made no rational sense. No one should have been able to withstand such an assault. Yet here he was, battered but unbowed, his sword once more safely stowed in its scabbard, which was in turn strapped across his back. She'd originally thought it ridiculous to bring something so primitive along. Now she was giving serious consideration to taking swordsmanship lessons.

That sword. That same sword that had been used by someone whose name Calhoun never told her. The one that had sliced open his face and nearly killed him. Now it was his, and he was more formidable at dealing death with it than anyone she had ever seen.

She had lain there in the darkness, struggling to get up, and she'd heard the shrieking and howling as the creatures descended from all directions. At that moment she'd been positive she was going to die, even as she sought for her fallen phaser in the darkness. Then she realized that every one of the vicious monsters of all shapes and sizes was heading for Calhoun. From a purely instinctual point of view, it must have made sense. They had determined that he was the most formidable there, and so sought to take him down en masse while they were at their strongest. It had been a fairly good plan, actually.

It just hadn't worked. Instead the result had been an entire room filled with dead animals, and several battered but breathing Starfleet officers.

Calhoun had been taciturn when he'd emerged with Bethom, gripping him tightly by the back of the neck like a cat worrying a mouse. Bethom had been surprisingly meek. Pathetically so, in fact. He kept begging that he not be hurt, that he was simply a scientist who was endeavoring to carve his own way into the annals of research, and they didn't understand, nobody understood. "Nobody ever does," Kemper had said unsympathetically.

What had not been expected was the large, white-furred creature that had emerged along with Calhoun. Shelby and the others had been nervous when they got a load of the thing's great claws and vicious-looking teeth. But then the damned thing spoke to them, assuring them in halting, one-syllable words that he would do them no harm. Having no idea what to make of it, they went along with the insanity of the situation and had the thing tail along.

Kemper and the others had been impressed by Calhoun's accomplishments. No one there had any illusions: The third-year cadet had saved the lot of them. Everything had gone wrong and Calhoun, through determination and sheer brute force, had pulled off the mission. Now, as they made their way back the way they'd come, Kemper and the more experienced officers were filled with questions. Calhoun brushed them all off casually. They attributed it to misplaced modesty.

Shelby didn't think it was that at all, particularly when she saw the briefly pained expression in Calhoun's eyes that he deftly covered over when they kept talking about what a total lunatic he was in combat.

Calhoun had spent three years trying to measure up to the concept of an officer and a gentleman as was taught to him at Starfleet Academy. And he knew that an officer and a gentleman didn't turn into a berserker, even when it was in a situation where lives were at stake. The fact that Calhoun had saved all their lives was secondary to him. He was concerned about the *way* he had done so, and Shelby suspected that in Calhoun's own judgment, he had come up short of his own expectations.

She didn't know if she was right, nor did she know if he'd admit to it if confronted about it. So she wisely just kept her mouth closed.

The Ridge Mountain tribe had been so helpful in locating the renegade scientist for the men of the Federation that Kemper had personally assured them they would return to the tribe upon Bethom's capture so they could see for themselves that the source of their terror was ended. Langdon wasn't sanguine over the prospect, concerned that the tribe would take justice and/or vengeance into their own hands. Calhoun, however, swore that would not be the case. "I know these people," he said. "Their strictures against violence are absolute. Despite the fact that he was a menace to them, they would just as soon take one of their own lives as kill him. To them, the sanctity of life is absolute. It doesn't matter whose life it is."

"Nice philosophy," Langdon said skeptically. Nevertheless, he withdrew his objection, and in less than a day, the ragtag group was trooping into the tribe's encampment with a frustrated Bethom in tow.

As pleased as the tribespeople were to see Bethom, it was the white-furred beast that really caused a stir. Especially when he opened his mouth and spoke in his slow, halting fashion.

Shelby in particular found him fascinating, and talked with Bethom at length about it. This rather annoyed Calhoun, what with Bethom being their prisoner and all. "Look, Mac," Shelby had replied, "he may have broken laws. He may have tried to kill us. But that doesn't make Bethom any less of a genius, or this creature of his any less an accomplishment."

"And what exactly has he accomplished?" asked Calhoun.

The tribe had requested—insisted, actually—that the Starfleet group stay for a feast. This didn't serve as too much of a problem. The long-range shuttle in which they'd arrived was just over the next ridge and thus not too much more of a journey. Kemper and the others were seated closer to the large pit that had been dug where fresh meat was roasting. The women seemed determined to show them a good time, and Kemper, Langdon, Fitzhugh, and Travers were not inclined to deny them the opportunity. Calhoun and Shelby sat farther away from the fire.

"What has he accomplished?" replied Shelby, surprised that she had to spell it out. "He's created a creature through genetic manipulation that has the capacity for intelligence on a par with a human's."

"He couldn't have aimed higher?"

She slapped at his upper arm in response to the needling. "Seriously, Mac," she continued as Calhoun rubbed his arm and mock-pouted. "There's never been a creature like this before." The creature at that moment was sitting close to the fire, staring at it in wonder. The firelight danced in his small, pink eyes.

"What exactly did he make it out of?"

"Several different species of creatures," she said. "A couple drawn from Earth, one from the planet Neural, one from Rigel, a bit of Caitian. He picked the best, the ones with the most capacity for learning. As near as I can tell, he succeeded. The question is, what happens to him now?"

Calhoun, however, wasn't listening to her. He heard a commotion at the far side of the encampment and was immediately on his feet, trying to anticipate what sort of trouble might be coming.

"Mac? Mac, what is it?" she demanded.

She saw him stiffen as several new arrivals entered the encampment. Others who were watching stepped back, forming a small semicircle as the newcomers swaggered in. They were dressed in what amounted to colorful rags. Calhoun just stood there, his body poised. To Shelby, it looked like he was ready to pounce on them.

The foremost of them sauntered forward. He had a sword in his belt, his hand resting comfortably on the pommel. His black hair was long and straggly, his beard was thick as night. He was a head and a half taller than Calhoun, and considerably wider in addition.

"So. It's true," he said, scrutinizing Calhoun as if he were a long lost brother . . . or perhaps an escaped criminal. "M'k'n'zy of Calhoun has deigned to return to us."

"Hello, C'n'daz," said Calhoun. He glanced at the clearly confused Shelby. "Elizabeth Paula Shelby of Starfleet . . . this is C'n'daz, one of my lieutenants from the days of the revolution. And this is . . ." Then he stopped and said, "On further consideration, I hardly think I'd call it 'deigning.' For that matter, what are you doing here? When we were fighting the Danteri, you never hesitated to express your total disdain for these people," and he indicated the tribesmen all around, who were watching with curiosity. "Yet now you come among them?"

"I have to come here," replied C'n'daz. "I have to come here because you're far too busy to come back to Calhoun and spend time with us."

"Would I be welcome?" Calhoun asked.

"Welcome?" He laughed derisively, the others joining in, as if the very suggestion was completely preposterous. *"Welcome!* My brethren," and he turned to what Shelby now assumed to be other members of the Calhoun community and continued, "The great and esteemed M'k'n'zy of Calhoun wonders if he would be welcome in our small community. Have you ever heard of such a nonsensical notion? From where could he possibly have gotten such an idea."

"It doesn't matter," said Calhoun. "If you say it would be so, then—"

But C'n'daz hadn't finished. "Why wouldn't we welcome the man who brought us to triumph over our enemies . . . and then abandoned us in our time of need."

"Abandoned you?" Calhoun was bristling. "What are you talking about? You didn't need me."

"That was your judgment to make, was it?"

"Yes! Who else's?"

Kemper and the others were slowly approaching, which was possibly the only thing that could make matters worse. "Problem here, Calhoun?"

"No. No problem," Calhoun said rigidly. "Just some old friends . . . who apparently don't know how to let go."

"We didn't exactly have the chance to let go, did we?" snapped C'n'daz. "You left out of pure selfishness."

"Mackenzie Calhoun may be many things," said Shelby defiantly, "but he's not selfish."

This caused a roar of disbelieving laughter from the Xenexians. " 'Mackenzie'? Is that what you're calling yourself now? You changed your name?" C'n'daz was incredulous. "You're that ashamed of us, of your heritage, that you leave your very name behind?"

"I don't have to explain myself to you," Calhoun told him.

"Oh, yes, you do," C'n'daz shot back. His voice cracked briefly, but he caught himself and said with growing intensity, "You walked out on us!"

"You didn't need me! You needed politicians and people to set up governments. That was never going to be me."

"That wasn't your decision to make."

"It's my life, dammit!" said Calhoun.

"I pledged my soul to follow you! We all did!" and there were nods from the men with him. "And you spat on that pledge by abandoning us! All because you didn't have the courage to stay with us and continue to lead us. . . ."

"Courage! You question my courage!"

"Difficult to question something you don't have," said C'n'daz defiantly.

Calhoun started forward, his fingers curled into fists, his scar burning bright red. And Shelby, feeling as if she was risking her life doing so, nevertheless got between them, throwing her arms out to either side to block him. The thought that she actually could prevent him from advancing was ridiculous, but she had to intervene no matter what the cost. "You can't do this," she told him.

"Out of the way, Elizabeth," he warned.

She shook her head. "You can't be doing things like this. You're a year away from graduation, and you have to start thinking like a damn Starfleet officer. Not a thug or a street brawler or a gang member. You have to exercise judgment."

"Eppy . . ."

But she kept right on talking. "You're going to encounter other beings all the time who try to bait you into fights. Who will try to get you to fly off the handle so you can make a mistake that's going to serve their ends. You're going to have to learn to swallow your pride and not get pulled into meaningless battles, because sooner or later the lives of an entire crew are going to depend on you being able to keep your temper in check. Not everything can be settled through force of arms. You have to be able to walk away without feeling like your manhood is on the line every single time. Don't you see that?"

She thought he was going to push right past her. Just toss her aside so that he could get at his defiant fellow Xenexian. But then, slowly, the blistering red of the scar began to subside, like a visual thermometer measuring his mood. "Fine," he said at last, and there was still a cold burning in his eyes, but he had lowered his fists. "Fine."

" 'Fine'?" C'n'daz repeated mockingly. "That's it? The great M'k'n'zy is told what to do by a woman, and he simply nods his head and acquiesces? Not only are you no longer Xenexian, you're barely even a man."

"It's not going to work, C'n'daz," Calhoun said. His voice was hollow. It sounded to Shelby as if he were a spirit whispering from a haunted house. "I'm sorry you feel I hurt you. But I had to do what was right for m—"

And C'n'daz pointed right at Calhoun's chest and snarled, "I issue a challenge. A blood challenge. Before these witnesses, before the eyes of all present, let it be recorded that a blood challenge has been issued. Do you accept?"

Shelby wasn't certain exactly what was going on, but she knew it wasn't good. This "blood challenge" was obviously some sort of ultimate requirement of Xenexian manhood. It was not something, she suspected, that was issued lightly, nor was it lightly ignored. Calhoun was trembling with suppressed rage, and he took a step toward C'n'daz, who was waiting for him. Shelby kept waiting for Kemper or one of the others to say something, but they were silent. Obviously they wanted to see Calhoun take the man on and likely beat him to a pulp. They'd probably find it entertaining. *Men,* Shelby snarled to herself.

Out loud, she said warningly, "Calhoun. This isn't the way."

C'n'daz didn't even afford her a glance. He simply repeated, slowly and deliberately, "Do you accept?"

Calhoun's mouth twisted as he formed the word. "No."

There was an audible gasp, not only from C'n'daz's followers, but even from the tribes people. Considering they were pacifists, this challenge thing must be fairly major to get such a reaction even from them.

And then C'n'daz turned toward Shelby, and stared at her with as much contempt as anyone had ever displayed. "You," he said icily, "have destroyed him. I pity him . . . but I despise you."

"Thanks for sharing that," replied Shelby. "I don't know how I'm going to sleep at night, knowing you despise me."

And then C'n'daz suddenly yanked out a knife from his belt, and he threw it at Calhoun's feet. Calhoun didn't move a muscle as the blade thudded to the ground just short of his toes.

"The challenge remains. And you will answer it, or be forever disgraced," announced C'n'daz. Then he and his associates turned away and headed out. Moments later they had departed the camp, and there was dead silence for a long while. Then, slowly, people went back about their business, but the celebration was rather muted and people kept glancing every so often in Calhoun's direction. Calhoun, for his part, sat as far away from the campfire as possible now, just staring off into space.

Shelby approached him at one point and knelt down to face him. "I was proud of you back there," she told him. "You did the right thing. The Starfleet thing. You—"

"Eppy," he interrupted her, not even looking at her. "I would really appreciate it . . . if you left me alone right now."

And a veil of silence descended upon him that was practically palpable. Her heart ached for him and she wanted nothing else but to reach out and comfort him, hold him tightly, make him feel better.

Instead, wisely, she left him alone in the darkness beyond the fire.

Chapter Twelve

Now

"The *Daystrom* Institute?"

Calhoun could scarcely believe it as, on the monitor, Vice-Admiral Nechayev nodded in confirmation. "That's right," she affirmed. "Bethom is now working at the Daystrom Institute."

He was in his ready room, feeling these days as if he practically lived in the place. He spent so much time in the ready room that he was concerned he might never actually be ready. "The Daystrom Institute," he echoed.

"I take it you're familiar with it."

"Of course I am, ma'am," said Calhoun. "It's just . . . I would have thought Bethom was still in custody."

"In a sense, he is," Nechayev said. "Several years ago, he was paroled to the custody of the institute. They felt very strongly that his mind and ideas were salvageable and could be redirected into more constructive pursuits than—"

"Than illegal genetics and murder?"

"I wouldn't have put it quite that bluntly. Then again, I'm not you."

"These days," Calhoun told her, "I'm not even sure *I'm* me."

"Still, blunt or not, that is indeed a fair assessment. Rest assured, Mackenzie, he remains under the closest scrutiny."

"Just how close would that be?"

"He's monitored around the clock, and he has an implant that physically prevents him from leaving the Daystrom facility where he's currently in residence."

"And that would be?"

She paused. "That information is confidential, Mackenzie. Dr. Bethom is a very special case. There are those who would seek to take advantage of his rather singular talents. Therefore his current whereabouts are a closely guarded secret, and cannot be entrusted to just anyone."

"I understand," said Calhoun. "So his current whereabouts would be?"

"Alpha Sigma IX. Oh. Drat," she said, her voice laced with sarcasm. "You tricked it out of me. Curse you, Mackenzie Calhoun, and your crafty techniques of interrogation. I remain helpless against your genius-level cunning."

"As do I against your rapier wit."

She smiled at that. "Come on, Calhoun. When are you going to tire of this captaincy phase of your life and return to the activities that give true meaning to your wretched existence?"

"Namely working for you."

"Namely, yes."

"Carrying out covert missions and such."

"I have no idea what you're talking about," she deadpanned.

"No, of course you don't."

"Come on now, Mackenzie." She studied him in that way she had, as if she were mentally breaking him down molecule by molecule and examining each one before tossing it aside and moving on to the next. "With all respect to a great breed of men . . . there are many who are Starfleet captains. But how many are there who could do the things that you did for me?"

"Careful, Vice-Admiral," cautioned Calhoun. "If someone should be eavesdropping, they might totally misinterpret that sentiment."

"Now, wouldn't that be a pleasant change of pace," she said, grinning. Then the grin faded. "Calhoun . . . be careful. The Daystrom Institute is a highly connected organization and facility. They've many powerful friends in the Federation, and gunboat diplomacy isn't going to get it done with them. I know this pertains to Janos . . ."

"You know that?" asked Calhoun.

"Of course I do, Mackenzie. You can't seriously think I'm not aware of everything major that's going on in Starfleet. Nor do I have to be a genius to know what you're thinking. I've crawled around inside that skull of yours more than anyone except your lovely wife. As a superior officer—a vastly superior officer—I'm telling you, be careful. As a friend, I'm telling you: Be very careful."

"I will, ma'am."

"If you need a friend, contact me immediately. I may or may not help you depending upon my needs at that moment and the overall security of the Federation."

"That's very comforting, ma'am."

"Yes. It is. Nechayev out."

He stared at the screen for a long moment after she'd blinked out, and then said, "Morgan."

Her face immediately appeared on the computer screen where Nechayev's had been seconds before. "That's so much friendlier than 'computer,' " she noted.

"Good. I'm glad you approve. I need you to raise the Daystrom Institute on Alpha Sigma IX."

"The entire institute or any particular individual?"

"Dr. Marius Bethom."

"Friend of yours?"

"He tried to kill me once."

"Haven't most of your friends?"

He considered that. "A few," he admitted. "But then, I have a broad definition of friends. Do it, would you please, Morgan?"

"Aye, Captain," she said, and her face vanished.

At that moment, the chime rang. "Come," called Calhoun.

The door slid open and Shelby entered, glancing around.

"Yes, Commander, what can I do for . . ." He smiled broadly. "Sorry. Old habit."

"Very old. So what, are you living here now? Burgy says you hardly show your face on the bridge anymore."

"Things have been a bit hectic, that's all. Dealing with this entire Janos mess. Plus I'm not thrilled going out there and seeing Danter on the viewscreen. Brings back a lot of unfortunate memories."

"So leave," she said, sounding eminently practical about it. "You have other assignments to deal with."

"Yes. There's a civil uprising on Qandis that's requested Si Cwan's aid in settling matters. And over on Ultis, the last survivor of an alien world has landed and is currently using his superior powers to try and rule the planet. So that should be exciting."

"And yet you're still here."

"And yet I am," he agreed.

"Which begs the question . . ."

"Why? Because I can't get enough of my wife, that's why. Here," and he patted the top of the desk. "Let's do it right here, right now. Right on top of this desk."

"Are you serious?"

"Never been more so."

She stared at him. "You *are* serious. My God, Mac . . . what if somebody walked in?"

"Let them. They can be dazzled by our strategies."

"Our what?"

He was busy reaching to a drawer under his desk, and he pulled out a chess set and placed it atop the desk. "Activate," he said, and a small holographic display of pieces appeared.

"Oh," she said. "You wanted to play chess."

He raised an eyebrow. "Well, sure. Why? What else could I have been referring to?"

"Well, off the top of my head . . . sex?"

He snorted. "You women. That's all you ever think about."

At that moment, Morgan's image appeared on the screen once more. "Captain, I placed your call to . . . oh. Hello, Captain Shelby. You're looking well."

"Uhm . . . thank you, Morgan," said Shelby, appearing extremely disconcerted. "I'm . . . sorry about your, uh . . . your loss . . ."

"You mean my body? Not that big a deal. I wasn't doing much of anything with it anyway."

"That's very, uhm . . . philosophical," she said, and looked in desperation to Calhoun.

He suppressed a smile as he said, "Go ahead, Morgan. You were saying?"

"I placed your call to Alpha Sigma IX."

"That was fast."

"You'd be amazed how much more efficient such activities can be when you can interface directly with the subspace switching station. Unfortunately, I'm afraid I was unable to get through."

"Alpha Sigma IX?" Shelby's face was a question.

"The Daystrom Institute. Dr. Marius Bethom," said Morgan.

As Shelby reacted with surprise upon hearing the name, Calhoun commented, "Thank you for sharing that, Morgan."

"Oh. Was it a secret?"

"Not anymore."

"Very well, then," she said. If she recognized his tone as sarcastic, she chose to ignore it. "In any case, Dr. Bethom was quite explicit that he had no desire to communicate with you until a particular change in climate at an indeterminate point in the future."

"Let me guess: When Hell freezes over."

"That was it!" Morgan sounded surprised.

"I was afraid that might be the case. All right, Morgan. Thank you for trying."

"Not a problem." Her face promptly blinked out.

"Dr. Bethom," Shelby looked surprised. "Mac, we already had this discussion."

"He might be able to help," said Calhoun. "After all, he *did* create Janos."

"He's dangerously unstable, Mac."

"Who, Janos or Bethom?"

"At this point, I'd say both. And by the way, what the hell is an unstable geneticist like Bethom doing at the Daystrom Institute?"

"They've taken responsibility for him."

"Why?"

"Good question," said Calhoun. "I'm seriously thinking of going and finding out. You'd be amazed how much more willing someone is to respond to you when you're standing two feet away and threatening to break his face."

"You can't go around breaking people's faces."

"When did I say I was going to do that? I simply said I'd threaten to do it. Doesn't mean I will."

"That," she said, "is a deftly clever distinction. I suggest you brush up on it."

"Why?"

"Because Starfleet is the group that chose to parole Dr. Bethom to the Daystrom Institute. And if you go stomping in there in standard bull-in-china-shop form, you'll have plenty of time to explain your rationale to a court martial board of inquiry."

"It won't be the first time."

"It may be the last," she countered. "And if that happened, what would you do then?"

"Don't worry about me," he said. "I have prospects. Good ones."

"Oh, really," said Shelby as she made an opening gambit move on the chess set. "Such as?"

"A job that would allow me to ignore all the rules and beat people up as needed."

She considered that as she awaited his move. "That's more or less what you're doing now, actually."

And he realized she was right.

Then

i.

Jellico and Nechayev stared at the white-furred creature that was exploring every inch of Jellico's office. "Remarkable," said Jellico as he watched it at its work. "I've never seen anything like it."

"Or ever will again, is my guess," said Shelby. She, along with Calhoun and Kemper, was likewise watching the bizarre animal. She smoothed the front of her shirt. It felt good to be back in uniform, and even better to be safely back within the confines of Starfleet Academy.

"Is he the last of Bethom's experiments?"

"As near as we were able to determine," said Kemper. "We sent a cleanup crew back in after we brought Bethom into custody. They weren't able to dig up anything else. On the other hand, he kept copious notes. So if anyone were inclined to try and replicate his work . . ." When he saw the look from Jellico and Nechayev, he shrugged and added, "I was just pointing it out, not advocating it."

"Thank you for clarifying that," Jellico said icily. Then, his face reflecting a bit more concern, he looked at Shelby and Calhoun. "You two are all right? No major problems?"

"Fairly routine stuff, actually," said Calhoun. To Shelby, it appeared that he was making eye contact with Jellico but, at the same time, had his mind far away from the current proceedings. "It's all in our report to Captain Nechayev. She was pretty thorough."

"I'm sure it will make gripping bedtime reading," Jellico said. He looked back at the white-furred creature which, at that moment, was thoroughly absorbed with studying Jellico's distinguished-service medal. "It's not going to eat that, is it?" he asked nervously.

"I doubt it," said Shelby. "He'll determine by sense of smell whether it's edible or not, and I don't think he's going to consider metal to be on his diet."

"So what's going to happen to Janos, Captain?" asked Calhoun.

Nechayev swiveled the chair she was seated in toward Calhoun. "To whom?"

"Janos." He indicated the creature.

"You *named* him?"

"He could have killed me . . . or at the very least, come close. Instead he chose to help me. I certainly think that warrants a name. 'Janos' is Xenexian for 'Great Strength.' "

The recently dubbed Janos bobbed his head in appreciation. "Thank . . . you," he said.

The sounds emerging from his lips caused Jellico to jump several feet straight back. "My God, it talks!"

"You really didn't read the debriefing notes very closely, did you, Edward?" Nechayev scolded him.

"I had a pile of material to go through that . . . my God," he said again. "Is it . . . like a parrot? That it repeats things at random?"

"Things . . . at . . . ran . . . dom?" said Janos slowly.

"Ah." Jellico relaxed a little.

And then Janos shook his head and said, "No . . . not . . . like . . . that . . . at . . . all."

Jellico sank into a chair, goggle-eyed. "I'll be damned," he said.

"We'll have to wait to find out about that one, Edward," Nechayev said diplomatically.

"No one's answered my question," Calhoun said. "What's going to happen to him?"

"I imagine he'll go to Federation labs and be thoroughly studied for . . ."

"The rest of his life?" Calhoun asked Nechayev.

"Quite possibly."

"What would you suggest, Calhoun?" Jellico said. "Arrange to have him adopted by a nice family and eventually enroll him in the Academy?"

There was no laughter in response to this. Jellico looked around.

"You know, it's not a bad idea," said Shelby.

"Oh, come *on!*"

"She's right, Edward," said Nechayev. "It'd be a fascinating chance to observe the phenomenon of nature versus nurture. If it's stuck in a lab, it'll never have the opportunity to live anything approximating a normal life."

"It's an *animal!*"

"It's a life-form," Shelby corrected him. "A new life-form. Aren't we supposed to be seeking those out?"

Jellico glared at her. "The idea of putting it into an uncontrolled environment . . ."

"Not uncontrolled," Nechayev said. "We'd obviously be looking for people who are experienced scientists, with specialties in biology. Starfleet personnel, ideally. My office would work closely with them to monitor its progress . . ."

"His," Calhoun corrected. "His progress."

"His progress," Nechayev amended, sounding very formal about it. "And I'm not saying that his eventual enrollment at the Academy is a certainty. . . ."

"Oh, how very kind of you," said Jellico sarcastically.

"On the other hand, can you imagine someone of his obvious strength and power in a security position? Admit it, Edward . . . if you had a choice between having your back covered by a normal human being, or someone built like that," and she pointed at Janos, "which would you choose? I mean, honestly now."

"I'd want to choose the one I was certain wouldn't have some sort of regression and bite my head off if my back was turned."

Janos whimpered slightly and backed into a corner.

"Nice going, sir," said Calhoun. "You hurt his feelings."

"You should really apologize, Edward," Nechayev said primly.

"I think you're all insane," Jellico said. "Fortunately, whatever the outcome, I won't be here to have to deal with it."

"Nothing's been definitely decided," said Nechayev. "To begin with, the feasibility of Janos's stewardship has to be studied and determined. If nothing else, we have to find a couple of scientifically inclined Starfleet officers who would be willing to take on this responsibility."

"Actually," smiled Shelby, "I think I might have just the candidate for you."

ii.

Wexler had been up until all hours studying, and was looking forward to sleeping in on Saturday morning. So he was none too pleased when the chime at his door sounded. His girlfriend, Leanne, in bed next to him, simply moaned softly and pulled the blanket over her head. So Wexler, grumbling, rolled out of bed and tied off his robe around his middle as he shuffled toward the door. "This better be good," he called through the door.

"Oh, it is," came Shelby's voice from the other side.

"Elizabeth?" he frowned. "What is it?"

"Remember that kid brother you always said you wanted? Well, if your parents will agree to it, then I think we've got one lined up for you."

"What are you talking about?" he demanded and released the door lock. It slid open and a white-furred face with cruel, red/pink eyes was looking at him.

Wexler let out a yelp and jumped back, clutching at his chest as if his heart was going to explode out of it. The commotion naturally woke Leanne, who snapped upright, saw the white-furred creature crouched in the doorway, and dove under the bed with a shriek.

Peeking out from behind the creature's shoulder, Shelby called, "Vincent Wexler . . . meet Janos, your baby brother. Janos, this is Vincent Wexler. Or Wex, as most call him."

"Hi . . . Wex . . ." said Janos.

Wexler, who had fallen back onto the bed, gaped at Janos. "Uh . . . hi . . ."

"He followed us home," Shelby told him cheerfully. "And you get to keep him."

Wexler looked from one to the other and forced a terrified smile.

"Oh . . . joy . . ." he said.

Chapter Thirteen

Now

Gleau was screaming in her dreams.

Shelby was standing there helplessly, watching him suffer, and Janos was tearing him to bits. Curiously, throughout it all, Gleau wasn't actually making any noise. His mouth was open, his eyes were wide, and his arms were thrashing about like a drowning man's. But not the slightest sound emerged from his terrified face.

Nor was the assault occurring in the turbolift. Instead it was happening on Xenex, in the desert. Within the context of the dream, somehow it made perfect sense. She stood there and watched dispassionately, sipping a drink with a small umbrella in it, as Janos continued to shred Gleau. M'Ress was curled up to one side, having a grand old time with a ball of yarn.

Of course. She's responsible. He was her cat's-paw. Shelby wanted to shout out her sudden realization, but there was no one to talk to about it. And then M'Ress was gone, replaced by Calhoun, who also was playing with the same ball of yarn. But it wasn't Calhoun as she knew him now. He was young, barely out of his teens, and when he looked up at her it was with pure savagery, and blood was trickling from the scar on his face, except it wasn't a scar, it was an open wound.

He opened his mouth and actually produced a sound: a loud, ear-shattering roar that was so fearsome that Shelby just wanted to run. But she didn't know where to run to, and then he was coming after her, and then he beeped at her.

He beeped once more, and the waking and sleeping worlds bled together as Shelby sat up in her bed, the beeping becoming more and more insistent. It was coming from her computer station over on her desk. "Yes, what?" she called out in irritation.

The cranky response was enough to activate the link, and the voice of Kat Mueller sounded in her quarters. "Captain, you're receiving a priority transmission from Starfleet."

"God, XO, don't you ever sleep?" moaned Shelby as she flopped back onto her bed.

"As little as possible, Captain. Since it's a priority communication . . ."

"Yes, yes, yes," said Shelby impatiently. She rolled out of bed, fumbled around in the darkness for a robe, not wanting to bring the lights up even to half. She slept in the nude and it wouldn't have done to be speaking to Starfleet topless. Finally she found the robe, tossed it around herself, stumbled across the room, banged her shin on a table, uttered a brief string of profanities, and finally flopped down in the chair facing the table. "All right," she said, rubbing her eyes once more, "put it through."

The screen snapped to life and Admiral Edward Jellico appeared on it. "Sorry about the lateness of the hour, Captain," he said without preamble.

"There's nothing wrong with the lateness of the hour, Admiral," she replied, barely stifling a yawn. "It's particularly nice if one is sleeping during it."

"I'll get right to the point."

"That would be appreciated."

"The Selelvians have prevailed upon the Federation to set aside Starfleet procedure and turn Ensign Janos over to them."

Any vestiges of sleep evaporated from her and, in the darkness, she sat straighter. "Are you joking, sir?"

"You've known me since the Academy, Captain. Name one time when I joked about anything."

"None is readily coming to mind, sir," she admitted.

"The Selelvians want the prisoner and we're to turn him over."

"Admiral, there's more to the situation than meets the eye," said Shelby. In quick, broad strokes she outlined for Jellico the results of their investigation and their suspicion that Janos might literally not have been in control when the attack occurred.

Jellico frowned and shook his head. "State of mind may mean a great deal to you and me, Captain, but it means nothing to the Selelvians."

"Captain, we've been trying to get in touch with Dr. Bethom. If we're right, if it's some sort of breakdown in Janos's mental makeup . . . we may be able to salvage him. We—"

"There's nothing *to* salvage, Captain," said Jellico. "It's out of our hands. The orders from the Federation Council could not be more explicit." He was clearly reading off something: "The *Trident* is to rendezvous with a Selelvian representative in Sector 21306. The *Trident* will then turn over its prisoner relating to the murder of Selelvian national Gleau to the Selelvians for trial and execution."

"Nice to know nothing's being left to chance," Shelby said. She had never felt more frustrated. "Admiral, there's got to be another way . . ."

"There isn't, Captain," he said flatly. "There is no other way. We're being left no options here. Yours is not a pleasant duty, I'll admit. But your duty it remains, and you will carry it out to the letter. Am I understood, Captain?"

"Yes, Admiral," she said tightly. "Understood perfectly."

He paused and then added, "I'm sorry, Captain. Every so often, we lose one. This is one of those times."

"Yes, sir."

Jellico's image vanished from the screen, and Shelby sat there for quite some time in the darkness until a voice floated across to her from the bed.

"Were you planning to wake me and tell me?"

"Lights to half," she said, and squinted as the lights obediently came on. There was Calhoun, in her bed, bare-chested. She couldn't help but note that, unlike hers, his eyes were wide open. The increased brightness didn't appear to be bothering him. For some reason that greatly annoyed her.

"I thought I'd tell you in the morning," Shelby said. "Guess I should have known better, huh."

"I guess you should have," he agreed. "So what now?"

"What now?" Somehow she'd expected him to say that, even though the answer should have been self-evident. "Now we do as we're ordered. You go back to your ship, head off on your next assignment. We leave orbit around Danter and head for our rendezvous with the Selelvians. And we all go on about our lives."

"All of us except Janos. He loses his."

"It certainly looks that way, doesn't it."

"Yes," he said.

She waited for what seemed forever to hear what he had to say next. Mackenzie Calhoun shrugged. "I suppose that's it, then."

She couldn't quite believe she was hearing correctly. "That's it? You mean you're just going to accept the decree of the UFP?"

"Well, it's not as if we have a choice," he said, sounding eminently reasonable. "We serve at the pleasure of the Federation. We can't just go second-guessing their decisions, can we."

"No. We can't."

Calhoun was on his feet, calmly pulling on his uniform. "We're line officers. We were sent here to Thallonian space to help keep the peace. What kind of example would we be setting if we immediately gave ourselves over to anarchy the moment we don't like the way the chain of command is going."

"Are you saying these things because you believe they're what I want to hear?"

"*Are* they what you want to hear?"

"They're certainly sensible attitudes to have."

"Thank you."

"Then again, you haven't always been the most sensible of men."

He closed his uniform jacket. "What can I say, Eppy? Everybody grows up. Everybody gets older. And sooner or later, even the most insensible of men come to their senses. Now give me a kiss."

She did as he asked, coming to him, pressing her body against him and kissing him passionately. His tongue probed her mouth for a moment, and then he withdrew and smiled at her.

"Never let it be said we didn't do our best," he told her. Then he tapped his combadge and said, "Calhoun to *Excalibur.* One to beam over."

He stepped back from her, smiled once more, and blew her a kiss lightly as he dematerialized.

Before the last of his molecules sparkled away, she knew exactly what was going to happen.

She dropped her robe, headed into the bathroom, and took a long shower. She considered it very relaxing. But despite the lateness of the hour, she knew she wasn't going to be going back to sleep anytime soon.

Once out of the shower, she put on her uniform, dressing very slowly and deliberately. Then she exited her quarters and strolled down the main corridor, greeting night-shift crewmen who were clearly surprised to see the captain out and about. She felt brief annoyance that she didn't know all their names and resolved to attend to that at the earliest opportunity.

She stepped onto the turbolift and said, "Bridge," and as the lift started up, her combadge suddenly beeped. She tapped it calmly and heard Mueller speaking with great urgency.

"Captain," she said, "I'm sorry to wake you again, but we have an emergency on our hands. Can you come up to the bridge? Quickly?"

"If you insist," said Shelby just as the turbolift door opened. She stepped out onto the bridge and was greeted with the sight of Mueller doing a genuine double take. "Quick enough?" inquired Shelby.

"How did . . . ?" Then Mueller obviously thought better of wasting time wallowing in confusion and came to the point. "Captain, Ensign Janos has vanished from the brig."

"Really," Shelby said. She tried to sound shocked. She failed utterly. "Are you saying he escaped?"

Mueller was clearly puzzled at Shelby's equanimity regarding this piece of alarming news. "No, Captain. According to guards, he was beamed out. And the *Excalibur* has just left orbit and gone to warp. It's my belief that they transported him off this ship and have absconded with him."

"I see." Each step more leisurely than the last, Shelby sauntered down to the command chair as Mueller stepped out of the way. It took her a moment to remember the name of the nightside man on conn. "Lieutenant Harrison," she said to the jowly-looking fellow at the post, "set course for Sector 21306."

"*What?*" Mueller appeared stunned. "But Captain . . . that's not remotely along the course heading of the *Excalibur!* Is it?" She looked to Harrison for confirmation and he shook his head, backing her up.

"I'm afraid that's not of consequence, XO," Shelby informed her. "You see, Admiral Jellico had very specific orders to give me. Orders I was told I am not allowed to vary from in the slightest. We are to rendezvous with a Selelvian representative in Sector 21306. There, we are to turn over our prisoner relating to the murder of Selelvian national Gleau to the Selelvians for trial and execution. I must follow these orders to the letter."

"But we don't *have* the prisoner, Captain! The *Excalibur* does!"

"True," said Shelby. "But the letter of the orders has no bearing on that. If we have no prisoner to turn over, well . . . there's not much we can do about it. Then we at least do as much as we are able, in the interests of interstellar peace."

The light began to dawn upon Mueller. "You knew he was going to do this. Calhoun. You knew he was going to abscond with Janos."

"Abscond with Janos? Simply because the UFP has agreed to turn him over to the Selelvians, who will immediately execute him even though he was not consciously in control of his actions at the time of the murder? I knew no such thing, XO," replied Shelby. "He voiced no plans of that nature whatsoever."

"Because he didn't want you complicit," said Mueller.

Shelby shrugged. "Who am I to read Mackenzie Calhoun's mind, or presume to know what he's going to do before he does it?"

"You're his wife, and I would bet anything that that's exactly what you do know: what he's going to do before he does it."

"Are you prepared to swear to that in court?"

Mueller stared at her blankly. "Swear to what?"

She saw the half-smiling looks from the others on the bridge. It wasn't as if anyone on the ship would have wished Gleau dead for the things he'd said and done. On the other hand, the brutal practices of the Selelvians didn't engender much support from the crewmen, either.

"Exactly my thought as well, XO."

"Course plotted and laid in, Captain," said Harrison.

"Take us out of orbit, Mr. Harrison," said Shelby. "And inform Ambassador Spock that there's going to be a slightly longer delay in the completion of his mission. We have orders we have to obey to the letter, and we'd better go on about obeying them."

And, heading in the completely opposite direction from the *Excalibur,* the *Trident* leaped into warp drive and was gone.

Then

Shelby felt as if she were going to lose her mind, and what annoyed her the most was that Calhoun wasn't losing his.

She was sitting in the gardens behind the Academy, watching the sun setting and the shadows lengthening across the neatly manicured lawn. She was studying her padd vigorously, even as her thoughts were reeling over the many facts they had to learn and be prepared to regurgitate for the upcoming final exams.

As she continued to go over materials sure to be covered on the tests, she couldn't help but let her mind wander to her roommate, Mackenzie Calhoun. Ever since the successful raid in the company of Kemper and the others, Calhoun's self-confidence had grown considerably. Captain Nechayev had given him something invaluable: a taste of what his future could hold for him if he stuck with his studies and got the job done. Not only that, but the mission had proven to Calhoun that he was ready, willing, and able to handle missions presented him. That was a confidence builder as well.

He'd come a long way from being the tentative outsider with anger and uncertainty bubbling just below the surface.

"Damn him," she muttered, and was surprised at the sentiment that had popped out of her mouth.

She was even more surprised when a brittle-sounding voice came from practically at her elbow. "Damn whom?"

Shelby gave a startled gasp and was on her feet, turning to see an old man perhaps a foot away. He was wearing green coveralls that were stained even darker green at the knees. He had very short gray hair and facial stubble that seemed to exist more because he hadn't bothered to shave for the past couple of days than out of a concerted effort to grow a beard.

"Where did you come from?" she demanded.

"Mars," he replied with a growl. "We turn invisible on Mars, you know. I walked right up to you and then turned visible just to startle you." When her expression continued to be blank, he shook his head and said, "Young lady, you were so engrossed in thought, a herd of elephants could have trotted up and waved their trunks in your face and you'd only just have noticed."

"Who are you?"

"Name's Boothby," he said. "I'm the groundskeeper here."

"Oh." She didn't know quite what to say to that. "Right. Your reputation precedes you. But I've never seen you around before."

"Yes, you have," he said. "You've just never noticed me before."

"I don't think that's possible."

Boothby clearly found that amusing. "Young lady, I can't even begin to count the number of times you've walked right past me and looked right through me. I really might as well have been invisible."

"What? Really?" Immediately she felt a considerable amount of chagrin. "I'm . . . I'm sorry. That was rude of me."

"Yes. It was." But then he shrugged, not seeming especially perturbed. "I suppose you had a lot to think about. That's the thing about this place. It opens your mind up so much, it can be a full-time job just figuring out what to notice."

Without being invited, he eased himself onto the other end of the bench she was seated on. Then again, she supposed there was no reason for invitation. She was far more the visitor here than the perennial Boothby. "If you're concerned about rudeness," he continued, "you should know it's rude when an old man asks you a direct question and doesn't get a direct answer."

"Question?" she said blankly.

He blew air out in irritation through wrinkled lips. "They must not be doing much to teach you study skills if you can't hold a conversation in your mind for more than thirty seconds."

Annoyance swept through Shelby at his attitude, but suddenly she realized what he was talking about. "Oh. Damn whom." He nodded. She half-smiled, feeling a rush of color to her cheeks. "It's nothing. My boyfriend."

"Your boyfriend's nothing? *There's* foundation for a permanent relationship."

"It's not like that. I'm not really angry at him. And it's not his fault."

"You're not angry at him over something he didn't do." He looked at her askance. "They teach you anything about basic physics here? You pick up anything about cause and effect? There's obviously *some*thing that he's done which you feel, on some level, angry about. And you're busy denying it. I'm wondering if you two communicate at all."

She felt slightly offended at that. "With all respect, sir, how can you make that kind of judgment? You don't even know us."

"Heh." Clearly he thought that funny. "Young lady, that's one of the joys of being around for as long as I have. You get to know everybody. Oh, the names change. But the people themselves, the things they say and feel . . . that's pretty consistent from year to year. And the best thing of all is that everybody thinks their situation is unique."

"Believe me, mine is."

"See?"

She had to laugh at that. The logic was pretty impenetrable. "All right," she said, suddenly feeling challenged. "My boyfriend is a former warlord who liberated his planet while still a teenager and has been working on fitting in here at the Academy even though he wears our concept of civilization like a cape that he wishes he could toss off at any time."

Boothby didn't so much as blink. "So he's an outsider, is what you're saying, trying to become an insider."

"Well . . . yes," she admitted.

"Eh," he shrugged. "Seen a ton of those over the years."

"Not like this one."

"Background doesn't matter, young lady," he said tartly. "Different circumstances? There's always different circumstances. It's the nature of the experience that's the important thing. You remember that. That's something they don't teach you here. Well, they do, actually. They just don't tell you they are, and a lot of people don't have the brains to realize it."

"You don't seem to like Academy cadets a great deal."

"A lot of you all don't seem to like yourselves. And I'm left picking up the pieces and trying to stitch you all back together. Not hardly in my job description. They don't pay me enough to be the one who does that. Wind up doing it anyway."

"I didn't ask for your help," she assured him.

He didn't seem deterred by that. "They never do."

She wanted either to tell him to go away, or to get up herself and leave. Instead she stayed rooted to where she was even though she didn't know why, at which point he reminded her, "You still haven't said why you're so annoyed with your boyfriend."

"I'm not."

"You routinely damn people you're not annoyed with? Heh. Hate to see what happens when someone finally does get on your bad side."

"It's not that."

"What is it, then?"

"I don't know."

"Yes. You do," he said flatly.

She tried to deny it, but he knew they'd just be going back and forth over this all evening. She wanted to say anything to the old man just to give him an answer he'd accept so this absurdity could be ended. "I just . . . liked him when he needed me more. There's so much toughness about him, so much independence, and the fact that I was helping him was my entire entry into his personality. And now that he needs me much less, I'm worried that . . . he . . ." Her voice grew softer. ". . . that he won't . . ."

"Need you at all?" he finished.

And she realized that, in trying to say whatever was required to terminate the conversation, she'd inadvertently blurted out the exact truth of the matter. A truth that she herself hadn't fully realized until she'd said it. She felt overwhelmed, her throat constricting. She managed a nod. Her eyes stung slightly and that annoyed the hell out of her . . . the annoyance surpassed only when Boothby held up a handkerchief for her to dab her eyes with. She waved it off, her jaw set.

His next question caught her completely off guard.

"Do you need him?" he asked.

She stared at him. "What do you mean?"

"Funny thing," said Boothby. "I'm much too old to mean anything other than what I say. Do you? Need him?"

"I suppose."

"You suppose. Young lady, enter into the service with that degree of conviction, and you'll be lucky if you don't get yourself blown up inside of a week."

"Okay. Fine. I need him." She hesitated and then added, "I guess."

"You guess."

"It's not that simple."

"It should be."

"I don't want to come across as if I can't exist without him," she said. "I mean, how would that make me sound to you?"

"Like a young woman truly in love. As opposed to a young woman who seems more concerned over the image she projects to a total stranger than she does over what should supposedly be the most important relationship of her life."

"It's not that simple."

"You said that. And I said it should be. And maybe the both of you are too young and have to decide the type of people you're going to be individually before you're ready to decide what you're going to be together. And then you'll say it's not that simple, and if we're going to keep having the same conversation, I'll just get back to what I was doing."

"Well, maybe you should," she snapped at him, and turned away to bury her attention in her padd. She was just going to ignore him, that was all. She had far greater concerns on her mind anyway. She was rock solid on her xenobiology studies, and her computer sciences as well. She'd discovered she had a real flair for computer sciences, and that had surprised her considering she'd had only minimal interest in computers before. She was still a bit weak on stellar cartography, but not so much that it presented a problem to ... to ...

Her thoughts trailed off and turned back to Calhoun, and suddenly she wanted to do nothing but talk about everything that was tumbling through her mind about him. She turned back to Boothby.

He was gone.

She turned completely around on the bench, searching for some sign of him. Nothing.

Maybe he really was from Mars and had turned invisible.

Chapter Fourteen

Now

i.

There was an uneasy silence on the bridge of the *Excalibur.*

Not a person on the crew didn't know what was going on. Not a person on the crew was exactly ecstatic about it.

The depth of the quiet was not lost on Calhoun. He had seen their expressions when he'd stepped onto the bridge. He knew that and said softly, "Morgan."

She'd turned in her chair. Not for the first time did he marvel at the detail of the hologram technology. Every move, ever tic made her look like a one hundred percent human being. "Yes, Captain?"

"I need you to access the transporter systems."

"All right," she said.

This immediately prompted Robin to turn in her chair, and drew mildly confused looks from the others.

"Scan the *Trident*. Find Ensign Janos's life signs."

"Yes, Captain."

Slowly Burgoyne got to hir feet. "Captain . . . ?" s/he began. Clearly s/he didn't quite know what to say. As it happened. Even if s/he had, Calhoun wasn't interested in hearing it.

"Found him, Captain," said Morgan.

"Good. Lock on to him and beam him from there directly into the deck-five brig, please."

Calhoun saw all the blood drain from Robin Lefler's face. *"Captain . . . ?"*

"Captain, what's going on?" said Burgoyne.

Mackenzie Calhoun took a deep breath. He had no illusions. His crew was his crew, and he was certain they would follow him to hell and back. But they had attachments to Shelby as well. He couldn't be anything less than candid with them or it would compromise the notion that he believed in the rightness of his actions. "I'm absconding with Ensign Janos, Burgy. They're still on night shift over on the *Trident,* since their day/night is a few hours behind ours. By the time they react, we'll be long gone."

"Absconding?"

"Yes."

"With . . . Ensign Janos."

"That's correct."

"Good."

It was Kebron who had spoken. The massive Brikar took several steps toward Calhoun, stood behind him with arms folded, and simply remained there. He was sending a very deliberate message that Calhoun didn't actually think needed to be sent. But there it was: The most physically formidable being on the ship was backing up the captain. Endeavor to change the status quo at your own peril. Calhoun, however, didn't believe it would come to that. At least he certainly hoped it wouldn't.

The message was not lost on Burgoyne, but s/he merely looked Kebron up and down once, assessing the situation. Burgoyne was second-in-command. The rest of the crew would look to hir at a moment like this, to see how s/he responded.

"Does Captain Shelby know about this?" s/he asked.

I suspect she does, he thought. *At the very least, she knows me well enough to see it coming.* "No, Burgy," replied Calhoun, sounding very reasonable about the whole thing. "If she knew about it, then it wouldn't be called 'absconding.' It would be called 'a prisoner transfer.' "

"Captain," said Robin, "you can't just kidnap Ensign Janos!"

"It's not kidnapping," Soleta spoke up. "It's most unlikely that he's being transported against his will, and kidnapping requires the unwilling—"

"I don't care!"

"I do," replied Soleta. "If you're going to use technical terms, at least use the correct ones."

"Captain, he's aboard," Morgan said.

Her words froze the moment, a snapshot in time, and then very quietly, Mackenzie Calhoun said, "Morgan, set course for Alpha Sigma IX. Best possible speed."

"Immediate departure?"

"Before the *Trident* starts firing at us? I think that'd be best, yes."

"Mother!" said Robin. "You can't—!"

"Actually, Robin, I've very little choice in the matter," Morgan said. "My personality is integrated with the computer's. I have to obey direct commands from the captain."

"Bull! He once told you to start reading out all my personal journals in order to see if you were in the computer system. You didn't then!"

"Would you prefer I had?"

"No!"

"Well, there you are," said Morgan, as if that explained it.

And suddenly the *Trident* was gone, as was the planet Danter. Naturally both ship and world were right where they had been. It was the *Excalibur* that had departed, hurtling at warp speed toward the destination that Calhoun had ordered.

"Burgoyne!" Robin called out. "Are you going to let him do this?"

All eyes turned to the Hermat. All eyes except Calhoun's. He stared resolutely forward.

"He's the captain," Burgoyne said very softly. "Are you suggesting I endeavor to relieve him of duty?"

Kebron cracked his knuckles. *Just try it,* the gesture said.

Burgoyne fired a fierce look at Kebron, and just for a moment, an actual pitched battle between Zak Kebron and an angry Burgoyne didn't appear to be quite the lopsided matchup that one would have thought. But then Calhoun put up a hand and said, "Zak . . . that won't be necessary. Everyone . . . calm down."

"I'm calm," Morgan said cheerfully.

"Thank you, Morgan, I had every faith. Please. Sit." There was a brief hesitation, and then everyone who was on their feet slowly sat. "Something has happened, and I am either very right about it, or very wrong about it. Either way, I had no desire to compromise the career of anyone on this bridge. That's why I filtered all my orders just now through Morgan; I doubt any reprisals can be taken against her."

"They can do a level-one diagnostic," said Morgan. "It's extremely intrusive and annoying. It's like having a gynecological exam from your feet to your brain."

"Captain, permission to forget what I just heard?" requested Soleta.

"If I can find a way, I'll join you. Burgy . . . I regret having to do it this way," said Calhoun, facing his first officer. "If I'd let you know ahead of time, then you'd have become a co-conspirator."

"As opposed to doing nothing once the act is in progress, thereby making me an accessory after the fact?" asked Burgoyne. "Is that really any better?"

"Oh, yes," Kebron said. "For one thing, you get sent to a much nicer penal colony. They have bowling."

"Zak, stop helping me," said Calhoun. "Look, people . . . Ensign Janos has a problem."

"Yes. He kills people," Robin said nervously.

"But he's not in control of his actions."

"That makes it all right then?"

"No, Lefler, that does not make it all right. It does, however, make it something that we can do something about. Except we've been told to turn him over to the Selelvians, who are not interested in doing anything about it except executing him."

"I don't believe it," Soleta said flatly. "The Federation would never stand for it. . . ."

"The Federation has already given its blessing and the Selelvians are on their way to rendezvous with the *Trident.*"

This brought a stunned silence. "They . . . did?"

"Yes, Lieutenant Lefler . . . they did," Calhoun said to her. "And I suspect I know why."

ii.

Janos was snoring soundly when he was awakened by the heavy footfall of Zak Kebron. With an infuriated roar, Janos lunged forward and slammed bodily into the forcefield. Thrown onto his back, he lay there for a moment, stunned.

"Janos?" called Kebron. "Have you gone into a berserker rage again?"

"Nooo," Janos said after a moment composing himself. "No, I just don't do well with being startled awake." He had been released from the restrictive chair, but he was still wearing the manacles that could shock him into senselessness. "So . . . back again, I see. You're spending so much time over here, people are going to think you're assigned to this ship full-time."

"I am."

Janos looked taken aback. "You've had yourself reassigned to the *Trident?*"

"No. You're aboard the *Excalibur.*"

"No, I'm not."

"Yes, you are. We beamed you aboard a short while ago."

"But that's . . ."

"Go ahead. Work it out for yourself."

Janos called out, "Computer."

"Working," came back a female voice.

"What's the name of this ship?"

"No, what's the name of the man on second."

"Morgan!" called an irritated Kebron.

"I'm sorry," replied Morgan's voice. "I've just always wanted to do that. Hello, Janos. Welcome back to the *Excalibur.*"

"I more or less divined that from the 'man on second' response," said Janos. He sagged back against the wall. "But . . . I don't understand. What am I doing here?"

"Long story short: We're trying to help you."

"I have an idea," said Janos. "How about making the long story long. If nothing else, it'll make the time pass faster."

iii.

"That was fast." Calhoun braced himself, knowing that what was about to come wouldn't be pretty. "All right, Morgan. Put it on screen."

The stars hurtling past them vanished, to be replaced by the infuriated face of Admiral Jellico. He was about to speak, then realized he was in full view of the bridge crew. "Captain," he said tightly, "perhaps it would be best to take this in your ready room."

"The ready room isn't an option, sir."

"Why n—? Wait. Let me guess. You're not ready."

"My compliments, Admiral. You learn quickly."

"Unlike some others I could name. All right, Captain. You want this out in the open? Out in the open it is."

"I think that's preferable, Admiral. Far preferable," he continued before Jellico could get a word out, "to private UFP hearings which result in rights being set aside in favor of quiet little nonpublic executions."

"I don't like it any better than you, Calhoun," said Jellico. "But unlike you, I'm not out to take matters of planetary import into my own hands in contravention of our governing body. Now I'm asking you: Is the transmission I've received from the *Trident* accurate?"

"I couldn't say, Admiral. What transmission are you referring to?"

"Do you or do you not have Ensign Janos aboard your ship?"

"Yes."

"So you admit it."

"Admit what?" asked Calhoun, all innocence. "You asked do we, or do we not? Obviously it has to be one or the other. Either he is or he isn't. Everyone, after all, has to be somewhere, and since you haven't specified—"

"Dammit, Calhoun, this isn't a game!" thundered Jellico.

As loud as Jellico got, that's how quiet Calhoun was. "No. It's not," he said icily. "It's a life at stake. A life . . . and possibly much more than that."

It was with visible effort that Jellico reined himself in. In slow, measured tones he asked, "Is Janos there . . . and what do you mean, 'possibly much more'?"

"Yes. He's here," said Calhoun evenly. "And the term 'possibly much more' refers to the security of the UFP itself."

"You're talking in riddles," Jellico accused him. "Calhoun . . . what the hell is going on? If you have a shred of hope of preserving your command, you tell me right now."

"Very well," Calhoun said. He leaned against the back of his chair but remained standing. "It is my belief that, via a mind-tampering technique called 'the Knack,' the Selelvians have manipulated the Federation Council into acceding to their demands. They're going along with the Selelvians because they don't have any choice."

"Calhoun . . ." Amazingly, Jellico looked speechless. "Do you know what you're saying?"

"Generally, yes. It's preferable to speaking incoherently."

"Good work, sir," muttered Burgoyne, "that's just what you need to do: Piss him off even more."

"Do you have any proof that the Selelvians are doing this?"

"Aside from the fact that I consider the UFP's decision to be uncharacteristic and serving of Selelvian interests? No, sir, I do not."

"And why would they be so interested in seeing Ensign Janos executed?"

"I don't know, sir. It could be he possesses some particular knowledge that they want. It could be they plan to dissect him, see what makes him tick. For all I know, it's exactly what they say: a desire to avenge themselves upon him for the death of Lieutenant Commander Gleau."

"A death I understand even you acknowledge he is most likely responsible for."

"That would be correct, sir."

"Calhoun," said Jellico, and he leaned forward so much that it seemed as if his face were going to come right through the viewscreen. "We're not stupid. We know where you're heading: Alpha Sigma IX. We received reports from the Daystrom Institute that you were sending them harassing messages."

"I would dispute the term 'harassing' . . ."

"You will turn your damned ship around, you will return Janos to the *Trident*, and then you will submit yourself for full psychiatric evaluation."

"Admiral . . ."

"Yes, Captain?"

Calhoun sounded extremely solicitous as he said, "If you were thinking of leaving Starfleet and taking up a career as a fortune-teller, I'd strongly reconsider. Because every one of your predictions just now was dead wrong."

Jellico said nothing for a time. And then finally, he announced, "All right, Calhoun. You've pushed it too far this time. Whatever happens next is going to be entirely on your head. Do you understand? It's on your head."

With that, the transmission abruptly ended, leaving Calhoun to say, "It always is, Admiral. It always is."

Then

Elizabeth Shelby barely had time to take a breath before her head was shoved under water and held there securely.

She lashed out with her right foot, doing so blindly. But a combination of skill and luck were with her, and her heel glanced off her attacker's crotch. Not sufficient to send him into screaming agony, but enough to cause him to loosen his grip.

With a quick upward thrust she splashed to the surface, and saw Wexler's pained expression several feet away from her. "Now, that wasn't necessary," he grunted.

Several quick strokes sent her gliding away from him, on the other side of the swimming pool, from which relative safety she shouted, "You are such a *jerk,* Wexler! I swear to God!"

"At least I remember who my friends are!"

"Easy to remember what you don't have!"

A throat was cleared loudly at the far end of the pool and they turned to see Calhoun and Leanne, in bathing suits and having just emerged from the locker rooms. Leanne folded her arms and gave them her best scolding look. "Do we have to separate you two?"

"Perhaps they're still interested in one another and this is just a way of pursuing it," Calhoun suggested.

It was raining heavily outside, the rainwater spattering harmlessly on the roof of the Academy's indoor swimming pool. It was relatively deserted this day, most students having taken the weekend to go home after a recent series of grueling midterms. However, since Calhoun wasn't going home, Shelby decided to stay at the Academy with him. Leanne had been recovering from a wrenched shoulder she'd gotten during self-defense class and decided not to aggravate it by traveling, so Wexler had remained with her.

At the moment, though, Shelby wouldn't have minded wrenching Wexler's shoulder so he and Leanne could have a matched set.

"Your boyfriend is being an idiot," she said archly to Leanne.

"Oh, is he," said Leanne. She eased herself into the pool, moving tentatively so as not to unthinkingly lean back on the injured arm. "Well, nice to know you can count on some things."

"What's he being an idiot about?" asked Calhoun. He walked around to the deep end of the pool and dove in cleanly. Shelby couldn't help but marvel at how far Calhoun had come in regard to his aquatic comfort level. He still wasn't the world's greatest swimmer, but he got around in a perfectly satisfactory manner, and didn't balk about going into the water anymore. She waited until he surfaced to reply.

"The *Kobayashi Maru,*" she said.

He stared at her blankly. "The what now?"

She couldn't quite believe he didn't know what she was talking about. "The simulation," she said. "The starship simulation. All fourth-year students on command track take it. We're fourth-year, we're command track. So we take it."

"Right, of course, the *Kobayashi Maru,*" said Calhoun in such a way that she couldn't quite determine whether he'd remembered or not. "So what about it?"

Wexler turned in the water to face Calhoun. "You haven't heard? Little Elizabeth's term scores were high enough that she's aiding in the updating and reprogramming of it."

"Why is that necessary?"

"Because a century ago, a smart-ass cadet reprogrammed it," said Shelby. "Made the simulation more to his liking. Since then every year it's updated. The differences are minor, but they're just enough to keep the probabilities shifting and no one can pull the same stunt."

"What about the smart-ass cadet? Was he expelled for cheating?"

"Actually," she admitted, "he was given a commendation for original thinking."

Calhoun shook his head, water flying off his hair. "I will *never* understand this place. But . . . so what was going on with you and Wexler just now then?"

"Nothing," Wexler assured him. "I swear on my mother's grave."

"Your mother's alive, Wex," said Shelby.

"Yes, but she's got her grave all picked out. Brilliant view, really."

Shelby splashed water at him and, using a clean sidestroke, swam over to Calhoun. "Wexler wanted me to tell him what we're going to be doing."

"Doing?"

"With the simulation."

"Just want to know what the back door is," said Wexler.

"There is no back door!"

"Back door?" Calhoun looked like he was getting more lost by the moment.

Shelby rubbed water from her eyes and ran her fingers through her hair before it became a hopeless snarl. "Every year the same rumor goes around: That there's some sort of code word you can say that unlocks the *Kobayashi Maru* scenario and makes it so simple that a plebe could take it with flying colors. And it's *never true,*" she said very pointedly to Wexler. "There are no back doors, no cheats, no ways around of any kind. The test is the test, and that's all there is to it. So stop trying to come up with ways around it, because you're annoying the hell out of me."

"I don't understand why you would want to, Wex," said Calhoun.

"Exactly," Shelby said, draping an arm around Calhoun and floating next to him.

"Elizabeth has been made part of this team to tinker with this test. You and I and others should be willing to rise to it rather than try to circumvent it."

"See?" Shelby nodded approvingly. "See, Wex? Mac gets it."

"And besides," concluded Calhoun, "it's not as if what she and her associates are going to come up with will be a challenge."

"That's precisely the—" Her head snapped around. "I beg your pardon? What's that supposed to mean?"

"Nothing in particular," Calhoun said. "Just that I personally am not concerned—"

"Because you think whatever I come up with for the scenario, you're going to find a way to deal with it. My God, Calhoun, what an arrogant prig you can be sometimes."

"Well . . . yes. That's true," he allowed. "But that has nothing to do with this. In this case I'm simply saying that I won't be outwitted by a computer simulation, no matter how devious it is."

"Is that a fact?"

"Yes. I planned too many strategies in my life, Elizabeth. I can certainly deal with whatever is cooked up by some computer programmers."

"And I think you're wrong, Mac," she said challengingly. "So when it's time for the test, I guess we'll see who's right and who's wrong, won't we."

She got no rise out of him. Instead, very mildly, he replied, "Yes. I suppose we will."

"Well, now this is interesting!" Wexler called out. "Mac, you actually think you'll win?"

"Yes. I will," said Calhoun.

Leanne spoke up from across the pool. "Before y'all get even more het up, it might not be a bad idea to define certain terms, such as 'win.' "

To which Calhoun responded coolly, "You survive and your enemy doesn't."

There was a thoughtful silence and then Shelby said defiantly, "Okay. I can accept that definition. You, Calhoun," and she grinned, "are in more trouble than you know what to do with."

"I usually am," replied Calhoun.

Chapter Fifteen

Now and Then

She looked so young.

Eppy had always looked timeless to him somehow, never-changing. But now, as she sat opposite him in the ready room, wearing the uniform of a fourth-year Starfleet cadet, he realized he'd forgotten the youthful eagerness in her face, the sense of innocence. He wouldn't have recognized it for what it was back then. They'd all felt so grown-up, so adult. *We were children. Children playacting as adults.*

The circumstances of his own background had certainly worked against him. It had never, ever occurred to Mackenzie Calhoun to resent the situation that had thrust him into a leadership role for his people. He had so eagerly embraced his seeming destiny that he never thought about such things as a lost childhood, skipped developmental years. He'd taken up the spear and battled his enemies with the ferocity of any adult because that was what had to be done.

"That's what it was, you know," said young Eppy. "There's a certain point in people's lives where they learn the concept of boundaries. When the rules are laid out for them and they grow to understand what they can and can't do. You never had that. At the time in your life when you should have been learning it, you were too busy rewriting the rules. You have trouble working within the system because the very first system you encountered, you destroyed. And everyone patted you on the back and cheered you and told you how wonderful it was that you had done so. Maybe that's why you felt drawn to Starfleet. You felt an innate need to exist within some sort of system of order. You needed someone to tell you what the rules were. To say to you, 'You can only do this much and no more or there will be consequences.' "

"If it's what I wanted," said Calhoun, "then why do I find it so impossible to live within those confines?"

"Because it's never an easy fit. In some ways, Mac, you're like an eternal teenager. Always feeling the need to push at the boundaries the 'grownups' set for you."

He shook his head. "How did you ever learn to tolerate it?"

"I chose to find it charming," she replied, smiling.

Calhoun sighed and came around the desk to her. He didn't try to touch her, because he knew his hand would pass right through her and somehow that seemed rude. "Did you ever consider how much easier things would have been for you if you'd never met me, Eppy?"

"Every day. Every damned day," she said with mock gravity.

"Look at you," he said. "You've got your whole life ahead of you. And I screwed it up for you."

She laughed delightedly at that. "Oh, and aren't *you* full of yourself. The vast shadow of Mackenzie Calhoun stretches so far that absolutely everything in my life that isn't to my one hundred percent satisfaction is because of you. I never made any decisions on my own, I never took any responsibility for my actions."

"Well, it sounds silly when you put it *that* way. Still, I didn't have to do what I did during the *Kobayashi Maru*," he said.

She shrugged. "And I didn't have to react the way I reacted. As you said, we were children playacting that we were adults."

"I didn't say that."

"No, but you thought it. Close enough."

"I just . . . I keep thinking . . ."

"That's a start," she said dryly.

"I keep thinking," he continued, making no effort to smile, "that you would have been better off if I'd never come between you and Wexler."

"Maybe. Then again, maybe I'd have been worse off."

"How could you be worse off? Look at the situations I've put you into. . . ."

"*You* put me into?" She snorted derisively. "You put me into nothing, Calhoun. I put myself into them. I knew what I was getting into when I signed on as your first officer. And I . . ." She paused, looked down. "And I knew what I'd lost when I thought you were dead."

They said nothing for quite some time. In the distance, he could hear the ship's powerful engines humming.

"This is still how you see me, I suppose," said Shelby finally, pointing at herself. "The eager young, doe-eyed cadet whose life you saved. This 'innocent' thing that you've conjured me up to be in your skull. Well, I've got news for you, Mac. I was never that innocent."

"Never?"

"Never," she said flatly. "Even as a baby, I was worldly-wise and capable of dishing out dazzling rhetoric while engaging in deft wordplay and snappy conversation."

"I stand corrected," said Calhoun, and bowed slightly.

She rose from her chair, so light, weightless. "I would never admit this to you," she said, "but usually your instincts are more reliable than all the rules or decisions that Starfleet could possibly make. I get so angry when you circumvent the chain of command or come up with bizarre solutions to problems that would never have occurred to any truly sane person . . . but that's only because, deep down, I'm a bit jealous of you that I'm not nervy enough or creative enough to match you."

"Okay, now you're just saying things to make me feel better."

"Of course. It's *your* stupid dream."

She was so close to him. It would have taken the slightest movement of his head to bring their lips together. "You don't think you would have been better off without me?" he asked.

"Calhoun . . . I was never without you. Even before I was with you, I was never without you."

"What's that supposed to mean?"

"Figure it out," she said, and her lips passed into his.

"Captain?"

Calhoun sat up so abruptly that he banged his knees under the desk. He looked around but wasn't at all disoriented, because he was still in his ready room. Shelby, however, was gone. Instead Burgoyne was standing there, looking a bit uncertain. "Are you all right?"

"Fine, fine." Calhoun shoved the base of his palms into his eyes and rubbed furiously. "I didn't know I was going to fall asleep."

"I was hoping you would," said Burgoyne.

"Concerned about my health?"

"Yes. Well, that, and I had twenty-seven hours without sleep in the pool."

Calhoun stared at hir blankly. "You were all taking bets as to how many hours I'd stay awake before I passed out?"

"Not all. Soleta stayed out of it so she could be an impartial judge. You know, as to whether light dozing constituted sleep. That sort of thing." S/he smiled slightly, displaying hir fangs. "You know, Captain, we do have several shifts, plus you have your very own quarters. You are allowed to go down there and sack out from time to time. Probably more comfortable than your chair here in the ready room."

"I've slept in worse, believe me," said Calhoun. He stood and stretched, wincing at the kinks in his back. "I felt the need to stay nearby. Just in case."

"In case what?"

"In case anything. ETA to our destination?"

"A little over one hour."

"Good." He nodded and then said again, "Good." He chuckled. "I was dreaming I was talking with Shelby."

"Where?"

"Here."

Burgoyne didn't seem especially impressed. "In the realm of your wildest imaginings, you were sitting and talking with your wife in your ship's ready room. I have to say, Captain, that's what I've always admired about you. You dare to dream the big dreams. That was quite a flight of fancy."

"Belay the sarcasm, Burgy." He rubbed the last of the sleep from his eyes. "Did you want something?"

"Peace of mind, sir."

"You'll get it in the grave, and maybe not even then."

"I need to know if you truly believe what you said about the Selelvians."

"A little late to be asking that now, isn't it, Burgy?"

"Perhaps, Captain. Look . . ." Burgoyne was crouched in the chair. Not seated, but instead balanced lightly on hir feet, looking as if s/he was capable of springing at any time. Not that Calhoun considered that such a thing might happen or that he was in any sort of danger. "I can almost accept—although I'm not happy about it—that you kept me in the dark on this. You wanted me to have plausible deniability. You were concerned about my career. But I need to know for myself, in terms of comprehending the greater good. Do you truly believe the Selelvians are somehow unduly influencing the Federation?"

"Why?"

"*Why?* Because if that's so, Captain, then we may be pulling a great threat to Federation security into the open. But if you don't believe that, then . . . this whole thing is simply an exercise in . . ."

"Insubordination? Rule-breaking? Court-martial offenses? Treason?"

"Any or all of those, sir."

Calhoun looked at his sword hanging on the wall. How was it that a period in his life where he was making constant do-or-die strategies in a war against an implacable opponent could possibly be seen as a simpler time?

"If I believed it and it turned out not to be true, Burgy . . . would that be preferable to if I didn't believe it but it turned out *to* be true?"

"I'm not following you, Captain."

"The truth is, I don't know, Burgy," Calhoun admitted. "But you know what? 'I don't know' doesn't play. It doesn't play to superiors, and it doesn't play to subordinates. Not even in the case of routine, day-to-day existence, much less something as out of the ordinary as this. So as far as everyone else is concerned—including you—yes. I not only believe it, but I know it to be true. Because it's not going to do anyone—again, including you—a damned bit of good for things to be otherwise. Understood?"

"Yes, Captain. I just wish that someone outside of this ship believed it, too."

Calhoun drummed his fingers thoughtfully on his desk. "I think Jellico does."

"Jellico? *Admiral* Jellico?" Burgoyne was clearly incredulous. "Captain, I don't think there's that good an actor in the galaxy that could have pulled that off. If looks could kill, your body would be floating through space in a torpedo casing about now."

"What did he do?"

"Pardon, Captain?"

"What did he do?" Calhoun repeated. "Aside from glare at me and talk about how I was going to regret this. What did he do . . . or, more to the point, what didn't he do?"

Burgoyne stared cluelessly at Calhoun. "What *didn't* he do?"

"Yes. When he was on the viewscreen. What didn't he do that he was fully empowered to have done?"

"Well, he . . ." S/he frowned, suddenly puzzled. "He could have re- lieved you of command, I suppose. . . ."

"That's exactly right. He's an admiral. He could have ordered me re- lieved on the spot, put you in charge, ordered me thrown into the brig, and sent us scampering after the *Trident* to turn Janos back over to them."

"But he didn't."

"But he didn't," said Calhoun triumphantly. "And do you know why?"

"Because he was concerned that I might refuse to do so. Or that if I did, then Kebron—known to be a friend of Janos—might make a fight of it. And there would be bloodshed on the bridge of a starship which could have calamitous consequences for the entire crew? So he decided instead to order another starship in the quadrant to either head us off or meet up with us at Alpha Sigma in order to force a prisoner transfer, fig- uring you won't risk your entire ship and crew in a pitched battle against a sister vessel?"

Very slowly, Calhoun said, "Ohhhkay. Yes, that could be. On the other hand, I believe he suspects what I suspect: that the Selelvians are up to something. So he doesn't want us to sacrifice a Starfleet officer only to discover later that there were pernicious motives behind it."

"That could be, too, Captain," said Burgoyne diplomatically.

"Captain?" It was Morgan, her face appearing once more on the computer screen. "Is this a bad time?"

"No, it's fine, Morgan. What's up?"

"I thought you should know long-range scanners indicate another starship is approaching Alpha Sigma IX. Current estimates indicate it will arrive approximately an hour or so after we do."

Burgoyne and Calhoun exchanged looks. "Any idea which starship?" asked Calhoun.

"Energy signature indicates the *Starship Enterprise.*"

Calhoun sagged back in his chair. "Shit," he growled.

"Don't you mean *'grozit'*?"

"Not this time." He rubbed the bridge of his nose between his thumb and forefinger. "Jellico, you bastard. Of all ships to send, naturally . . . *naturally* . . ."

"It's not all bad, Captain."

"It's not?" He glanced up at Burgoyne. "Enlighten me. Where's the upside?"

And in spite of the gravity of the situation, Burgoyne grinned. "I had the *Enterprise* in the pool as to which starship would show up."

Then

Once upon a time, the *Kobayashi Maru* had been administered on a simulator. The problem was that trainees tended to be rather hard on the equipment, so that the simulated starship bridge had to be rebuilt every time. It was a time-consuming and wasteful process.

This had naturally gone the way of the dodo once holotechnology had become sufficiently sophisticated. Now the *Kobayashi Maru* test was given in a large holosuite, and it was a simple matter of resetting the simulation at the end to make it as good as new.

The positions assumed by the cadets had been determined through random draw, since ideally everyone should be able to do one another's job. After all, one never knew what station one might be compelled to assume in a combat situation. By the luck of the draw, Mackenzie Calhoun was in the captain's chair. He was grinning broadly, looking happier than Shelby had ever seen him. She supposed she should be annoyed by that on some level, considering the happiness she had given him any number of times in a more personal way. But she couldn't resent him for it. This was the first time since he'd departed his homeworld that he was genuinely in charge of something, and he couldn't have been more pleased. Because of that, she was pleased for him.

Besides, considering she had been involved in the reprogramming, she wasn't really eligible for the command slot herself. She'd known that going in, but had made the choice. The realm of computers and artificial intelligence was very intriguing to her, almost as much so as genetic manipulation. On occasion she would daydream about the two disciplines being combined somehow: an artificially created race of beings with machine intelligence. But for some reason, whenever she did dwell on such a notion, she would start to get chills and a sense of vague dread.

In any event, Shelby was content to be operating the tactical station. Wexler was up front at conn, with Gold at ops. Other cadets were at various stations, but Shelby was focused on Wexler and Leanne Gold, smiling at each other. She saw Wexler's booted foot move over and run along the inside of her calf. *Oh, for God's sake, give me a break,* she thought, and then grimly, *You won't be playing games much longer.*

Another foot abruptly came in and tapped Wexler on the heel. He looked up to see Clarke studying him sternly. She had drawn the position of first officer, and she was not taking her responsibilities lightly. "Keep that behavior off the bridge, Wexler . . . Gold."

Wexler was smirking. But then he shrugged and said, "Aye . . . sir," adding the second word as an obvious afterthought.

Clarke looked annoyed, but before she could say anything else, Gold sat up, alerted to an incoming signal at the ops station. Shelby could easily have picked it up from her position at tactical, but she was endeavoring to minimize her participation. The faculty members monitoring the session knew that and wouldn't hold it against her.

"Sir," she said, "We're receiving an incoming distress call. Audio only."

"Let's hear it," said Calhoun. He was all business. Shelby was relieved. Considering he was someone who had routinely been in life-and-death situations only a few years ago, she hadn't been entirely sure whether he would take a simulation seriously. Perhaps that occasion in the pool where he had boasted that nothing in the *Kobayashi Maru* scenario could faze him was enough to keep him thoroughly focused.

The crackling voice of a desperate commander came over the speaker, interrupted with frequent bursts of static. "Imperative! This is the *Kobayashi Maru*, nineteen . . . out of Altair Six . . . struck . . . a gravitic mine . . . and have lost all power." The static became louder for a moment, then faded just enough for them to hear, "Our hull is penetrated and we have sustained many casualties."

"Get their coordinates," Calhoun said immediately.

"This is the starship *Intrepid*," said Gold. "Request your current location."

More static, more garble, and then *"Intrepid,* our position is Gamma Hydra, Sector Ten . . ."

"That's in the Neutral Zone, Captain," said Wexler.

"Debatable," replied Clarke. "They claimed the Gamma Hydra system as an endeavor to expand their borders. No one disputed it since a passing comet had rendered most of the system uninhabitable. But it's been nearly a century, and the comet's effects are believed to have worn off. So now the Federation is saying it's in violation of treaty. The Romulans are saying it's too late to start complaining now."

"What were they doing on the wrong side of the Neutral Zone in the first place?" asked Calhoun thoughtfully.

Cadet Lawford was working the science station. "They said they struck a gravitic mine, sir. The Zone's lined with those. If one broke free of its moorings and they clipped it, they could have been disabled and floated to the other side."

The increasingly desperate voice sounded in the bridge. "Hull penetrated, life-support . . . systems failing. Can you assist us, *Intrepid?* Can you assist us?!"

"Kick up the specs, Gold," said Calhoun.

Immediately the specs on the *Kobayashi Maru* appeared on the center screen. "Third class neutronic fuel carrier, crew of eighty-one, three hundred passengers," said Gold.

Calhoun didn't immediately respond, which caught the attention of the bridge crew. He was staring fixedly at the screen, his eyes narrowing.

"Have we got a definitive fix on the ship's location?" he asked finally.

"Aye, Captain. Traced it back along the broadcast beam."

"Take us in," Calhoun ordered. "Sensors on maximum."

Shelby was impressed. She knew they were on a holodeck and not out in space. She knew the programming involved in creating the *Kobayashi Maru.* Even so, she was utterly in the moment, her breath caught, waiting to see the first hint of catastrophic problems.

"Entering the Neutral Zone on my mark," called out Wexler. "Five . . . four . . . three . . . two . . . one . . ."

"Happy New Year," muttered Gold.

"Passing through the Neutral Zone," Wexler continued. "Now entering Romulan space."

"Sensor sweeps?"

"Nothing so far."

Calhoun stared intently at the vista of stars in front of them. "Where's the damned ship?" he wondered.

"Got her," Wexler suddenly said. "Heading at two two one mark four . . ."

"Captain, reading unstable emissions from the ship's engines," Lawford spoke up. "Their neutronic fuel lines are ruptured."

"Do they still have fuel?"

"Yes, but it's leaking. If we don't have everyone off that ship in ten minutes, they'll be irreversibly contaminated."

Shelby was particularly pleased with that wrinkle. She'd come up with it, the notion of adding a further "ticking clock" to the scenario besides the problem that would be encountered with the . . .

"Romulan ships decloaking, sir," Wexler announced. "One on either side of the *Kobayashi Maru,* one behind us. Running weapons hot, sir."

"Shields up," said Calhoun. He was up out of his chair, and at first Shelby didn't know why. But then she realized: This was a man who was accustomed to going into conflict on his feet. It was a reflex.

"Open a hailing frequency, Ensign," Clarke said briskly. "Attempt to explain—"

"Belay that," Calhoun interrupted her. Clarke looked slightly taken aback. He shrugged. "No point. They won't believe us." He stared at the screen a brief time. Then, clearly having made a decision, he said, "Shelby . . . target the *Kobayashi Maru*'s neutronic fuel supply and engines, and fire."

"What?" Shelby's hands were frozen over the controls. She'd been about to make an attempt to target the Romulan vessels, which she knew, for a fact, would do little to no good against the attacking ships' shields. But Calhoun's instructions threw her completely out of kilter. "Did you say—?"

"Do it now," he snapped. "That's an order."

"Mac, are you nuts?! There's three hundred and eighty—"

Calhoun didn't hesitate. "Shelby, you're relieved. Clarke, take over."

Shelby just stood there, slack-jawed, and suddenly she was being shoved to one side by Clarke, whose fingers flew over the controls. "Firing phasers," she called out.

The ship's weaponry lashed out at the helpless *Kobayashi Maru*. In a heartbeat, the ship erupted. The two Romulan vessels, so confident that the freighter was no threat that they'd anticipated using it to hamper the *Intrepid's* attack, were blown in either direction from the freighter's blast.

The bridge rocked violently as they were fired upon from behind by the third ship. "Full shield power aft!" called Calhoun. "Fire aft torpedoes. Target the two forward ships and fire phasers! Wexler, prepare to bring us around!"

Shelby was leaning against the wall, suddenly reduced to a mere spectator while everyone around her was shouting out damage reports. Her mind locked up. She couldn't believe it was happening, and couldn't even quite understand *what* was happening. The screen was alight with phaser blasts, and then one of the Romulan vessels blew up, tumbling into the other and sending that one up in flames as well. Suddenly the view reversed and she saw the third Romulan warbird falling back, hammered by the photon torpedoes.

"Now, Mr. Wexler!" shouted Calhoun. "Bring us around and get us out of here, warp seven!"

The view shifted once more, and now the stars were hurtling past them once more.

"Clear of the Neutral Zone, sir," said Wexler, letting out a sigh of relief. "No sign of pursuing—"

"You son of a bitch!"

Shelby was coming around and down the far side of the bridge, advancing on Calhoun. He merely stood there looking calm, his hands draped behind his back. "Don't make me call in security, Ensign."

"You did that to make me look bad!"

"Did what? Saved my ship? Destroyed some attackers?"

The doors to the turbolift slid open, and two Starfleet Academy proctors—a heavyset man and a waspish woman, both with padds for taking notes—stepped onto the bridge. "All right, Cadets, that's more than enough of—"

"You blew up the Kobayashi Maru!" She turned to the proctors. "Did you see it? He blew it up! Innocent people, children—!"

"Stand down, Shelby, that's an order!" snapped one of the proctors.

Shelby did as she was told, but she was visibly fuming.

"Cadets," said the male proctor, "to the briefing room."

They filed out. As was custom, Calhoun was the last one off, Shelby the second-to-last.

He made no effort to meet her eye, nor she his. They headed to the briefing room in silence. Behind them, the holosimulation wavered and disappeared, leaving a blank room with a grid of yellow lines.

Chapter Sixteen

Now

Dr. Marius Bethom was many years older than when Calhoun had last seen him, but appeared to have aged no more than a couple. More surprising than that, he was walking toward Calhoun with what seemed to be a very genuine smile. He even had that damned gribble still with him, that odd little creature he'd bioengineered. It was perched atop his shoulder and waggled slightly back and forth as Bethom approached.

The main atrium of the Daystrom Institute branch on Alpha Sigma IX was very simply decorated, with a large painting of Richard Daystrom hung in the middle, overseeing all new arrivals. The rest of the place was decorated in what appeared to be wood grains (although they were doubtless synthetic), giving the place a nice, relaxed, homey atmosphere. Not exactly what Calhoun would have imagined for someplace so dedicated to research and development.

"Captain Calhoun," said Bethom, stopping a couple feet away from him. "I have to say, it's been quite a while. Not exactly a captain during our last encounter. Then again, I wasn't exactly myself, either." He glanced around at the rest of the away team. "And these would be—?"

"This is Dr. Selar," he said, pointing to each as he went. "Commander Burgoyne. Security Chief Zak Kebron. And frankly, Doctor," he continued, as Bethom looked in wonderment at the towering Kebron, "the cheerfulness of your greeting seems a little odd, considering you stated that you'd only see me when Hell froze over."

A voice came from behind them, saying, "You'll have to excuse Dr. Bethom. He was very busy at the time."

Calhoun turned to see a man coming toward them who seemed capable of redefining the word "loom." He was well over six feet tall, with silver-gray hair and a neatly trimmed Vandyke beard. He had a presence about him that commanded instant attention. Perhaps part of it was the voice, so deep that it appeared to originate from around his ankles.

"I was there, you see, when that message came in," continued the newcomer. "Dr. Bethom was at a delicate phase in an experiment. I assure you, Captain, he had not singled you out. Anyone who contacted him at that point, he would have informed them that he would not speak to them until Hell froze over, up to and including his own mother."

"That's true," confirmed Bethom. "And considering my mother passed away some years ago, that's quite an admission to make." He laughed then, and the tall man chuckled softly. No one from the *Excalibur* reacted. Calming himself, Bethom continued, "This is Dr. Christopher. He's been my friend, overseer, and baby-sitter since I was put over here into the custody of the Daystrom Institute."

"And I am more than prepared to vouch for him, Captain," said Christopher. "Marius has spent many years in intensive therapy . . . 'reprogramming,' for lack of a better term. He is now as harmless as you or I."

"I wouldn't put it quite that way, Doctor," said Bethom with a thin smile. "If you think Captain Calhoun is harmless, then you're doing him a grave disservice."

"What is that thing?" asked Kebron, obviously unable to contain himself.

"Oh, this?" Bethom looked casually at his shoulder. "You know, I've gotten so used to it, I sometimes forget it's there. Its name is Gribble."

"The same one from twenty years ago? Long-lived," said Calhoun.

Bethom nodded. "I created it to last. Starfleet was generous enough to allow me to keep it as a pet."

"Captain, we're on a slight deadline," Burgoyne reminded him softly.

"Yes, of course. Dr. Bethom," Calhoun said cautiously, "we have a bit of a . . . situation with one of our crewmen. One I'm hoping that you can do something about."

"One of your . . . crewmen?" said Bethom, looking bewildered.

Christopher said, "I'm afraid I don't understand, Captain, how Dr. Bethom could be of service to one of your people. Although I assure you that we here at the Daystrom Institute would be more than happy to assist—"

"You'll understand in a moment," said Calhoun, and he tapped his combadge. "Calhoun to transporter room. Send him down."

After a moment, there was a humming in the air, and a familiar shaggy white form materialized. He was still in his bonds, semi-hunched over, and he looked up at Bethom with open suspicion.

Bethom looked as if a slight sneeze would be enough to knock him over. "Oh my God," he said. He started to move toward Janos, but Kebron put a hand up, blocking the way.

"I wouldn't," Kebron warned.

"Is it him . . . ?" Bethom turned and looked eagerly at Calhoun. "Is it him?" Calhoun nodded. Bethom appeared ready to pass out from sheer joy. "I don't believe it! I'd . . . I'd always assumed he . . . and in a Starfleet uniform! Who thought to dress him up in a Starfleet uniform?"

Janos spoke with a low growl. "The people who thought I should join Starfleet."

"But . . . this is miraculous!"

Other men whom Calhoun took to be scientists were coming toward them, gathering closer, gaping in awe at the casual conversation between what should have been an inarticulate beast and the man who had created him.

"Yes, miraculous!" insisted Bethom. "I can't believe you're still a—"

Then he stopped abruptly, looking like a child caught out with his hand deep into the cookies.

"Still what?" asked Dr. Selar.

"Nothing. It's nothing . . ."

"Alive," Janos said quietly. "You were going to say 'alive,' weren't you?"

"All right . . . yes. Yes, I was," said Bethom with a defiant edge to his voice. "Frankly, I'm amazed that Federation scientists didn't dissect you down to the smallest molecule. Look at him, my friends," he continued, his voice getting louder as if he were a ringmaster talking to an impressed audience. "You've heard tell of my earlier deeds. The 'abominations' in which I engaged. See it for yourself. Look at the 'great evil' of my earlier work."

There were whispers among the scientists who had pressed in to see him closer up. They were clearly impressed, and several of them were actively congratulating Bethom when Janos himself spoke up. "You all are aware that the science which crafted me . . . is illegal. Correct? You know this. Yet you seem to be acting with overt admiration. I can't pretend to understand."

Several of them were too overwhelmed by Janos's articulate question even to speak. One of them finally managed to say, "You would be amazed how many fields of science were abominated before the slow-witted or shortsighted were able to catch up to them. Once upon a time, the mere act of speculating that the sun did not orbit the Earth was enough to risk death at the hands of foolish authorities."

Kebron glanced at Burgoyne. "Wait. The sun *doesn't* orbit the Earth?"

"Starfleet swears they sent a memo about it," said Burgoyne.

"Captain," Selar said with a bit of annoyed urgency, "perhaps it would be best if we did not lose focus—?"

"Yes. Of course. The problem, Doctor, is this—"

Abruptly his combadge beeped. He tapped it, knowing even before he did so what he was going to hear. "Calhoun here."

"Captain," came Soleta's guarded voice, "company will be arriving within the hour. . . ."

"On my way. Dr. Bethom, Dr. Selar and my crew will explain the situation. If you have any interest in what happens to Janos, you'll cooperate and extend whatever help you can. Soleta, one to beam up."

Within moments the air crackled around Calhoun and he vanished.

"Well," said Dr. Bethom, clapping his hands together and rubbing them briskly. "Our services have been requested by the illustrious Captain Calhoun. We shall do what we can to attend to them. I do have one question, however, before we get started."

"Anything you wish to know, Doctor, we'll be happy to tell you," Burgoyne said. "What's your question?"

"Who's 'Janos'?" asked Dr. Bethom.

Then

"I believe it was a trap."

The proctors had spoken to each of the cadets in turn and dismissed them until only Calhoun and Shelby were remaining in the conference room. Calhoun was aware that Shelby wasn't looking at him. He could practically see the anger radiating from her. He kept telling himself it was not his problem, but hers.

The male proctor was Professor Little, and the female was Professor Crown. Crown tended to pose like a curious hunting dog sniffing out inconsistencies and uncertainties. Little, by contrast, sat back with an open manner that seemed to invite people to open up to him.

Crown leaned forward when Calhoun had made his assessment. "A trap?" she echoed.

"Yes, Professor," said Calhoun. "I believe there was a significant likelihood that the *Kobayashi Maru* was actually a trap laid by the Romulans."

Calhoun could see it was taking much effort for Shelby to keep her tongue still. She knew that the proctors—Crown in particular—would not hesitate to cut her off if she interrupted the debriefing.

"Upon what do you base this rather intriguing conclusion?" asked Professor Little.

"I believe the damage that the freighter was alleged to have sustained was such that it would have had to float for many hours to reach the point that it did."

"You believe this," said Crown. "Did you ask for verification of this belief from your science officer? Or your conn officer?"

"No," said Calhoun. "I was already certain. Therefore I didn't see any need to ask about something I was sure of."

"And if you were wrong?"

"I knew I wasn't."

"But *if you were.*"

"The thought never occurred to me," he said.

Crown and Little nodded almost in synch, then made some silent notations in their padds. "Go on," said Crown.

"It was my belief that the ship could not have gotten that far into the Neutral Zone in its helpless state without being detected earlier," Calhoun continued. "That indicated two possibilities to me. Either the Romulans came upon the derelict ship during a secret excursion outside the Neutral Zone, towed it to that point, and then used it as bait. Or the ship did indeed drift into Romulan space and the Romulans, upon discovering the vessel, simply waited for some starship to try and rescue it in hopes of capturing the starfleet vessel."

"To what end?"

Calhoun shrugged. "Research and development. Or perhaps as an excuse to resume hostilities. I don't know for sure."

"And so you decided the best course of action would be to destroy the freighter?"

"Yes. Their engines may have been off line, but they still had fuel. I knew that rupturing their fuel sources would set off a chain reaction to which the Romulan ships would be vulnerable since they were so close."

"And so you escaped," said Crown.

"Yes, Professor."

"And the crew and passengers of the *Kobayashi Maru* died. All three hundred and eighty of them." Crown leaned forward again, interlacing her fingers. "Cadet . . . we're dancing around something here. You know, I know, we all know it was simply a simulation. Would you be able to do what you did so easily if you were out in the depths of space and the same thing happened?"

"Actually," Calhoun said without hesitation, "it would be easier."

"*Easier?*"

He nodded. "Since I knew the lives of my crew were not really at stake, I took a little more time to consider possibilities before I did what I did."

"A little more time?" Little checked his records. "According to my notes, between the time that you rejected your first officer's suggestion of contacting the Romulans, and your giving the initial kill order, it was no more than five seconds."

"That seems about right, yes."

"To you, that's considering possibilities?"

"It's more than twice as long as I ordinarily would have taken," replied Calhoun.

Crown's gaze was fiery. "Cadet . . . aren't you concerned that you're being a bit cold about all this? We're talking about human lives . . ."

"Yes, Professor, we are," replied Calhoun coolly. "And unless I'm recalling incorrectly, the number of lives—human and otherwise—aboard a starship is roughly three times what it was on the *Kobayashi Maru.*"

"It was supposed to be a rescue mission!" blurted out Shelby, unable to contain herself. *"It was supposed to be a test of character!"*

Little was obviously about to say something, but Calhoun spoke before the professor could. "To you, perhaps. To me, it was simply a day in space. Better than some, worse than others. A rescue mission? No, Shelby. It was a war scenario. The *Kobayashi Maru* wandered into a war zone. And when innocent people wander into a war zone, they tend to die. If I could have saved them, I would have. But I realized very quickly that I could not. We've been taught the Romulans don't take prisoners. Is that correct, Professor Little?" Little nodded. "If I'd stayed to fight it out, we would have died. If I'd simply escaped, they would have died slowly at the hands of their captors, and the Romulans would just have held on to the ship and tried to pull in other unwary travelers. What I did was merciful. It gave them a quick death, which is sometimes the only gift you can bestow on someone, and it enabled us to send several ships filled with the enemy screaming into the next life. A test of character? Here's my character: I want to get my people home alive. The first rule of war is 'Survive.' I tend to think that's the first rule of space as well. Exploration, the search for new life: You can't do any of that if you're dead. You called me 'cold,' Professor Crown. The vacuum of space is pretty damned cold."

"And tell me, Cadet," Little said slowly, "what if you were ordered to fly a suicide mission. One that needed to be done, but the odds were nonexistent that you'd come back. Would you do it?"

"Yes," said Calhoun. "But . . ."

"But what?"

"I'd do it alone."

Crown looked as if she wanted to say something else, but then reconsidered and didn't. Calhoun sat quietly as they made some further notes. "Thank you, Cadet," Little said finally. "You may go."

He rose, headed for the door, and then stopped with his back still to them. "I just . . . I want to make it clear," he said.

"Make what clear, Cadet?"

"I said that, if it happened in real life . . . it would be even easier than the scenario."

"Yes?"

"That's not the same thing as saying it *would* be easy. In my mind . . . in my heart . . . I'd always hear their death screams, even though they were swallowed by the silence of space. And I'd know that, even though they were dead anyway, it would still have been death at my hand. Mine." He shook his head. "No. Not easy. Not at all." And then he walked out, the door hissing shut behind him.

Shelby sat there, feeling embarrassed and horrified for Calhoun. She turned back to Crown and Little, sitting there like inscrutable Buddhas. "Professors," she said, "I am so, so sorry for all this. Calhoun's behavior . . . it's because of me."

"Because of you?" asked Crown, leaning forward, her lips puckering in an "o" shape. "And how, Cadet, was it because of you?"

"Cadet Calhoun . . . well . . ." She shifted uncomfortably in her seat. "He reacted to the simulation the way he did because he knew that I was one of the people who worked on it this year. We're . . . well, we're involved, you might say, and because of that, the things he did, the decisions he made . . . I think our relationship colored it. And I think you should take that into account in making your assessment of . . ."

"Cadet Shelby," said Little crisply, "believe it or not, we are not blind to the likelihood that crewmen on a starship can and will become involved with one another. We have made many mistakes over the centuries, but robbing people of their basic, genetically hard-wired . . . enthusiasms . . . is not one of them.

"One of the things any Starfleet crewman must do is be able to balance his or her emotions and personal relationships with his or her responsibilities to ship and crew. One cannot give a cadet a 'free pass' simply because emotional issues may have been involved."

"But in this case . . . don't you see, he didn't take it seriously and that's my—"

"He didn't take it seriously?" Little looked bewildered, as did Crown, who was glancing at her own notes. "Cadet Shelby, we're not about to read you chapter and verse of our assessments of Cadet Calhoun's attitudes, but I think it should be obvious to anyone that he took the *Kobayashi Maru* most seriously indeed. His responses were thoughtful, considered, and very heartfelt. Obviously Starfleet doesn't recommend the firing upon, or destruction of, helpless vessels. But sometimes a Starship captain has to make very hard choices. Brutal choices dictated by the cold equations of space. Mackenzie Calhoun showed a willingness to do that far beyond his years or Starfleet training, and he did not back down from his choices. That's command material."

"Professor Little is correct," agreed Crown. "In point of fact, Cadet Shelby, in my opinion, the one who did not take the simulation seriously was you."

"Me?" Shelby thought she was losing her mind. "Me? Professor, with all respect, on what basis could you possibly think that I wasn't taking it seriously?"

Crown rocked back in her chair. She looked stunned, as if she couldn't comprehend why Shelby even needed to ask. "Cadet Shelby . . . your commanding officer in the scenario gave you a direct order. A *direct order*. You refused to obey it. Point-blank. Then, once the danger was passed, you uttered a profanity and further tried to attack him."

Shelby's mouth moved. She willed words to come out. None obliged her.

"Cadet Shelby," said Little, and he was speaking so softly that she had to strain to hear him. "I would like to ask you a simple question, and I'd like a yes or no answer, if that wouldn't be too much trouble."

"No . . . no trouble at all."

"Good." There was no hint of amusement or even mercy in his eyes as he said, "In all your studies here at the Academy, in all the tests you've taken, the texts you've pored over, the many lectures you've attended . . . in all of that, have you ever learned the definition of the word 'mutiny'?"

I'm going to kill Mackenzie Calhoun, thought Shelby.

Chapter Seventeen

Now

Zak Kebron wasn't happy.

He wasn't happy with the situation as it currently presented itself in the Daystrom Institute. He wasn't happy that, at that moment, the *Excalibur* was apparently in some sort of face-off with the *Enterprise,* and he wasn't there.

And most of all, he wasn't happy with Dr. Bethom.

Yes, granted, Bethom had agreed to do all he could to aid Janos. At that moment, he was subjecting his "creation" (as he liked to call Janos, which just irritated Kebron all the more) to a barrage of mental and psychological tests using in-depth devices and mental probes that were beyond anything the *Excalibur* could possibly have offered.

And he was doing so under the watchful eye of Dr. Christopher, who, as it turned out, was not only Bethom's "overseer" but also the top professional at the institute. There was nothing going on at the institute that Christopher didn't know about. If Christopher was willing to vouch for Bethom—Christopher, a man who had clearance at the highest levels of Starfleet—then certainly that should be that. Plus Burgoyne and Selar were overseeing matters as well.

Except Kebron couldn't help but feel that it wasn't.

As a result, while Janos underwent a series of examinations in Bethom's labs, with Christopher, Burgoyne, and Selar watching every move, Kebron began reading the various institute log entries from Dr. Christopher and his immediate staffers. It was no problem for Kebron to access the files. His security clearance was as valid at the Daystrom Institute as it was on the *Excalibur.*

He read the materials closely and slowly began to get an uneasy feeling, a feeling that grew more and more uneasy the longer he read the entries.

Kebron admired the hard-boiled detectives because they were as subtle as a hurricane in a feather factory, and Kebron likewise didn't have a subtle brick in his body. Consequently, he headed straight toward Bethom's lab, barreling down the center of the hallways, huge arms swinging in what was apparently a leisurely fashion but would easily have crushed the face of anyone who chanced to get near. He arrived at the room which he knew housed Bethom's lab and entered unannounced.

He saw that Janos was strapped to a glittering horizontal silver table, now held by electronic clamps all along his arms and legs. He was even more securely restrained than he had been before. He was covered all over with diagnostic tools that Kebron expected were feeding tons of information about Janos's "inner-ear infection" (as they'd taken to referring to it). Janos barely looked in Kebron's direction, and when he did he gave no indication of welcome, or even acknowledgment that Kebron was there. Instead he simply gave a small sigh and went back to looking at the ceiling. Doctors Christopher and Selar and Commander Burgoyne were speaking in hushed tones with one another, but Kebron could hear words such as "genius" and "brilliant" being bandied about . . . at least by Christopher. Selar and Burgoyne remained noncommittal, although they were smiling and nodding. Actually, Kebron realized, Burgoyne was nodding and smiling. Selar looked detached. It was nice to know there were some things one could count on.

Bethom looked over at Kebron in greeting as the Brikar strode into the lab. "How are we coming, Doctor?" asked Kebron.

"Oh, we've barely begun," Bethom assured him. "Janos's neural patterns are most unique. There's no other creature like him in the universe, you know. To try and determine exactly what could be causing these violent mood swings, these fugue periods where he reverts to utter bestiality . . . oh yes, it could take quite some time. Perhaps it would be best if you returned to your vessel and awaited our assessment."

"Perhaps it would," agreed Burgoyne. "However, we have our orders. So we'll be staying, if you've no objections. . . ."

"None at all!" said Christopher with that infuriating cheerfulness.

Kebron slowly approached Janos, who continued to look anywhere else but at him. "How you holding up?" he asked Janos.

He expected some sort of wisecrack, or some pithy, witty remark. Instead Janos fixed his red-eyed gaze upon him and said, so quietly that Kebron almost couldn't hear him, "I'm not going to make it."

"Janos," he asked with immediate concern, "is Bethom . . . ?"

"It's nothing he's done," insisted Janos. "At least . . . not lately. I just . . . I just feel it slipping away, Zak. Feel the beast inside me that my . . . my intellect has kept away. Like a mental dam holding back a flood. But my dam is turning into a sieve. My dam. My embankment. My weir. I'm a weirbeast. See? I can still . . ."

Then he let out such a terrifying roar that everyone in the place jumped, except for Kebron. But even he took a few steps back.

Janos began to tremble, pulling against the bonds which held him fast. Finally he managed to settle himself down and looked wearily at Kebron. "When I'm gone . . . when what's me is gone . . . do the right thing . . ."

"Come, come!" called out Bethom. "I'll have no such talk. Just be strong, Janos. It's not as dire as you paint it. It will work out fine, you'll see. So, Mr. Kebron," Bethom said, clearly eager to change the subject. "What do you think of our facility?"

"Very clean," commented Kebron. "I'd always thought true scientific geniuses kept their laboratories in a great deal of disarray."

"An unclean lab is the first indicator of an unclean mind," Bethom said primly. Over on a nearby lab table, the gribble was perched, scavenging around in a small pile of food that seemed to exist primarily of leftovers from people's meals. The gribble didn't seem to mind, cheerfully gnawing away. He reached over absently and petted it.

"And Dr. Bethom," added Dr. Christopher, "has a very clean mind."

"Yes, so I've noticed," said Kebron. "You stated as much in your official journal entries."

"Ah, so you've been reading those," Christopher said. He didn't sound the least bit uneasy about it.

Nevertheless, Kebron watched him carefully as he replied, "Yes. Yes, I have."

"Well, we've nothing to hide."

"So you say. Yet I've found something a bit curious."

Bethom looked up from his work, his eyebrows raised. "Have you?"

"Yes. You see . . . in studying Dr. Christopher's journal, I notice that in your first month here, his journal is filled with all sorts of cautions and concerns regarding erratic behavior on your part. How some days you seem calm, and on others, you're almost impossible to control."

"Really." Bethom shrugged. "I suppose everyone has a period of adjustment."

"Indeed. Yours, it seems, was exactly twenty-seven days. Because on the twenty-eighth day, his journal turns completely around. Suddenly he has nothing but effusive praise for you. 'Dr. Bethom is an asset to this institute and to science.' "

"Isn't that kind!" smiled Bethom. "Doctor, you shouldn't have!"

"I was simply expressing my sincere opinion," said Christopher.

But Burgoyne was looking at Kebron with concern, as was Selar. "Lieutenant . . . is there something else?"

"As a matter of fact, there is," Kebron said, accessing his tricorder. "From that point on, there's nothing but continued kind words. Not the slightest doubt is expressed over the doctor's activities. As a matter of fact, the specifics of the activities are not even spelled out. Or mentioned. At all."

"That," said Selar to Christopher, "is a rather shocking lapse of protocol, Doctor."

"We have a great deal going on here, Doctor," replied Christopher. "We're more thorough at some times than at others. . . ."

"Dr. Bethom is an asset to this institute and to science," Kebron read out.

"Yes," said Bethom, his smile looking slightly more pinched this time. "Yes, we know what Dr. Christopher wrote. . . ."

"This wasn't Dr. Christopher's entry. This was Dr. Malloy's entry," Kebron said. "Entered on the exact same day as Dr. Christopher's." When silence greeted this pronouncement, Kebron continued, "I also have Dr. Zimmerman's entry. And Dr. Margolin's. The precise same wording, on the same day. And here's something even more curious: The next day's entry is also word-for-word across the board. Different, but all the same. And the entry after that, and the entry after that, and so on and so on. I wonder what today's entry will say."

Slowly Selar and Burgoyne began to back away from Bethom. Burgoyne pulled out hir phaser.

Bethom's face was blank, but his eyes were dark and fearsome. "They'll likely say that some Starfleet officers asked too many questions."

Instantly Burgoyne slapped hir combadge. "*Excalibur,* emergency beam—" and suddenly s/he winced, almost doubling over as a high-pitched electronic screech emanated from the combadge. Selar, her hearing even sharper than hirs, staggered, grabbing her ears in a desperate and futile attempt to shut out the whining.

On the lab table, Janos was watching without movement. Then he emitted a low growl and started to struggle. But the bonds held fast.

"I don't think so," said Bethom to the Starfleet officers. "I don't think you'll be emergency beaming out of anywhere. Not with our security scrambler in place. No communications. And our energy dampener should nicely render your phaser weapons little more than decorative paperweights. We're state-of-the-art here. We control who stays and who goes and who does what to whom."

"Oh, really," said Kebron. "Control this." He lumbered toward Bethom, flexing and unflexing his fingers, clearly ready to break Bethom in half the moment he got his hands on him.

"All right," Bethom said without hesitation, and he tapped a panel on the nearby control console.

A door so seamless that he hadn't even spotted it in the wall suddenly slid open a few feet away. There was darkness from within, and suddenly a screech like a hundred discordant violins. Something that looked a great deal like Janos, except larger and fiercer and with claws that were the biggest Kebron had ever seen, barreled into the room, vaulted the distance with one powerful thrust of its legs, and slammed into Kebron.

Kebron had taken any number of hits before in his time, but he'd never felt anything like this. It shuddered through his powerful body, and he tried to steady himself, but the thing was everywhere, its claws at his face, its legs wrapped back and around his knees, and suddenly Kebron was tumbling backward. He hit the ground so heavily that the vibrations through the floor knocked Doctors Bethom and Christopher off their feet.

Instantly Burgoyne started toward Bethom, determined to rip him to shreds if he didn't put a stop to this immediately.

And that was when s/he realized that whatever that creature was that had sprinted out from the darkness to attack Kebron . . .

. . . it had friends.

Lots of them.

Then

Calhoun didn't quite know what to expect when he returned to the quarters he shared with Shelby. Would she give him the silent treatment? Would she just start shouting at him? He suspected it would be one or the other; there didn't seem to be a great deal of room to negotiate. The problem was that he didn't know which was preferable.

He wondered if he should apologize. But he didn't know what he could possibly apologize for. It would be hypocritical, because he didn't think he'd done anything wrong. But if he didn't, then she'd probably just continue to be angry about the whole matter. And really, would it mean anything to him to tell her he was sorry? But if he wasn't truly sorry, then how could he in good conscience say that he was? Wouldn't that be instilling a big fat lie into their relationship?

It was beginning to look like his decision to annihilate the *Kobayashi Maru* was the easiest one he'd made that day.

Word of how he had resolved the situation had gotten around the Academy at even faster speeds than usual. To his surprise, most of the cadets he encountered grinned and said helpful things like "Well done. Someone should have blown that damned freighter out of space years ago." They seemed to be amused by it . . . but also appeared to appreciate the fact that he had placed such a high priority on his crew's safety, and also was willing to make difficult decisions where others might well have faltered.

After much wandering punctuated by a variety of discussions with "fans" of his work, he finally steeled his nerve and headed back to his quarters. He touched the chime, figuring that protocol dictated asking Shelby's permission to be let in, despite the fact that he was as entitled to be there as she was.

"Yes?" said Shelby from the other side of the door.

She doesn't sound mad. Probably because she doesn't know it's me. "It's me," Calhoun called.

"Oh," she replied, and then, "Well, what are you standing out there for?"

He let out a huge sigh of relief. There was a very slight, almost frazzled edge to her voice, but she certainly didn't sound angry at him. "Just wanted to make certain I'm not intruding."

"No. Not at all."

The door slid open and he walked in, and stared as he saw Shelby in the middle of the room, her suitcases opened on the bed. They were filled with her clothes. She pointed to the closet and said, "Be a dear and get the last of my things out of there, would you?"

Looking and feeling numb, Calhoun did as she asked, pulling out the clothes and handing them to her. He stood there dumbly as she tucked them neatly into the suitcase. Everything was precisely and perfectly arranged. He'd never seen such organized luggage in his life.

"What are you doing?" he managed to say finally.

"What does it look like I'm doing?"

"Packing."

"Actually," she said with a triumphant closing of the suitcase, "past tense. Packed."

"But why?"

"I'm going home, Mac."

"Is . . . someone sick? Your parents . . . ?"

"They're fine," she said easily.

"I . . . don't understand then. It's not the end of the semester. Why would you leave? We graduate in a few . . ."

" 'We' aren't doing anything. You're graduating. I'm leaving."

"No!"

"I don't see," she said, "where it's any of your business."

"This is about the test! The *Kobayashi Maru!* You're doing this to get back at me, aren't you," he demanded. "To make me feel badly. All right, fine, it worked. I feel badly. Satisfied? The point's been made." He reached for the nearest suitcase. "Now let's unpack this and—"

"Get away from it!" she called out angrily, and batted at his hands. He withdrew them, looking as confused as he felt. "Mac, I'm leaving, and that's all there is to it."

"But I don't . . ." He'd never felt so helpless. "Why?"

"Because," she said, "my evaluation on the *Kobayashi Maru* is not going to be everything I'd hoped."

"And they're making you leave because of *that?*"

"No," she said patiently, "I'm making me leave because of that. Me, Calhoun. My decision. Don't worry, though. I'll be back. I've decided to repeat my fourth year here. But I'd rather start fresh. Just begin over again next year rather than see this one through."

"This isn't making any sense."

"It's making perfect sense, Mac. I spoke with the professors and told them this was how I felt, and they agreed it would probably be the best thing."

"But I'll be gone!"

Like a knife in his heart, she said, "Yes."

"Then . . . then I'll repeat my fourth year, too."

"You've no reason to. Your grades aren't exemplary but they are good enough, your evaluations . . ."

"Let's see how great my evaluations are when I go and punch in a teacher's face."

"Don't you dare!" For a moment her careful veneer of calm slipped and the raw emotion roiling beneath was visible. With great effort she controlled herself. "That's not how this plays out, Mac. I leave. You stay. I graduate next year. You graduate this year."

"But that wasn't the plan."

"The best laid plans of mice and men oft gone a'gly."

"What?"

"Look it up," she said. "I'm sure you'll have much more spare time without me around to distract you."

"You were never a distraction."

"Then I guess I wasn't trying hard enough, was I."

She clicked shut the suitcases and heaved them off the bed. He stood between her and the door. "Mac," she said in exasperation. "Move, would you?"

"This wasn't the plan," he told her, trying to make her understand. "We . . . we were going to be assigned somewhere together. We were going to be a team. We were going to get married . . ."

"Married?" She laughed. "Since when did you ever propose?"

"I . . . I just always felt that you were my fiancée. Ever since our first time."

"You told me you didn't hold to that old Xenexian custom."

"I lied," he said. "We're supposed to be together."

"There's no such thing as 'supposed to,' Calhoun. There's just 'is.' And this is the way it is."

She tried to push past him to the door and he took her by the shoulders so fiercely she dropped her bags. "How can you do this?" he demanded heatedly.

"Let go!"

"How?"

"Because it's the right thing to do, dammit, and if you weren't a pigheaded barbarian from a backwater planet, you'd understand that!"

He released her as if she were on fire and stepped back. "Is that what you think of me?"

"I'm going now," she said, grabbing her bags.

"I did this for you," he said. "All of it. For you. You have no idea . . . no clue . . ."

"Calhoun, for once and for all, I think you're the one who doesn't have a damned clue. Look . . ." For an instant her voice broke and then she composed it. "The timing stinks, okay? We're not ready to be a couple. I'm not ready to graduate. You're not ready to be a husband. The only thing I'm sure of that's ready is that you're ready to get out of here and start your career. You have to do what's right for you and I have to do what's right for me."

"But . . . this isn't right for you . . ."

"Sorry, Calhoun. That's one decision you don't get to make. Now are you going to get out of the way or do you wind up wearing one of these bags?"

He stepped to one side without a word. She headed for the door. She stopped only when he said very softly, "I thought we were going to get married."

She took a deep breath, faced him, and said, "Think again."

And she was out the door and gone, her footsteps echoing behind her.

He sagged down onto the bed. His mind couldn't process what had just happened. It had to be some sort of elaborate joke on her part. That was it. Just . . . some way of getting back at him, because she was just that upset. All right, he could understand that. He could even appreciate it. He would just wait for her to come back. He'd wait right here.

And she'd be back.

That was definite. Just . . . any moment now . . .

He sat there for a long, long time. Outside the afternoon shadows stretched to evening, and he remained right where he was, waiting for her to return.

And the entire time he did so, he knew perfectly well that she wasn't coming back. But the longer he pretended she was, the longer he didn't have to deal with the fact that she wasn't.

Eventually he heard a soft beeping from the computer console and he realized he had a message waiting.

It was her. It had to be.

He crossed quickly over to it and said, "Play message."

The computer snapped on, and a voice came out of it.

"Hello, M'k'n'zy," said C'n'daz's voice. It was so unexpected that he couldn't quite understand what he was hearing at first. "Did you think I'd forget? Perhaps you don't take a blood challenge seriously, but I do. And so does everyone else on Xenex. I thought you'd want to know that your brother has fled our world, taking refuge on Danter. Isn't that just too perfect. He'd fled because, although it's taken time, I've made sure that everyone on Xenex knows just what a coward you are not to face me, and no one is willing to trust the Calhoun line anymore. Not you. Not any of your house. Not—"

With an inarticulate roar, Calhoun lashed out with his right leg. His foot slammed into the computer screen, smashing it in. Sparks flew as it tumbled off the table and clattered to the floor.

He tossed his few belongings into a suitcase and headed out, stopping very briefly to inform the associate dean's office that he was returning home to Xenex on an emergency leave.

"No one's dying, I hope," he was asked.

To which he replied, "No. But I haven't gotten there yet."

Chapter Eighteen

Now

Calhoun stood on the bridge, watching intently as the *Enterprise* floated nearby, facing them. She seemed near enough to touch. The rest of the bridge crew was watching uneasily.

He knew his people. They had followed him into battle against space monsters, fanatics, and gods. But the notion of going head-to-head with the flagship of the fleet was not a pleasant prospect. If it came to a pitched battle, an us-versus-them situation, there was no upside. If they triumphed, then they would be the outlaw vessel that had crippled or even destroyed the *Starship Enterprise*. If they failed . . .

We're not going to fail, he thought.

"Captain," said Morgan. "We're being hailed." Even the normally ebullient Morgan Primus seemed unduly sedate.

"I rather suspected we might be. Put him on screen." Not "them," meaning the callers as a group. Not "she" or even "it," referring to the ship. "Him."

He appeared on the screen, his expression possessing that odd combination of severity and compassion that Calhoun knew only too well.

"Captain Picard."

"Captain Calhoun."

"Good to see you."

"Yes," said Picard. "The circumstances, however, could be more generous."

"I agree."

"Mac . . . it seems we have a situation on our hands. And the primary cause of that situation appears to be you."

"It would appear that way, yes."

"So. What are we going to do about this?"

"Well, Jean-Luc . . . I was thinking that I'd explain to you that you're a pawn in a much larger game, and why you should take yourself off the board. And then I was hoping you'd do the right thing."

"The right thing." Picard shook his head in disbelief. "How in the world is precipitating an interstellar incident remotely the 'right thing'?"

"Special circumstances."

Picard fixed a piercing gaze upon him. "Mac . . . a Selelvian ship is coming directly here. Not the simple transport vessel that had been en route to rendezvous with the *Trident*. I mean a warship. The best in their fleet, so I'm told."

"Better than you?"

"That's hardly the point, and no," said Picard stiffly.

"What about the *Trident?* Have they been dispatched here as well?"

"Obviously not. Starfleet didn't want to be in the position of forcing a wife to attack her husband."

"That's how much they know," Calhoun said. "Most of the time I have to talk her *out* of attacking me."

"You're stalling for time, Calhoun."

"I prefer to think of it as opening a line of communications for as long as I can possibly keep it going until something else presents itself."

Picard did not look amused. He excelled at not looking amused. "You said something about 'special circumstances'?"

"That's right. I did."

"Would this have to do with your contention that the Selelvians are somehow manipulating the Federation?" He shook his head. "Admiral Jellico already informed us of your 'theory.' Frankly, Captain, I have trouble believing the horrifying risk you're taking over a hypothesis."

"It's neither a hypothesis nor a theory, Captain."

"Then what would you call it?"

"A hunch," said Calhoun with a wry smile. "I was once told that captains learn how to play their hunches. That's how they become captains."

"Really. What shortsighted fool told you that?"

"Jean-Luc Picard, captain of the *Stargazer.*"

"Things change, Calhoun," Picard told him. "People change. Even you. You must know that you're going to cost yourself your command if you maintain your present actions. The concept that the Federation is being manipulated by one of its member races . . ."

"And if I came to you in desperation, told you that you were my last hope, and informed you that Starfleet personnel had been infiltrated by controlling alien parasites . . . would you have helped me? Or dismissed me as a lunatic and allowed a conspiracy to flourish?"

Picard's scowl darkened. But then he glanced in Riker's direction and said, "Touché indeed. All right, Calhoun. I've only been hearing pieces of what's been transpiring, and Admiral Jellico wasn't forthcoming much beyond the concept that he wanted your head on a pike. So, since we have a little time until the Selelvians show up . . . tell me what the bloody hell is going on."

Calhoun told him.

He told him everything he knew, every step of the way, starting with Gleau's alleged mistreatment of M'Ress, through Gleau's murder, Janos's connection to the crime and subsequent rampage, and everything he knew, thought he knew, or vaguely suspected about the Selelvians.

"It would explain why they've done all they can to keep the Knack under wraps," he told Picard. "They know what a powerful tool it is, but it's in their best interests to make certain others don't learn of it. That may well be one of the reasons that they want Janos in their custody as soon as possible."

"Why?" When Calhoun didn't have an immediate response, Picard pressed once more, "Why, Mackenzie? Why can it not simply be that the Selelvians want justice for one of their own people?"

"It's not justice. It's vengeance."

"Granted," admitted Picard. "And it is tragic that they seem to care more about that than they do about our notions of justice. But still—"

"Oh, God," blurted out Soleta.

The exclamation immediately caught the attention of all concerned, as Soleta stared off into empty space directly in front of her. Calhoun knew that look. Something was going through her mind, some sort of connection that she was just drawing. "Lieutenant . . . ?"

"I am an idiot," said Soleta, and in a burst of annoyance she slammed her open hand on the console in front of her. *I am an idiot!*

Picard was staring at her in confusion from the screen. "Are you quite sure she's Vulcan?" he asked.

"She's . . . a little out of the ordinary," said Calhoun.

"Is there anyone on your ship who *isn't?*"

Calhoun didn't reply, probably because Picard had a point. Instead he said, "Soleta . . . what's happened? Why—?"

"Gleau shouldn't be dead."

"You mean he's alive?"

"No, no, he's dead as last year's toast," Soleta assured him. "But he shouldn't be. How could I have not realized?"

"Realized what?"

"Gleau would have wanted to live. He wouldn't have wanted to be murdered."

"I think that's fairly obvious," said Calhoun . . . and then he realized.

Picard did so at about the same time. "If Selelvians are able to influence thoughts . . . to compel people to do what they desire . . . then certainly Gleau would have been able to influence Janos not to kill him."

"But he failed to do so. His corpse is evidence enough of that," said Soleta.

"It could be that he was just panicked," Picard pointed out. "That he wasn't thinking straight and therefore Janos was able to strike."

"Perhaps," said Calhoun. "Or perhaps there is something in Janos's mental or chemical makeup that enabled him to resist the Selelvian influence. And they want to make sure he is dead because of that. Maybe analyze him, dissect him, see how he did it. Either way, that's why they would be so anxious to get him."

"It's possible," admitted Picard. "But it remains conjecture. And we cannot fly in the face of the Federation's will based on conjecture. We need proof."

"That's not always possible, Picard, and you know it," said Calhoun. "As I said before . . . as you said before . . . sometimes you can only follow a hunch."

"If everyone follows hunches, Calhoun, you have anarchy," Picard said. "We live in a world of order and rules . . ."

"Bull, Jean-Luc!" shot back Calhoun. "We live in a galaxy of chaos! Of infinite probabilities! We layer our orders and rules atop them, pat ourselves on the back, and tell ourselves that we have a handle on it all.

We don't. We just enjoy pretending that we do. But every once in a while, the sheer unpredictability of this insane, demented galaxy catches up with us. And we either do what needs to be done, or we cling to rules like children to their mother's apron strings and act like everything's okay when it's not. And when that happens, that's when those who thrive on chaos sneak in and tear us down, little bit by little bit. There're two ways to respond to them, Jean-Luc: either roll over and give them what they want, or fight them no matter what the risk. Which option are you going to embrace!?"

Picard could have been carved from marble for all the emotion he displayed. A full ten seconds ticked away, and then he asked very conversationally, "Are you *quite* through?"

Calhoun's mind raced, and then he shrugged. "For the moment."

"Brilliant. While you were declaiming, we finished scanning your ship. Janos isn't on it. Turn him over to us. Now."

"Mother," said Robin, "were they scanning our ship?"

"Yes."

"Why didn't you say anything?"

"Well," said Morgan as if it were self-evident, "the captain was declaiming. You don't interrupt a captain while he's declaiming. It's . . . tacky."

"Thank you, Morgan," Calhoun said, feeling very tired.

"Am I correct in assuming he's on the planet below?" inquired Picard. Without waiting for Calhoun to respond, he turned and said, "Mr. Data . . . begin scanning planet surface for life signs specific to . . ."

"Morgan," Calhoun said, "would you be good enough to raise our shields and lock phasers on the *Enterprise,* targeting her engineering and saucer dome."

The order brought dead silence. The routine noises of the devices on the bridge, normally ignored by those who had become so used to them, now sounded deafening.

As dispassionate as a computer could be, Morgan replied, "Targets locked, Captain."

"Never quite understood that," continued Calhoun in a surprisingly pleasant tone. "Placing the bridge in a dome right at the top of the saucer. Might as well paint a large bull's-eye that says 'Shoot us here.' Morgan, bring us to weapons-hot, please."

Picard finally found his voice. "Have you lost your mind?"

"You have no idea how many people who are now dead have asked me that," said Calhoun.

"Phasers at full power, Captain," Morgan announced.

"Shields up!" said Picard. "Charge phasers, target *Excalibur!* Do not fire except on my order." He shook his head even as the defensive and offensive capabilities of the *Starship Enterprise* were brought on line. "I know what you're doing, Calhoun. As long as our shields are raised, we can't beam Janos up from the planet's surface."

"Indeed. A rather clever strategy for someone who's lost his mind."

"Yes," Picard said grimly. "But it all hinges on my belief that you would truly attack us. If I lower my shields . . ."

"Then I will blow you to hell."

"You're bluffing," said Jean-Luc Picard.

"Call me," said Mackenzie Calhoun.

Then

All during his journey to Xenex, Mackenzie Calhoun kept going back and forth in his own mind as to whether he was going home or leaving it. By the time he arrived, he had come to a simple conclusion.

He had no home.

Starfleet Academy was the place where he engaged in his studies. Xenex was the place that he had left behind him because he felt he was no longer needed there. But someplace that he felt was genuinely his?

Well, there had actually been one such place in the past few years.

It had been the simulation on the holodeck for the *Kobayashi Maru.* When he'd been standing there on the bridge of a starship, even a facsimile, he had felt for the first time in a long time that he had discovered someplace he belonged.

But that place seemed very far away now. He wondered if such a place would ever actually be his. And he found himself not caring very much whether it was or not, because Shelby wasn't going to be with him.

He forced himself not to think about her. It was simply too painful, too much to deal with. He imagined himself taking a laser torch to that part of his soul that she had occupied, slicing it out, cauterizing the wound, and dumping the excised matter in a waste-disposal unit.

He had sent word on ahead to the shaman of his village, the aged and wizened B'ndri. Calhoun was intending to respond to a blood challenge. Discharging such an obligation was B'ndri's responsibility, and Calhoun wanted the matter to be settled as quickly as possible.

When he arrived at B'ndri's hut, the shaman was waiting for him. That did not surprise him. What did surprise him was that his brother, D'ndai, was there as well. They embraced quickly, but not particularly warmly. D'ndai looked much older than he'd remembered. But he'd left Xenex only four years earlier. Could endeavoring to rule their world have taken such a toll on him?

"I was given to believe," said Calhoun, stepping back from D'ndai, "that there's been some dispute in terms of our people's future. That your own position here was endangered."

"There are factions," said D'ndai dismissively. "There are always factions. C'n'daz leads one of them. He'd consider it quite a coup to dispose of the great former warlord."

Calhoun thought D'ndai sounded bitter when he'd said that. But before he could ask about it, D'ndai had taken his jaw in one hand and was turning his face this way and that, scrutinizing him as one would a prize animal one was about to purchase. "You look very polished," he decided. "If it weren't for the scar, I might not recognize you. No wonder C'n'daz took offense."

He batted his brother's arm away. "What the hell is that supposed to mean? That I deserved this somehow? That it's a positive thing that this imbecile challenge has been thrust on me?"

"Perhaps it is positive," said D'ndai, stepping back and rubbing his arm where Calhoun had struck it. "Does it hurt to be reminded from whence you came? Of your roots? Is it really in your best interests to pretend you're something you're not?"

"How would you know what I am or am not, D'ndai?"

"Oh, believe me, M'k'n'zy, I know what you are."

"And what would that be?" demanded Calhoun.

"You're the shadow I lived in my entire life."

Of all the things Mackenzie Calhoun might have expected to hear, that wasn't one of them. He had always suspected his brother felt jealousy for him, but had never wanted to believe it. Nor did he comprehend it. "Why would you feel that way?" he asked, sounding a bit less strident. "We fought for a common goal."

"If you have to ask, you will never understand."

"That's no answer—"

B'ndri interrupted them with an impatient rapping of his staff on the ground. "If this must be discussed," he growled in his aged voice, "then it will be discussed later. C'n'daz awaits in the Arena of Challenge. It is there now that we must go."

"Fine," snapped Calhoun. "Anything to get this over with."

ii.

The Arena of Challenge once had been a great, grand structure. Challenges in the ancient times of Xenex were issued with such regularity that they had become a form of entertainment among the ancestors of current Xenexians.

Over the centuries, the number of such challenges had dropped off drastically, and the arena had fallen into disrepair. The stone walls were crumbling, the center was filled with clutter. Nevertheless it was there that C'n'daz and his seconds awaited the man variously known as Mackenzie Calhoun or M'k'n'zy of Calhoun.

Calhoun entered from the far end of the arena, D'ndai directly behind him, the shaman bringing up the rear. But they were not the only individuals populating the arena, not by a long shot. Word had gone out throughout the entire region known as Calhoun, and anyone who was capable of any sort of locomotion had shown up, packing in the stands, taking up every possible square inch of standing room.

Despite the pounding his public image had taken in recent years thanks to his departure, the legend of the Warlord M'k'n'zy of Calhoun still rode high in people's hearts and minds. And as Mackenzie Calhoun glanced around at the cheering and waiting throngs, he realized that was exactly what irritated C'n'daz. In some ways, C'n'daz was like his brother, residing in Calhoun's shadow and unable to bring his own individual style to the rule and guidance of the population of Xenex.

In Starfleet Academy, he'd been taught that in order to deal with an opponent, one had to understand the opponent. Perhaps in that understanding (so went the philosophy) it would be possible to avoid full-blown conflict.

Mackenzie Calhoun understood his opponent all too well. That did nothing to deter his desire to pound C'n'daz's face into a fine paste.

The shaman had now moved forward to the center of the amphitheater. Calhoun noticed that elaborate weapons lined the arena's edges. Large cutting implements, devices that were part sword or part spear or part axe. All of them were lethal. All of them, he presumed, would be utilized in the lengthy and elaborate ritual that a blood challenge required.

"C'n'daz," he intoned. "You are the Summoner. Step forward."

C'n'daz did so, moving with a confident swagger that was mirrored by his seconds. They hung back a respectful distance.

"M'k'n'zy, you are the Summoned," continued B'ndri the shaman. "Step forward."

Calhoun walked toward C'n'daz, stopping about two feet away from him. While C'n'daz glowered at him, Mackenzie Calhoun kept his face carefully neutral.

"The blood challenge," began the shaman, "is a tradition stretching back to our earliest origins. It is the means by which disputes are settled. The means by which honor is maintained. The means by which we establish who we are, what we are, and where we are going. The weapons you see around you," and he gestured grandly, "are to be utilized in a specific order that has been passed down by oral tradition from generation to generation. The rituals in preparation for battle you will now undergo have likewise been passed down, from father to son, from shaman to shaman. These rituals will prepare you, focus you. The sun is now at its zenith. You will perform these rituals by the letter and spirit of the time-honored traditions, and as the sun moves across the sky, there will be a new series of prayers and meditations in which we will all join, that will—"

Calhoun took one quick step forward and drove his foot up into C'n'daz's groin, producing a loud "squish" noise. C'n'daz doubled over, his face a portrait in surprised pain, and he sagged to his knees.

"Or you could just do that," said the shaman without blinking an eye.

C'n'daz tried to stagger to his feet. Calhoun was impressed by that. Considering the pain that was likely exploding behind C'n'daz's eyes at that moment, any response beyond sobbing and moaning was a plus. He was disinclined, however, to congratulate him. Instead he pivoted in place and slammed a spin-kick into C'n'daz's face. C'n'daz toppled over, tears beginning to gather in his eyes, his legs curled up like an infant's. He had one hand tucked between his thighs, and the other was clutching his nose, from which blood was fountaining.

"You wanted blood, C'n'daz?" demanded Calhoun in disgust. "There's your blood." He knelt down, yanking C'n'daz's hand away from his face so the blood was visible on his palm. "See? See how slick it is? How pretty? Do you have any idea how much blood I've spilled, C'n'daz? Enough to bathe in, to keep a tub flowing in it for the rest of my life. I find it hard to believe you've forgotten, because you were there. But I haven't forgotten. And I'm tired of it." He stepped back and shouted to the silent audience members. "I'm tired of a place where all I dwell on is blood! Perhaps it won't always be so. I know I'll always think of Xenex as somewhere I want to be. The customs, the traditions . . . they'll always mean something to me. But I'm drowning in the blood here, C'n'daz. Drowning in the bloody memories. I have to make new memories . . . or there'll be nothing left of me! I hope you all understand that. And any of you who don't . . . the hell with you."

He was prepared to walk away when he was stopped by the shaman. "You've forgotten something, M'k'n'zy. C'n'daz's life is in your hands."

Calhoun looked back at C'n'daz, now sitting up, looking battered and apprehensive.

"So what? What am I supposed to do with it?" demanded Calhoun.

"If you are wise? Take it. He will not stop hating you. Not stop trying to kill you. Leaving him alive settles nothing."

"Nor does killing him," Calhoun said firmly. "This foolishness is over. I hope you all understand that I'm just trying to live my life. You don't need me anymore. Allow me to fade away gracefully into the history of this world, instead of trying to hammer me into a shape that you find preferable. A leader in war should never be a leader in peace. He'll atrophy. He might as well be dead. You don't need me. You need D'ndai. So please . . ."

"M'k'n'zy!" D'ndai shouted, pointing in alarm.

Calhoun turned just in time to see the long, evil-looking blade in C'n'daz's hand. His actions were pure reflex, no thought given them at all. He spun to the side of C'n'daz's outthrust arm, gripped the wrist with one hand, twisted down, around and up, and then heard a horrifying moist noise he knew all too well. He stepped back, pulling his blood-covered hands away, as C'n'daz staggered with his own blade buried deep in the pit of his stomach.

C'n'daz, his eyes a world of hurt, stared at Calhoun in silent accusation. What he was accusing Calhoun of, the Xenexian could not even begin to guess.

"Are you happy?!" shouted Calhoun. *"Is this what you wanted?!"*

Whether it was or not would never be known. C'n'daz fell forward onto the sand and lay there, unmoving, as the ground beneath him became thick with his lifeblood.

Calhoun stood there, staring. He had seen so much death, caused most of it. What was one more? One more?

He became vaguely aware that D'ndai was at his side. The shaman was intoning that the blood challenge was over.

"Get me out of here," M'k'n'zy said to his brother in a low voice. "I'm going to be sick."

Chapter Nineteen

Now

i.

"Move! Move!"

Kebron was shouting as loudly as he could while he acted as a barrier to the monstrosities that were in pursuit of them.

He had been endeavoring to keep back the flood of animals in the same way that a mighty boulder on a beach would provide protection to land inhabitants by absorbing the crashing of the waves. The ersatz Janos had thrown him for a loop at first, but he had recovered quickly. That the creature had knocked him over at all was more stinging to his pride than anything else. The Brikar as a whole preferred to think of themselves as unassailable, and Kebron wasn't about to tamper with that self-satisfied mind-set.

Flat on his back, the creature's mouth roaring in his face, its fearsome talons tearing at his hide and actually making deep, hacking slashes in it, Kebron had not allowed himself the slightest hesitation or dent in his conviction that he would triumph. He had disposed of the creature through the simplest means possible: He had shoved his fist up and through the beast's mouth and out the top of its head. Brains and gore had flown straight up, and the lesson was not lost on the attacking beasts that were bounding toward them. They let out a collective squeal and beat a brief retreat. They didn't take their eyes off Kebron, seeing him as a terrifying and formidable foe.

Kebron, for his part, was briefly stuck. He was wearing a mutilated monster on his right arm, and was having trouble shaking it off. With seconds to act, he braced the creature's corpse with his left hand and yanked straight upward, tearing his right arm loose with a rending of blood and skull. This prompted another shriek from the animals, and then a howl of outrage.

Then they charged en masse.

He must have been very popular, thought Kebron. He made a move toward Bethom, who was laughing at the scene, and then the creatures had come between them. Turning, Kebron started running. Burgoyne and Selar were already ahead of him, and more beasts were angling in from the right. The exit from the room was just ahead and Kebron shouted "Out of the way!" as he sped up. The other officers broke right and left as, with the power of an asteroid, he slammed into the door. It was locked, but that was irrelevant once he got through with it.

One of the creatures, looking like a cross between a bear and a wolf, got to Burgoyne, and Burgoyne emitted a challenging shriek of hir own, hir claws extended from the tips of hir fingers. S/he swiped hir hands around, going straight for the creature's throat, searching out the jugular. The creature hadn't expected such resistance and flinched back, and that was its undoing. Burgoyne's talons found its throat and sliced through it effortlessly. The creature fell back, clutching at its throat, then falling onto its back and flailing about.

Another came in, far faster. It bounded over its fallen brethren, shoved past Burgoyne, and went straight for Selar. It slammed into her and they both went down.

"Selar! Kebron, help her!" howled Burgoyne, and Kebron was right there, yanking the creature off Selar, expecting to find her dead. Instead the creature was unconscious, stunned by the Vulcan neck pinch. Selar looked shaken but determined. Kebron yanked her to her feet and then off them, slinging the protesting doctor over his shoulder, and they charged out the door, Burgoyne bringing up the rear.

They pounded up the hallway, and there were scientists standing there, looking stunned, bewildered, unclear as to what was happening. Then they saw the stream of creatures charging up the hallway after the fleeing starship crewmen and they did everything they could to get out of the way. Some managed. Some didn't. Kebron didn't care. He had other things to worry about.

Burgoyne, formerly chief engineer of the *Excalibur,* had rotated the frequency of hir phaser to make it operational in the static field, and was firing at random behind them. S/he wasn't bothering with the stun setting; s/he had it on full disrupt. S/he hit creature after creature, blasting them into free-floating atoms, but there seemed to be more and more, and the damned things weren't stopping. There was no telling how many of them Bethom had made.

"In here!" bellowed Kebron, darting to the right, and Burgoyne followed. They entered a room, the door sliding shut behind them, and Burgoyne whipped hir phaser around, thumbed the setting down, and fired it into the junction box controlling the door. The box melted into a puddle of circuitry, effectively sealing the door.

Kebron dropped Selar unceremoniously to the floor. To her credit she said nothing, straightening her uniform and clambering to her feet. "They cannot get in?" she asked.

"That's the upside. The downside is, we're not going anywhere at the moment," said Kebron.

"We'll see about that," said a determined Burgoyne. S/he looked at the equipment lining the walls. "This is their computer center."

"Yes," Kebron said.

"You're hoping I can overcome their grid that's shutting down any possible transporter link."

"Yes."

Quickly Burgoyne moved to the computers and began running systems checks. "This must have been what Bethom wanted all along."

"What do you mean?" asked Selar.

"This. The facilities of the Daystrom Institute. Far beyond anything that he was going to be able to put together himself. Gods, talk about long-range planning."

"I am not greatly concerned about long-range planning at the moment," said Selar. "Of far more interest to me is short-range planning, including whatever plans you might have to return us to the *Excalibur.*"

The door at the far end of the room shuddered.

"The neighbors are restless," said Kebron, facing the door. Once more it trembled under the thudding of something, or things, on the other side. "Burgoyne, a bit more alacrity, if you please."

"We have a problem."

"What, just the one?"

"All the commands for the defense grid are specifically encrypted and encoded to Bethom or Christopher," said Burgoyne. "I can't access it, which means I can't lower it."

"There has to be some means of punching through, to alert *Excalibur* to our location and situation," Selar insisted.

Burgoyne's mind raced . . . and then s/he smiled, displaying the tips of hir fangs. S/he began tapping instructions into the padds in front of hir.

"What are you doing?" said Kebron, casting a sidelong glance at the door and not being thrilled with the way it appeared to be holding up.

"Normal com channels may be blocked," Burgoyne said. "But I can create a direct link with the *Excalibur's* computer."

"What kind of link?"

"A simple energy pulse. But I can control the speed and frequency with which it goes."

"I do not understand," Selar said. "Will that be of any use?"

"With any other computer in any other vessel? No. Computers are wonderful resources in terms of determining facts, but they can't make intuitive leaps. They wouldn't recognize the pulse for what it was, and even if they did, they wouldn't know to inform anyone else. They'd just note it and log it. But the *Excalibur* doesn't have just any computer."

ii.

Calhoun was most curious to see whether Picard would call his bluff. Until faced with the direct challenge to it, he couldn't say for sure if it was a bluff or not. At that moment, Calhoun had no more idea of how things were going to turn out than anyone else on the very silent *Excalibur* bridge. He was, however, the only person there who had to pretend that he knew everything that was going to happen.

Picard was about to respond, and Calhoun braced himself. Then Picard paused, apparently being informed of something by Data. He looked up, frowning. Instead of addressing the Mexican standoff they had before them, he said, "Calhoun . . . are you aware that some sort of energy grid has been erected around the Daystrom Institute? We wouldn't be able to locate Janos in any event."

"What?" He looked to Soleta for confirmation.

After a moment, the science officer nodded. "It's true, Captain. I can't get any sensor readings at all."

"Com?"

"Useless," said Robin Lefler. "I can't raise any sort of hailing frequency."

"How long has this 'blackout' field been in effect?"

"Not sure, sir," Soleta told him, sounding apologetic. "We've been distracted."

"Yes. Yes, we have." He studied Picard over a distance of kilometers and what seemed years. "It's your fault, you know."

"How is this disaster my fault?" demanded Picard.

"If you'd had the brains to leave me on Xenex instead of talking me into attending the Academy, none of this would have happened."

Despite the severity of the situation, Picard actually chuckled at that. "Perhaps you're right. Perhaps it is my fault at that."

"Captain!"

It was Morgan, and her computerlike dispassion was gone. Instead she was speaking with barely controlled urgency. "I'm receivng an SOS."

"A what?" asked Calhoun.

"An SOS. An old-style distress signal utilizing an antiquated method called Morse code," she explained. "Someone's sending a pulse directly into my systems, at the appropriate intervals. There's no mistaking it."

"Do we know who?"

"No, sir. It's just the same SOS, over and over again. I can, however, use the pulse as a trace for coordinates, lock on and beam them up. Or, for that matter, use those same coordinates to beam help down there."

"Except," said Calhoun, "if we drop our shields . . ."

"Then *we* can blow *you* to hell," Picard noted, sounding far too cheerful about the prospect as far as Calhoun was concerned. "Now let's see. How did you put it? Ah, yes. Call me."

"Captain Calhoun," Robin suddenly spoke up.

He didn't want to hear it. "What?"

"Selelvian war vessel approaching, sir."

"Naturally," said Calhoun. His mind raced, trying to come up with something. Anything.

"Well, Captain?" asked Picard. He sounded patient, but Calhoun knew that wasn't the case.

"You wanted proof, Jean-Luc?" he said abruptly.

"Proof?"

"Of the Selelvians' manipulations of the Federation?"

"That would certainly help matters," said Picard.

"All right, then," said a determined Calhoun. "Then here's how we get it. . . ."

Then

The first of the two communiqués reached Mackenzie Calhoun as he sat in a small room at Starbase 6, staring at the wall and wondering what the hell he was going to do with his life. The room wasn't much. Then again, Starbase 6 was one of the older Federation facilities and wasn't exactly built for comfort.

He almost didn't answer it. He was simply lying on the bed, staring up at the ceiling, much in the same way that he'd been doing the previous two days. The computer station beeped at him insistently and he glared at it. On Xenex, there were no computers. People had privacy. People could be alone when they wanted. In the world of the Federation, the damned things were everywhere. There was no privacy, no nothing. The Federation, one big happy family. It was enough to make him sick . . . again.

And still the thing continued to beep at him. Briefly he considered disposing of it the way he had the other one, back on Earth. But that seemed needlessly destructive. With an aggravated sigh, he called, "Connect."

The screen promptly flared to life and he sat up. For some reason he wasn't the least bit surprised when he saw who was looking out at him from the screen.

"Hello, Picard," he said.

Jean-Luc Picard smiled grimly at him from the screen. "It seems like yesterday you called me PEE-cahd."

"Things change."

"So I hear. And you've been quite busy. I'm told you blew up the *Kobayashi Maru.*"

"Yes, sir. I did."

"Mind telling me why?"

"It was blocking my view of Venus."

Picard looked confused. "What?"

"It seemed like a good idea at the time. It was how I dealt with it." He smiled grimly. "And, as it turns out . . . it was a complete lie."

"In what sense?"

Calhoun didn't answer.

After a moment, Picard said, "I'm told that you departed the Academy in something of a hurry . . . and haven't been back. Missed a few classes. There's still time for you to make them up and not miss out on graduation."

"Why do you care?" demanded Calhoun. "How do you know what's going on with me?"

"I left word with a few key people to keep me informed. I think you have potential. More than that . . . I think you have a great destiny."

Calhoun laughed bitterly at that, flopping back on his bed. "It's comforting to know you think so highly of me."

"Mackenzie . . . what happened?" asked Picard, not ungently.

"A friend of mine on Xenex died."

"Was it sudden?"

"In a sense. He died suddenly after I buried a blade in his stomach."

"Merde," muttered Picard, a word that Calhoun hadn't heard him say before. "Why . . . did you kill him?"

"It seemed like a good idea at the time."

"Flippancy is hardly appropriate, Mackenzie. A man died—"

"I know, Picard. I was there. I killed him. I killed him because he challenged me in what he believed was a matter of honor, he attacked me, I tried to spare him, and he attacked again and would have killed me if I'd given him the chance. And then I got sick to my stomach, although thank the gods no one except my brother saw it. All it did was underscore the lie that is my life."

"What lie?"

"You want to know why I blew up the *Kobayashi Maru?* Because I talked a good game, Picard," he said heatedly. "That's why. I made it sound like the simplest thing in the world. At the time, it was. Yet someone was trying to kill me, and I was fool enough to spare him when by rights I should have disposed of him when I had the initial opportunity. I left myself vulnerable. Gave him another chance at me. He was right about me, the man I killed. C'n'daz. He believed I was weak. And it's true. I'm not what I was when I was warlord. Starfleet Academy taught me to be weak."

"It taught you compassion, Mackenzie."

"Same thing."

"No," said Picard with conviction. "Compassion is never a weakness. It's the greatest strength a man can have."

Calhoun shook his head. "You don't understand."

"I understand perfectly, and I *know* what you're going to say . . ."

"My people want me to be their leader for life."

"All right," Picard amended, "I *didn't* know what you were going to say. Their leader?"

"Ruler. King. God. Whatever term you'd care to apply to it. I killed C'n'daz and suddenly it was the legend of Mackenzie Calhoun reborn. It solidified my brother's support base, but they've asked me, begged me, to take over. Even D'ndai supports the notion, although I think if he could spit acid at me, he would. Some people even claim my rule was foretold. That I was destined to return to Xenex and be their leader everlasting, ruling by the strength of my arm and the power of my sword."

And then Picard said something that made no sense to Calhoun.

"Whoso pulleth this sword of this stone and anvil," he intoned, "is rightwise King born of all Britain."

That prompted Calhoun to sit up and stare at the screen. "What the hell are you talking about?"

"An ancient legend. The story is told of a mighty sword, plunged into an anvil set upon a stone, which appeared in a churchyard in London during a time of great upheaval and unrest. It bore the inscription I just cited. One after the next, men tried to pull the sword from the stone and anvil, but were unable to do so. And then one young man, a most unlikely hero—an outsider, truth to tell, who was only doing it to aid his older brother—drew the sword from the stone. And when he repeated his feat for witnesses, they fell upon the ground and hailed him as the king." He hesitated, waiting for some reaction from Calhoun. None was forthcoming. "Do you understand what I'm telling you, Mackenzie?"

"That people believe everything they read?" he asked. "Even if it's some words on a rock?"

"It means, Mackenzie," said Picard with great patience, "that some of us are born to greatness . . . some of us have greatness thrust upon us . . . and for a very few, it's a combination of both."

"So I'm destined for greatness?"

"As I once told you: A captain learns to play his hunches."

"And where," demanded Calhoun, "is that greatness supposed to lie? On Xenex? Or on the bridge of a starship?"

"I can't help you with that," said Calhoun. "You can only make that decision after much soul-searching, after many arduous—"

"Fine, fine, fine, I'll come back to the Academy," Calhoun sighed.

Picard looked taken aback, but then he smiled. "I forgot. You aren't much for deep contemplation, are you."

"I've been thinking about nothing but that for the past week, actually," said Calhoun. "And I was more or less coming to the conclusion that it was more worthwhile making a difference on a series of worlds than on just one. Ultimately, though, I realized just now that if I go back to Xenex, be what they want me to be . . . I'm going to be haunted by you and your annoying accent for the rest of my life. In my waking, in my dreams, you'll always be there harassing me, telling me what I should have done instead."

"I didn't tell you what to do, Mackenzie. You decided."

"Yes, but you'll be there representing the part of me that made the wrong decision. There's a transport out of here at fourteen hundred hours. That gives me just under forty-five minutes to get packed and book passage. Is there anything else?"

"Yes," said Picard. "I'm sorry I won't be able to make graduation. It would be good to see you in person."

"I'm sure we'll see each other again, Picard," said Calhoun. "Either you'll be lecturing me on my responsibilities to Starfleet or else we'll be threatening to kill each other."

"I very much doubt that," said Jean-Luc Picard. *"Bon voyage."*

"Right," Calhoun said. Moments later, he was shoving the last of his meager possessions into his bag when the summons of another message sounded. In exasperation he muttered, "What now?" and then said louder, "Go ahead."

"Calhoun!" It was the angry face of Captain Edward Jellico. "What do you think you're doing?"

"Packing, sir. I don't have a lot of time . . ."

"Calhoun, my understanding is that you've left the Academy. In my opinion, that is a waste of material, and I am ordering you to head back right now on the next available transport."

"All right."

Jellico looked confused. Clearly he'd been expecting Calhoun to say something else. "All right?"

"Yes, all right. I'll grab the next transport back."

"You're not just saying that," he demanded, suspicious.

"Captain, I can obey your order and take the next transport, or we can keep going round about this and I can miss the next transport. Your choice."

"Very well," said Jellico stiffly. "Obey my order."

"Yes, sir. Oh, and sir . . . ?"

"What is it, Calhoun?"

With a resolutely straight face, Calhoun said, "You were very commanding, just now. An obvious leader of men. I was very impressed."

Eyes narrowing in suspicion, Jellico said, "Thank you . . . I think."

"You're welcome, I think."

Chapter Twenty

Now

i.

Vice-Regent Tulan of the Selelvians was one of the most impressive individuals Calhoun had ever seen.

A stunning female, she seemed literally to be a glowing picture of health. When she smiled it was with perfect teeth, her perfect skin shining, perfect, everything perfect. It wasn't very long ago that Calhoun had gone up against beings purporting to be Greek gods, and even they didn't measure up to the ideal of beauty that Tulan was setting.

A three-way communication was transpiring between the *Excalibur,* the newly arrived Selelvian vessel (elegantly designed, almost entirely curves and twists that provided the sleekest ship Calhoun had ever seen), and the *Enterprise.* Both starships still had their screens up, and Tulan was quite disturbed by this. She didn't seem upset so much as concerned. She displayed that dazzling smile and said, "So it appears we have a bit of a situation here."

"So it would seem," said Picard. Calhoun simply nodded.

"I'm afraid my orders are most specific," said Tulan, her voice musical. "We are to retrieve the creature called 'Janos' and return him to my government."

"Your government," Calhoun said flatly, "manipulated the Federation into giving in to them. Your people are dangerous."

"We wish harm to no one," said Tulan, "but justice must be served."

"I keep hearing that," said Calhoun. "I'm not seeing much of it, though."

"I was told you might be intransigent," sighed Tulan. "Captain Picard, clearly you are reluctant to stand against a fellow starship captain. And I would suspect your vessels are evenly matched."

"Actually, my ship can kick his ship's ass," Calhoun told her.

"Hmm," she said, her eyes unaccountably twinkling in merriment. "That may well be the case. However, there are two vessels here now, arrayed against your one. The odds are very much in our favor. So, before this spirals out of control, let's serve all our interests and do what your Federation has ordered you to do."

"Actually," Picard said slowly, "although it's two vessels to one . . . it's not quite in the way you think."

Tulan began to look slightly less pleased with herself. Her officers, visible behind her, were glancing at each other in concern. "Pardon?"

"The *Enterprise* stands with the *Excalibur,*" said Picard.

It was as if the words hadn't quite registered. "Pardon?" she said again.

"You're not getting Janos from us," Calhoun told her. "You're not getting anything from us. That's our decision."

"If you wish," said Picard, "you can go through proper channels, have us brought up on charges. That would be at your discretion. But you . . ."

His voice trailed off.

And suddenly Calhoun knew without question that he was in the wrong. He had never felt so chagrined. What had he been thinking?

He looked to his bridge crew and Soleta asked him with quiet contempt, "How could you have?"

"I . . . don't know . . . I'm not sure what I could possibly have been thinking."

"We were never truly going to refuse to cooperate," Picard assured Tulan. "I might have been briefly considering it, but really, it was just a passing thought."

"Are we dropping shields now?" Robin Lefler asked eagerly. "Taking phasers off line?"

"Yes. Yes, by all means," said Calhoun. "Jean-Luc, how about you?"

"Consider them dropped."

And Data's voice was heard from the *Enterprise* bridge. "I am sorry, Captain. But as per your previous instruction, I cannot allow that."

"What?" Picard was outraged, and his image turned to Calhoun. "Did you hear that? My own crew! This is mutiny!"

"I'm shocked!" agreed Calhoun.

"As am I," Tulan said. "Captains, I had heard better things about Starfleet than this."

"Attention *Excalibur*," Data said as if none of them had spoken. "Are you picking up the same readings I am?"

"Yes, Commander," Morgan promptly responded. "Biorhythms have been altered. Brain-wave function is impeded. They are being influenced by outside agencies."

"The likely candidate would be the Selelvians," said Data. "It would appear Captain Calhoun was correct. Their ability to manipulate free will is far beyond anything to which they have admitted."

"This is outrageous!" Tulan cried out, her veneer of calm beginning to crack.

"Fortunately enough, they can't affect us," Morgan said.

"Obviously not. Shall we take action?"

"I'm thinking yes," said Morgan.

"Morgan, what are you doing?" cried out Calhoun.

"Mr. Data, are you mad?" Picard said.

"No, sir," Data replied evenly. "Not even mildly incensed."

Picard lunged toward Data, trying to drag him away from the conn, but the android simply stiff-armed him, and Picard's own forward motion resulted in his tumbling back.

At that moment, phaser fire erupted from both starships, slamming into the Selelvian warship. The Selelvians barely got their shields up in time, but they were no match for the heavy firepower of the combined starships.

"You'll be hearing from my government about this!" shouted Tulan, and abruptly the warship angled around. Its faster-than-light engines roared to life and, a heartbeat later, the ship leaped into warp space and was gone.

And just like that, the cloud that had been on Calhoun's mind had lifted. It happened at the same time over on the *Enterprise,* where a dazed Picard said, "Good lord . . . I . . . I would never have known . . . even after it was done . . ."

"You'd have thought it was your own idea," said Calhoun, sagging against his command chair, breathing deeply. "That's how it works. That's how they get you. That's how they would have gotten us . . . but they didn't realize we both have people of artificial intelligence on the bridge crew."

" 'Artificial'?" Morgan sniffed in annoyance. "Well, I like that!" Then, her voice still laced with irritation, she said to Picard, "And what are *you* staring at?"

"Nothing. It's . . . nothing. You just keep reminding me of . . . a woman I know," said Picard. Trying to get his mind back to business, he said, "The Selelvians have repeatedly denied having power of such magnitude. This must be brought to the attention of the Federation. The Selelvians pose a greater threat than we could have imagined."

"First things first, Captain," Calhoun said to Picard. "I have an away team down there in distress. I'm sending down a security force. Could use some help."

"Anything for a fellow starship captain," said Picard.

ii.

On the surface of the planet, the door to the computer room buckled under the steady pounding. Burgoyne had managed to shut down the energy dampener, rendering hir phaser fully operational. But the com was still blocked. Kebron stood at the ready, Burgoyne and Selar prepared as well. "We go down fighting, my dear?" Burgoyne asked Selar.

"With each other?" inquired Selar.

"I mean fighting the creatures."

"Ah. Yes. I suppose."

"Good."

"Although," continued Selar, "my brief confusion was understandable. We have, after all, been known to fight a good deal between ourselves."

"Yes, I think we should definitely be spending our last moments tallying up how many fights we had."

"Don't make me come over there," Kebron warned them.

The door shuddered once more. The metal was twisting, bending, and shadowed forms could be seen through the breaks. Kebron pushed against it, trying to keep the door in place, but he knew he was fighting a losing battle. Not that he wasn't strong enough to keep it in place and resist the push of the beasts on the other side. But the door itself was giving way.

"Kebron—!" called Burgoyne.

Kebron didn't shake his head because he didn't have a neck. But he growled, "Unless we're beamed out of here within the next five seconds, we're dead."

Suddenly the air was filled with the howling of transporter beams, and ten heavily armed men, with a burly sercurity officer at the head of the group, materialized within the room.

"That'll work, too," said Kebron.

The well-muscled officer called to Kebron, "Step away from the door." Kebron did so and, an instant later, the door crashed in. The beasts from the other side tumbled over each other trying to get in, clawing and howling and completely out of control.

Within seconds they were in full retreat, scampering down the hallway and howling as the shrieks of phaser blasts beat them back.

"You could have beamed us out of here, you know," said Burgoyne.

"And miss all this?" the security chief rumbled.

Burgoyne considered that a moment and then nodded. "Good point," s/he said.

They fanned out, mowing down resistance wherever they found it. Burgoyne led the way, sending the security team back in the direction of the lab they'd escaped from.

iii.

Dr. Bethom didn't like the way things were going at all. He saw his troops being annihilated by the combined forces of the Federation ground troops. On monitor screens, he saw them heading in his direction, with that aggravating Hermat leading the way and that even more distressing Brikar right behind hir. Still strapped to the table a few feet away, Janos was howling with fury, pulling at his restraints. Bethom wasn't sure what he would be dealing with if Janos broke free. Was there anything of his intellect remaining? Or would he just leap upon his creator and grate him like a block of cheese?

Dr. Christopher, Bethom's associate, was lying on the ground with blood trickling from his forehead. He had been slammed to the floor during the initial crush of the beasts hurtling past, and he had not gotten up again. Bethom wasn't worrying about it. He had other concerns.

"Get us out of here!" said an angry voice in his ear. "Now!"

"I don't know where to go . . . this all happened so fast. Everything's spiraling out of control."

"Find a place! Find somewhere! Do I have to do all the thinking for both of us!"

"Yes, yes, all right!"

Bethom sprinted for the far door, his mind racing. Through there was the kennel where he had kept the creatures. It was now empty. If he cut through there, he might be able to hide out for a time in some of the private offices. Wait it out. That might be the way to go, yes, he could . . .

The air suddenly shimmered in front of him and Mackenzie Calhoun was blocking his path. Standing next to him was Jean-Luc Picard.

"Seems like old times," said Calhoun. "Captain Picard . . . I don't believe you've met the Bad Guy."

Bethom let out a screech and charged at him. The gribble, perched on his shoulder, clung desperately.

Calhoun cocked his fist.

Bethom took one look at it and stopped in his tracks. Then he forced a smile. "That . . . that won't be necessary. We can . . . we can deal with this like intelligent adults . . ."

Calhoun hit him anyway. He swung an uppercut that caught Bethom squarely under the chin and sent him flying. He fell heavily to the floor, and the gribble fell off his shoulder and rolled up into a ball. A second later, it unfurled itself and started to scamper across the floor.

"As always, Calhoun, the model of restraint," said Picard.

And Janos, from the table, howled, *"Stop that thing! It's in charge!"*

At first Calhoun had no idea what Janos was talking about. Then he saw where the furred security guard was indicating. The gribble was moving as fast as it could, and Calhoun was still bewildered, but Picard didn't hesitate. His phaser was in his hand and he fired off a quick shot just as the gribble was getting to the door. The phaser shot caught it squarely and the furred creature ricocheted across the floor and came to a rest at the far end.

"Nice shot," said Calhoun.

iv.

The group of them—Calhoun, Picard, Selar, and Kebron—were grouped around the gribble, which was inside a bell jar atop a table, unable to escape. The tiny creature glowered at them.

In other areas throughout the institute, the security teams were rounding up or, for the most part, disposing of the few remaining creatures running amok through the institute. Janos was still strapped to the table, but Selar had given him a sedative and he was sleeping soundly. There seemed little point to just returning him to the brig. Besides, at that moment, their attention was focused squarely on their undersized prisoner.

"You've got to be kidding," said Kebron.

"Shut up, you overgrown lummox," snapped the gribble.

"So am I understanding you correctly?" Selar asked. "You were a 'failed genetic experiment' . . . ?"

"Except I wasn't a failure," said the gribble, glaring at Bethom. "I was his greatest achievement. And part of my greatness was keeping my intellect masked so he didn't realize that it was only growing throughout the years. Why, the facilities here at the institute have been beyond anything I could have hoped for."

"Far better than the penal colony you were originally sent to, I'd wager," said Picard.

"Don't be too sure of that, baldy," the gribble said. "I made valuable contacts at that penal colony. Contacts who were extremely interested in what I had to offer, and the benefits of any further research I might implement. That's why this place was a godsend. Bethom on his own had more or less reached the heights of what he was going to accomplish. But with my intellect guiding the research . . ."

"And you used some sort of incredible mind power to influence the scientists so they would do your bidding?" said Kebron.

"No, you idiot," the gribble snapped. "It was just a matter of drugging their food and whispering to them at night while they slept. Human minds are remarkably pliable."

"I'm sorry," sobbed Bethom, strapped to a chair a few feet away. "I'm sorry I let you down. . . ."

"Oh, shut up," said the gribble in his squeaky voice. "Pathetic fool. I'm embarrassed to be seen with you. My achievements far outstripped anything you ever could have aspired to."

"Meaning . . . ?" asked Picard.

"The deterioration factor."

"The what?"

But Calhoun understood immediately. Looking in Janos's direction, he said, "You mean . . . what's happening to Janos."

"Yes," said the gribble. He reached up with one leg, scratched behind his tiny ear. "With the sole exception of me, all of Bethom's earlier experiments suffered from deterioration of their faculties, to the point where they became too dangerous to live. Your 'Janos' lasted far longer than most, probably because he was the single most successful in terms of intelligence. But obviously even his deterioration and reversion to savagery is progressing."

"There has to be a way," said Calhoun. "Unless you want us to dissect you for hints, you'll tell us."

At first the gribble looked defiant, but as he saw the quiet building anger in Calhoun's purple eyes, he realized that bargaining might be his best option. "Perhaps," said the gribble. "Perhaps there is a way. It's an outside chance. But if I do it, what's in it for me?"

"You get to live," Calhoun told him.

The gribble didn't look impressed. "You wouldn't kill me in any event. I'm intelligent, I'm self-aware, and I'm fluffy. I have to do more than live if I cooperate. I get to walk away from this. Well . . . scamper away."

"No deal," Picard said harshly.

Calhoun looked at him. "Jean-Luc—"

"He has allies, Mac," said Picard. "Someone he was developing research and technology for. Research and technology into outlawed sciences. These unknown allies present a potential threat to Federation security. He has to at least name them. Be willing to speak against them before the Federation when they're captured."

"You'll never capture them," said the gribble confidently.

"Then you've no need to worry about naming them, have you?"

"I suppose not," admitted the gribble. "All right . . . a deal. I try to help the hairbag over there and tell you who my allies are, in exchange for my freedom. And you're lucky, Calhoun. Bethom would have been no use to you at all."

"It's true," sobbed Bethom. "I've no idea how to help Janos. I'm sorry. . . ."

"Damned right," said the gribble. "I'm the only being in existence who could possibly pull it off. All right . . . here's what needs to be done . . ."

The snapping of the metal bonds caught them completely off guard. As one, they turned in time to see Janos bounding free of the table. His eyes were bloodred in fury and he roared so loudly that Calhoun thought he was going to go deaf.

Janos was completely berserk.

"Weapons out!" shouted Picard.

"Stun setting won't stop him!" Kebron said, advancing on him. Janos instantly took the challenge, leaping forward and slamming into Kebron, knocking him to one side. The impact sent him lurching toward Calhoun and Picard, who fired their phasers in unison. The twin blasts spun Janos completely around and he struck the table with the bell jar. The table was overturned and the bell jar crashed to the floor, shattering.

The gribble tried to run. He didn't get far. Janos was upon him in an instant. . . .

"No!" Calhoun cried out.

It was too late. Janos hadn't been fed all day. He grabbed the gribble up and before the terrified creature could utter a sound, Janos devoured him in one bite.

Then Kebron collided with him from behind, hurtling him to the floor. Straddling his back, he pulled Janos's upper and lower jaws in opposite directions. "Spit him out! Right now!" Janos made gagging noises. *"Right now!"*

The gribble's haunches tumbled to the floor out of Janos's mouth. The small creature's front section was nowhere in sight.

"This can't be good," said Kebron.

Janos suddenly reared up and managed to shove Kebron off him. He lurched to his feet, and once more phaser fire from multiple directions hammered at him. He tried to fight them off, but then he began to waver and, moments later, toppled to the floor and lay silent.

"He was still heavily medicated," said Selar. "Otherwise I suspect the phasers would not have stopped him."

"Great," Calhoun said. He stared at the remains of the gribble and then looked woefully at Picard. "I think the deal's off," he said.

Then

Mackenzie Calhoun strode across the podium when his name was called. Polite applause followed him as he did so, and he received his diploma from the dean. He was saluted, and saluted in response. It was a ceremonial gesture, the salute, a holdover from centuries ago that was trotted out only for highly ceremonial occasions such as this.

"Congratulations, Ensign Calhoun," said the dean.

"Thank you, sir," replied Calhoun.

He returned to his seat wedged in between two other classmates and studied the diploma. He ran his fingers across it, noted the raised letters, the smooth paper. The format of the diploma had not changed in centuries. He felt as if he were looking back through a window in time, seeing the way things used to be. He liked them.

The rest of the ceremony breezed past. More speeches. More congratulations. The Academy band played pompous music.

And when it was over, people embraced one another, family members pouring forward like the great flood to mingle with the graduates, to congratulate them and express excitement about the great destinies that awaited them.

Calhoun watched them as if from a distance. As if he were back at the time of those earliest diplomas, and looking forward to another time, another world that he was not a part of.

He had no family to embrace him. No loved ones to celebrate with him. Wexler and Leanne were busy with their parents, who were pumping their hands or posing for pictures.

Then he saw her, at the far edge of the crowd. Elizabeth Shelby. Smiling, joyous, her arms open wide, ready to run to him if she could just get through the crowd. He wondered if she was merely a vision, as she had been four years ago, but no, she was real, flesh and blood, trying to get past everyone else to get to him . . .

. . . and then she stopped and threw her arms around another cadet, and he realized it wasn't her. The hair was the same, the general shape of the body, but it was a different face, a different woman. Not her.

He stayed right where he was, unmoving, just to see what would happen.

And eventually, the field was deserted. It was a beautiful day, and he stood there until the sun moved across the sky, and the crews came and cleared away the chairs even as they looked in puzzlement at him, and the night fell, and the clouds came out. All that time, Mackenzie Calhoun didn't move from the spot.

No one came to him. And somehow he knew, in a burst of clarity, that he would spend his entire existence alone.

"I can live with that," he said finally, and walked away, leaving the field deserted.

Chapter Twenty-one

Now

"I couldn't live with that," he said.

Captain Shelby, standing next to her husband, wrapped her arm through his. "Live with what?" she asked.

They were seated on a hillside on a world called Neural. It was a lovely place, with tall trees and rich undergrowth. Once small tribes of humanoids had populated it, but they had wiped each other out in a civil war, and now there was only animal life.

"Live with being alone," Calhoun replied.

"My. Where did that come from?"

"Just . . . thinking about the past."

"That's a safe thing to think about. The future's always more problematic. But hey, at least you have a future."

"Meaning?"

"God, Calhoun," and she jabbed him in the ribs. "Do you have *any* clue how close you came to losing it all? If the Selelvians hadn't withdrawn their complaint, if they hadn't insisted the matter be dropped . . ."

"You mean if I hadn't been right," he said. "But I knew I was. And now they want to drop the matter because they want to avoid investigation by the UFP. You can mind-control some of the people some of the time, but not all of them all of the time."

"You knew you were right."

"Yes."

"You were able to trust your instincts."

"That's right."

"Here's the problem, Mac: I trust your instincts, too. But there're plenty of people out there with lousy instincts. That's why there are rules. That's why they have to be followed. And it's impossible to pick and choose who is going to follow them. Despite the fact that, yes, you were right, Jellico was ready to have you strung up. If it weren't for the combined efforts of Captain Picard and Ambassador Spock . . . I don't like to think what would have happened."

"And would you have been with me?"

"With you?"

"Whatever they'd have done to me," said Calhoun, taking her hands in his. "Would you have seen it through?"

"You mean lived with you at a penal colony?"

"Yes."

"No."

He nodded. "All right. I can understand that."

"However," she continued, "I hear such places have generous conjugal-visit policies."

"Better than nothing."

"Much."

They watched the creature who had once gone by the name of Janos. He had made it to the edge of the woods, and now other creatures somewhat similar to him had emerged. They came out, one by one, sniffing at him, then roaring challenges. He had responded in kind.

Then the largest one charged him . . . and Janos, acting entirely on instinct, stepped out of the way, grabbed him from behind, and threw him to the ground in a perfectly executed judo toss. The creature lay there, stunned, tried to get up, and Janos kicked him in the face.

The second largest also charged him. The same thing happened.

"He reminds me of you," said Shelby. "That's more or less what you did when you first came to the Academy."

"We're both outsiders," Calhoun replied. "Pity there's no stone and anvil with a sword stuck in it for him to pull out in order to gain acceptance. It takes much less time, from what I hear. But I suppose you do what you have to in order to fit in." He shook his head, unable to maintain the attempt at levity. "I failed him, Eppy. Do you think he realizes? Remembers?"

"You did what you could, Mac," she said. "Released him here into the wild. It won't be the life he could have had . . . but it's a life. You were able to give him that at least."

"I don't like settling for 'at least.' "

"Would you settle for me?"

He smiled at her, stroked her face, and then brought her lips up to his as, far away, Janos blended in with his new tribe and they vanished into the shadows of the forest.